PRAISE FOR CINDY

"Set in 1963, in the coal-mining town of J
Cindy Morgan weaves the threads of the r
Grace's life through her interactions with f their divided
community. Against this backdrop of cultural change and uncertainty,
Grace's coming-of-age story is told. I've never experienced a more
intimate and fascinating portrayal of these times in a story told with
such empathy and compassion."

AMY GRANT, Grammy-winning singer-songwriter and author

"Cindy Morgan is an award-winning singer and songwriter, and her
prose is as lyrical as her music. This heartbreaking coming-of-age
story eloquently portrays the hellish and heavenly nature of Kentucky
life in the 1960s with great detail and sensitivity. Morgan's story will
make you grateful for the Word's healing touch, the complicated
bonds of family and friendship, and the power of air conditioning on
a scorching summer day. What a delicious slice of Southern fiction!"

ROBIN W. PEARSON, award-winning author of *A Long Time Comin'* and
Walking in Tall Weeds

"*The Year of Jubilee* is such a compelling and powerful story that it is
clear Cindy's gift includes more than just music. I would now describe
her as simply a brilliant and expressive writer."

MANDISA, Grammy-winning artist

"Some stories are told; others, like *The Year of Jubilee*, are woven into
the reader's heart. With honesty and bravery, a compelling coming-of-
age heroine confronts ignorance and racial prejudice in the deep South
while wrestling with her own past demons—and learning the price of
forgiveness. A beautiful story wondrously told!"

TAMERA ALEXANDER, *USA Today* bestselling author of *Colors of Truth*

"*The Year of Jubilee* is a poignant coming-of-age story set during a turbulent
time in our country's history in the 1960s. This one is sure to stir your heart."

T. I. LOWE, bestselling author of *Under the Magnolias*

"Cindy Morgan takes us on a barefoot walk into the heart of Jubilee, Kentucky, as her authentic characters fumble toward love and justice in the divided South. Vivid with style and substance, Cindy Morgan's debut novel is a down-to-earth masterpiece."

SANDRA McCRACKEN, singer-songwriter and author

"Cindy brings empathy, a poetic perspective and a resounding hope that calls from the depths to this story. It's the story of her family, and the story of all of us who have loved and lost and grieved and tenaciously clung to hope. All of us who have experienced Jubilee."

SISSY GOFF, bestselling author of *Raising Worry-Free Girls* and cohost of the *Raising Boys and Girls* podcast

"In this emotional, heart-gripping and soul-stirring novel . . . the reader gets to travel back in time on a journey of redemptive healing and forgiveness. *The Year of Jubilee* is a must read, especially for anyone struggling with seeing the world around them through the eyes of another!"

LYNDA RANDLE, award-winning singer-songwriter and author

"A brilliant story, woven with beautifully crafted characters and rich, colorful detail. Your heart will be stirred as you come to see through the eyes of the insightful narrator, and learning of her family, her life, and her struggle to understand God will inspire you to contemplate your own journey in new ways."

GINNY OWENS, musical artist and author of *Singing in the Dark*

"Cindy Morgan's debut novel *The Year of Jubilee* struck so many personal chords within me, transporting me back to a small-town life in the hills and hollers of Kentucky. . . . A story that will tantalize your heart and soul to the very end!"

DONNA JORDON, Eagleville Bicentennial Public Library (Cindy Morgan's local librarian)

THE YEAR OF JUBILEE

THE
YEAR
OF
JUBILEE

A NOVEL

CINDY
MORGAN

Tyndale House Publishers
Carol Stream, Illinois

Visit Tyndale online at tyndale.com.

Visit Cindy Morgan online at cindymorganmusic.com.

Tyndale and Tyndale's quill logo are registered trademarks of Tyndale House Ministries.

The Year of Jubilee

Copyright © 2023 by Cindy Morgan. All rights reserved.

Cover photograph of house copyright © Erika Brothers/Arcangel. All rights reserved.

Cover photograph of girl copyright © pixdeluxe/Getty Images. All rights reserved.

Cover photograph of birds copyright © JC Shamrock/Getty Images. All rights reserved.

Cover photograph of car bumper by Josh Rinard on Unsplash.com.

Author photo taken by Julee Duinee, copyright © 2022. All rights reserved.

Designed by Jennifer Phelps

Edited by Sarah Mason Rische

Published in association with the literary agency of Browne & Miller Literary Associates, LLC, 52 Village Place, Hinsdale, IL 60521.

Unless otherwise noted, Scripture is taken from the New King James Version,® copyright © 1982 by Thomas Nelson. Used by permission. All rights reserved.

Proverbs 14:13 in the epilogue is taken from GOD'S WORD®, copyright © 1995 by God's Word to the Nations. Used by permission of God's Word Mission Society. All rights reserved.

The Year of Jubilee is a work of fiction. Where real people, events, establishments, organizations, or locales appear, they are used fictitiously. All other elements of the novel are drawn from the author's imagination.

For information about special discounts for bulk purchases, please contact Tyndale House Publishers at csresponse@tyndale.com, or call 1-855-277-9400.

Library of Congress Cataloging-in-Publication Data

A catalog record for this book is available from the Library of Congress.

ISBN 978-1-4964-7597-8 (HC)
ISBN 978-1-4964-7598-5 (SC)

Printed in the United States of America

29	28	27	26	25	24	23
7	6	5	4	3	2	1

FOR SAMUEL MORGAN

NOVEMBER 7, 1966 – OCTOBER 31, 1971

THE FEAR OF DEATH FOLLOWS
FROM THE FEAR OF LIFE.
A MAN WHO LIVES FULLY IS
PREPARED TO DIE AT ANY TIME.

MARK TWAIN

PROLOGUE

There are some moments in your life you don't forget. Even when your eyes grow dim and your skin is thin like a moth's wings, you can find them there, buried deep. You dust them off, and they shine like new again. Even now, in my middle years, I only have to crack open the cover of my red journal, and though the ink is fading, the words remain.

I remember.

I remember the feeling of my father's rough shirt beneath my bare legs as he lifted me onto his shoulders and up to the window of Isaac's hospital room. I remember the white walls and silver railings along his bed. I remember Rojo in my arms, still, with only the sound of his soft clucking as we peered in through the glass. The crest atop his head as red as blood against the windowpane. I remember thinking Isaac looked like a bird in a cloud, covered in a mound of sterile white sheets and blankets. I remember long clear tubes from a machine, feeding liquid life into his tiny bird arm.

I remember his lips moving as he looked up at us, and I wondered what he was saying.

I remember my mother in her pale-blue dress standing beside him, holding his hand with a river of sorrow in her eyes. I remember the sound of my heart beating like a drum in my chest and the smell of the rain as it held its breath before relenting.

I remember how we stood there as it started to rain, afraid of breaking the spell we were in. I remember the rain becoming a flood and our lives getting swept away in it.

I remember.

1
CONSTANCE

The minute I saw Miss Adams, I was keenly aware of my lingering eighth-grade awkwardness, my nails bit down to the quick and my clothing meant for comfort instead of fashion. The other girls in her class were also well turned out in their dresses, makeup, and padded bras. I was still in my training bra and trying to tame the frizz in my bush of curly hair. I had come to her midway through the year, skipping from eighth grade into the ninth at the recommendation of my teacher, who felt I was bored and needed to be challenged.

Miss Adams was my new ninth-grade English teacher, fresh out of college and new to Jubilee. All anyone knew was that her daddy was a prominent doctor from down in Mississippi. She was exactly what any principal in a small Southern town would have prayed for, the quintessential Southern woman—real marriage material. Her nails were a soft shade of pink; and her hands, like her figure, were slight and ethereal. When she spoke, her drawl was like sugar rolling off her tongue—the way folks with money from the Deep South speak, nothing like the jagged edges Kentuckians spit out. Instead of saying *mother* and *father* with a strong *er* sound at the end, she said *mutha* and *fahtha,* and it made you want to crawl up in her lap and purr.

I remember one day in class, just as the winter relented and the blossom of spring was in the air, she announced we would be taking a field trip and that all we would need was our imagination and a good pair of walking shoes. This was no problem for me or any of the boys in the class, but some of the girls, like one prissy girl named Emoline Bluin, had worn their good church shoes to school.

"You will have to suffer through or go in your bare feet," Miss Adams told them.

Sitting on a large quilt under a magnolia tree behind the school, she read us poetry, asking us to listen with our eyes closed and our hearts open. No teacher in this small hick school had ever taken a class on a nature walk to read poetry. Whether boy or girl—didn't matter—we were all a little in love with her.

The world blossomed in color and detail when Miss Adams read literary fiction, poetry, and historical novels. I was never bored like I had been in my other class. She took us on expeditions through time. As she recounted important moments and people, the posters of historical figures on the walls came to life. I could hear their voices speaking through her.

We all adored her. That was, until the last day of school.

We were minutes away from the bell that would take us into summer.

"Attention, please."

Miss Adams stood in the middle of the room, her voice breaking into our restless energy. I noticed that her voice warbled a bit in her throat and she reached for a small glass from her desk and took a dainty drink of water before proceeding.

"Before the bell rings, I'd like to read you something to think about over the summer break. Something that seems fitting for the times we are living in."

She held up a book for us to see. "This is *The Winter of Our Discontent* by John Steinbeck."

She cleared her throat, pressing the book to her chest before holding it out in front of her to read. "'I wonder how many people I've looked at all my life and never seen . . .'"

She raised her head, eyes on us, as the book lay open in her hands. A small murmur of disinterest was rumbling from the boys on the back row.

"Boys," she said, zeroing in on them. Her icy stare froze their words in their open mouths as she waited for silence.

She continued to read. "'No man really knows about other human beings. The best he can do is to suppose that they are like himself.'"

She let the book close and took a deep breath, her eyes bright and leveled with ours. "Most of you realize, there is much unrest in the South, fear of things changing. School integration is happening all across the country. We don't know if next year, this school could possibly embrace the idea of integrating—"

Eli Gunner shot to his feet. "You must be out of your m-m-m-mind if you think that's g-g-gonna happen!"

The boys erupted in laughter.

Eli came to school most days smelling as though he had not showered and devoured the warm lunch as if it was his first meal of the day. The stutter he struggled with made me think that God must have had it out for him.

"Eli!" Miss Adams stretched out her hand toward him. "I know it might seem unthinkable, but you might have to open your mind to something different than what you've always known."

I wondered if all the fantasies the boys had about Miss Adams were shattered in that single moment. In the South, there were two unforgivable sins: speaking poorly of the Holy Spirit and being a liberal. I knew Miss Adams was different, but it wasn't until that moment that I understood how different. Word would get around.

Miss Adams clapped her hands three times, and we fell quiet. She took a deep breath and pressed her palms together in front of her, as if poised to pray.

Emoline Bluin raised her hand quickly.

"Yes, Emoline!" she spit out, letting her irritation show.

"My daddy says it's because of the curse of Ham. You see, when Ham looked on his daddy Noah's nakedness, God cursed him by turning his skin black. All the coloreds are descendants of Ham and are cursed just like he was and that is why they won't ever be equals to the whites."

Miss Adams tipped her head sideways, drilling her gaze into Emoline's. Starting to speak, her voice caught in her throat and she had a small coughing episode. She reached desperately for the glass again, holding her index finger in the air to ask for a moment, and this time guzzled all of the water before responding.

"The proper term, Emoline, is *Negroes*, not *coloreds*. No offense to your daddy, but . . . that sounds like a justification to demean an entire race of people and ease his guilt over denying Negroes their constitutional and God-given rights."

The room let out a gasp.

Emoline's eyebrows scrunched together and her mouth gaped open; then she aimed her retaliation. "I don't think you know who my daddy—"

The bell rang.

Even with the victory of the scathing last word, the message Miss Adams had hoped to convey had landed like a turd in a punch bowl. Most of the kids scrambled to their feet, leaving Miss Adams and her lofty ideas in the dust behind them.

She stood at the classroom door calling out goodbye, hopeful, maybe, that someone would look back. No one did. I felt bad for her.

I'd started to get up from my desk to go when Eli ran past me and tripped on his untied shoelaces. He fell to the ground and his shirt, which he looked to have outgrown in junior high, slipped halfway up his back and revealed a purple bruise the size of a man's fist. He reached to shove the shirt back down as he got up, and I looked away so he wouldn't think I'd seen the bruise.

"Are you okay, Eli?" Miss Adams asked.

"Y-y-y-y-yes." And he rose quickly, running out of the room without tying his shoelaces.

This left only me and Miss Adams in the room.

"Grace, could I see you for a second?"

I gathered my things and walked over to her, my hands sweaty from the humidity.

She gazed out the door, deep in thought, and then asked me, "What did you think of what Emoline said?"

"Oh, I've heard that before, but my father thinks it's bad theology."

"Really? And your mother?"

I stared at her, unsure of how to even begin to explain the complexities of Virginia's theology.

She shook her head from side to side. "It was a shame that our time together in class had to end like that." Her gaze floated around the room, a look of disappointment piercing her eyes with a slash of gray. I longed to say something to make her feel better, but nothing came out.

Distracted, she reached into her desk drawer and pulled out a package wrapped in brown paper with a red string tied around it. She presented it to me. I carefully untied the string, and underneath the brown paper was a red journal with the outline of a bird on the cover. I heard a faint crack as I turned to the front page, blank except for what was written there:

Grace—

    Thank you for being such an engaged and curious student. I think life holds many possibilities for you.

                All the best,
                Constance Adams

Constance. I rolled her first name around in my mouth like a butterscotch candy. I had never heard such a grand name, and I decided that it suited her perfectly. Then before I thought better, I wrapped my arms around her waist, smelling the faint whiff of gardenias. She laughed, startled by my affection, and put a gentle hand on my shoulder.

"Thank you." The words stuck in my throat.

"I know how much you love reading, and I thought maybe you would enjoy writing down your own thoughts."

"I'm gonna miss you." I surprised myself by saying that out loud.

"I'll miss you too. I'm sad I only had you for a little while, but I'd love to keep in touch. Let me know how you are?"

"Thank you again." I hurried out, turning my face away from her to hide the unwelcome tears that were flooding my eyes.

I wiped them away and left out the front door, heading across the parking lot to the small, two-lane road that led to town. An uneven patch of ground tripped me up, but I managed to save myself from a nasty fall.

Instead of getting up immediately, I sat on the ground, replaying the moment with Miss Adams while I wiped the dirt and gravel from my clothes.

"You all right, Miss Grace?"

I looked up to see Miss Pearl, an older Negro lady who sold peaches out of the back of her truck along the highway across from school.

"Oh yes! Sorry, Miss Pearl. You caught me daydreaming."

"Daydreaming is good for the mind," she said, pointing her short dark finger to the side of her head. "Shows you got imagination. Wanna free peach?"

I was so thirsty, my mouth watered at the thought of it. I put the journal into my book bag, letting a truck pass, then crossed to her side of the road.

"Thank you, Miss Pearl. You're sure it's okay?"

"Yes, child. Take yo' pick."

I selected one that was ripe and ready for eating. "Thank you."

"You're welcome, child. You excited for summer?"

"Yes, ma'am." I smiled. Miss Pearl had gentleness in her mannerisms, but her eyes glowed with fire. I wiped the trickle of sweat on my forehead with my sleeve.

"It sure is getting hot," I said.

"Oh, that's a fact. I melt down out here, but they say the sweat is good for your health, so I must be reeeeeal healthy."

She laughed, exposing a missing front tooth. She wore an oversize bright-colored cotton dress to match her colorful personality. The rolls around her middle jiggled and made the dress jump nervously to the rhythm of her laughter. In that moment, I wondered what it would be like to sit in Miss Pearl's warm lap and let her motherly affection engulf me. Motherly affection was in short supply in my life.

I shook the thought loose.

"Miss Pearl, do you get hot sitting out here all day?"

"I reckon I do, child, but Mr. Oak here, he helps me out." She pointed upward and gently took hold of a leaf from the low-hanging branch she was parked under. A slight breeze caught her dress and the leaves, making them both shiver for a moment. I fought a sudden burst of emotion at her gratitude for the simple gift of a shade tree.

I wondered how long I'd been standing here talking. Virginia got upset when I took too long to get home. "Thank you for the peach, Miss Pearl."

"You welcome, baby. Be careful now; they some crazy people on this road."

"I'm gonna take the trail through the woods and wade in the river all the way back to town."

"A fine idea. I might dip my toe in the water after the school rush passes."

I ran back across the road and headed for the trees. I took a bite out of the peach. It was sweet and tart and reminded me of the peach preserves Grandma Josie used to slather on the hot biscuits she made. The juice ran down my chin and onto my shirt, but I didn't even care.

The real world fell away as I floated into the woods. The long-armed branches reached across to embrace each other. The shimmering leaves gathered into a verdant canopy overhead. The ground was dappled with patches of gold and shadow. The covering ended abruptly, and the blistering afternoon sun raged again. I walked the few short steps to the bank of the river.

I imagined Miss Adams would love woods the way I did.

She wrote that my life held "many possibilities." It made me feel proud—which concerned me.

Virginia said that you shouldn't think on compliments long or else they would grow a seed of pride in your heart. You should think of yourself as being of little or no importance to God; then you would never be tempted to be proud, which to Virginia was a cardinal sin.

I allowed myself to hold Miss Adams's words in my heart a few moments longer, taking my chances with God's displeasure toward me. It was, after all, a familiar feeling.

I made my way along the edge of the river, peeling off my shoes and socks. My bare feet sizzled as I crept into the icy water, feeling the current rush over my toes. Small crawdads darted away as I got closer.

I winced as my tender skin found sharp rocks along the edge of the riverbank where it flowed underneath the bridge connecting to Main Street. It would never do for Virginia to hear that I had been walking around town like a barefoot hillbilly. I hopped from the riverbank to a small patch of grass and lay back on the soft green cushion, seeing a castle and a shark in the clouds before the wind blew them away. Reluctantly, I sat up to put on my shoes and socks then crossed over the bridge toward town.

As I turned onto Main Street, I saw two men going into the Green Parrot Café. One's face was so black from coal soot I couldn't make out who it was. The other was a man I knew—Tater Beggins, a pig farmer who made it a normal practice to wear his dirty coveralls into the diner. The smell of cow or pig manure, coal dust, and three-day-old sweat wafting above the scent of burgers and fries was just an everyday occurrence.

Jubilee could be charming and even beautiful when the honeysuckle and dogwoods were in bloom. Tidy farms scattered with chickens, pigs, and cows dotted the outskirts of town. But about a half mile from the far end of Main Street was the eyesore—or the crown jewel, depending on how you saw it: KY Coal. Dust billowed from the large heaps of coal no matter the time of day.

Coal was as much a part of living in Kentucky in 1963 as fried chicken, corn bread, and buttermilk. It wasn't just the poor who worked the mines in Jubilee, it was anyone who had no means or desire to go to college or learn a trade or run a business. I looked into the window of the diner as I passed by. I saw Jerry Lawler, who had been a friend of Daddy's since they were kids. Jerry looked up, saw me, and waved. His teeth glistened like pearls against the coal soot that covered his face. Daddy told me that he and Jerry had worked their very first day together in the mines when they were just sixteen.

It was on that first day in the mines that Daddy discovered he had claustrophobia.

"Me and Jerry rode an elevator down into the earth, rattling and shaking, dropping deeper and deeper. We were looking at each other. I could tell he was scared like I was. I remember thinking that hell couldn't be much farther down."

Daddy never went back. Jerry had been working there ever since.

I kept walking and thinking how glad I was that Daddy wasn't a miner. I had heard too many stories of men dying of black lung. But Daddy said the miners deserved our respect for the courage it takes to ride down that shaft every day.

Those black chunks were the fuel of life hauled in by the bucketful for fireplaces and coal stoves. Virginia had begged Daddy to have electric heat installed, but he said it was still too expensive for us. The dust covered everything with a fine black film no matter how often you dusted.

But what I hated the most was the smell. It was in our clean clothes hanging out on the line and in our freshly washed hair. You couldn't get rid of it. But coal was just a part of life. When everyone smells like coal, nobody does, until someone comes along to tell you that you do.

There was certainly no need for burning coal in the sweltering heat of summer. I breathed in the wild, new freedom that only the first day of summer could bring. The air was rich with the smell of fried catfish and adventure. It was a magical feeling. I wanted to hold on to it as long as I could, so I was taking my time getting home. I knew that feeling would vanish the moment I stepped into the house.

Holding my red journal from Miss Adams against my chest, I knew there was no more stalling. I rounded the corner from town and turned onto my street.

2
VIRGINIA

Before the screen door could slam shut, her voice sliced through me.

"Grace?"

I took a deep breath and caught the scent of lilacs and Aqua Net—the smell of my mother, Virginia. I would never have dared call her by her first name to her face. I was careful not to call her anything to her face but *ma'am*. *"Yes, ma'am; no, ma'am."* I'd swallow the words of defiance that hovered at the back of my throat as I accepted whatever criticism or orders she doled out. But in my thoughts, she was never Mother, Mama, or Mom. She was simply Virginia.

At first glance, she was soft like a buttercup, but you only had to scratch the surface of the petal to find cold steel beneath. I feared her and dreaded her, and when I wasn't struggling with my feelings of anger toward her, I felt as desperate for her love as a drowning man in need of air.

Some days I imagined her greeting me with a hug and the smell of cookies baking in the oven. My daddy told me that there were many times when I was younger that she had done that very thing. That she had been a doting mother but that she was suffering from what he called "the change" on account of Virginia having a hysterectomy last year, due to some complications . . . My mind wandered back to a moment I immediately blocked out. Daddy said the surgery brought on the change a good fifteen or twenty years too soon. I had a feeling it was mostly because of me—and the thing that no one ever spoke of. I sometimes dreamed of a different Virginia, maybe from a memory buried deep. But now, in the blistering sun of reality, a feeling of dread greeted me like opening a door to a dark room. No cookies. Just lilacs, Aqua Net, and wrath. That was Virginia.

Obviously annoyed by my propensity to get lost in my own head, she repeated the razor-sharp words, but a little louder this time. "I asked you where have you been? If you have made me late, Grace Louise Mockingbird, you might as well go get your switch."

Virginia followed the tradition in the South of having your child select their own switch. The trick was, if you returned with one that could not punish to satisfaction, the parent would select another that would deliver a greater penalty than originally deserved. To spare the rod was to spoil the child, condemning them to hellfire before the age of accountability. "You'll need to look after Isaac until Daddy gets home. Sissy started her summer job at the Tri-Way Drive-In today."

Sissy, my older sister, was a not-so-sweet sixteen with a brand-spanking-new driver's license. My daddy liked to say that she "kept the roads hot." She somehow managed to escape the worst of the chores. It was plain that Virginia favored her, or maybe it was just the stark contrast of her anger toward me in comparison. Sissy and I were always messing up the facade Virginia had carefully crafted. The image she hoped to project to those in Jubilee who mattered.

I watched Virginia checking herself in the mirror. Her hair fell like waves of molasses, and her eyes were deep-brown chocolate drops, with thick butterfly lashes that she fluttered mercilessly at Daddy when she wanted something.

Aunt June had once said her figure was as shapely as a Coca-Cola bottle. Whenever we went anywhere in town, men took second and third glances. It was easy to feel invisible around her, and most of the time that was just the way I liked it.

Today she was a thing to behold in her Sears catalogue dress. It was a mint-green A-line, fitted at the bodice and accented by a pink belt that showed off her small waist. She wore stockings with a crisp straight line up the back of her shapely legs and pink pumps perfectly matched to her belt. The dress had cost Daddy nearly a day's wages, but he knew how much looking nice meant to Virginia, so he indulged her.

I wondered if like me, he longed for the momentary look of approval that ran across her face when you pleased her. Daddy made sure she had all the pretty dresses she needed to feel as though she belonged in proper society, though he always said Virginia could look beautiful in a potato sack. He even put up with her occasional nagging about wanting a bigger house in a nicer neighborhood, but there was a limit to what even he would tolerate.

To tell the truth, I lived for the moments when he said no to her because it made me think I wasn't crazy. She wasn't always right, and I wasn't always wrong.

Virginia gave her dress one final glance of half-hearted approval and swished through the kitchen door, looking at me suspiciously. I followed her and the dark cloud she kept close by into the kitchen.

She drained sweet tea from a small mason jar and turned her attention on me. "Grace, how do you become such a mess by the time you get home from school? Look at your pants! How did they get wet? Have you been in the river again? What a mess—and your hair!"

I looked down at myself, noticing the yellow stain on my blue shirt from spilling mustard at lunch, as well as the peach juice that had dribbled onto my sleeve.

Virginia had recently sent away for a copy of *Emily Post's Etiquette*. At night she would read it in bed, hair in rollers, and wake the next morning ready to give us all lessons on style, grammar, and dining manners. She had taken to setting a proper table, laying out all the forks and knives and different glasses for milk and juice and coffee, using every dish in the house. I hated this because it was my job to leave the kitchen spotless before I left for school.

Virginia walked out of the kitchen and came back a minute later, carrying a hairbrush and a cotton-candy-pink purse that matched her belt and shoes.

"Do you still know how to use one of these?" she said, handing me the brush. "How do you expect to ever get anywhere in the world looking like that?"

I half-heartedly brushed my hair, making little or no improvement.

She cleaned off the countertop that was already clean and nervously chattered.

"I have an SWS meeting. They are voting on the new secretary and I am one of the nominees. Do you know that the daughter of the president is in your class?"

I knew, all right. It was Emoline. Not only was her father the pastor of the largest church in Jubilee, but her mother, Cordelia, was from money and was the apple of Virginia's social-climbing eye.

The Southern Women's Society, or SWS for short, was a social club, thinly veiled as an organization that did good deeds for the needy in and around Jubilee. It was mostly tea parties and bake sales, but any woman in Jubilee who considered herself fit for society wanted in. Membership was by invitation only. Like most Southern social clubs, the political views ran to the far right, and if you weren't white and Protestant, you would not be receiving the teal-blue invitation that women in town prayed to see in their mailboxes. Sissy had overheard one of the high school teachers say that Miss Adams had received an invitation but had turned them down flat.

Handing me a recipe and a list of chores, Virginia started back in.

"I have set out the flour, egg, and buttermilk. Remember, roll the chicken in the buttermilk and egg, then the flour, then the buttermilk, egg, and flour again. When the Crisco is sizzling, put the chicken pieces in the skillet one by one . . . on medium heat."

I tried to take it all in, but her directions started to sound like a stream of noise from a faraway place. I had never been good at processing multiple instructions.

"The clothes in the basket in the back room need to be hung out on the line, and don't let the chicken burn. I hate the smell of burned food in here; and besides, it's wasteful."

Long before the end of her list, the magical feeling I had floated home in was gone like a toy boat down the river. This was my life with Virginia. Every chore I did was a small penance for the great sin I'd committed against her years ago. Would I always be a prisoner to Virginia and her lists?

She finished with a short "Bye," then took off, plowing her pink patent leather heels into the freshly cut grass, looking down at herself to make sure she was presentable for those she feared she would never measure up to. I took a deep breath, feeling relief wash over me as I watched her perfect figure disappear around the corner onto Cherry Street. In her presence, it was hard to hear my own thoughts or even find my own air to breathe. She used up all the oxygen in the room.

I stood on the porch, waiting until she was out of sight, then ran to steal a cold Coke from the secret stash Daddy kept in an old cooler in the shed. I plucked the red journal from where I'd hidden it behind the azaleas. If Virginia knew I owned a journal, she would make it her job to find it and read it when I was out of the house. I had to keep it a secret.

I traced the deep groove of the black bird's outline on the cover. I sat and let the porch swing drag my toes along the wooden boards, letting the weight of Virginia's expectations slip off my shoulders. I heard a crack when I opened the journal. I loved that sound. Then I found the page where she had written—

*Thank you for being such an engaged and curious student. I think
life holds many possibilities for you.*

All the best,
Constance Adams

I read her inscription over and over again, as if trying to absorb her
words into my skin. I thought of the eruption in class today. Those boys
and Emoline had been so rude to openly disagree with her. But I knew
Miss Adams had pushed the limits on what country folks in Jubilee
could tolerate. "Constance," I whispered to myself, feeling smug that
not even that prissy Emoline knew her first name.

I considered how different Miss Adams and Virginia were. They were
both very beautiful, but Miss Adams was much younger. Miss Adams
walked with a perky stride, confidence dripping from every word that
poured from her genteel lips. Virginia fussed and bothered over every
crooked seam and chipped teacup. Miss Adams was, after all, a working woman, whereas Virginia worked hard to fit in with the crowd of
women who depended solely on the provision of their husbands.

I looked back down at my journal, turned to the first blank page, and
picked up the pen I had found in the kitchen drawer. I wrote *May 29,
1963* at the top and sat staring at it. What should I write?

I set the journal open beside me on the swing and popped off the
top of the Coke bottle, letting the fizz slide down my throat, cold and
sweet, enjoying the momentary feeling of freedom and the possibilities
of the summer days ahead.

3

ISAAC

There were days with Virginia when I wondered if a life on the run might be a better alternative. But I did have a reason to stay. I had Isaac.

His walls were a soft blue. Pictures ripped from magazines he'd read were taped around the room—horses, planets, and mysterious ocean creatures. His cowboy boots were perfectly lined up at the foot of his bed. Little stray shoots of brown hair stuck out from beneath his cowboy sheets and moved to the rhythm of his breathing. I crept in and eased down beside him on the bed. Virginia said he had the stomach bug that had been going around.

Hanging over the top of Isaac's bed was a wooden cross he painted at Vacation Bible School last summer. It had a Navajo design, representing our Native American heritage, though our grandfather had been Cherokee. The teacher had scolded Isaac for that, telling him you couldn't mix being an Indian with Jesus. Isaac said it was his cross and he could do what he liked.

The little Navajo cross was peaceful against the blue wall.

I smoothed the blanket around him, careful not to wake him. He was seven years old and already in the fourth grade. When he was four, his kindergarten teacher noticed he'd finished his crafts long before the others. She peered over his shoulder and saw Isaac writing his name and creating little math problems to solve. While all the other kindergartners were working on the letters *A* and *B*, she saw Isaac reading *Clever Polly and the Stupid Wolf* to himself.

Virginia was called in to meet with the principal, nervous at the thought of embarrassment by yet another Mockingbird child. But to her surprise, the principal explained the observations of the teacher and asked Virginia's permission to have Isaac's IQ tested. When the test came back, he scored 150. They said only one kid in a few thousand had an IQ that high. They moved him into the first grade and then two weeks later moved him up again to second grade.

Honestly, they didn't know what to do with him. He craved learning and tended to find trouble when he got bored. Reading seemed to be the answer to keep him engaged. As his reading skills advanced, he read library books on just about everything that interested him. Western novels were his favorite, but he also read nonfiction—how car engines run, trains, swimming, horseback riding, and his favorites, space exploration and deep-sea diving.

The trouble was, he was so small. The bigger boys took great pleasure in picking on him. He stood his ground, doing his best to uphold his budding manhood. We feared he would get hurt, but he didn't seem to mind that. He was, after all, the grandson of Rowdy Mockingbird, who people said was one of the toughest men to breathe air. He died before we were even born. The way he died left a legacy, not only of his toughness, but also of his stubbornness. He died from an arm-wrestling match. After beating every local challenger, he took on a man three times his size. After a long battle, the giant man slammed Rowdy's arm down so hard that it broke and forced the bone through his skin. He was too proud to go see a doctor, as much as Grandma Josie begged him. The wound turned gangrene and then the poison got into his bloodstream.

Right before he died he told Grandma Josie he wanted his ashes to be buried at the base of an oak tree sapling, so that he would eventually be the strongest and tallest man in the hills through the life of that tree. I had visited the tree in Grandma's backyard, and it always made me wish I'd known him. Isaac was small like Rowdy, and Daddy said when he saw Rowdy's baby picture on the mantel at Grandma Josie's house, Isaac was his spitting image.

But something happened that would forever change the way those bigger boys saw Isaac. Spring of second grade, his class was offered a reward: If everyone passed the end-of-the-year math test, the class could visit the Carter family farm. When Isaac came home talking about it, Virginia worried since the farm had a swimming hole and Isaac had not done much swimming.

Isaac said, "I read a book about it."

"Well, reading is different than doing."

Isaac considered this, then asked, "What if I went with Daddy and Grace for swimming lessons?"

Virginia knew Isaac wasn't one to give up easy, and so she agreed. "If your daddy says you're ready, then I guess you can go."

It was a done deal. We both knew Daddy was an excellent swimmer and had taught me and Sissy to swim. Now it was Isaac's turn. The following Saturday we all headed off to the lake. Daddy was patient with him, like he had been with all of us. By the end of the day Isaac was swimming like a tadpole.

In class, Isaac offered help to anyone who needed it, to prepare for the test. Being just a kid himself, he was able to break the problems down in a way that another kid could understand. His small stature made his massive intellect less intimidating. When the day came to take the test, everyone passed.

The Carter family had dug out a pond that fed into the river. It was like something out of Milton's paradise: Trees hung like a wedding arch over the river, cherry blossoms shimmered in their bright-pink jackets while the butterfly bushes grew wild among the trees and along the riverbank, making the air thick with the sweetness.

There was a vine that had wrapped itself up and around to the very top of a giant walnut tree. It was strong enough to hold a good-size man and hung at the perfect spot where the pond met the river so that you could grab hold of the vine and swing in over the deep part and let go.

Isaac had recounted the story so many times, I had my own memory of it. The vine snapped and Butch Brogan, the largest of the boys that had bullied Isaac, missed the deep part of the pond, hit his head on a rock, and sunk beneath the murky waters. The current moved swiftly and started to drag him away. The dainty teacher and her students stood around while their screams echoed across the water.

Then Isaac jumped up and grabbed the piece of vine still hanging down and swung out, plunging under the deep water. Somehow, even with Butch being twice Isaac's size, Isaac wrapped one arm around his body, using the other to swim with perfect technique. Once Isaac reached shallow water, several of the other boys came to help carry Butch to the riverbank. Isaac pumped on Butch's chest a few times and then did the unthinkable: Leaning down, he put his mouth over Butch's and blew into it. This went on until Butch finally coughed out the river water and gasped for air.

There was a sense of awe around what Isaac had done. How could someone so small do such a large thing? I asked him how he'd known what to do to save Butch the way he did.

He shrugged. "I read a book about it."

I decided to let him keep sleeping while I hung the clothes on the line and then came back in to batter the chicken. I wondered if Isaac was ever gonna wake up. I crept down the hallway and opened the door to his room again. He was still sleeping. I tiptoed over and sat on the corner of his bed. Then I heard Rojo scratching at the back door.

Rojo had arrived on Easter Sunday. Aunt June, who was Daddy's older sister, pulled into our driveway that afternoon as we all sat on the porch digesting our large meal. She got out and immediately pulled a box from the back seat of her car.

"Happy Easter," she said, setting the box down on the bottom step of the porch. "Isaac, this is for you."

He stood up, excited. "What is it, June? What is it?"

"Well, aren't you gonna open it and find out?"

We could hear something inside scratching the sides of the cardboard box. When he opened it, there was a small ball of yellow fluffy feathers with a flash of red on its head. It bolted out of the box, but Isaac caught it.

Daddy whistled. "Would you look at that red crest. *Rojo!*" he said, rolling his *r* the way Zorro did in his movies.

"What does that mean?" Isaac asked.

"It's Spanish for *red*."

"Let's call him that! Let's call him Rojo!" Isaac said.

And we did.

Daddy built a small chicken coop in the back for him, but most of the time he roamed around the yard and did whatever he pleased. He was ornery to everyone except Isaac.

"Roorooroo!" came the call from the back door.

Isaac rolled over in his bed and opened his eyes at the sound, then looked up at me.

"Hey . . . why are you staring at me?" He yawned.

"Just bored. How are you feelin'?"

"I'm all right. Hope I'm not catching." He said this as he tried to tickle my arms and giggled.

"If you get me sick, I'll kill you. School is finally out!" I stood and danced around the room. "School's out, school's out. Aww, you missed the last day, Isaac."

"What a shame," he said, smiling. "Rojo! Stop scratching. I'm coming, I'm coming."

Then he looked at me. "Wanna race?"

He got up and put on some shorts and a T-shirt and we went outside. I hopped on my bike and Isaac put Rojo in the back of his red wagon. We raced down the sidewalk in front of the house. I let him win about half the time to keep it interesting. When Rojo's feathers lifted in the wind, he looked almost regal. People slowed down as they drove by, pointing at Rojo riding in the wagon. He was no ordinary rooster.

I looked back at Isaac laughing and running. He was my best friend in the whole world, and these days, since moving up a grade, he was my only friend. But he was enough.

4

THE FOX
AND
THE DEACON

I awoke the next morning to Isaac standing over me this time, smiling, with his small hand on my arm.

"Grace . . . Gracie. You awake?"

I forced my eyes to open. "Do I look awake? Isaac, I wanted to sleep in. I can't believe you woke me up. Go away." I buried my face in the covers.

"You gotta get up, you gotta see it! Come on, Grace. You're gonna miss it. Get up!" I could smell his little-boy morning breath as he leaned in closer.

"Okay. Okay." I forced my legs over the side of the bed. "I've got to go pee first."

He waited outside the bathroom for me. "Hurry, Grace, you're gonna miss it!"

As soon as I opened the bathroom door, he grabbed hold of my hand and pulled me down the hallway past the spare room where Aunt June slept whenever she visited. It was also our laundry room and where we stored the canned food. Right past it was the screen door that led to the backyard. We burst through it, but I stopped in my tracks. Rojo was sitting atop what looked like a small dog, except its tail was orange and fluffy.

"What in the world?"

"I heard a ruckus and looked out the window and saw Rojo hovering over it."

"What is it?"

"It's a fox."

"No way. Is it . . . dead?"

"I don't know," Isaac answered, his eyes never leaving Rojo. "But look at him, standing on top of that fox like he's conquered Mount Everest."

We inched closer until we could see that the fox was still breathing, his orange furry chest moving up and down. Then we saw a little stream of blood on his face. In a flash he came to and started fidgeting and spinning and putting his paws over his eye that had the blood on it, and then Rojo hopped around and started pecking on his other eye. That's when we noticed the fox's left foot was caught in some barbed wire that had come loose from the fence.

"Look at that, Grace. Rojo hogtied it with barbed wire and then pecked his eye so he couldn't see." Isaac was staring, amazed at this strange mythical creature of ours.

There were moments when Isaac forgot about logic and was like any other kid his age. I surmised that the fox had gotten tangled up in the barbed wire before Rojo found him. But it was much more fun to go along with the way Isaac saw it.

Rojo crowed proudly as he stood atop the poor fox. We laughed until we held our sides and water seeped from our eyes. I put my arm around Isaac's shoulders as we walked through the yard, feeling the wet grass between our toes.

We found Daddy drinking coffee in the kitchen and told him of Rojo's legendary battle. He went out, chased Rojo away, and tied a strip of an old T-shirt around the fox's mouth to keep him from biting him, then untangled him from the barbed wire and put him into a cardboard box.

"He'll easily work that strip off once he's in the box."

Over breakfast he told us his plan. "I'll carry him to another part of town and set him loose. He'll live; don't worry. They are tough to kill and even tougher to outsmart. You know what they say: you can't outfox a fox . . . No one except Rojo."

He laughed and blew on his hot coffee. Isaac threw his head back, laughing to imitate Daddy.

"How about you two come help me out at the garage?"

Isaac spoke through a yawn. "I think I might play with Rojo for a while then sleep a little more, but maybe I could get a ride with Sissy to the garage later?"

Daddy put his large hand on Isaac's head, feeling for warmth, then ruffled his hair. "You sure you don't wanna come, buddy?"

"Yeah, I'm sure."

"Sissy's here and your mama should be home soon from her garden club meeting. I'll call and check on you in a little bit."

I ran to my room and got dressed. Daddy said we'd let the fox go by the riverbank on the way to the garage. We backed out of the driveway in Daddy's blue Volkswagen, listening to the fox scratching against the cardboard box.

As we rode through our neighborhood, we saw Mr. Farris under a large straw hat, deadheading some yellow roses—a chore I guessed Mrs. Farris had given him. Other folks sat rocking on their porches, reading the paper and enjoying the cool of the early morning. I loved how it felt to be with Daddy. We rode in comfortable silence. Each free to breathe our own air.

I cranked the window down and stuck my arm out, feeling the air run between my fingers like water, watching Jubilee roll by. Bright-pink wild Alberta roses and purple lilacs lined the street. I lifted my face into the wind and felt the freedom of summer return. Daddy parked on the shoulder of the road where the forest met the river. He set the box on the ground and opened it. The fox took off running and never looked back.

"He looks happy to be free," I said.

Daddy smiled as he watched the fox run into the trees. "That's how God meant him to be."

We pulled into the garage under the sign standing high above his shop: *VW Repair.*

The small gas station that sat two doors down from our garage was brimming over with men leaning on hoods and slapping their knees at a joke somebody told. Others drank coffee from paper cups. They called out warm hellos to my father and waved at me as we made our way inside.

People called Daddy "the Bug doctor." He was the only mechanic for fifty miles who specialized in VWs. Daddy said that his customers were from all different backgrounds—history buffs, college kids, lawyers, professors, musicians. He seemed to take pride in his association with people of higher learning. Some locals said only liberals drove VWs. I wasn't sure what that meant about my father. The mystery of his unconventional ways revealed itself in layers. I dug down, chipping away for clues and uncovering artifacts of his history. Every layer revealed a different color and texture. But he was, by all accounts, superior to any other man I'd ever known.

I answered the phone, acting as his secretary. I organized his desk and played with the radio, exploring different stations while he attempted to fix a dark-green Bug in the garage.

It was a good morning until a VW came to a screeching stop out front in a storm of gravel dust, and a tall, hulking figure squirmed from behind the wheel. It was Old Man Drake. He stood and wiped a trickle of sweat from his forehead with a dingy white handkerchief that he pulled from his pants pocket, then slammed the driver's side door, as if offering a blow to a disobedient child.

I watched him unseen behind the bookshelf beside Daddy's desk.

Everyone knew Drake had no time for liberals or VWs. The car belonged to his daughter. He was a good twenty years older than Daddy and was known to have a white sheet and a hood in his closet at home. He also fancied himself a local radio personality since he paid for an hour of airtime to advertise deals and luxury items from the furniture store he owned, while featuring special musical guests, including his wife, who was quite possibly the worst singer on earth.

He walked in through the large bay door that stayed open when the weather was warm. I could tell his deodorant was giving out by the sweat rings that had seeped through his brown Western shirt. He wore a small bolo tie and dusty cowboy boots with sharp silver points. I got a whiff of body odor and Old Spice cologne, which made me want to vomit.

"Hello, John."

Daddy wiped his hands on a rag as he looked around the car to see who it was. "Hello, Drake."

Drake walked with his chest out, which couldn't compete with the round belly suspended over his skinny legs. He walked up to my dad, placing his hand on the top of the car Daddy was working on. He took a cigarette out of a pack in his jacket pocket and lit up.

"My daughter's car's been acting up." He paused to take a long drag off his cigarette, coughing as he exhaled. "The baby's down with the croup. If it were me, I'd sell that hunk of junk and get her a Ford." He tapped the long worm of ash off the end of his cigarette, tiny sparks flying like falling stars to the oil-stained concrete floor. "American-made is the only way, if you ask me."

Daddy clenched his jaw. "You can leave the keys over on that peg and I'll get to it as soon as I'm done with this one. It might be a while. If you'd like to use the phone to call for a ride, you're welcome to."

I could tell Daddy was hoping he would leave.

"Oh, that's all right. I'm in no rush."

Daddy's face registered his annoyance as he returned his attention to the open back hatch to work on the engine.

29

Mr. Drake helped himself to some coffee from an old tin pot and continued to hover over Daddy, as if he planned to advise him on any problem he might see. The radio was reporting news about President Kennedy and his views on integrating schools.

Mr. Drake let out a swear word to describe Kennedy that I had heard plenty of times at school. "He's a Socialist, maybe even a Communist!" Drake spat out the words like they were bitter in his mouth.

Daddy worked silently, not looking up. I assumed that Drake swore freely because he didn't notice me sitting there. I swiveled my chair around to watch him.

He looked up at the ceiling of the garage, releasing another tobacco cloud, then blurted out, "I ain't about to share no bathroom or eating place with 'em, no sir."

Daddy looked over at me. Our eyes met. He shook his head in disapproval.

Drake kept going. "Once we do that, they'll want to marry our women. Then we got all these mixed babies messing up the gene pool. What do they call 'em? Mulattos? That's what's coming next, you just watch and see!"

I looked at my own skin, much lighter than Daddy's, since Virginia's skin looked like peaches and milk. What was the name for someone like me that was part Cherokee, part Jewish, and part white?

Daddy gripped the hatch with his rag and slammed it shut. "Drake, you can either leave the car and get a ride or walk back to town, or you can bring it back some other time, because I am in no mood to listen to your mouth."

My breath turned to ice in my throat. Drake jutted out his chest and pressed it into Daddy, then backed off smugly, sizing up his opponent like some dirt under his fingernails. Daddy stayed calm.

"I shoulda known with that Injun and Jew blood in you that you'd be a Yankee sympathizer. I was hoping you'd come around, John, see it the way we do in the brotherhood."

I was pretty sure I knew what "brotherhood" he was talking about.

"Drake, in case you missed it in history class, the Confederacy lost the war."

"Well, some of us are still holdin' to the old ways. Just because some people have caved don't mean we all have to."

"I have work to do, and I can't do it when you keep running your trap."

Old Man Drake and Daddy stood nose to nose. I could barely breathe. Finally, Drake dropped his cigarette and ground it out with his shoe, then aimed a wad of spit on the floor beside Daddy's black work boots. He left a stream of cussing behind him and drove his daughter's car out of there. I was glad to see him go.

Unfortunately, I knew I'd be seeing him again come Sunday. He was a deacon at our church.

Daddy crouched down eye level to me. "I'm sorry you had to hear that, Grace."

"It's okay. But, Daddy . . . Miss Adams says that things are changing. Says that there's a good chance schools will integrate next year. Do you think she's right?"

His face showed a bit of surprise. "Did she say this during class?"

"Yep. None of the other kids liked it much."

He nodded, not surprised by this. "You sure think a lot of Miss Adams, don't you?"

I nodded.

"Well, she's not wrong. There is a good chance. But Drake and the others like him . . . they will fight it every inch of the way. It's amazing how his daughter turned out so nice. Goes to show that someone can end up very different than their raising." He added, "You can't change who your father is."

He squeezed my shoulders, then walked back over to the engine he'd been working on.

It was true—whenever I saw Drake's daughter, Miss Rachel, at church, her face was warm and open and you couldn't help but like her right away. I wondered if Miss Rachel felt the same about her father as Virginia did about hers. When I was younger, I would ask Virginia to tell me stories about him, but she always would change the subject. Before long I stopped asking. Thankfully my eavesdropping from the hallway filled in the gaps of her mysterious history.

Virginia's father, Willy, had come and gone like a bad toothache during her early childhood. Then when she was around ten years old, he left for good. Granny Bee and all her kids had worked through the summer months to grow a huge garden and canned everything under the sun, but by winter, supplies got low. Willy sometimes showed up on their doorstep needing a warm place to stay and some food, and Granny Bee always let him in. Maybe hoping this time things would be different. He had a big appetite so he would dig into seconds before everyone had their first helping. One time they got down to a single jar of green beans and a handful of cornmeal. With five mouths to feed, Granny Bee told him to go get a job. He disappeared into the night after everyone had gone to bed. She had to go begging at the welfare office, humiliating for a proud Kentucky woman.

To her credit, after that, she kicked him out for good. The only way to receive help was to divorce him, so she did. But being a divorced woman was a disgrace.

I tried to imagine how Virginia must have felt with a father who never supported her family and, worse, left them cold and hungry to fend for themselves. Maybe that was why she put so much energy into fitting in with the ladies from SWS. Trying to outrun being the girl with no daddy.

Swiveling around in my chair, I watched as Daddy hummed along to a song on the radio. God had chosen him to be my father. My heart felt like it would burst. I launched myself out of the chair like a rocket toward him. He caught me in his arms and spun me around, and it was once again a perfect day.

5

SUNDAY MORNING

We heard Virginia's voice echoing down the hallway from the kitchen.
"Sissy, Isaac, Grace, it's time to get up and get ready for church!"
She sounded almost pleasant.

I would have been suspicious of her good mood, except she had shared the reason at the dinner table last night over turnip greens, fried chicken, and cornbread.

"Cordelia put me in charge of running the bake sale. The proceeds will buy winter coats for the orphans over in Middlesboro. As y'all know, they are announcing the decision for the new secretary this week. I can't help but think she put me in charge because she knows it's gonna be me!"

Her smile was dazzling. Daddy had reached his hand out to smooth the side of her face and said, "Of course it will be you."

She called again but a little louder. "Sissy, Isaac, Grace, come on now, it's time to get ready for church!"

I could smell bacon frying and fresh biscuits. Virginia was humming a hymn in the kitchen. I wandered down the hall to find Daddy.

I opened the kitchen door and saw Virginia all decked out in her yellow chiffon dress with little pearl buttons all around the neckline. "Where's Daddy?"

"Now what kind of manners is that, Grace? No 'good morning, Mama.' Just 'where's Daddy?'" A trace of a hurt ran across her face.

"I . . . I'm sorry. Good morning." Then I waited. She never even looked up.

"Your daddy's in the backyard reading the paper."

I left as quietly as I could and ran down the hallway, out the back screen door, and into the yard. There was Daddy, under the big oak in his rocking chair with a cup of coffee and the morning paper propped up in front of him. I could see one of the headlines: "Willie Mays Slams Eighth Homer!" Just beside his chair was a worn black King James Bible his mother had given him when he was baptized. He had told me about his trip to the altar at a mountain revival when he was thirteen. Even still, Daddy was his own kind of believer.

Beside the Bible, Rojo sat quietly as if he was waiting to be read to.

"Hey, Gracie." Daddy put down the paper.

I rubbed my eyes and sat on the ground beside his chair, careful not to get too close to Rojo.

"Look at ole Rojo, waiting for his Sunday morning sermon."

I knew what this meant. It was, as far as I knew, my father's only flaw.

"Daddy, are you coming to church with us this morning?"

He took a long drink of coffee, then let out a deep breath. "Gracie, my church is here in the backyard with the Lord among the worms and the birds and Rojo."

He lifted my chin up to look in my eyes and smiled. I knew exactly how he felt. I would have rather mowed the yard with my teeth than go to church and face some of the uppity people at the First Church of Christ of Jubilee.

"Could I stay home too? I could sit here by Rojo and listen to you read!"

His smile drooped. "You know how important it is to your mama that you kids attend church."

"But she wants you to go too. Why is it different for us than for you?"

"I'm sorry, Gracie. It's hard to explain." He leaned over and kissed the top of my head. "You better start getting ready before your mama comes looking for you."

I got up and slumped back into the house. I understood why he didn't want to go, but I wished he would go just the same. Church was so much more bearable with him. I always felt so nervous when Virginia got around people at church. People like Old Man Drake and Cordelia Bluin who looked down on anyone who wasn't up to their standards.

When I was around ten, Virginia told Daddy that it was downright shameful for a woman and her children to attend church alone every Sunday. I heard them arguing in the kitchen from my usual spot in the hall.

"Virginia, if we could go to a different church, somewhere I didn't feel so . . . out of place . . ."

"But John! It's the nicest church in town!"

"Virginia, you know what I'm talking about."

"John, please, darling. If not for me, do it for the kids."

He gave in. That Sunday morning, he let us out at the front door of the church to find a parking spot.

He asked Virginia to save him a seat. He'd meet us inside.

I wondered why in the world Virginia chose a seat so close to the front. I kept turning around in the pew to watch for him. As he walked in through the double doors, his dark Native features stood out in our church like a neon sign. The church grew silent as everyone watched him walk down the aisle. His face flushed and he stared down at the carpet, too embarrassed to look up.

I wanted to run to him, show them how proud I was that he was my father, but I sat there rooted to my pew, betraying the man I loved most. He and Virginia argued about it in the backyard after church. I

35

could hear them through the window of my bedroom. After that, he only came on Easter and Christmas and an occasional Potluck Sunday.

Like him, I never felt like I belonged. At least if Daddy came with me, we could feel like outcasts together. But he could make his own choice. Virginia made mine for me.

I was going. He wasn't.

"Sissy! Let's go!" Virginia's good mood evaporated when Sissy decided to take forever in the bathroom. "Isaac and Grace, you two go ahead and get in the back seat. We will not be late . . . Sissy!"

Finally we were all piled into the car and on our way.

I hated Sunday school, but Sissy loved it for reasons of the flesh rather than the spirit. Taylor Bluin, Cordelia's oldest son and Emoline's big brother, helped out with her class. You never had to twist her arm to go. He had that perfect mixture of bad boy and Southern-gentleman charm that turned girls to mush.

Virginia thought Cordelia was grooming him to be a preacher like his daddy.

The reason I hated Sunday school was Emoline. As if being a bragger and a know-it-all wasn't bad enough, she had humiliated me in class earlier that year when I had first transferred to the ninth grade.

I tried not to hate her, but she made it so easy for me. I saw her standing in the doorway of our classroom. She greeted me with her usual warmth.

"Hello, Grace. My, my, did you sleep in that dress?" she said, turning her perfect little nose up at me. "Doesn't your mama have an iron?"

"Your face needs an iron." The words were out before I could stop them. Something about Emoline thawed my frozen tongue.

She got up close to my face. "Grace, it's not Christian to say such unkind things . . . when I was just trying to help. How do you expect to find a boyfriend looking like that? Since I obviously know how to make a boy notice me and you don't have the first clue."

"Fine by me. You can have them." I had witnessed for myself how shamelessly Emoline gushed and flirted with Douglas Henry and a couple other decent-looking boys in class.

"Well, if you ever want me to give you a makeover, I could give you some tips on how to attract boys."

"I bet you could."

Her eyes narrowed, her hands squeezing into fists. "So ungrateful! Don't come crying to me when nobody wants you." She stormed to the other side of the room.

An afternoon with Emoline would be an endless opportunity for her to belittle me. She was great at finding your weak point and grinding her elbow into it.

I noticed a group of boys surrounding Billy Raines, engrossed in something he was saying. He had been in my eighth-grade class and had always been nice. I moved closer so I could hear. He lifted his hand to wave at me and kept talking.

"I had to hide until nobody was looking then I jumped on right before it took off. Then I jumped off the train over at the old shoe factory at the edge of town."

The boys were guffawing with open mouths and giving him high fives, obviously impressed with his story.

"That's dangerous. Why in the world would anyone want to hop a train?" I blurted out, not meaning for the thought to reach my lips and fly into the air. They all turned sharply in my direction, annoyed by the intrusion.

"That's 'cause you're a girl," one of them said, rolling his eyes at the others.

I wanted to crawl under my chair.

Billy came to my rescue. "She's right, I guess." Shrugging his shoulder, then beaming a mischievous smile at me, he added, "But since when is playing it safe any fun, right?" Then he winked at me. I felt my stomach flip and averted my eyes, relieved when the Sunday school teacher called us to order.

Emoline sat by herself at the front. Being the preacher's kid, I wondered if she was always trying to be the perfect daughter her parents expected her to be. She was the first to raise her hand whenever a question was asked, which was annoying.

Halfway through, Cordelia peeked her head in the door. "Sorry to interrupt. I need Emoline's help with another class."

"Of course! Whatever you need," the teacher gushed. The Bluins had so much influence, most people wanted to be in their good graces. They were the closest thing to royalty that Jubilee had.

Emoline tossed a nasty look at me as she passed by.

I once asked Daddy how Pastor Bluin got to be head pastor of the largest church in town since I could hardly stay awake through his sermons. Daddy said he had "pull." Cordelia's daddy was the president of the bank.

I guess that explained why Cordelia's brother, Oden—or Dr. Oden, I should say—had just been appointed chief of medicine at Middlesboro General Hospital even though everybody knew that Dr. Clarke was just about the best doctor in all of Kentucky. Daddy said he graduated at the top of his class at Duke University, which had one of the most prestigious medical schools in the country. Dr. Oden, on the other hand, had come close to flunking out of the medical school in New Orleans. Even the Bluins had secrets to hide, but they had money and influence to smooth them over.

Daddy once asked Dr. Clarke why he ended up in a small town like ours. He said he used to spend summers with his grandparents who lived in Middlesboro and remembered the poor care they received as they aged. Small hospitals in the South often provided second-rate care because the best doctors left to work in the city.

When the bell rang for Sunday school to be over, I walked out into the hallway and met up with Isaac. As we headed toward the sanctuary,

Virginia was standing in the foyer talking to Cordelia and Emoline. She looked in our direction and waved us over. No way this could be good.

"That's a marvelous idea," I heard Virginia say as we got closer. "Grace, Emoline was just telling me about her sweet offer to give you a makeover. She says you were reluctant to agree." She stressed the word *reluctant* as her eyes bugged out at me.

Cordelia looked down at me with pity. I wasn't sure what to say, so I didn't say anything.

I stared at Emoline, who was smiling at me as if we were the best of friends.

"Grace, I'm sure you would just love to spend an afternoon getting a makeover, wouldn't you, dear?" Virginia's bulging eyes made it clear what my answer better be.

"Well, Grace," said Cordelia. "What do you say?"

Isaac nudged me with his elbow.

"Yes, ma'am."

"Yes, ma'am, what?"

"Yes, ma'am, I'd be happy for Emoline to give me a makeover." The words came out robotic, but it was all Virginia needed.

"How perfect." Virginia gave her most charming, plastic smile and clasped her hands together in delight. "Maybe we could have a visit while the girls are enjoying their afternoon. When should we do it?"

There it was. Her ulterior motive revealed.

Emoline chimed in, "How about tomorrow?" She looked up at Cordelia.

"Tomorrow is fine."

"Marvelous!" Virginia rushed to answer. "Say, eleven o'clock?"

"We'll see you then." Cordelia seemed as pleased at the thought of torturing me as Emoline did.

6

BANGS

Virginia woke me up tearing through my closet. There wasn't much to choose from. She paused on the brown jumper, holding it out in front of me on the hanger.

"What about this?"

I shook my head with determination. That brown jumper had been the cause of the most humiliating moment of my life. She relented and moved it out of sight to erase it from both our memories.

While she searched for a dress, she started lecturing me. "Be polite to Emoline. She is so nice to offer to do this. Maybe you two will become good friends!"

I rolled my eyes.

The words on the tip of my tongue were, *"I just hope I don't end up punching her."* But I squeezed my lips tight, swallowed hard, and tried to be the obedient daughter Virginia wanted me to be.

Finally, way in the back, she found a light-blue sundress that showed my growth spurt since I'd worn it last summer. She wrinkled her nose. "This will have to do."

Before we left, I heard Virginia in Isaac's room. I went to listen at the door. "Isaac, are you feeling poorly again this morning?"

Her voice was so sweet and tender. It reminded me of the last time she'd spoken to me like that—when I was about Isaac's age and had a bad case of the chicken pox. She sat beside my bed, spoon-feeding me small bites of vanilla ice cream, cooing, "There you go, my baby girl." That felt like another Virginia and another me. I couldn't imagine her speaking to me like that now.

"Isaac?" she prodded.

Isaac yawned a little before responding. "I'm just a little tired."

Her brows met in the middle and she placed the back of her hand on his forehead.

"No fever . . . well, all right then. Sissy's here. I'll tell her to look in on you. I left biscuits in the bread box for you."

"Okay, Mama."

I crept back down the hallway and slipped into the bathroom to inspect myself in the mirror. I dreaded the next two hours.

"Grace. Are you ready? Time to go."

Her voice was void of all the warmth she had for Isaac.

I came and looked up at her, saying nothing, hoping she would have a sudden rush of mercy and not make me go.

"Why are you just standing there? Let's go!"

* * *

The Bluins lived on Dogwood Lane, where the houses were surrounded by perfectly painted white picket fences and large shade trees. Wisteria vines, plump with pink and white blossoms, hung like a canopy over walkways and sidewalks. It was the nicest street in town. Their two-story Victorian home had fancy windows and a round turret on one end. A porch with ceiling fans wrapped around the front. A Negro maid in a crisp white dress with a black apron carried a large tray. She began setting the table with crystal glasses of iced tea and a plate of finger sandwiches and cookies.

I had never seen anything like it except in pictures from the Emily Post book that Cordelia had recommended to Virginia.

I met the maid's eyes and she smiled slightly before returning her attention to her work.

Virginia looked spellbound. "How lovely."

Cordelia greeted us as we walked up the porch steps.

"Hello, Virginia. Grace." She glanced down at her watch. It was eleven o'clock on the dot. "Grace, Emoline is inside. Follow me."

As we stepped in, I could feel myself shrinking.

Virginia was breathless. "Your home is spectacular."

Cordelia gave us a tour, guiding us left to a room she called "the parlor." I had never noticed before what large feet Cordelia had, compared to Virginia's tiny size six. I would have guessed her a size ten easy. She caught me staring at her feet and ruffled the bottom of her dress, as if trying to conceal them. She walked us to a gigantic painting of her children.

"I sent a photograph away to this famous painter in Minneapolis. As you can imagine, it was quite expensive, but it was worth every penny to have them immortalized. They look royal, don't they?"

It was impressive, though I thought the hands all looked too big and the noses too small.

Emoline came into the parlor and posed for a moment beside the portrait of herself. I noticed she was wearing the same dress as in the painting.

"Emoline, stand up straight!"

Her face flushed with embarrassment at being disciplined by her mother in front of us. She reached out for my hand and pulled me, running, behind her.

"Emoline! No running in the house!"

She slowed to a fast walk, looking back at her mother with disdain.

42

I followed her, staring up at the high ceilings and large windows. It was like something out of *Better Homes and Gardens*, which was Virginia's favorite magazine. She regularly circled items she loved and left it lying around open for Daddy to see. I had always loved my home, but now it seemed small and drab in comparison.

Emoline stood in the hallway with her hand on the knob of the closed door and took a deep breath before opening it. "And this is *my* room."

It was a dream in pink. In the center was a large poster bed with a pink canopy over the top. She had a collection of dolls that all looked strangely similar to her, with blue eyes and ringlets in their hair. They were lined up on a bookshelf. There were no books.

"Isn't it beautiful?"

Before I could stop myself, I whistled the way Daddy did when he saw something amazing. "It sure is."

For a split second she acted as though she were sincerely happy that I was there. It occurred to me that she had never seemed close with any of the girls in our class. But then again, neither had I. Maybe she wanted a friend but had no idea how to be one.

She led me into her closet, which was the size of my bedroom. There was a long row of dresses on hangers, with shelves built into the wall for shoes and hats. Eyes wide, I admired all of her dresses, praying she wouldn't bring up what had happened at school earlier that year.

"Now . . ." She turned me to a mirror on the wall. "Let's take a look at you. For starters, you never wear anything to accentuate your features. Look at this dress. It's just so plain and it's way too small and your hair just hangs there." She grabbed a light-green dress and held it up to me.

I looked into the mirror, noticing that the color made my skin glow.

"See how that sets off your plain features?"

Even when she tried to say something nice, she still ended up insulting me. She put the dress back and clapped her hands excitedly. "We have work to do. Work to do!"

I followed her back into her room, where she sat me down in front of what she called her "vanity." It was a small table with a fancy chair and lights around the mirror. It looked like something I'd seen in movie stars' dressing rooms. When I looked in the mirror with the lights around it, I noticed dark circles under my eyes. My hair looked even frizzier than usual.

"This mirror is designed to show all of your flaws so that you can fix them before you go out in public."

I was in hell.

She put one hand on top of my head and struggled to get the brush through my hair.

"Grace, do you ever brush your hair? Look at all these tangles."

I had brushed it, but it was a losing battle.

She rolled small sections of my hair onto the same kind of pink rollers Virginia wore to bed.

"Now, for makeup." She started with powder, then added pink eyeshadow and blush. "You have to fix yourself up so that boys will notice you."

"What if I don't care if boys notice me?"

"Grace, how in the world will you ever find a husband if boys don't notice you?"

I guess I never considered that.

I didn't want to criticize her, but the eye shadow was way too bright and my cheeks looked like they were bleeding. After a while she took the rollers out and brushed my hair out into soft waves. It looked a little like Virginia's, which shocked me.

"Now, let's see. You need a dress . . . follow me!" I walked behind her back into the closet.

I was secretly praying she would choose the green dress but no such luck.

"I never wear this old thing anymore. Put this on." She threw a dark-blue dress at me. "Go ahead. Change. I'm a girl. You don't have anything I haven't seen before."

I was wearing a hand-me-down bra of Sissy's and un-matching underwear. I could feel Emoline's eyes on me—nothing in my "make-over" nightmares prepared me for being in my underwear in front of Emoline. I turned around, facing the corner as she watched me pull the dress over my head. Finally I had it on. She came forward and tied the belt around my waist, pulling it so tight that it hurt.

"Ouch!"

"Don't be such a baby."

We stood close to each other. She was a head taller than me and her hands shook a little as she tied the belt.

"There's one last thing. Come on!"

Grabbing my arms, she pulled me behind her and sat me back down at the dressing table. I felt assaulted by my own reflection. If she added a curly wig and a red nose, I could have been a clown.

"Emoline, could you tone down the eye shadow a little? It's too bright."

"What? No, it's perfect! I have *one* final surprise for you."

She laid a curling iron on the glass top of the dressing table. I had only seen a picture of one in a magazine.

"You can curl your hair in a flash. I think there's a few pieces here in the front that need an extra touch-up."

I was nervous, but I sat still as she rolled my bangs into the iron. I leaned away from the heat, afraid she would burn my forehead. "Careful . . . it's hot."

"I've watched my mother curl hers a dozen times. Stop worrying."

She stood there twisting my hair around the hot silver surface. Suddenly my hair started smoking.

"Emoline, take it out . . . it's smoking!"

"That's normal. Just a few seconds more."

"Take it out!"

The smell of burned hair wafted into the air with small wisps of smoke. When she finally unrolled it, half of my bangs fell to the floor. The other part was scorched and singed. Both our mouths gaped open as we stared at the burned hair on the floor.

"Oh, I guess I did leave it on for too long." She slapped her hand over the laugh she wasn't trying very hard to contain.

I looked horrific.

Before I could say anything, she lifted a pair of scissors lying on the table and cut off the remaining fringes of my burned bangs almost up to my scalp.

"Stop!"

"I was just trying to get the burned parts off." Emoline tried to suppress her laughter as she looked at my reflection.

Was that freakish clown with no bangs in the mirror really me?

"You did this on purpose!"

"No, I didn't! It was an accident. I promise!" she declared, barely holding back a grin.

If I stayed there any longer, I would punch her, so I ran out of the room and onto the porch.

Virginia's mouth dropped open in shock. "Grace, what happened to your hair?"

"She burned it," came Emoline's voice from behind me. "I tried to tell her not to leave the curling iron on for so long, but she wouldn't listen."

I whipped around, not believing that she was turning this on me. She pleaded with a genuine look of fear in her eyes, but I did not care.

"She's lying!" I couldn't stop myself.

Cordelia exploded, "How rude and ungrateful!"

Virginia was mortified. "Grace, I want you to apologize to Emoline and Cordelia for your unthinkable behavior!"

"But I didn't burn it! She did!"

Virginia stood. "Grace! Not another *word*. I am so sorry for all of this, Cordelia."

Cordelia gave Emoline a questioning look before she turned back to me. "Next time, Grace, you'll learn to listen."

Virginia squinted against Cordelia's comment but immediately recovered. "Grace, go change back into your dress and give Emoline hers back."

"Gladly" flew out of my mouth before I could catch it. I ran back to Emoline's room and tore off the dress, leaving it in a heap in her stupid princess room, and put my own ugly dress back on. I ran out of the front door and off the porch to the car without saying another word.

Virginia followed me, apologizing the whole time. I hated them. I hated their house and Emoline's stupid makeup mirror.

When Virginia got in the car, it began. "Grace! What an embarrassment! We were having such a lovely time. How could you?"

"She lied! *She* burned my hair. She just didn't want to get in trouble and she knew you wouldn't go against Cordelia."

"Why, Grace, you are making this up."

"No! I'm not!"

She looked over at me and then composed herself. "I wonder if you just misunderstood Emoline," she said, exasperated and confused. "All this trouble. Cordelia probably thinks you have no manners. That reflects poorly on me."

"But I didn't do anything!"

"Quiet! I don't want to hear another word. There are more important things in the world than bangs."

"I hate you." It was out before I could reel it back in.

She let out a gasp as if my words had stabbed her, then she went quiet and I let the bitter words ring in the still air. Cordelia and Emoline stood hand in hand on the porch. Godzilla and her little protégé. Virginia waved goodbye stiffly, but I stared at Emoline, wishing I had punched her while I had the chance.

When we got home I went straight to the bathroom to see my burned and chopped bangs, my face looking ridiculous with all the bright circus clown colors. I washed the makeup off as best I could and stewed in my anger for the rest of the day. I guess I shouldn't have been surprised that Virginia would believe the perfect girl Emoline and not me. But I knew Daddy would believe me.

When he got home, I ran to the living room to meet him at the door. He zeroed in on my bangs. "Grace, what happened to your hair?"

Virginia spoke up as she walked down the hallway, drowning out my hope of being heard. "She and Emoline had a little mishap with the curling iron."

Daddy saw my face and lingered there as I stood shaking in anger. "I'm sorry, Grace."

Our eyes locked. Then Virginia broke our silent bond. "Her bangs will grow back. It's not the end of the world."

Maybe not to her.

"Grace, come help me with dinner, please."

I felt the rage boiling inside of me with no hope for escape, at least not as long as Virginia was around. I let the anger seep into my body. I wasn't sure where all of these words and emotions went when you swallowed them down, but I felt them in deep places hidden beneath organs and bones. Her refusal to let me tell my side of the story only showed how obsessed she was with Cordelia's approval. So I did what I always did. I told myself this too was penance for the wrong I'd done to her.

7

WATER
AND BLOOD

On Wednesday night, more than a week after the burned bangs incident, we got ready to sit down to a meal of pork chops, mashed potatoes, and fried green tomatoes. Earlier that day, Virginia had announced that she was planning a special dinner to celebrate a momentous occasion. None of us knew what she was talking about until Daddy pulled into the driveway.

Virginia rushed to the front door and said, "Better go see what your dad brought home!"

Isaac and I tore through the screen door, the rare sound of Virginia's laughter mixed with our stampede down the front porch steps. Daddy hoisted a cardboard box out of the back seat. We could see what it was by the picture on the front. We jumped and spun in circles, the bright-green grass digging into the soft bottoms of our bare feet. Televisions were just becoming commonplace in Jubilee. Our family had been saving for several months in an old mason jar that sat on the top shelf over the icebox. Daddy and Virginia had counted up the money two nights before. There was just enough to purchase a small set.

It was most definitely a momentous occasion. Even Sissy ran out to see. She started talking about a dance show called *American Bandstand* that she was *dying* to watch, though I was pretty sure she would have to get Virginia out of the house to do so. We followed Daddy up the steps.

As he worked to get it all set up, we buzzed around the small TV like bees around a honeycomb. To think we would have a little movie screen right in our house. Movie stars would be close enough to reach out and touch. They always seemed too far away at the Bijou.

Daddy set the TV up on the counter so we could all see it from the kitchen table. He adjusted the long silver antennae he called "ears." Virginia was humming a gospel hymn, decked in her apron and pearls as she stirred the giant pot of mashed potatoes, adding ample amounts of butter and sour cream. She was the newly appointed secretary of the SWS and in an unusually good mood. I was relieved that my whole bang fiasco had not prevented her from getting the position but still daydreamed about getting even with Emoline.

"Gracie, would you please set the table? Make Emily Post proud!" She spoke with sweetness as she gave me a smile and a wink.

I looked around to make sure she was talking to me.

"Sissy, can you fill the glasses with milk? Isaac, can you get the loaf of white bread for the table, darlin'?" We never ate dinner without a loaf of white bread on the table, though I wasn't sure why.

We worked in harmony, getting everything ready. Daddy's face beamed with pride for our happy home. A home without mice or squirrels running through the walls, the way he had grown up. Virginia walked over to him, wrapping her arms around his waist, and leaned in to give him a kiss. It almost took my breath away. I couldn't remember a time when she had shown open affection to him. I could see in that moment how much she adored him and certainly how over the moon he was for her. Those movie stars had nothing on Virginia with her hair up in a French twist and red lips that set off her milky skin and dark hair.

We gathered around the table, sitting in our normal places.

"First, we give thanks." Daddy smiled at each of us as we joined hands to say a brief prayer of thanks for food and health and the new television.

"And everyone said . . . amen!" we all chimed together. With his hand on the power knob, we counted down, "Three, two, one . . . Hooray!" A cheer went up when the picture came to life.

"Turn it up!" Sissy called out.

We were just in time to see the Beach Boys in matching plaid shirts singing "The Summertime Blues." Sissy practically fainted at the sight of them. Virginia rolled her eyes. We dug into the excellent dinner, watching the screen. Isaac was dipping his white bread into the mashed potatoes and gravy and laughing at Sissy singing along with the Beach Boys.

Virginia looked over and said, "Gracie, your hair looks so smooth. Did you do something special to it, dear?"

The word *dear* almost made me choke on my pork chop. I had smoothed my bangs down at the sides with bobby pins, trying to make my hair look like less of a disaster. "Y-y-yes. I put a little bit of lard on it."

Virginia's face twisted in confusion. I panicked to explain, afraid of bursting this beautiful bubble we were in.

"I took a spoon and got a tiny bit from out of the mason jar where you save the grease drippings. A while back Miss Pearl at the peach stand told me it worked, and it does, like a charm, but it makes it greasy if you put too much on, I guess. It was so frizzy today with all the humidity, I thought I'd give it a try."

Isaac looked from me to Virginia, as though he were watching a Ping-Pong match, waiting for someone to miss the return.

I added, "Miss Adams says Miss Pearl is a very wise woman."

Virginia's eyes widened and her lips were pursed with a comment when Daddy shushed us to listen.

The bottom of the screen read *CBS News* and a man named Walter Cronkite spoke. "Last night President Kennedy addressed the unrest that has reached a boiling point in Southern states." Images flashed of

Negroes sitting at lunch counters and a hateful-looking man surrounded by state troopers, blocking the door to keep a Negro girl from enrolling in the same college as whites.

The screen returned again to Walter Cronkite, who continued, "The unthinkable violence against the children you see here was suffered at the hand of one of the South's most notorious segregationists, Bull Connor."

Grainy black-and-white images appeared of what seemed to be an ocean of children walking in their Sunday clothes. We sat wordless when the picture changed to streets full of children running from fire hoses held by police; the force of the water ripped clothes and nearly the skin off little brown boys and girls hunkered down in corners trying to escape. Police officers were swinging their clubs at young boys to force them into the waiting paddy wagons. Water flooded down the street. The camera zoomed in on a boy crying and holding his head with a streak of blood trickling down into his eyes. Daddy sat stone-faced, shaking his head.

The TV switched to a clip of a man standing at a pulpit, shaking his fist.

"Who is that?" Sissy asked.

"The police commissioner in Birmingham, Bull Connor. He hates Negroes at the risk of hell and damnation."

"John, please!" Virginia protested.

"It does no good to shelter them from the truth." He said this softly and kept watching.

I thought of Miss Pearl, how kind she was to all the kids at school even when they walked right by, never acknowledging her, or worse, said mean things. And I thought of Mr. Hutch down at the gas station, who Daddy always spoke to. Daddy told me he walked with a limp because he took a bullet in the Army during the Korean War. He always called me "Miss Grace" and would ask, "Would you like a jawbreaker, Miss Grace?" His voice was scratchy and soft, and he had kind eyes.

I wondered how those police officers and firemen could hurt these children when it was their job to keep them safe. Fear and sweat trickled down the back of my neck.

Virginia shot from her chair and switched the TV off.

"Virginia, why did you do that?" Daddy's voice sounded annoyed.

"Because I've heard enough of this . . . and there's nothing to be done about it anyway."

"Miss Adams says—"

She jerked her head in my direction so fast I thought it might fly off her neck. *"Miss Adams says, Miss Adams says!"* she spit out. "Grace, you'd be wise to take caution who you listen to, especially the likes of her."

I jolted back, feeling as though I'd been slapped. Why was she attacking Miss Adams? I started to say something else to defend Miss Adams, but Daddy shook his head in warning to me.

Daddy, Isaac, Sissy, and I cleared the table and washed the mountain of dishes while Virginia disappeared into the backyard. She was probably picking out a switch for me. I didn't care. My anger had gone from a simmer to a full boil. Just as I got back to my room and was about to put on my nightgown, Virginia called me back to the kitchen impatiently.

"Grace Louise, bring shampoo and a towel to the kitchen sink."

My stomach sizzled with acid. I took my time going into the bathroom, expressing my own subtle protest. I stiffly brought them to the kitchen. She stood at the sink and with a single hard turn of the faucet, the water gushed from the tap.

"No daughter of mine will be walking around with lard in her hair. Lean your head over . . . over!"

How many times had I heard her say, "No daughter of mine"? My anger mingled with despair. I was a reminder of the past she could not wash away. Hating her would feel so good.

"And whoever is putting these lofty ideas in your head, Grace, let me remind you that you live under my roof and are to follow my rules."

I knew the "whoever" she was referring to.

"Grace, keep your head still!"

The water chilled me to the bone. I shivered. "It's cold."

"That's right it's cold. There's no sense wasting hot water when cold would do just as well," she said, her voice as icy as the sink water.

She scrubbed my scalp until I thought it would bleed. When she was finished, I wrapped the towel around my head. I couldn't help the hot tears falling down my face as I ran to my room.

I heard a quiet knock.

"Grace . . . it's Isaac. You okay? Can I come in?"

Isaac slipped in through the crack in the door that I made for him. I sat on my bed and turned my head away from him. I didn't want to meet his eyes. I mindlessly stared at the drawings he had made for me that were taped to my pale-green walls, warm tears falling on the bare skin of my legs.

He shuffled to my bedside and sat down beside me. "I think your hair is nice, Grace."

I could see how much he wanted me to feel better, and that made me want to feel better, if not for me, for him. I put my arms around his neck and hugged him so tight I was afraid I'd break him.

Isaac returned my hug, then grabbed the deck of cards from my bedside table. "Hey, I read a book about card tricks and I've been practic-ing." He shuffled the cards and spread them out in a fan. "Pick a card!"

We sat in my room while Isaac amazed me with card tricks. I thought of Daddy and Virginia kissing. I thought of the children marching. How brave they were.

* * *

In the middle of the night I heard Virginia crying. I got up quietly and listened outside their bedroom door. I heard the rumble of Daddy's voice, soft and comforting. I heard him ask, "What reminded you?"

Her answer was so soft I strained to make it out. "The water and . . . the blood." She cried even harder.

An ache rose up in my chest. I knew I was the cause of her suffering. How could she or God ever forgive me, and what right did I have to be angry at her? There was a debt to pay.

Whatever happened, I had it coming.

8

RED BOOTS

Virginia's eyes were red and swollen in the morning. I wasn't sure if anyone else had heard her, but Isaac was especially quiet, which made me think he had. Sissy was still sleeping. Daddy asked me and Isaac to go along with Virginia to town and help her carry home gardening supplies. Isaac and I ate oatmeal by ourselves in the kitchen while Virginia and Daddy were in the backyard making a list before Daddy left for work.

Isaac slid his hand across the table and placed it in mine. I squeezed his hand. Virginia came through the hallway calling, "Kids, are you ready to go?" We heard the screen door open and then shut. We scrambled out, nervous about keeping her waiting.

On the drive to the hardware store, any trace of what happened the night before was gone. The children's march and her emotional breakdown were all folded and tucked away neatly in a drawer. By all outward appearances this was a normal Thursday morning. She was chipper and buzzed about her flowers, hoping they would be chosen to be photographed by the garden club for Jubilee's weekly paper.

"Mayella Thompson, the mayor's niece, has a breathtaking rose garden that will be tough to beat, but who knows!"

Isaac asked from the back seat, "Mama, what is your favorite flower?"

"Hmmm . . . my favorite flower . . . that would have to be a daylily. They are a dazzling yellow and only in full bloom for a single day before they begin to fade."

"That's sad," I said.

"Yes, it is." Our eyes locked in the rearview mirror.

Her happy voice was betrayed by a sarcastic bite.

Then Isaac asked, "Do we have any at home?"

"In the backyard. They bloomed in the spring."

"I guess we missed it," Isaac said.

Virginia looked away from me. The tension she had tucked away gathered into the ghost that was always floating between us.

At the store, Isaac and I followed her through the aisles to the greenhouse in the back, where they kept annuals and perennials. There by the dahlias and echinacea was my makeover buddy, her face transformed by the earthy smell of blossoms. She didn't see us walk up behind her.

"Emoline, stop daydreaming and let's go!" Cordelia's voice broke in, shattering her floral dream.

Emoline turned, her breath catching when she saw us, realizing we had heard her mother's reprimand. She was holding a flat of yellow and orange begonias in her arms and did not meet my gaze.

Isaac spoke first. "Those sure are pretty flowers."

"Thank you, Isaac."

I looked at Isaac with obvious confusion and disapproval and then followed with a sarcastic question. "Since when did you guys become such good friends?"

Emoline snapped back at me, "Is it such a shock that you don't know everything, Grace?"

Isaac giggled at this, which evoked unexpected laughter from Emoline. I wanted to throttle him. How could Isaac be nice to her after what she had done to me? I had told him the whole story the night it happened.

I let my eyes drill a hole into hers and then his, willing myself not to touch my bangs.

Cordelia was turned out in a pink floral frock with a pink straw hat and a man-size pair of pink sandals.

"Cordelia, aren't you a vision in that coluh," Virginia said with forced charm, leaving off the *r* on the end of *color*. I tried not to roll my eyes.

"Hello, Virginia." There was an awkward pause. "Just picking up a few things for my garden. Did you watch the news last night?"

"Yes, we just got a new TV."

A fact Virginia seemed a little too anxious to share.

This was not lost on Emoline. "Y'all are just now getting a television? We've had one in the living room for over a year, and my daddy just bought another one for the kitchen."

A lopsided grin with a slight nod of her head showed Cordelia's approval of Emoline's boast about their family's superior status.

Cordelia's next words seemed casual, almost bored. "Things are the way they are for a reason. Those Northerners are known to be godless heathens, going in for all manner of sin. I'm just so thankful we have it straight here in the South, aren't you, Virginia?"

A moment of indecision ran across Virginia's face before she nodded in agreement.

"We'd better be on our way . . . lots of gardening to do," Cordelia said, clearly done with the conversation. As she passed by me, she stared at my bangs and clucked her tongue to remind me how rude I had been. I wanted to give her an earful but I knew better. Even without a threat from Virginia, Cordelia was a grown-up and the preacher's wife. To back-talk an adult was almost as bad as taking the Lord's name in vain. It was a cardinal sin of Southern manners.

I looked over at Isaac, who was in a daze watching Emoline walk away. Did Isaac have a crush? On Emoline?

At the till, Rank Gunner and Brady Boon sat on each side of a barrel with a checkerboard between them, talking to Mr. Handy while they played. Virginia pushed her cart up, and Mr. Handy rang up the items one by one.

"Hello, Mrs. Mockingbird, kids. How are y'all today?"

"Fine, thank you, Mr. Handy."

He reached under the till and handed Isaac and me each a small sucker.

"Thank you!" Isaac and I chimed together. He had always been such a nice man.

Rank Gunner, the father of my classmate Eli, leaned back in his chair, putting his red cowboy boots on the top of the barrel, and spit into a small tin can. He looked Virginia up and down in a way that made me want to gouge out his eyes. A bit of black tobacco juice pooled in the corner of his mouth. I thought of the bruise on Eli's back.

He tipped his hat to her. "I couldn't help but overhear what you and the preacher's wife was saying."

Virginia continued to place the things from her cart onto the counter. She looked his way but did not respond.

He leaned back and tipped his chin up in the air, dribbling more tobacco juice and a stream of smugness down his face. I heard the jingle of the front door but was too distracted by Mr. Rank's ranting to turn around and see who had entered the store. "You just got to remind them who they is and who is boss."

He rose up, bringing his red boots back down to the floor in a loud thud. He licked his thumb and put it over one of the black checkers. "You gotta keep your thumb on 'em all the time."

He laughed, his teeth stained brown and crooked like swinging doors collapsing in the middle.

I wanted so much to stand up to Rank and tell him what Miss Adams had told us, but the words were nailed down inside me. Rank jerked his head toward the front door and looked with disdain, which made me turn to see what had become the brunt of his disgust.

Daddy's friend Mr. Hutch stood with his little girl, who looked to be my age. Their sad eyes both found mine. Hutch's large hand trembled as he turned his daughter around and out of the store. I wanted to run after them and say something, but what?

Rank spat into his can, watching Hutch limp away, and grunted, "Good riddance," his ripe hatred on him like his body odor and his name.

Isaac quietly stepped closer, picked up one of Brady's checkers, and jumped a line of Rank's checkers, moving into the king position.

"Hey, what do you think you're doing?" Rank's anger flared, but Brady was snickering and nodded his approval, patting Isaac on the back.

Isaac peered intently into Rank's eyes.

I noticed a small grin of satisfaction on Virginia's face. "We better be going. Good day, Mr. Handy."

I shrunk back in shame, wishing I had done something to stand up for Hutch the way Isaac had. But I was too scared of making Virginia upset. Too afraid of what Rank Gunner might do. I loathed myself. Was it good manners or cowardice that kept me from speaking out?

When I got home, I retreated to my room and wallowed in my self-loathing, which lasted through the weekend and made church on Sunday even more miserable than usual.

* * *

On Monday afternoon, Virginia called Isaac and me into the kitchen. "Kids, your daddy's on his way home from the garage. When he gets here, you need to leave him be, give him some space."

"What's wrong?" Isaac asked.

"Just do as I say, please." She turned her back and continued chopping a pile of raw vegetables on the counter.

As we left the kitchen, we heard the phone ring and Virginia say, "Hello, Cordelia!"

Isaac's eyes locked with mine. "You okay, Grace?"

I shrugged.

"Why have you been in your room all morning?"

I couldn't explain, so I changed the subject.

We heard the sound of tires on the driveway gravel.

I whispered, "Do you want to go see Daddy?"

He nodded.

Our curiosity wouldn't allow us to follow orders, and since Virginia was on the phone, this was our chance. We watched through the back screen door as Daddy walked to the shed. We eased out, careful not to let the door slam behind us.

When Daddy was upset, he always went to the shed.

Rojo was pecking in the dirt under the old oak tree and followed us through the yard like a dog would.

We could hear the twang of country music on Daddy's radio with the twisted wire hanger that he had fashioned into an antenna. As we peeked in around the doorway, we saw him hammering nails into a bench he was making for Virginia's garden.

Rojo made a clucking sound and Daddy turned to us.

"You kids need something?"

We hesitated, then ran to him, wrapping ourselves around his waist. He placed an arm around each of us, his shoulders slumping.

"Daddy, did I do something wrong?" Isaac asked.

"Was it me?" I asked.

"It's not either of you. Y'all go play and take Rojo with you."

He turned away from us and went back to his hammering.

Virginia and Daddy fought in the kitchen for a long time that night. Their voices, hissing in strained whispers, were easily heard if you sat close enough. Isaac came out and joined me in the hallway and we both listened. Even Sissy, who Daddy said could sleep through an atomic bomb, roused and came to the doorway of her room before she lost interest and went back to bed.

"John, I do not approve of this! Folks in town will think we are troublemakers. I have worked so hard to finally fit in . . ." Virginia lowered her voice. "You know whose husband is a member, don't you? This could cost me my position. I'm finally being accepted, John. All that work, out the window, for something we can't change anyway."

"Virginia! There are some things that matter more than what Cordelia thinks." He slammed his fist on the kitchen table, which rattled the coffee cups and saucers.

Isaac and I smacked our hands over our mouths. I couldn't remember a single time when Daddy had spoken that sternly to Virginia or with any of us. We snuck back to our rooms. I lay in my bed, unable to sleep. I was comforted by the train whistle blowing high and lonesome. With my windows open, it sounded close by. A part of me wished I could jump on that train and ride away from all of this.

9

RED HOOD

The next morning, I threw off the tangle of sheets and wiped beads of sweat from my forehead as I heard Daddy's voice: "Sissy, Isaac, Grace—time to get up."

We all rolled out like soldiers into the hallway; his voice had an "I mean business" quality. I was nervous his mood would turn even worse. Virginia was nowhere in sight. A large pot of oatmeal sat ready on the stove. He asked us to dress quickly, eat, and come meet him on the porch. We did as we were told.

Sissy, who was the last to get dressed, appeared in the kitchen, ate her oatmeal, and ignored us as usual. We felt a little lower than dirt around her. It was a gift she had. Isaac wasn't eating much.

"Aren't you gonna eat your oatmeal, Isaac?"

"I don't feel hungry."

I put the back of my hand on his forehead the way Daddy sometimes did. It didn't feel any warmer than mine, but it was already so dang hot it was hard to tell. I was sure he felt nervous like I did, though it didn't seem to affect my appetite.

When we finished eating, we washed our bowls and left them on a towel to dry on the counter. Daddy was sitting on the front step sharpening a pencil with his pocketknife. Rojo hovered close by, pecking at an ant that was desperately trying to outrun his beak.

"Everybody ready?" Daddy said without ever turning around.

"Yes, sir."

In a shaky voice, I gathered the courage to ask what we all wanted to know. "Where are we going?"

"There's a demonstration in town."

"What kind of demonstration?" Isaac asked.

"That's what we're gonna go find out."

We walked to town, and by the time we arrived on Main Street, lots of folks were lined up on the sidewalks. Obviously, word had spread. Standing beneath the shade of awnings, we waited in front of Betty's Beauty Shack, the early morning heat scorching the tops of our heads.

Daddy craned his head, looking for someone.

City Hall stood in the center of the town square where Main Street ran into a roundabout, with a small police station on one side and the firehouse on the other. There were businesses on each side of Main Street. The Bijou Theatre, Green Parrot Café, Nickel Thrift, and the post office were on one side. Handy Hardware, Puckett's Grocery, Betty's Beauty Shack, Edland's General Store, and the barbershop were on the other. A few blocks away, I saw Hutch and his family walking past the offices of KY Coal. His wife and two kids created a tight chain—the girl I'd seen a few days ago and her little brother, who was even smaller than Isaac. The kids stared at the ground, but Hutch and his wife, who had worn a yellow flowered dress and white and yellow hat, moved with their heads high, their eyes staring straight ahead. They walked with purpose to the front of Nickel Thrift and stopped.

Daddy reached back to hold hands with me and Isaac and made eye contact with Sissy, then crossed the street to where Hutch and his family were standing. Sissy followed close behind, letting out a sigh of frustration every now and then.

"Good morning, Hutch." Daddy gave a polite nod to Hutch's wife.

Hutch's voice came out rough and shaky. "This is my wife, Hazel. Hazel, this is John, who I told you about before." She gave a small nod to him and smiled at Isaac and me. Sissy ignored all of us. Hutch squinted against the sun and asked, "You sure about this, John?"

Daddy nodded. "Yes, I'm sure."

We claimed our spot only a few feet away from Hutch and his family. I wondered what Hutch meant by his question and then realized we were the only whites on this side of the street. I felt the fear creep up my spine.

Looking behind us, Isaac's eyes grew large, his mouth falling open. "Daddy, Grace, look!"

A sea of brown faces marched toward us. There must have been more than a hundred people. Children held tight to their parents' hands. They hummed a tune in time with the sound of their footfalls, and it sent a chill down my arms.

Suddenly the argument Virginia and Daddy had the night before made sense. We were choosing a side, but against who? We squeezed in like sardines, shoulder to shoulder on our side of the street, stretching back past the post office and the Bijou. I stood on my tiptoes to watch as they kept coming.

Across the street, people leaned against the front window of Handy Hardware, shooting loathing glances our way. It was unimaginable that we had not chosen the white side of the street. Taylor and Emoline Bluin gawked at us as Cordelia whispered in the ear of another woman, both of them shaking their heads in disapproval. Emoline shot daggers in my direction but dropped her hand low and gave a small wave to Isaac. He waved back.

"Isaac!"

"She waved. I had to wave back."

"No, you didn't!"

Daddy bent down and whispered, "Kids, settle down."

I saw other people from our church standing close to the Bluins. I was sad to see Mr. James, the school principal, join the growing crowd of white faces.

A man called out, "Hey, John Mockingbird, do you got more than Injun in yo' woodpile?" The group of men around him burst into laughter.

Daddy clenched his jaw. Everyone stared at us.

My fleeting moment of pride for not sharing the same side of the street as Emoline melted into a sweaty fear. I looked up at Daddy and slipped my arm through his.

Taylor Bluin motioned for Sissy to come over. I muttered a small curse under my breath when she broke ranks and silently crossed the street, glancing back at Daddy for a moment. Isaac and I looked at each other and then up at him.

The words were out before I could stop them. "That little traitor."

Isaac poked me in the ribs with his elbow. I was embarrassed that I had said it out loud.

Daddy squeezed my hand, then spoke softly so I could hear. "It's her choice. Y'all have a choice just like she does." I gripped his hand and clung to him like I was glued to his legs.

A voice like butter on a hot biscuit filled the air behind us.

"Would y'all have room for one more?"

Miss Adams looked as good as she smelled in a lavender-colored dress.

"Hey, Miss Adams."

"Well, hello, Grace. And this must be Isaac, who I've heard so much about."

Isaac nodded politely but averted his eyes, turning shy. I had forgotten how beautiful Miss Adams was.

She turned around and extended her gloved hand, "Hello, Hutch, Miss Hazel, Yully, Eustace."

Hutch removed his hat and smiled. Hutch's wife spoke up. "I sure do loves that color on you."

Miss Adams reached back, squeezed her hand, and silently mouthed, "*Thank you.*"

I introduced her to Daddy as well. He tipped his head in her direction. Dr. Clarke appeared at the corner and pushed through the crowd to stand between Hutch and Miss Adams.

She gave Dr. Clarke a fetching smile, which he returned.

The sweat, tension, and humidity were running down our faces. I wiped my forehead on the sleeve of my shirt.

Miss Adams seemed more chipper than normal, almost giddy as she chatted to Dr. Clarke, who listened quietly. Behind us the sound of marching and loud voices erupted at the head of Main Street. There were about fifty sheets and hoods in all. They carried crosses and handmade signs that read *White Is Right* and *Segregation Now Segregation Forever.*

The hoods they all wore came to a sharp point at the very top and had two round circles cut out of the face, making their eyes look, in contrast, like narrow slits. They were an eerie sight. The blast of an engine revving up and a horn blaring made me jump. An old truck carried three men in sheets and hoods who held the rebel flag and the Kentucky flag in the back of the truck bed. The one in the middle wore an identical robe and hood, except it was red.

Daddy looked down, noticing us looking at the red-robed Klansman. "He wears a different color to show his superior rank. That is the robe of an Exalted Cyclops, which means he's the head of the local chapter."

Isaac and I were wide-eyed, fascinated and terrified by it all. But we felt safe standing beside Daddy.

The Klansmen drove their trucks to city hall and parked. A small platform held a podium with a microphone and a large speaker. This was where the mayor spoke before the lighting of the Christmas tree. Sheriff Teeton stood ramrod straight with a few other officers. His hand was resting on his holster.

I remembered Daddy telling me that you could tell the identity of the Klansmen by their shoes, and what blamed idiot wouldn't change the shoes they walked around in every day if they didn't want to get found out? I paid close attention to their shoes and recognized three pairs. A pair of old brown dusty cowboy boots with silver tips that I had seen in Daddy's shop. Next, the bright-red boots I had seen propped up on top of the barrel at Handy Hardware. He must have chosen his red boots to match his red robe. And finally, a pair of black patent leather men's shoes, nice and polished. I had seen those many times pushing into the plush baby-blue carpet on Sunday mornings. The fact that he was not standing with his family seemed to be a sure confirmation who it was.

Red Boots hopped out of the back of the truck onto the platform. He strode to the microphone. I tried peering into the eyes of the other Klansmen who stood around him. Red Boots tapped on the mic several times before he leaned in to speak. His voice was nasal and thin, but he tried to make his presence more powerful by using sweeping hand gestures as he spoke.

"As y'all know, there's a lot of trouble going on. People thinking that things is gonna change . . . like we been hearing about down in 'Bama . . ."

He paused to let the smattering of shouts from the other white sheets ring in the air.

"That ain't the way it's gonna be here." More approval from the eye slits. "We are assembling here to inform you that things are staying the way they always have, and there are plenty of good Christian folks here that agree with me!"

More noise from the white sheets and the white side of the street.

"Yeah!"

"That's right, brother."

"Amen!"

"Just remember who owns yo' houses and gives ye yo' jobs. All that can go away. This is a reminder to ye not to get any big ideas up in yo' heads."

One white sheet served as a kind of cheerleader, lifting his arms in the air to rev up the other white sheets.

"Y'all best remember yo' place, or we'll have to remind ye where it is!"

Some hisses and shouts and boos erupted from the brown faces behind us.

Red Boots shouted at them, "Now shut that up, you hear me? Y'all are lucky to even be living here."

He stopped to accept the applause and cheers from his followers in the white hoods. I wondered if the stoic faces of Mr. Handy and a few of the other shop owners meant they were uncomfortable with what the Klan was doing but too nervous to openly rebuke them. Or maybe it was a quiet show of solidarity with the Klan. It was hard to tell.

"Excuse me!" A refined voice rose above the crowd. *"Excuse me!"* The sharp blast cut through the noise, and the crowd fell silent.

"Excuse me, but this isn't just *your* town. As far as I can tell, these folks pay taxes just like you."

There were grunts and gasps from the crowd. Not only because of what had been said, but because of who had said it. Miss Adams. A woman. Smart-mouthing the Klan leader. I was having a flashback to the last day of class. But this was borderline insane.

"What's yer name? I don't believe I know you."

I heard Mr. Hutch whisper behind her. "Miss Adams, you better hush now; just let it alone."

But she kept going. "My name has nothing to do with this. It is unconstitutional for you to deny any citizens their rights as taxpayers. These are good, decent folk; they have rights. A right to speak up, a right to vote! A right to attend our white schools and be treated in hospitals. What makes you think you're big enough to take away those rights? Do you think you are more powerful than the president? After all, these are *his* orders."

My mouth dropped open. Miss Adams held nothing back. Being witness to such a tongue-lashing was unnerving. I took a step away from her and hid behind Daddy.

Red Boots glared directly at her. His followers yelled.

"Woman, keep your mouth shut!"

"Are you crazy or just stupid?"

Red Boots spoke again. "I don't give a rat's behind what that Commie president says."

A small rumble of approval came from his hooded followers.

"Whoever you are, you'd be wise to keep your yapping mouth shut."

I looked over to see the principal of the school sneering at Miss Adams. Why couldn't she just stay quiet?

Sheriff Teeton walked to the podium and took the mic from Red Boots, then, facing him and the other hoods, said, "All right, you've made your point and exercised your right to assemble."

Red Boots raised his arms high in the air and the white sheets did the same. They burst into a rally cry: "White Pow-er! White Pow-er!"

The sheriff capped his hand over the microphone. A piercing shriek echoed out of the square black speaker. Red Boots clamped both hands over his ears. This effectively silenced him and the audience so the sheriff could be heard.

He brought his mouth close to the microphone. "This demonstration is now over. Everybody go home or go back to work. And if any of you are thinking of starting some trouble, me and my deputies are armed and ready. We don't want no trouble, so just go on home now."

We all knew that lawmen in Kentucky were not to be trifled with. Daddy said most of them could shoot the whiskers off a squirrel a hundred yards away. The Klan marched their way back up the street. Red Boots and his herd honked their truck horns, waving the rebel flag high in the air. Daddy looked back at Hutch and they shook hands, saying nothing.

"Hey, Miss Grace," came a low, raspy voice from behind me.

I turned to see Miss Pearl and a teenage boy standing beside her.

"This here's my grandson Theo. Theo, this is Miss Grace. I think y'all are close in age."

"Hi," I said and extended my hand, which he took in his. It was warm and soft. His skin was like coffee with too much cream and his eyes looked like green marbles. I couldn't deny that he made me feel a little weak in the knees. I shook it off and turned my attention back to Miss Pearl.

"Theo is gonna be helping me with the peach stand this summer."

"Oh, that's great. I'm hoping to get a summer job too."

"Good for you, Miss Grace. Make you some spending money! Well, I sure do appreciate you and Mr. John being here. And is that yo' little brother?"

"Yes, ma'am." Daddy and Isaac stood talking with Dr. Clarke a few feet away.

She took my hand in hers and squeezed it tight. "Come see us now. We be moving from the school since there ain't no traffic in summer. We're moving out by the old trailer park."

"Okay."

She put her small pudgy hand on my face. "You have a good day."

Her smile made me feel like there was hope in the world, even with the terrible thing we had just witnessed. Theo lifted a hand to wave goodbye. I did the same and had to pry my eyes away from his.

I turned to see Miss Adams shaking my father's hand. I went back to his side just in time to hear him say, "Ma'am, I have no right to give you advice, but you might want to consider going to visit your family or making yourself scarce for a few days."

Her charming smile wilted and she bit her bottom lip. The smooth skin between her brows squeezed into an S shape.

Daddy rescued her from the awkward moment with a question. "If you don't mind me asking, have you had dealings with the Klan before? You seemed mighty sure of yourself."

Finding her words as quickly as she'd lost them, Miss Adams answered, "Enough to know that the lot of them are buffoons."

Daddy nodded in agreement.

"Mr. Mockingbird, I stand by what I said. What happened here today is wrong; of that I am sure."

"I'm sure right along with you, but it doesn't change that these people are dangerous. Grace thinks the world of you—just want you to be . . . cautious."

Miss Adams bristled against his fatherly advice. "I have spent enough of my life being a silent witness to the injustice imposed on the innocent. I will no longer be that person."

Daddy considered what she said. "But if your rebuke makes things worse for the innocent you are trying to defend, is that really helping?"

She seemed caught off guard by this. I thought he made a good point. Her turn—"'Evil men flourish when good men are silent.' Ever heard that?" She held his gaze. "Mr. Mockingbird, bringing your family to stand with our Negro citizens took courage, and I admire you for it, but it's going to take a lot more than standing silently to see real change."

Daddy peered at her quizzically. "I didn't mean to insult you, Miss Adams. Just asking an honest question—which, by the way, you didn't answer." He smiled, which melted her icy stare.

Her eyes softened and she smiled back. He offered her a truce—a handshake. She extended her beautiful, dainty fingers and shook his rough mechanic's hand.

He turned back to us. "Come on, kids. Time to go."

I tried to meet Miss Adams's eyes, but she had already turned to walk away. I hoped she wouldn't hold what Daddy said against me. Besides Daddy, she was my favorite grown-up.

Daddy looked weary. He reached for my hand and Isaac's, and we walked back toward the house. Sissy lingered with Taylor. I waved at her to come with us, but she shook her head and turned back to him.

Isaac and I held our questions as we walked home. We could both feel the weight of what had just happened. All I had to do was think about Hutch standing in the doorway of the hardware store with his little girl to understand why Daddy would risk standing on the Negro side of the street. As much of a coward as I was, even I couldn't have stood on the other side. How could Sissy have done such a thing? I enjoyed my temporary feeling of superiority over her.

We passed Mr. Farris on his front porch whittling away on some little critter that would end up at the Nickel Thrift. He threw up a hand at us as we walked by. Daddy gave a small nod. It was strange to see him sitting there with no idea of the life-changing moment we had all just experienced. Maybe that's what happened when you got older. You avoided stress and danger. Daddy and Miss Adams had walked straight into the eye of the storm. I held my head a little higher. Maybe Isaac and I could afford to be a little proud of ourselves for staying. Some might say that it was irresponsible for Daddy to let us go, but I didn't care.

As we walked to the porch, I could hear Virginia's raised voice through the kitchen window. "You can't be serious! Why would anyone do such a thing?"

I had a feeling the Jubilee gossip network was working overtime.

Daddy whispered, "Kids, why don't you go see what Rojo's up to in the backyard."

We watched him cautiously open the screen door. Isaac and I walked to the backyard feeling bad for what Daddy was in for. We crept back around once he was inside and listened underneath the kitchen window.

"John! Do you realize what everyone is saying? You were standing right beside her! I told you not to go!"

"Virginia, Teeton had everything under control. Don't get all worked up."

"Worked up! You have no idea how much restraint I'm showing. I can't believe you are dragging us into this! And our children, John?"

"Virginia, I wanted them to see what hate leads to."

"No more! I'm done talking about this."

The kitchen door slammed. Isaac and I ran to the backyard, afraid we would be caught listening. The front door opened, and we peeked through the bushes in the backyard and watched Daddy drive away. Virginia stuck her head out the back door. She saw us but said nothing. I wondered where Daddy had gone.

A while later, he returned and lifted a couple brown paper bags out of the passenger seat.

We ran to help. "What did you buy?"

"Oh, I just thought I'd give your mom a break in the kitchen tonight."

"Can we help?" Isaac asked.

"Sure. We can let your mama relax, and we'll fix dinner."

He pulled out green and red peppers from the bag. He went to the wood crate and got a large white onion. He asked us to rinse everything and said he would chop. He got out the giant cast-iron skillet and fried ground beef, onions, and peppers and then added two cans of red beans. When it was all done, he smothered it in cheese. It smelled delicious.

We set the table and brought the white bread.

Virginia had been weeding and watering her vegetable garden since he left. Daddy called through the back screen door for her to come in. She tried to suppress a smile, seeing the table set properly with a steaming skillet of what Daddy called "hash" in the center.

We said grace and ate. We didn't talk much, but who could talk when the food was this good? I think even Sissy would have loved it. Daddy had saved her some and put it in the icebox.

I couldn't remember seeing Daddy cook before. I wondered why he didn't make dinner more often, so I asked him. Virginia answered before he could. "Because that is my job. I'm the wife, so I'm the cook." She seemed almost offended by the question.

"But sometimes I cook." I couldn't believe I had challenged her.

"That's because you're a girl. I'm teaching you how to do these things for your family one day." She dabbed her mouth with a napkin, looking annoyed and sure of her next words. "Women need to know what their role is. It keeps you grounded, and you learn better than to mouth off when you should just stay quiet!"

"Virginia, calm down," Daddy said as he rested his hand on her arm, which she jerked away.

"Don't tell me to calm down. Do you realize what people in town are saying about that woman?"

"What woman?" I asked, feeling as though I should duck. That was twice I had interrupted her.

"Your troublemaking teacher, that's who!"

"But I like Miss Adams."

"Which is troubling! Do you realize the entire town now thinks our family agrees with her because your father took you down there and stood by her?"

I wondered if Virginia was mostly concerned about what Cordelia thought since we all saw which side of the street she was standing on.

"I don't want you to have anything more to do with her."

"But . . ."

"No buts! She is trouble, and that's the last thing our family needs right now."

I fought the urge to cry. Miss Adams was the first grown-up besides Daddy to see potential in me. She treated me with respect. Virginia knew this. Each time I talked about Miss Adams, I could feel tension from her. Was she jealous or threatened? The thought of not seeing Miss Adams again was devastating.

Daddy placed his hand on my shoulder. His eyes said, *"Let it go."*

Virginia wiped her mouth, pushed away from the table, and stood. "I think I've had enough. Thank you."

Once she was gone, I looked over at Daddy, my eyes pleading for him to disagree with her.

"Grace, I know how you feel about Miss Adams, but for right now, I think your mama may be right."

Involuntary tears dripped onto the cold hash on my plate. I sometimes wondered if Virginia's goal in life was to take away everything that made me happy. Maybe because of what I had taken from her. Isaac was so quiet, his large eyes watching me.

"Tell you what, kids—I'll do the dishes, and I have a job for both of you. Wait right here." Daddy went into the kitchen and came back to the table with a small mason jar. "I want you both to catch as many fireflies as you can and put them in this jar; then when it's dark, we'll release them together."

It was just about dusk, the firefly hour. I wondered where they went after dusk. They were mysterious. We took the jar and headed to the front yard. As far as I knew, fireflies only existed for our pleasure. We ran with the dry grass scraping our toes as we tried to capture them in our hands while their brief light betrayed them. Each one we caught we gave a name beginning with a different letter of the alphabet.

Daddy had come out and watched us as he swayed on the porch swing. He had known exactly what to do to remind me that life wasn't all bad. There was still summer. There was still magic. Pretty soon the jar was full, and we were only up to *M* for Molly. We brought the jar to him. He admired it as we tried to recount all the names from Adam to Molly. He led us to a part of the neighborhood that had no streetlights so the sky was inky black. He held up the jar and unscrewed the lid. It was like our own Fourth of July. They floated up like sparks. We stood there till all the sparks were gone. Then we walked home in silence, not wanting to break the moment of wonder.

* * *

Hours later, when the whole house was asleep, a soft murmur of voices then a pound on the door broke into our dreams. We rolled into the hallway, groggy and unsure why we were awake. Looking out the living room window, we saw men in white sheets loading into the same truck from the rally. They whooped as they revved the engine and disappeared out of sight, tires squealing.

Daddy moved cautiously toward the front door. We all leaned forward, watching as he opened it slowly.

"John, be careful," Virginia whispered.

His eyes narrowed and squinted at something below.

"What is it?" Virginia hissed.

He opened the door wide for us to see.

"Oh my Lord!" Virginia threw her hand over her mouth.

The stench burned my nose as we edged closer. There on the soft worn wood of our porch was a dark pile of human waste. Virginia stumbled back, gagging. We all started to gag. Daddy's face was red and his breathing was fast.

"Now do you see, John?" Virginia began crying.

"Hush, Virginia."

He looked at me, Isaac, and Sissy, his eyes full of apology. "Everybody go on back to bed. I'll clean up."

Virginia, who had run to throw up in the toilet, came back with a wad of toilet paper on her nose. She shook her head erratically and darted words through her sobs, clenching her nose in a tight fist. "John, how are we supposed to sleep now? Or feel safe?"

"I'll go down early tomorrow and talk to Teeton about it." He turned to us. "Kids, please, go back to bed."

We obeyed. Sissy dragged into her room without response. As I walked Isaac back to his room and tucked him into bed, I heard Daddy sigh deeply.

Isaac looked up at me, tears brimming in his large eyes. "Hey, Grace, do you think you could stay with me for a while?"

"Yeah, sure."

He edged against the wall, making room for me in his twin-size bed.

I wrapped my arms around him, swallowing my own fears and disgust for what they had done. Wishing we could rewind the night to our fireflies and erase this awful feeling. We both finally drifted off to sleep, wanting it to be a bad dream.

* * *

The next morning a knock at the door woke me up. I was careful not to wake Isaac as I slipped out of bed. Who would come so early? I wondered if it was Sheriff Teeton.

I got up and tiptoed down the hall. Virginia was standing on the porch talking to a short, dark-haired woman with a little blonde girl who looked to be four or five years old.

I edged closer, trying to hear.

"No, she ain't doing good. We wanted to make sure ya knew, and I was a-needing to come to town anyhow, so we thought we'd stop by to tell ya."

It took me a minute to register that it was her sister Retha. Their hair was the same rich molasses color and even their figures were similar, except Retha was a good head shorter than Virginia. But instead of a stylish A-line dress, she wore tight blue cigarette pants and a sleeveless turtleneck blouse that hugged her petite frame nicely. She held a cigarette in one hand, extending her pinky out as she flicked the ashes into the grass. Her hair was teased and sprayed into perfection. Good looks ran in the family; that was certain.

Virginia opened up the screen door, motioning for her to enter. "You all are welcome to come in."

"No, we best be going. Joe Joe needs the truck," Retha said, taking another deep drag off the cigarette.

Virginia gave them a hug and they turned and walked down the steps to a truck parked in the driveway. Daddy's car was gone. Virginia stood there watching them drive away. I crept back to the hallway and then into the bathroom and waited till I heard her voice in the kitchen. She must've been on the phone.

I came out of the bathroom quietly and rested my head against the wall of the hallway and listened.

"They just left. She said that Mama's had a bad fall . . . Yes, I think I'll go in the morning."

A while later, Daddy came home for lunch and we heard more details.

"They're not sure what happened. Retha said she was in the kitchen and thought Mama must have slipped on some lard. Anyway, I am going to visit her tomorrow."

Before I could think better, I asked, "Could I come along to see Granny Bee?"

She stared at me for a moment, then said, "Yes, that would be fine."

Daddy glanced over at me, surprised. Then he turned his attention to Sissy, who had slept in till almost lunchtime. "Sis, what are your plans for tomorrow?"

"I am working the lunch shift, so I have to be there early to do prep."

He looked over at Isaac. "You want to come to work with me tomorrow?"

"Sure!"

I was glad we weren't talking about what happened last night. It would have suited me to pretend it never happened. Instead I thought of the fun I'd be missing, being with Dad and Isaac. I regretted ever volunteering to go with Virginia, but I was curious about her side of the family. There were so many unanswered questions about them.

I lay in my bed that night feeling panicked. Being trapped in a small car with her. What would I say? Would she bring up Miss Adams? What would I say to her family? I had only visited Granny Bee a handful of times, and it had been at least three years since I had gone to a family reunion at her house. I hoped I would be able to remember all of their names. Virginia had kept them and her past at a safe distance. But I felt drawn to them. Like they were a missing puzzle piece to my life.

10

THE HILLS

We left early, hoping to get back in time for dinner. It was an hour and a half drive up into the hills. The air was so hot and sticky that my fingers swelled like little sausages in boiling water and a pool of sweat gathered under my legs, but my mouth was as dry as cotton. I would have given anything for a drink of water. My heart hammered in my chest as I tried to think of what to say. Virginia seemed lost in thought. As we drove up Main Street out past KY Coal, I thought of a question I could ask her.

"You glad Daddy ain't a miner?"

"Yes. I'm glad he isn't a miner. Not *ain't*, Grace. Yes, I am very glad."

"Me too."

There was silence a while longer. I reached up to feel for my bangs that had finally grown out a bit. Last night, after my bath, I snuck into Virginia's room and borrowed two of her rollers. I smoothed my wet bangs around them, using bobby pins to secure the rollers in place, and slept on my back. When I took out the rollers, tight little corkscrew curls bounced back, and it looked ridiculous. Thankfully the curls had relaxed and now shaped my face nicely. I admired the bangs from the tiny side mirror of the VW. Feeling the awkward silence, another question came like a gift from the patron saint of daughters. It was as much of a surprise to me as it was to her.

"Was Daddy your first love?"

Her tense jawline softened into a faint smile. "Your daddy was about the best-looking man I'd ever laid eyes on." She rested her arm on the frame of the window, the wind lifting small golden hairs from her skin. "But more than that, your daddy treated me with respect—as an equal. Honestly, I don't know what would have happened if he hadn't come along."

"What do you mean?"

"I mean, your daddy saved my life." She wrung her hands on the steering wheel. I had never seen her so jittery. Maybe she wasn't so glad to be going back to the hills.

I thought about the words *your daddy saved my life,* letting them linger in my mind.

As we drove the narrow, winding road into the hills, she pointed out houses where she knew people or where a relative lived. We drove past a tiny white church that she had attended as a girl. There were small gray shacks that leaned to one side. Trailers sat at the tops of steep dirt roads. The trees were full and green and created a canopy over us. The smell of honeysuckle growing along the road wafted in the windows. I saw old couches, rusted-out iceboxes, and bags of garbage dumped in the deep ditches. I wondered why anyone would want to junk up such a beautiful place.

When we finally arrived at Granny's, I was struck by how different her mountain home was, compared to those in town. Built from rough-hewn logs, stacked on top of one another and sealed with homemade concrete. Gray, weathered steps led up to the covered porch, where a small bucket of water with a metal dipper sat in the shade by the front door. I wanted to pour the whole bucket over my head.

"Is it okay if I have a drink?"

"Yes, that's spring water."

I quickly plunged the dipper into the bucket and brought the water to my lips. It was sweet and refreshing and a hundred times better than the water we drank at home. Virginia surprised me by having a drink too. She straightened her dress, inspected me for a moment, then reached for the doorknob.

I had not been to Granny's house in years. Virginia used to visit by herself monthly, but she hadn't been in a while and never talked about her visits except to say Granny Bee had aged a lot since she had married Thomas, her second husband. Thomas was different than Willy, but in some ways worse. He was not from Kentucky. He came from up north in Michigan and talked through his nose.

At first the family was taken by how much he loved to be with the grandchildren. Willy never had much interest in any of the kids, so at least Thomas had one appealing trait. Retha, Nell, and Irene were all too happy to hand their children off to him at family gatherings so they could gossip and eat in peace. That was until Thomas volunteered to take Caroline into the woods for "an adventure walk." At some point, Caroline ran from the woods and up the stairs to the house. Finding Retha, she crawled up into her mother's lap, sucking her thumb, and remained silent for the rest of the visit.

Later that night when Retha was tucking Caroline into bed, she said, "Caroline, baby, is something wrong?"

Then Caroline told her mom about what happened in the woods. Retha stormed out of the room and found her husband, Joe Joe, in the garage working on his truck and told him the whole story.

Joe Joe punched a fist on the hood of his truck, making a large dent. "He's gonna die for this!"

He grabbed his rifle and jumped in his truck and rounded up a few of his buddies. They drug Thomas out of the bed in his long johns at gunpoint, made him strip naked in the front yard, and beat the daylights out of him. The only reason Joe Joe didn't put a bullet in him was because his friend Dorsey calmed him down.

"You'll spend life in prison because of this scum pervert. It ain't worth it."

Granny refused to believe it. It was too much for her to think she had chosen another reprobate. Ever since then, Thomas and Granny Bee had been uninvited to all family gatherings. Granny Bee was left with Thomas as her only company. Choosing a man over your own kids and grandkids was hard to forgive, especially if that man's lust led him to do something evil. Like an old tree trunk with deep roots, Granny dug in, refusing to budge.

Now that Granny was in a bad way, whatever family would come around was all she had left to care if she was dead or alive or somewhere in between. Suddenly I wished I was back at the garage with Daddy and Isaac. I was terrified to be in the same house with Thomas.

Virginia opened the creaky screen door. Her brother, Junior, and his wife, Nell, were sitting on a couch in the small living room. I stayed close behind Virginia, which felt strange.

Granny's house smelled of bleach and biscuits. The furniture was sparse but efficient. Nothing about the house was welcoming, especially not the large man who sat on the couch picking at his teeth with his fingers. Thomas came through the kitchen doorway into the living room.

Virginia's voice was stiff and businesslike. "Hello, Thomas, Junior, Nell."

Junior barely looked up at us but offered a limp *hey* as he cleared some phlegm out of his throat. Nell waved her small hand briefly, then let it fall back in her lap. Junior was enormous compared to her mouse-like frame.

"Hi, you guys." Thomas's voice fit his weasel face—narrow nose and small black seeds for eyes. He came over to me and leaned down till he was in my breathing space. His skin was pasty white and his hair, silver with streaks of oily brown strands, was plastered onto his head. His large dentures sagged out of his small weasel mouth. I took a step away from him.

"Grace, would you like a piece of candy?"

I shook my head, unable to find my voice.

"We are here to see Mama." Virginia put her hand against my back protectively.

It was the first time I could remember her touching me like that in years.

"Is she in the bedroom?" she asked Junior, ignoring Thomas.

Junior spoke without making eye contact. "Yep." He hitched his thumb behind him. "Back yonder."

Even I was surprised by how little they cared about us being there. Virginia was the second-youngest of all the siblings and as different from them as lace is from burlap. Irene was the oldest, then Junior, Virginia, and Retha, the baby. I could see why Virginia didn't visit much.

Thomas interjected, "Yes, in the back room." His nasal voice put my teeth on edge.

I followed her along the narrow hallway to a bedroom at the back of the house. When we stepped into the room, Irene was sitting by the bed. She was what I'd heard men call "voluptuous," her curves accentuated by the tight red shirt and black skirt that looked a couple sizes too small. Her hair was bleached and dyed a shiny yellow blonde like Marilyn Monroe's, though no one would have ever mistaken Aunt Irene for Marilyn.

Nell slipped in behind us and sat down across from Irene. She was dressed in a faded mustard-yellow dress with a high collar, and her mousy brown hair, pulled back, had threads of gray running through it. She sat with a blank expression on her face.

Irene rose to greet us, speaking with such speed that I could hardly keep up. "Is this Gracie? Land sakes, you are growing like a weed. I can't hardly figure out who you look like though. Not as pretty as your sister, that's for sure. And boy, you've got some short bangs, don't you?"

Nell looked at us both and then, as if remembering her manners, said in a slight voice, "Virginia, you should come sit here." She stood from the chair nervously, offering a shy smile that made me think she was the nicest of all the relatives. She moved to the corner of the room by a small window. I was grateful for the view of the woods outside.

Virginia guided me with her hand on my back around to the other side of the bed. She sat in the chair and I stood beside her. Granny lay there, like a wax doll. The steady rhythm of her chest moving up and down was the only evidence that she was alive. Her skin was smooth and soft. Her hair was mostly gray but still had a few dark streaks that hinted at the beauty she once was. Even in her late sixties, she was striking. I could see a lot of Virginia in her. I heard Junior clearing his sinuses in the living room.

Nell walked to the door and said, "I'll give y'all some privacy."

Once she was gone, Virginia started asking questions. "So how did this happen?"

Irene answered with bullets of rapid-fire words. "Well, Thomas was the only one here when it happened." She widened her eyes and pursed her lips as if his name tasted bitter in her mouth. "What he *said* was Mama was making fried chicken and some drippings from the pan spilled onto the floor when she was pouring them into a jar to save for frying potatoes. She was leaving the kitchen to go to the outhouse, in a little bit of a hurry, I guess, and she slipped and fell. Hit her head hard on the wood floor. She ain't woke up since."

Virginia softly caressed the milky skin of Granny's limp hand. "Mama. I'm here. It's Virginia."

Irene couldn't help herself. "Virginia, she can't hear you, you know."

"I'm not so sure about that. I've read stories about people coming out of a coma and recounting back to the family exactly what had been said."

"That's a crock of bull." Then Irene's voice turned to a whisper. "I'll tell you something else: I am starting to wonder if old pervert boy out there is the one who done pushed her and made her fall. Maybe Mama's gotten a little old for his taste."

When Irene said this, Granny Bee's feet twitched back and forth.

"Irene, that is enough! We don't want to upset her."

"I am just telling you, I think something rotten is going on. I also wonder if he's got some insurance money out on her."

Virginia decided to change the subject. "Has a doctor been here yet?"

"No. Thomas keeps saying there ain't nothing a doctor can do. I did think about going to the witch doctor up here to see if she had any ideas."

Virginia sat there silently, weighing it out. "We need to get a doctor to see her."

"*Psh*, Virginia. Mama and Thomas ain't got no money to pay no doctor. Besides, old Thomas's truck ain't been running for a while, and I wouldn't want to put her in Junior's pigsty of a vehicle. Your car's too small, and well, my boyfriend dropped me off on the way to the pool hall and I am not about to ask him to take her."

Virginia dropped her head in frustration.

Irene became animated. "I met this really great guy in the bar where I work. He's a truck driver, makes good money." I'd overheard that Irene was an "exotic dancer" and changed boyfriends as frequently as her underwear.

Virginia walked me back into the living room. Nell was sitting on the couch, knitting. "Where is Thomas?"

"I'm here!" He appeared in the kitchen doorway, as if he'd been eavesdropping.

Junior lumbered up the porch steps, returning from the outhouse.

"Thomas, we need for a doctor to see Mama."

"I don't see what good a doctor would do. We don't have any money to pay, so I think the best thing for us to do is wait and see. I'm sure she'll heal up in a few days."

"This could be serious. Potentially life-threatening."

Junior walked in the door and returned to his hollowed-out spot on the couch. Nell twisted her body to peer over the back of the couch at us. I stood slightly behind Virginia, feeling the rising tension. I nervously edged away from them. Nell and I met eyes.

"There is a good doctor in town," Virginia said. "A brother of a good friend of mine. We could take her."

It dawned on me that she must be talking about Cordelia's brother, Dr. Oden. I wondered why in the world she wouldn't rather have Dr. Clarke treat Granny Bee.

Thomas was shaking his head wildly back and forth. "No, no, no, no. I am her husband. She has made her wishes clear to me. I think it's best to wait."

"What wishes?"

"She told me if anything ever happened to her to make her just lie there like a vegetable that she wanted to just go on home. I think we need to honor her wishes."

"A doctor might be able to give her medicine or at least tell us what is wrong."

"I told you, that is not what your mama wanted, and I mean to protect her wishes."

By now, Irene had come out of the bedroom and into the living room and was standing beside me with a crazy smile on her face. She looked insane. Like she was enjoying this. Nell and Junior were both turned around on the couch now, giving the conversation their full attention.

Virginia got up into Thomas's face and exploded. "She is *our* mother. What makes you think you are the only deciding factor for her care?"

"Because I am her husband, and legally, *I* decide! Not any of you. And furthermore, this is both your mama's and my house, so if you're not going to abide by her wishes, maybe you should leave."

"What makes you think this is yours? You didn't pay a dime for this house. As far as I can tell, you're living off Mama like a parasite."

Thomas cut her off. "Shows what you know—she added my name to the deed, so I have as much right to this house as she does. None of you have any claim to this house, so you can get that idea out of your head!"

Junior and Irene both stood and moved toward Thomas, but Virginia was lit up. I had never seen this side of her—the unhinged side.

"I pray the fires of hell down on you if our mother dies. God will get you, Thomas. For everything. He sees all the secrets you've been hiding away. It's all on your head."

Thomas backed away from her, furious, but his eyes showed fear. As though every terrifying word Virginia had spoken found its mark.

Junior poked his finger in Thomas's chest and said, "If anything happens to her, you're dead."

Irene's eyes were wild with excitement. "That's right, you disgusting perv!"

"Out! All of you, out! I will not be spoken to like this in my own house."

Junior, Irene, and Nell spat out a few choice names at him before they stormed out the front door. Only Virginia stayed.

"Wait for me outside, Grace."

I gladly stepped out onto the porch. Through the open door I saw her return to Granny's bedroom. Virginia was totally different from everyone in her family. For that I was grateful. I waited on the porch, waving goodbye as Junior, Nell, and Irene backed down the narrow dirt driveway. When Virginia finally came outside, she was wiping away tears. I tried to remember the last time I had seen her cry.

"Let's go, Grace."

The car felt like an oven. I quickly twisted the crank to roll my window down. The trees offered shade, but nothing could protect us from the suffocating humidity. As we backed down the driveway, I tried to imagine Virginia as a girl, playing in these woods. Did she like the forest like me?

Her sadness was as thick as the air. I wanted to say something to make her feel better. "I'm glad you stood up to Thomas."

"Thank you, Grace," she sighed.

"Why did Granny Bee marry *him*?"

She shook her head and twisted her hands on the steering wheel. "There are some women that cannot stand to be without a man. Mama was always easy pickings for a man with charm."

"Gross."

"I couldn't agree more."

"You sure are different from all of them . . . but you're beautiful like Granny."

She reached across and squeezed my hand.

A single tear escaped from my eye and I was afraid if I said anything else, I would ruin the moment, so I said nothing.

11

TRI-WAY

The next morning, I had so many thoughts about the trip to Granny's, I sat in the backyard under the oak tree and wrote in my red journal. Rojo sat beside me with his feet under him, making cooing sounds every so often. In some ways, Rojo was like a cat. He loved you on his terms, but he had some sort of sixth sense about Isaac. I reached over and gently smoothed down the rooster's feathers. He closed his eyes like he might take a nap.

Virginia leaned out the back screen door. I quickly hid the journal under my bare legs and held it above the grass, careful not to get dirt on the pages. "Grace, Isaac is gonna try and go back to sleep. He's not feeling well. Maybe the stomach flu again. I gave him some crackers and soda water. He needs rest, so don't tempt him to come out and play."

"Yes, ma'am."

She kept going. "I'm leaving in a few minutes for a meeting. Your daddy will be home early since Sissy is working. I've left directions for you to start dinner before I get back. Understood?"

"Yes, ma'am." I dreaded the long day without Isaac, but I certainly didn't want the stomach flu, so I decided to follow her orders. Desperate for something to do, I climbed over the fence of our backyard and escaped into the woods. Daddy had cautioned us not to, since it was summer and the likelihood of snakes was high. I made careful steps, avoiding anything with venom, including the poison oak, and decided to gather some wildflowers and look for quartz. The mountains were full of it, and every now and then you could crack open an ordinary-looking rock and find a sparkling treasure within.

I came back with no quartz, but I had gathered a handful of spring beauties and another plant with a row of tiny white bells that looked to be weeping. I found a mason jar, filled it halfway with water, and arranged them as best I could, then placed the bouquet in the center of the table. I found some cold fried chicken and a pitcher of sweet tea in the icebox. I stood eating with the door open, then poured myself a glass of tea. I noticed the note Virginia had left on the counter but decided that torture could wait. I headed out to the porch to drink my tea.

Our mailman, Walter Cummings, who also attended our church, was walking toward our box. I set the glass down and ran to meet him.

"Hey, Mr. Walter."

"Hello, Miss Grace. It's another scorcher."

"Sure is."

"Whew! I'm melting like a snow cone in hell!"

I giggled a little and he belly laughed, pleased with his commentary on the heat. He had a sackful of different phrases he used—a few for each season. *Melting like a snow cone in hell, hotter than the devil's armpit*, and *hotter than two hamsters farting in a wool sock* were his summer favorites. I always looked forward to his brief visits to us; even on a day as strange as this was, with the memories of yesterday hanging in the humid air, there was comfort in routine.

His blue postal uniform was drenched in sweat and he continually adjusted the mailbag slung over his shoulder. "Later, gator!"

"After while, crocodile!" I quipped back. He threw his hand back to me and made his way to the neighbors next door.

I carried the mail into the kitchen and sorted through it. There was a Sears catalogue for Virginia and a letter from Aunt June addressed to me. I felt something round and bumpy inside. I quickly opened it.

Dear Gracie,
    I'm coming to visit you this summer and teach you about herbs and flowers. Be good till I get there!

                                                                Love,
                                                          Aunt June

She included a packet of sunflower seeds, which were her favorite. Good ole Aunt June. She had always been my favorite relative, even though she could be a little kooky.

The box fan was turned backward in the window, humming, pulling out the hot air. I put on an apron and got out the flour, baking soda, baking powder, milk, eggs, salt, and pepper, as well as a pack of minute steaks from the icebox. Pretty soon I was up to my elbows in flour and trying carefully to follow Virginia's directions for battering chicken-fried steak.

I heard Daddy's Bug pulling into the driveway. I looked out the window, relieved to see him. I waved and he waved back.

"Hey, Gracie." He looked at me with a smile as he came into the kitchen. He added some flour to the tip of my nose, then kissed the top of my head. "Well, you look like quite the chef."

I laughed.

"Where's Isaac?"

Before I could answer, we heard the toilet flush and Daddy walked out to the hallway.

I heard him ask, "You feeling okay, Son?"

I walked out of the kitchen to see them in the hallway, Daddy crouched down on his knees and Isaac resting his head against Daddy's shoulder. Daddy moved his large hand along Isaac's tiny back.

"Yes." Isaac stretched his arms with a wide yawn. "My stomach was upset this morning."

"And how about now?" Daddy felt his forehead.

"I think it's better now."

"You hungry?"

"Yeah, a little."

"What about you, Grace?" Daddy turned to me in the kitchen door. "Chef Grace is in the midst of making us dinner, but I had another idea. What do you say we drive over to see Sissy at Tri-Way, have a burger and a shake? I think it's too hot to cook, don't you?"

I threw my tea towel and a handful of flour up in the air in agreement. "Yes, sir!"

Isaac laughed at me.

Daddy stood, looking down at his watch. "Your mama's meeting will be over pretty soon; let's drive by and see if she wants to come along too."

Isaac and I squeezed in the back of the blue Bug with Daddy up front. We stopped by the community center where SWS met and picked up Virginia. As we drove, I could see Daddy glancing back every now and then at Isaac with a concerned look on his face—the kind of look your parents have when they're thinking of something you're not old enough to know. Isaac leaned against the window. His skin looked ghostly, like you could almost see right through it.

Daddy looked through the mirror and asked, "Isaac, how about a cheeseburger?"

"Yeah . . . I guess so," he said with a little yawn in the middle.

Virginia had been quiet since we picked her up at the meeting, but as soon as the town limits were behind us, she started talking.

"I tell you, those SWS ladies think they know it all. So sure of themselves. Like they know exactly what the poor in Jubilee need.

What do they know about being poor? All of them are a bunch of Southern belles."

I wondered if Virginia's trip to the hills had sparked something in her.

Within Virginia, there were two feelings at war: she felt both beneath and above the SWS ladies at the same time. It wasn't the first time we had heard her turn on the SWS ladies after a meeting. But it never took long before she was once again desperate for their approval. In all her waffling, though, she never criticized Cordelia. As she ranted on about it, Daddy kept his hand on the wheel, giving the occasional nod and smile, while glancing back at me and Isaac in the rearview mirror.

We pulled up to Tri-Way, and there was Sissy leaning into the side of Taylor Bluin's cherry-red Chevy convertible. We all held our breath as we watched Virginia slap her hand over her mouth.

Sissy looked like she'd stepped out of a calendar with her golden hair cut into a flirty bob, shapely bronze legs in a short skirt and shirt unbuttoned to the point that you could see the hint of her blossoming womanhood underneath. Instead of tucking in her shirt, she had tied it so that you could see a little patch of sunbaked skin around her nineteen-inch waist. All those hours of lying out in the backyard with iodine and baby oil had paid off big-time.

"Now, Virginia, calm down. Maybe that's what they asked her to wear," Daddy said.

I didn't want to say anything to get Sissy in trouble, but I happened to know that she made a regular habit during the school year of leaving the house wearing an outfit Virginia approved of, but with other clothes stashed in her school bag. She would leave early enough to head straight to the smoking porch at Jubilee High, where a few of her girlfriends would stand around her in a tight circle puffing away so she could change without being seen.

When Sissy turned around, the bronze color drained from her face.

Virginia got out, rattling our teeth when she slammed the car door behind her. She plowed over to Sissy, with Daddy close on her heels to referee. I couldn't hear what all was said, but arms were flying as the battle raged between them.

Taylor started his engine while all this was going on and decided to rev it up three or four times before he squealed out of there. Sissy turned away from Virginia and Daddy to watch him drive away. If Taylor was grooming to be a preacher, Lord help us.

When Daddy and Virginia returned to the car, we sat in silence.

"All right, what does everybody want?" Daddy asked with forced cheer. "I'm gonna have a double cheeseburger with onion rings and a chocolate shake. How about you, Gracie?"

Sissy finally found the courage to take our order. I noticed that she had managed to pull her skirt down so the hem was a little closer to her knees, buttoned up the shirt to the second button, and tucked it into her skirt.

Daddy searched the radio to find some music. "My Boyfriend's Back" by the Angels came on. Daddy and I were nodding our heads to the music, but Virginia said good Christians had no business singing the devil's music and could Daddy please change the channel to something decent like the gospel station. I knew from hearing Virginia talk with Cordelia that "the devil's music" was anything with a beat. Virginia had been raised in a hellfire-and-brimstone culture in the hills. If you enjoyed it, it was bound to be sinful.

Daddy and I met eyes in the rearview mirror. He turned the dial to the gospel station to keep the peace.

The station was playing the local hour—popular with folks in town who had aspirations of being famous singers but lacked the talent or drive or both. This was their chance to shine. It was also a way for preachers to get the Word of God out to the shut-ins and elderly who were too sick or too old to come to church. And also for the heathens who would never dream of darkening a church door but might listen to a sermon on the radio. As soon as we heard the fiery voice of the preacher, Daddy said, "That's Cooter."

Cooter Conley was a well-known Holiness preacher in Jubilee, though he had never had any formal training. That was the way of Holiness preachers. He was nineteen years old and about the best-looking man in all of Kentucky—certainly in all of Jubilee, or at least better looking than any I'd ever seen. I remembered shaking his hand when Virginia took me and Sissy to a revival last summer. He took my hand and smiled. When he looked at Sissy, you'd have thought he had lost his ability to speak. Sissy had giggled and Virginia broke the trance they were in.

"Enjoyed your sermon, Cooter. Let's go, girls!"

Cooter was the kind of person you'd enjoy sitting on the porch talking to, but something changed when he stepped behind the pulpit or the radio microphone. He'd hold his King James in one hand and lift the other to the heavens, like he had fire shut up in his bones.

Cooter had been wild as a young teenager. He'd play hooky from high school and drink a little moonshine. A lot of folks just assumed he would turn out like his daddy, Jack Conley. I heard Daddy once say that Jack Conley was as good-looking as Cooter but was "bad to drink and bad when he drank." He'd stagger home drunk on moonshine bought with the money Cooter's mama, Leola, made from taking in laundry. He'd wake up the whole house yelling and beat Cooter's mama while the kids huddled in the corner, crying.

One night when Cooter was around fourteen, Jack came home drunk, yelling and knocking Leola around like he always did. He was cussing Leola and calling her awful names that kids should never hear their daddy say. Cooter jumped up out of bed, ran to the kitchen, and got the big round cast-iron skillet that his mama made biscuits in every morning. Just as Jack raised his fist to render what might have been a fatal blow to Leola, Cooter whacked him in the back of the head with that skillet with all the strength he had. The force of it sent Jack spinning around. He turned to Cooter with a look of disbelief in his eyes, then dropped like a hammer to the floor. Out cold.

The whole house was up by now. Leola was weeping and crying and kneeling on the floor, calling out Jack's name. Cooter asked his mama how she could weep over someone as wicked as Jack Conley. She stroked Jack's dark hair back over his forehead and said, "Because I love him." Jack was still breathing, but no one knew what to do, until their mama made all the kids go back to bed. When they woke up the next morning, Jack Conley was gone. No one except Leola was sad to see him go. Not long after that, Cooter, being the oldest and the only boy in the house, started working in the coal mines when he was barely fifteen.

The following summer, Cooter attended a tobacco barn service up in the hills, where a circuit preacher would come through once a month. The preacher talked about sin and that Jesus was willing to forgive you for whatever bad things you'd done and give you a fresh start. At the end he gave an altar call, inviting people down to the front who wanted to repent of their wicked ways. Cooter walked the aisle, tears streaming down his face, and knelt down at a straw and tobacco altar. I wondered if he felt guilty a lot, wondering if he might have killed his own daddy, or at the very least made him leave.

There were folks who weren't willing to believe that his transformation was genuine, choosing rather to believe that Cooter would eventually give in to the destiny he had been born for.

"Daddy, do you think Cooter will end up the way people say? I mean, he used to be so wild."

Daddy thought for a moment. Virginia stared at him, waiting for the answer.

"'Show me a man without vice, and I'll show you a man without virtue.' I'm paraphrasing Abraham Lincoln."

"What does that mean?"

"Basically he's saying that when a man looks like he's perfect, most likely he's not. I'd rather know a man who's had some troubles you can see, instead of a lot of things hiding in the dark."

I thought of Pastor Bluin hiding under the Klan hood.

I noticed Virginia looking at Daddy. She leaned over and kissed him on the cheek.

He smiled back at me and Isaac and said, "I think she likes me."

Virginia softly punched him in the arm like a teenage girl feeling shy.

The little Volkswagen was hot. Virginia started fanning herself and Isaac and I stuck our noses as close to the open windows as we could for fresh air. As I looked out, I noticed Hutch and his wife and two kids walking toward Tri-Way.

Daddy lifted his arm out of the window and waved to him. Mr. Hutch smiled and waved back. His teeth reminded me of freshly fallen snow. I wondered if Hutch had heard about the Klan's visit to our house. Daddy told us that Sheriff Teeton said nothing else had been reported, which was surprising, considering what a scene Miss Adams had made. I imagined Miss Adams must live on one of the nicer streets in Jubilee, seeing as her family had money, but come to think of it, I had no idea where she lived.

Hutch and his family walked around to the back of the drive-in to the door where the sign read *Coloreds Order Here*. It was the first time I thought about how it must make them feel, to have to order from a different door.

Our burgers and shakes finally came, but as we sat there eating, I noticed that Isaac hardly touched his food.

"Isaac, aren't you gonna eat some of your burger?"

"My stomach hurts."

"Maybe try some of your vanilla shake. That'll make it feel better."

He took a little sip and sat there for a moment with the straw to his lips, but then he started coughing. Daddy turned around in his seat, and so did Virginia. Then Isaac was gagging, and that's when we all saw it.

Red and bright. Splattered on the white seat all the way down to Isaac's blue cowboy boots. Blood.

Daddy jumped out, panicking, to push the seat forward so he could lift Isaac out. I tried to help but I felt frozen in place, staring down at the blood and Isaac. As Daddy lifted Isaac from the seat, careful not to hit his head on the car, Isaac collapsed. Daddy was yelling, "Isaac! Isaac!"

Virginia was screaming, "Oh, God. Oh, God."

Hutch appeared behind Daddy and picked up Isaac's little boot that had dropped to the ground.

People got out of their cars to see what was happening. Sissy was standing with her hands over her mouth a few feet from Daddy, and I sat in the back seat, frozen.

Sheriff Teeton's car was parked a few spaces over from us. He ran over with a mouthful of onion rings and some ketchup spilled down his shirt. He took one look at Isaac and told Daddy to bring him to the squad car and for us to follow them to Middlesboro Hospital just up the road. Daddy laid Isaac gently in the back seat, holding his head in his lap. I will never forget the look on Daddy's face. It was as if he was staring out from a black hole.

Hutch took a step forward and handed the little blue boot to me and watched us as we drove away. Virginia, Sissy, and I followed the squad car with its lights flashing all the way to the hospital. Each of us mumbling our prayers, rocking back and forth.

Feeling the darkness settling in.

Isaac. Please, God, don't take Isaac.

12

RED BIRD

I am sitting on the edge of a small chair next to the living-room window, hypnotized by the sound of Virginia's low-heeled shoes clunking across the hardwood floor and the sight of a red bird perched on the other side of the window. As bright as a cherry on a sundae. It looks at me, cocking its head to the side, as if to say, *"Are you okay?"* I sit motionless, wanting so badly for it to come closer, to whisper some truth about the universe to me in the high, lonesome notes of its song. Some explanation for this misery, this ache. It looks at me one last time, then lifts its wings and disappears for a moment into the fire of the Japanese maple in our yard. I have seen this bird before. Daddy says unlike other birds, they never leave; from the hottest day in summer to the coldest, brownest day of winter, they come pecking at the earth, reminding you that some things are constant. Some things don't leave or change. As he hops from branch to bush, I hear Virginia on the phone, and it pulls me back to the awful reality of what has happened. Cordelia has called to find out what the doctor said about Isaac.

Dr. Clarke was on duty when we burst through the ER doors. He instantly began barking orders at the nurses to get Isaac stabilized. After running several tests, he came to meet us in the waiting room and asked us to follow him somewhere more private. He took us into a tiny chapel with a low ceiling, carpet, and padded pews. We sat on the front pew as he leaned against the altar. The cross hanging behind him gave a strange comfort. He removed his glasses and rubbed his eyes.

"I don't know any easy way to say this. Isaac has a mass in his stomach. I think it might be malignant."

"What do you mean, 'malignant'?" Virginia asked.

"It's cancer."

The word hung in the air like a thick fog.

"From what we can see on the X-ray, he has a large tumor in his stomach. We need to send him to the children's hospital in Memphis. They are the best at dealing with this sort of thing. I have a friend who is a surgeon there. I can call him and let him know we are sending Isaac." Dr. Clarke put his hand on my shoulder before walking away.

I lay in bed last night hating that word—*cancer*. Now Virginia was in her bedroom packing. I left the red bird and came to stand in the doorway of her room as she closed the latches on the old brown suitcase that hadn't been used in years.

"Can I make you a cup of tea or something?" I was thinking that's what Emily Post would do at a time like this. Virginia looked up at me, without ever answering, attempting a smile that wilted on her lips, as though she understood what I was trying to do. For a moment, she saw me. She heard and understood that I was trying to connect. But then, in the next moment, it was gone.

"Aunt June is coming to stay while we are gone. You and Sissy can look after yourselves this evening. She'll be here early tomorrow. Make sure you help her make dinner and keep the garden up and the house cleaned."

She stood in front of me, leaned down, and brushed my cheek with a wisp of a kiss. I breathed in the smell of motherhood and sorrow and was overwhelmed by the urge I felt to reach out and put my arms around her. But I didn't. I was suddenly aware of how much I needed her, but I knew there was no room or energy for my needs. The small sliver of hope I had felt when we drove back from Granny Bee's withered. Why would I expect anything from her when she was giving everything she had to Isaac? I felt ashamed and selfish. I had to think of Isaac. Isaac was all that mattered. I swallowed my tears and steeled my heart against this feeling.

She walked out onto the front porch, stiff and dry-eyed. Daddy pulled into the driveway. As she stood on the bottom step, the red bird came and lit on the grass a few feet from her. She watched it for a moment before plowing across the yard, the bird darting away. Daddy and I had already said our goodbyes. An ambulance would transport Isaac to Memphis. Daddy and Virginia would follow. I wanted to run to Daddy, but he was in a hurry not to keep the ambulance waiting. Daddy waved to me as he got out of the car to help Virginia with her bag.

I felt a chill run over my body. Who knew a June day could feel so cold?

The red bird must have known. Maybe that's why he came.

13

AUNT JUNE

In the morning, I was sitting on the back step watching Rojo dig for a worm. Sissy was still sleeping since she'd gone to bed late the night before. She'd spent close to thirty minutes on the phone with a boy, or so I guessed from all the giggling I heard. Probably Taylor. She had managed to stretch the phone cord all the way to her room. She sat with her back against her closed door.

That would never fly with Virginia, or even Daddy for that matter.

I heard a car door slam, heavy steps on the front porch, not walking but marching. I ran to see, still in my PJs and socks. As I slid through the hallway into the living room, Aunt June was opening the screen door, with her horn-rimmed glasses and her red hair flying in all directions as if she had rolled out of bed and driven straight here. I wasn't even sure if she had changed out of her nightgown.

Aunt June was big on comfort. It was only on rare occasions that she let any concern for what others thought creep into her mind. In her arms she carried a variety of paper bags and old satchels. Aunt June didn't believe in wasting money on luggage when a grocery bag would do just as well. Her underwear and Kern's bread had shared the same traveling arrangements for years.

"Well, my little Gracie Lou, look at you how you've growed! You've got that silky brown hair just like your mama's and beautiful brown eyes, and look at those bangs."

I ran my fingers through them self-consciously. "That's kind of a long story."

"Well, I like them." She kissed me on the forehead. "Sets off those pretty eyes." She placed her hands on my shoulders. "Oh, Gracie. How are you holding up? I can't hardly believe this." She gave me a hug and then pulled a handkerchief from her bra and blew her nose and wiped her eyes. "I love that sweet boy. Lord knows I do."

She gave me another hug. "We are gonna just hang in there together, aren't we, my girl?"

I nodded, feeling better just having her there. Aunt June brought with her a kind of fearless optimism mixed with a strong dose of reality. I loved her for both. June was a blazing golden beam through my sky of dark clouds.

"You need help carrying anything in?"

"Yes, sweet baby, can you run out to Beauty and grab my Bible and my bag of vegetables and herbs out of the back seat while I get settled in? We need to get them in the icebox or they will wilt in this heat before you can say Jack."

Beauty was the name of the 1960 Cadillac Eldorado Aunt June had bought fresh off the lot three years earlier with the insurance money her husband left her when he passed. She loved that car like it was her own child. It stretched out so long, she either had to hang it out into the street at the end of our short driveway or hang it into the yard at the front. It looked like a rocket, black and shining with a white top and fins on the back.

June held to the "cleanliness is next to godliness" principle in the house, but apparently not when it came to her car. Then again, Aunt

June didn't cotton to rules much in general. The back of her car was full of books and slips of paper and shoes and religious pamphlets. Somewhere between a "What Is Hell and Are You Going?" tract and a size-nine-and-a-half moccasin, I found the brown bag she'd sent me for, her white King James peeking out the top with little bags of herbs that smelled so strong they made my stomach turn. I carried the bag into the house and heard Aunt June talking to Sissy in her room.

"I bet you're beating off boyfriends with your good looks, and look how tanned you are!" June stood with her hands on her hips. "Lord, I'd give anything for your blonde locks," she said as she raked her fingers through her fire-red hair.

Sissy was sitting up in bed rubbing her eyes, still half asleep while accepting the barrage of compliments from Aunt June, when she and I both saw something on the bedside table: a pack of Camel Lights that she had left out last night since she knew the coast was clear with Virginia away. Feeling a sudden need to protect June's wholesome idea of Sissy, especially given June's strong views when it came to smoking, I broke in.

"Hey, June," I said, rustling the bag around to make noise and turn her attention to me. "Why don't you come in the kitchen and tell me about these herbs and natural cures?"

"Why, I had no idea you were interested in that. I would love to!"

Sissy shot me a surprised and grateful glance.

June forgot all about Sissy's golden locks, the presence of the Camels flying under her notice. She followed me into the kitchen with a stream of chatter about bloodroot, slippery elm, and something called "black cohosh" that she said she'd been making into a tea for her feminine issues. She'd brought some herbs for Virginia too.

We sat around our small Formica table for over an hour while Aunt June made her ginseng tea and I listened to her chatter. My mind drifted as I wondered what was going on in Memphis. Somewhere between breaths, June read my thoughts.

"Gracie, are you thinking about Isaac?" She shook her head and took a deep breath. A painful expression ran across her face. "I remember how scared I was when Benny got the lung cancer. Him laying there with barely room for a breath in his lungs and pleading for just one puff off a Winston. I begged and begged him to quit those things, but he said nothing was ever gonna make him quit, so finally, I just had to give it up to God."

"But, June, why would we give it up to God if *He's* the one who did this?"

"Gracie, I understand your anger." She sipped her tea. "I was so angry when Benny died . . . but finally . . ." She sighed deeply, then said, "I just had to let it go."

"But I don't want to let it go! I want answers. Why someone like Isaac? He is . . . special."

June fetched some toilet paper from the bathroom for me. I blew my nose and dried my face. My breath stuttered out of my chest as I asked, "Why would God do this?"

She put her hand on my shoulder and waited for me to calm down, then spoke softly. "I'm sorry, Gracie. You know how I feel about him." She burst into tears, then reached inside her bra and pulled out a handkerchief again to blow her nose. "I know this is a different situation than when Benny was sick. I just meant that I understand feeling helpless. And for what it's worth, I do believe God allows us to suffer, but I don't believe He causes it."

"But *why* does He allow it?"

"This old preacher woman in the hills spoke at Benny's funeral, and she said that when God says no, it's because He wants to give us a greater *yes*. Maybe there is something we're all meant to learn. But I personally think that God allows suffering because He wants to show us something beautiful."

"What do you mean, 'something beautiful'?"

"I mean that the most beautiful experiences of our lives often come after we have walked through the deepest valleys." She placed her hand on mine in the middle of the table. "I will tell you that I cursed Benny *and* those cigarette people. I shook my fist at God and whatever it was in Benny that made him want those things more than a deep breath or another day with me. He couldn't get free of them cigarettes, and I couldn't get free of wanting him to. I guess we were each bound by our own wants, but in the end, each man or woman chooses what he will or won't be a slave to."

"What beautiful thing came out of Benny's death?"

June took in a deep breath and stared out the window. "I learned that we have to love the people in our life for exactly who they are, faults and all. There is a great freedom in that . . . being merciful, because the mercy we extend is the mercy we receive."

I felt as though my heart was cracking open, but I wouldn't let it. What mercy had Virginia ever shown me for the awful thing that happened years ago? She had let me live under a cloud of dread and guilt. She had never once said, "It wasn't your fault" or "I forgive you." She just let me make a home in my misery.

June took a long drink from her teacup. "Gracie, we don't always have a choice about what happens to us, but we always have a choice about how we respond."

"Miss Adams, my teacher this year, read to us from a book about how it's important to know what someone else's life is like—how the world looks from someone else's point of view."

"Had you ever considered that before?"

"Well, maybe not, at least not until she brought it up."

"Miss Adams sounds like she knows what she's talking about. Hallelujah! I'm glad they've got at least one teacher down here with some humanity."

I heard Sissy's steps, right before she threw open the kitchen door. She had on an outfit similar to the one from Tri-Way that sent Virginia into a fit.

June turned and looked her over. "Oh my, aren't you looking so cute? Where are you off to?"

I guess Aunt June didn't get as worked up about short skirts.

"I'm meeting up with some friends before I go to work."

"Can I make you something to eat before you go?" she said, rising from her chair.

"Ahh, no thanks, Aunt June, I'll just make a quick peanut butter and jelly sandwich to take along."

"Oh, I'll make it. You just sit here at the table. I'll only be a jiff."

Sissy and I exchanged a conciliatory glance.

Nobody ever wanted Aunt June to cook. You just never knew what sort of strange thing she might make. Sandwiches were the safe bet when June was around.

"Will you be home for dinner? I thought I'd make a big pan of chicken goulash with some okra I brought from my garden."

"Oh, sorry, June, I am working at the drive-in tonight. Looks like it's just you and Grace for dinner." Sissy gave me a satisfied grin and I shot her back the evil eye.

Goulash. Why did it have to be goulash?

Sissy wrapped the sandwich in a napkin and took it with her. June headed back to her room and spent the afternoon getting unpacked and settling in.

Later in the day, I was standing in the kitchen watching Aunt June pull vegetables out of the brown bags she'd brought from home to make our goulash supper. I was dreading it, but I hated to hurt June's feelings. Then she turned to me like a lightbulb had gone on in her head.

"I feel like a chili dog and French fries. How does that sound, Gracie?"

I quickly accepted, furiously nodding my head as she shoved the goulash fixin's back into the icebox. We decided to walk to town since it was turning into a nice evening.

As we walked, she pointed out different wildflowers growing up through cracks in sidewalks and by the sides of houses. She knew the names of every flower, which ones you could eat and which were poisonous to humans but not to birds. This was something she and Virginia had always loved to talk about.

Folks sat on their front porches, fanning themselves, throwing a limp hand up in the air as we walked by. Mr. Farris sat on the steps of his porch, leaning over his large belly, whittling away on some new creation. His wife, Mrs. Farris, who I had never seen without her brown wig, red lipstick, and pearls, had just walked back into the house. She always smelled of cooked onions and mothballs. She was known to be a tidy housekeeper and a terrible cook. Nobody at church socials ever wanted to eat the liver and onions she brought. Poor Mr. Farris. I wondered if he got tired of eating all that leftover liver and onions.

He was a nice man, quiet, who always looked to be on the verge of smiling. The little animals he whittled were so lifelike I marveled at them. He didn't know it, but I bought his carvings whenever I saw them at Nickel Thrift, and not just the animals. I had a nice collection on my dresser: a deer, a rabbit, a squirrel, a turtle, and a little cross with a lily cut out in the middle from Easter last year. A whole collection of original artwork for less than fifty cents. I thought I should save up my allowance and pay him more.

"That's Mr. Farris," I said and told Aunt June about the carvings he made.

"Well, let's see what he's making today."

He looked up and broke into a full smile as we walked up his sidewalk. "Hello, Grace. Who do we have here?"

June thrust out her right hand. "I'm her aunt June. Come for a visit."

"Nice to meet you, Aunt June." He looked at me as if weighing his next words. "Grace, I heard about Isaac. I'm so sorry to hear he's . . . sick."

I nodded, but wanting to change the subject, I asked, "What are you making today?"

"Oh. I'm not really sure. Sometimes it's a mystery. I let the wood tell me what it wants to be."

"I love your little figurines. I buy them when I see them at Nickel Thrift."

He seemed surprised and pleased by this. "Thank you, Grace. I guess I make so many of them, the missus ends up taking them down to the thrift store. She doesn't like my old critters cluttering up her house."

"Well, I'm sure they are very nice," June said. He nodded his thanks.

As we walked away, June said, "I feel bad his wife takes his figurines to the thrift store."

"Yeah, me too."

We turned onto Main Street and passed by the Bijou. There were two men on ladders changing the movie playing on the marquee. We stood and watched them until the full title was revealed. "*Dr. No*," June read. "Supposed to be a good one."

We turned the corner to the Green Parrot. Inside, the tables were scattered around the room with red-checked tablecloths and a real daisy in a small jam jar at the center of each tabletop. Sometimes Daddy would take me and Isaac here after work when Virginia was busy with SWS and Sissy was busy ignoring us.

I tried to disappear behind my menu as June's wild red hair flopped around. She spoke to the waitress in a loud voice like they were old friends. "Honey, would you look at your skin. It's milky smooth. Do you use a special cream?"

The waitress, Lila, was a talker like Aunt June, so she was more than happy to answer. "I use cocoa butter just like my mama, but the real secret is that I stay out of the sun. Us redheads, you know . . . we burn so easy."

"Oh, don't I know it."

I knew for a fact that June was not a natural redhead, and her skin, like Daddy's, had an earthy brown undertone.

I could hear little snippets of conversations around us. "I hear he's sick" and "such a shame" and "they were asking for trouble." I felt embarrassed. What was it to them? I wished I had the guts to tell them to keep their noses out of our family's business.

The door to the café opened and a family I'd never seen before came in. But this was no ordinary family. All conversation tapered off and everyone turned to look at them: a mother, father, and a boy, who was about my age, with moon-blue eyes and ringlets of golden hair circling his face like the sun. They were dressed in their Sunday best. Like celebrities, the two grown-ups smiled and nodded at folks as they walked past to find a table. The boy watched his feet.

When the waitress came to bring our food, Aunt June asked her in a whisper, "Do you know who they are?"

"Yes, honey. I am surprised y'all haven't heard. That boy is the famous child evangelist Golden Shepherd. Everyone calls him 'The Golden-Haired Miracle Boy.' Ain't that neat? He's only fourteen years old, and his mama and daddy are both preachers. Their names are Mary and Joseph Shepherd. Can you believe that? They said at three years old, little Golden was filled with the Holy Ghost while taking a bath. There with his rubber duckies he started speaking in the tongues of angels. They say he has divine powers of healing. You should hear him preach! You wouldn't believe it!"

June's face beamed, and she asked, "Where are they from?"

Lila leaned down closer and lowered her voice. "I'm not sure where they're from, but I hear they are renting a place out at Shady Creek. They drive a big gold Chevy."

June said, "Gold?"

"Yep, gold."

She kept jabbering on, excited at the idea of a celebrity in her restaurant. Then she looked down at me. "Grace, I heard about your brother. I'm so sorry." She reached down and set her hand on my shoulder. "Maybe you should take him to one of their revivals?"

After we finished our hot dogs and fries and were waiting on the bill, Aunt June lifted herself up from the table.

"June, where are you going?"

"Don't worry. I'm just going to go introduce myself."

"But June, *wait*," I said desperately, not wanting our family's troubles on display to these strangers and the whole restaurant, but she was determined.

"Grace, now don't worry, I'll be back in a jiff. Here's money for the bill."

I sunk down in my seat, grateful for the large dessert menu that had been left on the table. I could hear bits and pieces of her words, enough to know that she was telling them about Isaac and asking if they had a revival in this area or if they made house calls. The mother and father seemed mildly interested in what June had to say, smiling and nodding between bites of French fries. The boy with golden hair looked past the conversation with a blank stare on his face.

After June had more than worn out her welcome, she returned and sat down to wait on our bill. "I had a good talk with them. They said they'd be happy to let us know about the nearest revival."

The waitress came to collect the check and the money. As we waited on change, the family stopped by our table.

The mother spoke up. "We will be advertising the dates for our revival in the local paper, so keep a watch for that."

"Well, thank you so much," June gushed.

The dad held a straw hat in his hands and smiled with dingy yellow teeth. The white shirt under his green suit jacket had the top two buttons undone. I could see the glint of a silver chain mingled with brown and gray chest hair. His skin was the color of glue against his black hair. The mother, though small in stature, towered over him. A tight, thick bun sat firmly on the top of her head. Her cheekbones looked sharp enough to cut paper.

The strange couple nodded politely to onlookers while the Golden-Haired Miracle Boy stared at his black patent leather shoes—preacher shoes. They looked so strange on a boy his age. His eyes drifted to mine. They were so mournful I wished we could be friends. He didn't seem like a miracle boy. He seemed like a boy in need of one.

14

BISCUIT EATERS

Aunt June decided to move the television to a small card table in the corner of the living room so that we could lounge on the couch and watch the news at the end of the day. She relaxed with her feet up on the coffee table as we watched. I was wearing the soft, white nightgown with little blue flowers that Grandma Josie had made me before she passed.

June dabbed her forehead with a handkerchief she'd pulled from the front of her nightgown.

"Aunt June, do you have a lot of those?"

"A lot of what?"

I pointed at the white handkerchief in her hand.

"This? Oh my, yes! I have a whole pack of these. I use a fresh one every day and bleach the daylights out of them when I wash them."

She patted me on the leg and giggled to herself a bit as she picked up her knitting.

Walter Cronkite stared into the camera like he was talking right to us. I liked his face. "Today, President Kennedy electrified the world with his *'Ich bin ein Berliner'* speech, delivered near the notorious wall dividing East and West Berlin."

The screen flashed to the president in a dark suit, leaning over a bank of microphones. Aunt June, eyes growing wide, paused her knitting to say, "Wooo-weee, is he a looker or what!"

The warm voice and accent filled our living room with his words: "Freedom is indivisible, and when one man is enslaved, all are not free." His eyes looked tired and full of emotion.

"I like him," I said to June.

"Oh, so do I! And isn't his voice so soothing?"

I nodded in agreement.

The newsman returned to the screen. "In other news, three days ago Dr. Martin Luther King Jr. led the Walk to Freedom in Detroit, Michigan, drawing a crowd of 125,000." Footage from the march splashed across the screen.

June shook her head, occasionally letting out a sigh, while knitting at lightning speed.

"Aunt June, did you hear about what happened to us . . . after the Klan rally?"

June screwed up her face like she might vomit. "Yes, your daddy told me—makes me want to gag, those lowlife, white trash racists!" Her knitting got more frantic.

In spite of the awful memory, June's colorful language made me giggle a little under my breath.

"Actually, your daddy gave me Sheriff Teeton's number in case there was trouble . . . but I'm sure we won't need it. He said the sheriff went over and had a little talk with them sorry, no-good, sons-a- . . . biscuit eaters."

"June! For a minute I thought you were gonna say something else."

She winked at me then leaned forward to turn up the volume a little.

I wondered if the Klan folks had heard about Isaac and would leave us alone. Surely even they would have enough decency to do that.

At the end of the broadcast, the reporter ended with, "And that's the way it is. This is Walter Cronkite for *CBS News*; good night."

June got up to turn the television off.

"I wonder how Isaac is doing. They haven't called yet."

"Oh, Gracie, I know you must be worried sick."

The phone rang and June nearly jumped out of her skin. She ran to the kitchen to answer it. I followed her.

"Oh, John, it is so good to hear your voice. Gracie and I were just wondering how y'all were . . . Uh-huh . . . Oh, I see. Is that good? . . . Okay. Okay. Well, I guess we have to be grateful for any good news. She's right here. You want to speak at her?"

I jammed the phone to my ear. "Daddy!"

"Hey, Gracie. How's everything going?"

"We're doing all right. How's Isaac?"

"He's okay right now. He just came out of surgery. The doctors said he came through like a champ."

"Oh, that's good, right?"

"Yes . . . he's got a long road ahead, but the doctors here are excellent. They're taking great care of him. Are you being good for Aunt June?"

"Yes, sir. I'm trying to."

He laughed a little. It was good to hear his laughter.

I heard someone talking in the background. It sounded like Virginia.

"I think the doctors are coming to talk to us, so I better go. Grace, I love you. You, Sissy, and Aunt June look after one another, okay?"

"Okay, Daddy. Will you tell Isaac something for me?"

"Sure thing. You name it."

"Tell him that Rojo misses him almost as much as I do, and we can't wait for him to come home . . . Daddy? You there?"

"I'm here. I'll make sure to tell him."

"Love you, Daddy."

"Love you too."

The line clicked and I stood there longing for more.

We walked back into the living room and sat on the couch.

June broke the silence. "Well, I'm glad the surgery was a success."

"Yeah, me too." Then more silence.

"How about I pour us a cold glass of tea?"

"Okay."

I followed her back into the kitchen and watched as she took two glasses from the cupboard and filled them with ice and the sweet, amber liquid.

We had just brought our tea back into the living room when we heard footsteps coming up the porch steps. The screen door slammed open and Sissy came through the doorway.

She was trying to push past June, who was carrying her glass in one hand.

"Hold on there, Sis."

"Let me pass, June."

"Sis, are you all right? What happened to your face?"

Sissy's mascara was streaming down her face and she had the beginnings of a black eye. Blood and a large red scratch stretched down her arm.

"Have you been in a fight? Land sakes, your mama and daddy are gonna kill me if you're hurt." June reached her hand toward Sissy's face to get a closer inspection.

"No!" Sissy raised her voice. "I'm all right. I just got into a fight with a girl down at Tri-Way."

"What girl?"

Sissy paused a bit and answered, "Just this girl from Middlesboro."

June stared at her bruises. "What did this girl say?"

"She called me the b-word, and I . . . I let her have it. That's it."

June inched closer to Sissy. "Hold on now; let me take a look at you." She pushed a little harder for details. "What size girl was this?"

"June, stop nagging me! I just want to go take a shower. I'll be fine." Sissy swore under her breath and ran her hands through her hair in frustration.

"All right . . . calm down now. Can I at least make you something to eat?"

"No. I'm not hungry." Sissy headed back to her room and then into the bathroom. Aunt June watched her walk away.

I heard the shower start, so I crept to the bathroom door and put my ear up against it.

"What do you hear?"

I came back to the living room and whispered, "Sounded like she's crying. Do you think she's okay?"

"I don't know."

"Me neither."

We weren't in the mood for tea anymore, so we turned the lights out and went to bed with the faint sound of Sissy's sobs mingled with running water drifting down the hallway and into our dreams.

15

NICKEL THRIFT

A few days had passed since Sissy's fight. The bruise was starting to turn a nice purplish color, which she did her best to cover with makeup and sunglasses. Since she worked outside at Tri-Way she could get away with wearing sunglasses all the time. She must have gotten up early, because she was already gone when I woke up.

June and I sat across from each other at the table, finishing breakfast. I could hear Rojo at the back door scratching. He seemed lonesome for Isaac.

June broke the silence.

"Grace, I think we need an outing. I have been wanting to go to the Nickel Thrift since I got into town. You feel like going with me to see what kind of treasures we can find? Maybe some of those little figurines your neighbor makes."

"But it's so hot."

"What's new about that? Honey, this is the South—hot is something you learn to live with."

I had steered clear of the Nickel Thrift ever since Emoline had embarrassed me in front of the entire class a couple months ago. I raised my hand to my bangs, feeling the spiral of curls plastered against my forehead from the humidity.

"I'm not feeling up to it. And besides . . . I'm a little nervous of running into people right now."

"What people?"

"Well, just people . . . kids from school."

"Why is that? Gracie Louise, are you ashamed to be seen at the thrift store?"

"Just something that happened at school."

"What happened?"

"It's a long story, June."

"I've got all day."

I took a deep breath and started.

"Awhile back, Virginia came home with a little brown jumper dress for me. It was really nice. I was kind of surprised Virginia would shop in the Nickel Thrift. She sure never shops there for herself, but she said she was walking by and saw it through the window and couldn't resist going inside to see if it was my size. She said she knew picture day was coming.

"There was a rip under the arm, but Virginia sewed it up. Then she washed, starched, and ironed it. It was like brand-new.

"Anyway, I had never seen anyone in my class wear it before. Virginia seemed so proud of it, I didn't want to disappoint her. And besides, I couldn't imagine anyone in Jubilee, as poor as most folks were, ever donating anything so nice.

"On picture day I was actually excited to wear it. It had only been a few weeks since I'd moved up into ninth grade. Still feeling like the new kid, I guess. I walked into Miss Adams's classroom and then . . . Emoline saw me."

"Who is Emoline?" June asked.

"She is Cordelia's daughter and she's in my class."

June rolled her eyes when I said Cordelia. "Oh, boy, I can see where this is going."

"Anyway, Emoline made a beeline for me and said, 'Well, Grace Mockingbird. That sure is a nice dress.'

"I thanked her. Then she said, 'Came all the way from Nashville, Tennessee.'

"She moved in closer to my face and said, 'It's very expensive.' I wanted to crawl under my desk and die.

"'You know how I know? Cause it's my dress! My mama donated it to Nickel Thrift when it got a big ole rip right here.'

"She lifted my arm up with a look of triumph, followed by confusion when she saw the neat seam. Most of the kids laughed. I wanted to run back home and throw that dress in the trash, but what was the point? The damage was done."

June stood there with fire in her eyes, shaking her head. "Mm, mm, mm. Durn little turd. I wish I'd been there. I'da bent her over my knee and gave her a *whack*!"

"Now do you see why I don't wanna go?"

"I do. But, child, we can't be a prisoner to what other people think. Why, that was downright wasteful, sinful even, to throw out a good dress because of a little tear. You and Virginia were being good stewards of your money. There ain't a thing for you to be ashamed of."

Maybe she was right, especially after what Emoline had done to me with the curling iron, which June didn't even know about yet. I wished I could be more like Aunt June or Miss Adams and not care so much about what other people thought.

"I'll go."

"That's my girl!" She gave me a hug, then went back to her room to change out of her nightgown.

We walked to town, hanging a right onto Savannah Street. As we crossed over from Savannah to Main, just in sight of the front door of the Nickel Thrift, I heard a voice behind me.

"Grace!"

It was Miss Adams. She was wearing a white pantsuit with a mint-green scarf in her hair and those cat-eye glasses she had on the day of our class picnic. I introduced Miss Adams to June.

"Well, what a pleasure to meet you! Grace has told me about some of the important things you've been teaching her in class. Thank the Lord for teachers like you."

"Well, thank you, June." Miss Adams was taken aback by Aunt June's compliment.

"I've come for a visit with Sissy and Gracie while their mom and dad are in Memphis with Isaac."

Miss Adams's face mirrored some of the sadness that I felt at the mention of Isaac's name. "I am so sorry about your brother, Grace. I heard from Mr. Hutch what happened."

A lump formed in my throat.

She bent down and put a hand on my shoulder. "I've got an idea. How would you like to come to my house next week for a visit? We'll have afternoon tea."

When she said "afternoon tea," she clasped her hands together in delight. She looked up at June.

"Oh, I think that would be wonderful, wouldn't it, Grace?"

Miss Adams smiled. "Aunt June, you should come too."

"Well, how nice. I'd love to!"

Miss Adams took our number and said she'd call to make a plan and give June directions to her house. I felt sick, knowing that Virginia and Daddy had forbidden me from seeing her. But everything was different now. That was before Isaac.

We waved as Miss Adams walked away.

June said, "Sweet fancy Moses on buttered toast, she is a knockout!"

As we opened the door to Nickel Thrift, I wrestled with how I could keep June from telling Virginia and Daddy that we were going to Miss

Adams's house, but as Grandma Josie used to say, "Cross that bridge when you come to it." It was a risk I was willing to take.

At the back of the store, where they kept vases, teacups, and saucers, I found another one of Mr. Farris's figurines. It was a little lamb. Aunt June found a dress for church since she'd packed in a hurry and hadn't brought enough for the trip.

On the walk back home, June said she wanted to pop into the market for a few things to make for supper. I told her I'd wait at the front of the store. I read the want ads and flyers posted next to the "leave a book, take a book" shelf.

There was a flyer covering up a lost dog poster of a Collie named Phoebe.

ASK YOURSELF THIS IMPORTANT QUESTION:
What have I personally done to maintain
SEGREGATION?
We need your support in these dangerous times.
A community meeting is to be held this coming
Saturday at the community center.
If you are a concerned citizen and want to protect your rights
for segregation, please attend.
Saturday night at 6 pm.
The White Citizens Council of Jubilee

I had overheard Daddy tell Virginia that many of the people on the White Citizens Council were merchants and business owners—people of influence in the community, not just your run-of-the-mill redneck Klansmen. He said that was what made them so dangerous.

I heard June walk up and felt her breathing as she read over my shoulder. "If that don't beat all! What a bunch of jackasses." I couldn't help but giggle at her swearing.

She stormed out the door, the bell ringing loudly as we pushed through. I hurried behind her. She fumed all the way home.

I hoped I'd remember to ask Miss Adams what she thought of the White Citizens flyer when I saw her. No doubt, Miss Adams would have plenty to say on the subject. I thought of the heated exchange between her and Daddy. What if she pushed me on where I stood? Did I know where I stood? It made me nervous thinking about it, but I still wanted to go.

* * *

After our trip to town we spent the rest of the day cleaning until we could have eaten dinner off the floors. I figured it was June's way of working out her frustrations. The sheets were washed and dried and smelled of green grass and sunshine. When the work was done we took cold showers and ate a simple dinner of corn fritters and green beans and slaw. After dinner, June and I sat on the porch in our cotton nightgowns, with the smell of lemon and Pine-Sol on our fingertips. We wiped the sweat from our foreheads with our sleeves and drank Coca-Cola while we watched the fireflies show their brief light. We were the good kind of tired that you can only feel after a day of hard physical work is behind you. June checked her watch and said it was time for the nightly news, which she never wanted to miss. There was more talk about Dr. King and something called a "March on Washington," where people from all over America were gonna come to Washington to hear him speak.

They showed a short clip of him preaching a sermon. It was like the sky was splitting open and heaven was coming down. I thought even Cooter Conley would be impressed.

June sat in her nightgown and men's socks, leaning as close to the TV as she could. "My goodness, he makes the hair on the back of my neck stand up. Gracie, wouldn't it be something to go to Washington and hear him preach? Maybe me and you ought to get in old Beauty and go."

I imagined Aunt June with her flaming hair in a sea of brown faces. The thought of it made me smile. I knew, of course, that it was just talk.

June and I looked up as Sissy let the screen door slam behind her. She breezed past us with a short "Hey" and disappeared into her room, where she stayed holed up whenever she was home. Aunt June said that was part of being a teenager—you needed a lot of time by yourself to think about yourself. After the news June drifted off for a nap, snoring in spurts. She mumbled in her sleep. I suppressed a giggle. I felt bored. I got up to walk to the back door and instead found myself at Sissy's door. I was guessing she would tell me to buzz off. She had made it clear that her room was off-limits to me.

I knocked as softly as I could, careful not to wake June. "Can I come in?"

I braced myself for her usual tongue-lashing, but instead, she opened the door and motioned for me to take a seat on the bed. My legs went stiff and wouldn't move until I willed them to. I had become so used to us loathing each other. Her unexpected kindness was so strange, I felt like I was watching it happen to someone else.

I sat on her bed and leaned back against the white headboard. She was wearing only a pink bra and matching pink panties with a satin pink robe that was open in the front. She was tanned, lean, and shaped as if God himself had sculpted her until she was flawless. I wondered what it would be like to look the way she did. I kept these thoughts to myself as I watched her apply her makeup and perfume with precision—for what reason, I didn't know, since all any of us planned to do was go to bed. Even with the bruises still fading to yellow from the fight, she was stunning.

She turned around and looked at me. "Do you want me to put a little makeup and perfume on you?"

I sat not knowing what to say. She motioned me to the mirror and leaned down to apply some light-pink eye shadow on me. She was so close, I could smell her musk perfume. Her skin was warm and soft and her breath smelled like cigarettes and Juicy Fruit gum. She was doing a much better job than Emoline had.

"You know, Gracie, you're a pretty girl. But more than that, you're smart, and smart is better than pretty."

I couldn't remember one nice thing she had said to me recently. Her sudden warmth moved me in a way I had not expected, and I felt moisture spring to my eyes. I cleared my throat and tried to shake the emotions loose by asking a question. "You really think so?"

She added a little blush to my cheeks and perfume on my neck. I had always been her bratty sister. But in this moment, we were bound by something greater; it was there in the pools of her eyes as she turned me around to see how I looked with glittery pink eyeshadow and rosy cheeks in her dresser mirror. It was a longing, there in her dark-brown eyes, the same as mine.

I went to bed without washing my face. Letting her softness and mothering carry me into my dreams. Wishing it could have lasted a little while longer.

*   *   *

We got up with Rojo crowing through our windows. Aunt June wanted to be at church early. "I'd rather be an hour early than a minute late."

Sissy said she didn't feel good and wanted to sleep a little longer. June told her not to sleep the day away and that there were fresh biscuits in the warming oven if she got hungry.

We walked into the sanctuary, which had been built only three years earlier. It was large enough to seat two hundred people, with stained-glass windows and a baby-blue cloud of carpet. I saw Emoline as she passed our aisle, but gratefully she didn't see me.

While Pastor Bluin preached his sermon, June and I struggled to keep our eyes open. When it came time for testimonies and prayer requests, Aunt June shot up her hand and told them about Isaac's situation and asked for everyone to keep him in their prayers. Mothers listened closely and shook their heads. Old ladies dabbed away tears with their handkerchiefs. I tried to be invisible.

The pastor cleared his throat and nodded awkwardly without saying much else. At the end of the service, he included Isaac's name in the long list of those in need of prayers. I wondered why he didn't ask for healing, instead saying we would "trust in the Lord during these difficult times." Even though I was embarrassed by Aunt June blurting out our family's private struggles, I thought he could have at least given Isaac his own prayer. His condition was much more serious than the return of Mr. McElhaney's best hunting dog. Pastor Bluin was no Dr. King.

16

RUBY'S ROLLER RINK

By the time we got home from church, a drizzle had started that continued on and off all day, but the blue sky broke through the clouds Monday morning. June and I got up early and gave Virginia's flowers and vegetables a little water for good measure. Aunt June poured the water from an old can, proclaiming, "Cucumbers need a *lot* of water. The Lord sent just enough rain to tease 'em but not a full drink!" We checked on the herbs June and I had planted earlier in the week, then walked to Handy Hardware and bought netting to place over the beds to keep the birds out.

After we'd finished with the netting, June and I were taking a break on the porch when the mailman came. For some reason he decided to carry the mail to the porch.

"Well, how nice of you to bring that to us. How are you today?" June fussed over her red hair.

I spoke up. "Hey, Mr. Walter."

"Hey, Grace." But his eyes were glued on June. "Hello, I'm Walter

Cummings," he said extending his hand to shake hers. "Who might you be?"

"I'm June. Grace's aunt."

"You from around here?"

"No, I live up near Berea, but I came to spend some time with Gracie while her parents are away."

"Oh, that's right. I heard about what happened. Very sorry . . ." He kept staring at June, then said, "I declare you've got the prettiest red hair."

June blushed almost as red as her hair and let out a giddy, "Thank you, Mr. Walter." She was glowing.

He cleared his throat. "That reminds me, speaking of red . . . I saw a flyer in the post office saying that Puckett's Strawberry Farm is open. You take a bucket and pick as many strawberries as you like. They charge by the gallon."

"That's a wonderful idea, isn't it, Grace? Maybe we'll go pick some strawberries today! Thank you so much, Walter."

"Well, it was nice to meet you, Miss June. You girls stay cool! It's so hot, the chickens are laying hard-boiled eggs!"

June giggled and slapped her knee. "That's a good one, Mr. Walter!"

He beamed. "Thank you, Miss June. Maybe I'll see you around?"

"Maybe so," June responded, unable to suppress a girlish grin as he walked away. Then she turned to me. "What are you staring at?"

"I'm staring at you staring at Mr. Walter."

"It's nice to know I haven't totally lost my appeal." She giggled. "Okay, Gracie, we better get going before the heat melts our enthusiasm."

We hopped in Beauty, windows down, and rolled up to the strawberry farm that was already humming with folks walking into the field. We picked two buckets of strawberries and made it home before noon. June decided we should make jam while they were fresh.

"Strawberries lose some of their sweetness if you put them in the icebox before you can them." She put aside enough to make a strawberry shortcake for dinner. We didn't have the small canning jars she liked, so we drove to town again, bought the jars, and came home to start the jam.

We put the strawberries in a large pot with sugar, lemon, and pectin and let them come to a boil while I washed the jars and put them in a separate large pot of boiling water. We were burning up in that kitchen. June put the box fan in the window and turned it backward to pull out as much heat as she could, but it didn't really help.

Sissy finally rolled out of bed when we were in the thick of it. Her eyes widened, seeing the huge mess we were making. "What are y'all doing?"

"We are canning, darlin'. Would you like to help?"

"Wish I could, but I have to get ready to go to drill team practice." She popped a giant red strawberry in her mouth, then another.

"What are you up to tonight, Sis?" June asked while she stirred the preserves.

"I'll be working late at Tri-Way, so I probably won't be in till after y'all are in bed."

"You be careful, okay?"

"Sure thing." Sissy grabbed a handful of strawberries before she left the kitchen.

"Hey! You don't know how much work it was to pick all of these."

Sissy rolled her eyes at me and disappeared with a drawn-out "bye" trailing behind her.

June winked at me.

"June, this is a lot of work for just a few jars of jam."

"Oh, but Gracie, there is nothing like waking up on a cold winter morning and making a pan of biscuits with butter and then cracking open some strawberry jam. It's like summertime in a jar. You'll remember this day and the work it took to make it."

June saw the world in a way that made the work seem like an adventure. I had a tendency to wait for the other shoe to drop, always expecting that the worst possible thing was the most likely thing to happen. I wished that I could see the world the way she did.

When we finished canning, we were drenched in sweat. We took more cold showers and put on fresh clothes. By then we were starved, so June picked a tomato, red and warm from the sun, and made us a true Southern lunch. A tomato and mayonnaise sandwich on Wonder Bread. It was heavenly.

With no idea what to do for the rest of the day, I remembered that I had seen an ad at the grocery store for the skating rink's nighttime hours.

"June, what would you think about going skating tonight?"

"Ooh . . . that sounds like a broken leg waiting to happen."

"You're strong and fit. You've got nothing to worry about. Why, you'll probably be a better skater than me," I said, batting my eyelashes at her.

"Listen to you, trying to sweet-talk me into it." She chuckled. "It's been a long time since I went skating. Benny and me used to go . . ."

"Please, June! Pleeease!"

"Well . . . why not! Let's do it. But if I'm gonna skate tonight and not end up on my backside, I need a nap."

June napped and I hung out with Rojo while he lay under the shade tree. I sat in Daddy's chair and thought about Isaac.

"You miss Isaac, don't you, buddy?" I reached down to smooth the feathers on his back, and he let out a low, satisfied rumble in his throat. "I miss him too." I fell asleep in that chair with Rojo at my feet and dreamed about Isaac and me playing in the backyard.

"Gracie! Darling, were you sleeping out here? Bless your heart. It's five o'clock. We better eat something and get ready to go."

I stretched my legs out and yawned, said goodbye to Rojo, and ran inside. June made us fried baloney sandwiches, using the rest of the garden tomato we had eaten for lunch. She burned the baloney just enough to bring out the flavor and slathered it in mayo. After we ate, we changed into jeans to protect our knees and brought some thick socks to wear with the skates. Mr. Walter would have thought June looked downright adorable in her jeans.

It had been a while since I'd been to Ruby's Roller Rink. Daddy sometimes took me on Saturday afternoons when he was all caught up at the garage. Sissy usually went on Saturday nights with her friends and didn't seem to have an ounce of guilt about leaving me behind. I was excited that June was willing to try it out.

When we arrived, there was a man in the front booth taking the money and giving out skates. Usually Ruby was there. She had a sweet, full face—big and round like the rest of her. Ruby always called you "sweet baby" and made you feel welcome. This man was ghostly thin with a sickly face and a few greasy strands of hair covering his balding head. He had little white dots that covered his spindly arms. I wondered if those were burns from cigarettes like the one dangling out of the side of his mouth. A long strand of ashes shivered at the tip.

The rink smelled like dirty socks. Lights flashed, and the speakers boomed out, "Walk Like a Man." June and I found a bench and put on our skates. June kept glancing around. The place looked much different in the daytime. There were a few windows where you could see outside, but at night, it was dark and musty with the haze and smell of cigarette smoke. I tried to ignore it, deciding nothing was going to spoil the good time I was so ready for.

"Hey, June, I'm gonna skate around the rink a few times to get warmed up."

As the music played, I spread out my arms and pretended I was flying, letting the sadness of the last month lift off my shoulders. The music was loud and exhilarating. I lost myself in the moment. There was hardly anyone skating. I closed my eyes, feeling the music and the wind of my speed.

I opened my eyes to take a corner and saw her. Saw them.

Wearing shorts so short I was sure their cheeks nearly peeked out from the bottom, Sissy and her two best friends, Tina and JoJo, were burrowed into a dark corner. Their legs, brown from the sun, looked even more tan in white shorts. Their T-shirts were tied at the waist. And all three of them were smoking cigarettes and sitting on the laps of some rough-looking boys. They were laughing. A stream of smoke escaped through Sissy's lips.

I didn't know what to do. I didn't want June to see, but then again, I did. Why was Sissy on someone's lap? Virginia would have a stroke. Then the boy started kissing Sissy, big sloppy kisses with their mouths open. He had one hand on her thigh and the other around her tiny waist.

I skated furiously to the edge of the railing and yelled, *"Stop!"*

Sissy was so jolted when she saw me that she fell off the boy's lap, the weight of the skates pulling her down. I didn't notice that June was coming up behind me.

June stood swaying in her skates for a moment, then took me by the arm. "Let's go, Grace."

I resisted, but she was stronger. I was trying not to fall as she pulled me away. I struggled to look back at Sissy, who was still on the ground. People were skating around us and staring. I should have been embarrassed, but I was too mad. We skated across to where our shoes were.

"I'm sorry, Grace. I don't think this place is for you or me."

We returned our skates to the front counter. I looked to see if Sissy was watching us, but her back was to us now.

"Leaving so soon?" the attendant asked with a new cigarette in the corner of his mouth.

"Don't you have any rules in this place? There are things going on that parents would not approve of."

His eyebrows gathered in the middle; then he shrugged.

June pointed at the microphone sitting in front of him. "I would like for you to call someone to the front, please."

He took a puff from his cigarette, then blew it out sideways before asking, "What's the name?"

When Sissy appeared at the front, her face was smeared with mascara and pink eye shadow. June turned to me and whispered, "Grace, can you wait by the door, please?"

"But, June!"

"No arguing, Grace; just give me a minute."

I backed away to the door, never taking my eyes off them.

June put her hand on Sissy's shoulder, but she shrugged it off. I could hear June ask, "Honey, are you . . . ?" but the music drowned out the rest. Sissy was shaking her head and closing her eyes, refusing to listen. June tried to touch her shoulder again, but Sissy threw her hands up as if to say, *"Don't touch me,"* and skated away.

June watched her for a minute, then turned back to me. "Grace, let's go."

"Sissy isn't coming with us? How can we leave her here?"

"I'll explain, but not now. Let's go."

We rode home in silence. I was too mad at June to speak.

I stood in front of June in the kitchen with my arms crossed, the obvious question burning in my eyes. I saw the jam jars lined up on the counter to cool, and before I knew what I was doing, I grabbed one and threw it down. The jar broke into jagged pieces, and the red jam splattered all over the floor. It looked like blood.

"Grace! What in heaven's name are you doing?"

"Why did you leave her there, June? You should have drug her out by her hair! That's what Virginia would have done."

June took a deep breath. "I don't know how Virginia chooses to deal with things, but . . . I am not Virginia."

"Isaac's in the hospital fighting for his life, and she's out whoring around!"

"Grace! Your language!" She put her hands on my shoulders and smiled. "It's gonna be okay, Grace. Now, help me clean up this mess you made."

After the broken glass and jam were swept and wiped from the floor, we sat at the kitchen table, drinking the cocoa June made for us.

"Gracie, girls Sissy's age . . . well, she's . . . sowing her wild oats."

I had heard that expression before, like when people talked about Cooter Conley in his younger days.

"If I humiliated her and drug her out of there . . . well, she would just be back tomorrow night. She has to decide that she wants something better for herself. No one else can make her want that. Your parents left me in charge, and that's the choice I made."

She took a sip of cocoa before continuing. "Sissy's at an age where it's hard to talk about your feelings, even though you are pretty much walking around like one big raw nerve exposing all your feelings. Sissy hasn't said two words to me about Isaac. I kind of wonder if this is her way of dealing with it . . . by acting out."

I sipped my cocoa, letting the warm drink bring a moment of sugary comfort. Maybe she was right.

"Now, we better go to bed. Tomorrow is our afternoon tea with your teacher."

I had almost forgotten. At least I had that to look forward to. I was sad that all the good, mothering feelings Sissy had given me last night were gone so quickly. Just when things were looking up . . . the other shoe dropped.

It wasn't until we were in bed with the last light turned out that I heard the front doorknob twist and Sissy's guilty footsteps tiptoeing into her room. She might have gotten away with it for now, but just wait till Virginia got home.

17

WHO IS MY NEIGHBOR?

The next morning, June was sick.

"I bet I caught a bug from that nasty skating rink last night. Oh, Gracie, I don't think I can get up out of this bed to go to Miss Adams's house."

"But, June . . ." I felt all the excitement that had been building to get a glimpse into Miss Adams's world deflate like a birthday balloon. I had so many questions. How did she decide to move to Jubilee and why wasn't she afraid to stand up to the Klan in front of the entire town? Now I wouldn't get to know any of that. I was sure the disappointment was etched into my face. I left her room without saying anything else, afraid I might cry.

"Oh, Gracie, honey, I'm so sorry. Please come back."

Sniffing back my embarrassment at almost breaking down in tears, I regained my composure and went back to her room.

"Now come here, darlin'." She pulled me into a hug. I could barely breathe with all her red hair up my nose. She patted me on the back. "I just don't know what to tell you."

Then the answer sprinkled down like snow on Christmas.

"What if Miss Adams is willing to come pick me up?"

"Gracie, aren't you the smart one to figure that out! I am going to lay right here in bed. You get her on the phone, and I'll come talk to her."

Aunt June explained everything to Miss Adams, who said she would be happy to come pick me up. I gave June the biggest hug I could muster. She pinched my cheeks and said, "I like that you didn't give up."

Once again, I had the unfamiliar feeling of pride. Why was it that other women in my life, like Miss Adams and Aunt June, found it so easy to build me up, but Virginia only ever managed to tear me down?

Mixed in was a nagging guilt over hiding the truth from June that I was forbidden to see Miss Adams. Was June's getting sick God's way of stopping me from going? But what could it hurt?

I spent the morning bringing hot tea, soup, and crackers to Aunt June in bed. She sneezed and coughed and really did seem miserable, but whatever bug she had, it didn't affect her appetite.

I wondered if Miss Adams and I would have anything to talk about outside of class. Would it be awkward? Would she be easy to talk to? Last night I'd dreamed that Miss Adams and Daddy were happily married. Virginia was nowhere to be found, as if she'd never existed. I woke up feeling guilty for the happiness I felt in the dream.

When I answered her knock on the screen door, Miss Adams was wearing blue jeans and a flowing white top with a light-blue scarf in her hair. June came to the edge of the living room in her robe and thanked her from a distance.

"Miss June, is there anything I can get you before we go?"

"No, honey, but thank you. Grace has been looking after me all day. She's a great little nurse."

I gave June a quick hug and she waved us off. "I want to hear all about afternoon tea!"

And then she sneezed.

We snuck out the door. Miss Adams and I giggled over Aunt June. She was hilarious, even when she wasn't trying.

We drove through neighborhoods in the older and wealthier part of town. Streets with sidewalks and large oak trees that gave shade from the heat. White picket fences with pink and yellow roses climbing up trellises surrounded the yards. There were large front porches with ceiling fans. I was thinking there was something familiar about this street when we passed a house with a turret and wicker furniture. It was Emoline's. All of those angry feelings resurfaced in my chest.

I couldn't resist asking, "Miss Adams, do you live on the same street as Emoline?"

"Ahh . . . no. This is the easiest route to my neighborhood."

"What neighborhood do you live in?" I knew Miss Adams's daddy was a doctor. I figured she could afford to live in the nicest part of town, even though teachers didn't make very much money, from what Daddy had told me.

"I live just a few miles up ahead."

We took a turn down a road toward the river on the east side of town. We slowed to a stop in front of the train tracks, waiting for the train to pass. I had never been in this part of Jubilee, and as we crept over the tracks, I began to feel even more confused about where we were going.

There were no more tree-lined streets, picket fences, or flower gardens.

On the other side of the tracks was a bare dirt road exposed to the afternoon sun. A Negro man was walking to the river with a fishing rod over his shoulder. He was wearing overalls with just an undershirt beneath. The sun and sweat glistened like diamonds on his brown skin.

Miss Adams looked over at me. "Have you ever been to this part of town, Grace?"

"No, ma'am."

"I guess I thought with your daddy and Hutch being such good friends, you might have."

"No, ma'am."

The sidewalks disappeared into deep potholes that dotted the road. Miss Adams drove slower. The houses were smaller. They didn't have paint, just weathered planks of wood.

My stomach churned, thinking of what the Klan had already done from Daddy just standing on the same side of the street as Hutch. The thought of Rank Gunner finding out that I was spending time in the Negro part of town with Miss Adams made me very afraid.

Up ahead the neighborhood changed. There were people sweeping their porches and walkways. Even though the houses weren't fancy like the ones on Emoline's street, they were tidy and welcoming with home-made flower boxes full of bright-colored petunias. It reminded me of my street. Lots of folks sat outside in the shade under trees and on porches, talking with their neighbors. The men wore wide-brimmed hats, and the ladies laughed as they cooled themselves with church fans.

Miss Adams waved at a few folks, who smiled and waved back. Others let her pass by without returning a wave. A short, stout lady stood on the top step to her porch, arms crossed, shaking her head at Miss Adams. I looked from her to Miss Adams. She furrowed her brow. "That's Hashbrown. She cleans house for the mayor. She isn't crazy about me living here."

Miss Adams slowed down, and we pulled up to a small yellow house with a climbing pink rosebush cascading over a white picket fence. Her friendly front porch had two wicker chairs with a mason jar of roses on the small table between them. As I climbed the porch steps, a fluffy brown dog inched his way to me, wagging a stub of a tail.

"Can I pet him?"

"It's actually a she. Let's ask her." She dropped to a knee and scratched the top of the dog's head. "What do you say, Maggie? Can Grace pet you?"

Maggie placed her brown furry face on Miss Adams's knee, drinking in her love.

"Call her to you."

I bent down, making myself smaller. "Hey, Maggie." She looked to Miss Adams for approval. I moved forward and lowered my hand slowly, carefully smoothing the fur along her head. She whimpered a little bit, then started to wag her stub.

"See there, a new friend, Mags!" Miss Adams ran her hand along the dog's back.

"What happened to her tail?"

"That's a sad story." She looked down at her tenderly. "Maggie's former owner was a cruel man. He would punish Maggie by slamming her tail in the door. When a friend of mine found her by the tracks, she was nothing but bones, and her tail was eaten up with infection. The veterinarian I took her to wasn't able to save her tail, but she does okay without it."

I scratched Maggie's head once more.

Sweat was trickling from the top of my head all the way down my back. When Miss Adams opened the screen door for us to go inside, I felt a rush of cool air.

I couldn't stop myself from audibly gasping. "Ahhhh. You have an air conditioner!"

Miss Adams laughed.

I told her, "My daddy says he prefers open windows and fresh air, opposed to 'bought air.'"

"Your father is very strong in his ideas, isn't he?"

"Yes, ma'am, he is." I wanted to change the subject, feeling nervous about where it could lead. I stepped into her living room.

Her couch had big, soft pillows and a glass coffee table with more roses from her garden. A cozy fireplace along the center of one wall was filled with candles instead of a fire. A large rug with intricate designs covered most of the floor. There were bookshelves that ran all the way down the hallway. I read some of the titles as she led me to her kitchen, which smelled of warm cookies and brown sugar. The sun cast a golden light in through the open window. A small breeze made the leaves of the herbs growing on the windowsill shiver. If I ever had a home when I was a grown-up, I would want a kitchen exactly like this.

At the kitchen table, she had set two pink placemats with a mint-green teacup and saucer on each one. She lifted a glass tray of cookies and placed it on the small, square table.

"Grace, I'm not much of a baker, but I hope you like peanut butter." She poured hot tea from a mint-green teapot that matched the cups and saucers. "Have you ever had English tea?"

"No, ma'am. Is that different from sweet tea?"

"Well, English tea is made of a higher quality tea leaf than the kind we buy to make sweet tea, and it's served hot with milk and sugar. It might seem strange to drink something hot in the summer, but people in England and around the world have been doing it for centuries. Want to give it a try?"

The thought of milk and hot tea did sound strange, but if Miss Adams wanted me to try it, I would.

She added two sugar cubes and some milk, then gave me a tiny spoon to stir it with. I watched as she lifted her pinky when she raised her cup, and I did the same. It was different. She picked up a cookie and dipped it in her tea. I did the same. I loved it.

"Grace, have you heard from your parents how Isaac is doing?"

"Yes, ma'am. They called a few nights ago. They said his surgery went well, but they don't know when he'll be coming home."

She nodded as she swallowed her tea. "And you have an older sister, right? How is she doing with all of this?"

I looked at her with the memory of the night before at the skating rink still fresh in my thoughts. It must have been written all over my face.

"Is something on your mind, Grace? . . . Oh, listen to me! I'm sorry for asking you so many questions. Maybe you'd like to ask me a question?"

One rose to the top of my mind and was out of my mouth before I could stop it. "I was just wondering why you lived in this part of town. Aren't you afraid of the Klan?"

Miss Adams tilted her head to one side and took a deep breath before answering. "Well, if I paid attention to your daddy's advice, I certainly should be."

My eyes got wide, half surprised and feeling a little defensive of him, but she smiled and winked at me as she sipped her tea. "To answer your first question, I guess I moved into this neighborhood because I wanted to do something to mess up the tidy line that we Southerners are so accustomed to. I grew up in Mississippi in a culture of rigid Southern manners, country clubs, debutante balls, and finishing schools. Everything was turned out just so. I knew about the Klan, but I guess I was sheltered from it. My family, because of my father's work, had the means to whitewash over anything. Why, I was practically raised by Miss Cookie, a lovely woman who was our help. They called her Cookie because she baked the most glorious peanut butter cookies, much better than these!"

"What was her real name?"

Miss Adams swallowed the bite of cookie in her mouth, looking off to the side, trying to extract the name from her memory. "It also started with a *k* sound . . . Ca . . . Carlotta! That's it!"

I dunked another cookie in my cup and gobbled it down.

She kept going. "I always heard my parents speak to Cookie very politely, and yet there was a clear line drawn between who was the server and who was the served. I didn't even recognize that the world could operate differently until I left for college."

Miss Adams poured more tea into our half-empty cups.

I sat drinking in warm, sweet tea and every honey-coated word that fell from her lips, imagining what it must have been like to grow up the way she did.

"You see, I was the only daughter, two brothers. My father thought

THE YEAR OF JUBILEE

I should marry well. He would say, 'Constance, what is the point of wasting time and money on a college education for a woman? Let your future husband worry about that.'"

Miss Adams shook her head and bit her bottom lip. "I wanted to prove him wrong. I will never forget what he said when I told him my first choice was the University of Chicago."

She leaned back in her chair and let out a husky laugh followed by a masculine drawl, "'Now, Constance, darling, don't get your hopes up. U of C is one of the most difficult schools for even the smartest men, much less . . . a woman.'"

She snapped back to herself and let out a deep sigh.

I was mesmerized. "What happened?"

She left the kitchen for a moment and returned carrying a silver frame that held a diploma. Her eyes sparkled with pride.

> The trustees of the University of Chicago
> have conferred on
> Constance Adams
> the degree of Bachelor of Arts

"Wow . . . you did it."

"My father had to eat his words. Going to Chicago—it was like going to another planet. And talk about opening my eyes. Instead of a Negro maid, I had Negro professors who *I* answered to—serious intellectuals who were leaders in their field. At one of the first integrated universities in America, I had many Negro classmates. It was just . . . accepted. Then my junior year, I roomed with Dinah, who was also an English major, and Negro, who became one of my closest friends." She left the room again and returned with a photo of the two of them in their graduation gowns.

She traced her finger on the glass of the photo, the smile on her face wilting as she closed her eyes against a memory.

"But what changed everything was a young boy named Emmett Till."

"Who is that?"

"He was from Chicago—just fourteen when he was killed by white men while visiting the South. It happened only a few years before I arrived—my professors that showed a film about it in class had actually attended the funeral. Oh, Grace . . ." She closed her eyes again, as if aching at the memory. "It was an open casket, just fourteen years old . . . the most unspeakable cruelty. They said that one out of every five people had to be carried out after viewing what had been done to that poor boy. And can you guess where the crime occurred?"

I shook my head, unable to find any words.

"Home sweet home, Mississippi. It was impossible, after seeing something so . . . horrific, to ever be a part of segregation again. I guess that's why I chose to live here."

He had been barely older than me. The adults said I was still just a child. Then so was Emmett. A child, killed by grown men. The weight of it settled on my heart like a brick, sinking down to the dark river bottom.

"Are your neighbors okay with you being here?"

She winced and smiled awkwardly. "It's been a mixed reaction. Hutch and his family have gone out of their way to be neighborly. Some of the others . . . I'm slowly trying to get to know them." She sighed. "Grace, here I am going on and on. How are you doing? You must miss your brother so much."

"Isaac is pretty much my best friend in the world. In some ways, he is the only close friend I've ever had."

"I'm so sorry. Has it been a challenge to make friends?"

"Girls my age are usually interested in different things than me. Just hard to find someone who understands."

Miss Adams nodded.

Feeling exposed, I asked another question. "Miss Adams, why did you choose to teach in Jubilee instead of going back to Mississippi?"

"My godmother married a man from Middlesboro. She called to wish me well after graduating and mentioned she'd read in the paper that they were in need of a high-school teacher in Jubilee. I just couldn't face Mississippi . . . needed to blaze my own trail, I guess. So I drove to Jubilee, applied, and they hired me on the spot."

I had never known anyone like Miss Adams. She was so inspiring in the way she thought about life. It wasn't just the drudgery of a day-in, day-out life. She was living for a purpose.

"But what if people find out where you live?"

"Mr. Hutch and Miss Hazel helped me start a rumor that I was doing volunteer tutoring for Negro children as a part of a new mandated government program. That's been enough to explain why folks see me driving into this neighborhood."

"But when you spoke out at the rally, weren't you scared? What if they find out?"

"I've known for quite some time that Rank Gunner was the leader of both the White Citizens Council and the local Klan. I do feel afraid, and Grace, Hutch told me about what happened at your house." She grimaced. "I'm so sorry. I feel sort of responsible for that."

"It wasn't your fault," I said.

Then she reached her hand across the table to mine. "Helen Keller said, 'Life is either a daring adventure or nothing.'"

"Who's that?"

"A woman who became deaf and mute when she was only a toddler. She went on to become one of our great writers and thinkers. But she didn't accomplish anything by being afraid."

All I could think about was how afraid I was that Isaac wasn't going to make it. That was a thought I couldn't face.

"But how do you fight the fear when it's so overwhelming?"

"Grace, for most of us, there comes a time when not facing your fears becomes worse than the fear itself."

With those words still hanging in the air, a knock came at the back door right off the kitchen. Miss Adams rose to answer. I sat still, afraid of who it might be. Had June started to feel better and driven over? I knew Miss Adams had already given her the address.

"Hello, Hutch and Yully; y'all come on in."

Hutch and his daughter stepped in the door. I remembered seeing her that day at the hardware store and then at the rally, and later on that awful day at Tri-Way.

"Yully, I want you to meet Grace. Grace, meet Yully. I believe you two are about the same age."

I stood quickly and walked over. Yully and I stared at each other. I extended my hand.

She looked at me nervously then slowly lifted her hand and we shook, our eyes locking.

"Hey. Nice to meet you, Yully."

Yully nodded, a hint of a smile on her lips, but she didn't speak.

Miss Adams opened the door wide. "Won't you join us? Let me make you both a cup of tea."

"Oh no, we didn't come to stay. I just wanted to ask about little Isaac. Miss Grace, how's he doing?"

"He's still in Memphis at the hospital . . . Daddy called to say the surgery went well . . ."

I wasn't sure what else to say. I remembered Mr. Hutch holding Isaac's little boot. We had been drawn together by that awful moment in a way that was difficult to explain.

His dark, sad eyes had so much compassion in them.

"Just wanted you to know that our family is praying for Isaac. You let us know if you ever need anything."

"Yes, sir. I will."

"We best be going. My wife sent this over." He had been holding a round package in his hands. "Chess pie. She figured you two might like to have some pie with yo' English tea."

"How thoughtful. Thank you, Hutch, and thank Miss Hazel for

me too." Before they left, Yully skipped forward and gave Miss Adams a side hug. Miss Adams hugged her back. "Yully, wait right here; I have something for you." Miss Adams went into the kitchen and came back out a couple minutes later. She handed Yully a tea towel with a lump in the center.

"Some peanut butter cookies. I hope you enjoy them."

"Thank you." Her voice was like a puff of smoke. They were the first words I had heard her say.

They headed out the door.

Seeing the world through Miss Adams's eyes made me wonder what it would be like to be Yully. To walk around in her skin for a day, the way Miss Adams talked about on the last day of school. Maybe Yully wondered the same thing about me.

I wondered how Miss Adams could be so brave and risk so much for something she believed in. I wondered if I could ever be that brave. I wondered if the wrath of Virginia would always prevent me from doing anything truly daring. I felt small and cowardly next to Miss Adams.

On our drive home, as we turned onto Main Street toward my neighborhood, I saw the boy with golden hair and blue eyes walking behind his parents into Handy Hardware. He was wearing a short-sleeved, white button-down shirt and black pants and those same preacher shoes. I thought he must be so hot and miserable.

Miss Adams's voice broke in. "Do you know that boy with the blond hair?"

"Oh, I don't know him personally, just heard about him. He's a famous traveling child healer, Golden, the Miracle Boy."

"Hmm. Is that right?" Her voice was tinged with doubt. "I wonder how they manage his schooling with all of that travel."

He disappeared into the hardware store and I sunk down into my seat, suddenly feeling exhausted from the day.

Miss Adams delivered me to the front door. June thanked her profusely as we waved goodbye from the porch, watching her drive away.

June peppered me with questions about what Miss Adams's house was like and what we'd done. I was careful to say how pretty the house was and all about the English tea and cookies. She seemed delighted that I had enjoyed such a grand day out.

I figured leaving out part of the truth wasn't as bad as lying. I was praying that Daddy wouldn't call for a couple days so that June wouldn't think to tell them about me going to Miss Adams's house. I tried to think of how to ask June to keep it between us, but there seemed to be no way to do that without revealing that I had been forbidden to see her. After what Miss Adams had shared with me today, it almost seemed worth it.

* * *

The next morning as I walked down the hallway for a drink of water, I heard June talking with Daddy from the phone in the kitchen.

"Oh, John!"

I crept and placed my ear close to the kitchen door. I could hear her sniffing away tears as she listened. My heart was racing. Why was June crying? Suddenly June telling Daddy I had gone to Miss Adams's house didn't even matter.

She blew her nose and answered, "The girls are doing fine. Grace has been my little helper."

I eased into the kitchen, June looking up and then away from me as she wiped her tears with a handkerchief. I stood waiting. Desperate to know what was wrong with Isaac now.

"I will be praying, John." Then she hung the phone back on the wall.

"What is it, June?"

"Gracie . . . your daddy said the doctors are worried 'cause Isaac's been running a fever. He's had it for a couple days now. They say that he might have an infection, which is dangerous with his condition. We just got to keep praying, Gracie."

I ran out of the kitchen and out the back door and grabbed Rojo up

147

in my arms and cried, letting my tears run down over his feathers. He was strangely still and let me hold him without squirming. I sat down in Daddy's chair under the oak tree and started talking to the rooster. He clucked a couple times, and I set him down in the grass. He pecked at the ground and sat there peacefully.

Fear washed over me.

"We have to help Isaac. He has to come home, Rojo. He just has to. Aunt June says to pray, but why does that feel like doing nothing?"

I laid my head back in the chair, feeling the wind blowing in the old oak. The sun was glinting through the leaves showering me with a soft golden glow. *Golden.*

18

HELL'S
TRAILER PARK

I lied to Aunt June. And it was easier for me than it should have been.

I reasoned again that leaving out information wasn't the same as a lie. Besides, the good that could come out of it far outweighed the wrong of telling a small lie. Okay, maybe not so small.

When she was outside and couldn't hear the phone ring, I pretended to be at the end of a conversation with Mr. Farris asking me to come help him with some chores in the yard. When June came back through the kitchen door, I hung up before she could confirm the details of my fake conversation. "I am impressed with your can-do attitude, Grace. A summer job is a great idea." She added milk to her coffee as I told her I could ride my bike over. She thought that would be fine since it was only a few blocks away. I told June it would be an all-morning job and I wouldn't be home till a little before lunchtime.

I avoided looking into her eyes. My stomach churned with guilt. I had been so mad when Sissy lied to us before, but this was different. The situation with Isaac called for action. I couldn't let anything stop me from helping him, even if it meant lying.

Nearly an hour later I stood, holding the handlebars of my bike as I waited for the train to roll by so that I could cross the tracks. It felt like an eternity in the heat. I saw it make a stop, not far from the crossing, at the old shoe factory. When it started moving again it chugged along, slowly gaining speed. Finally I was clear to cross. I turned my bike onto the potholed street of the Shady Creek Trailer Park. A shirtless little girl covered from head to toe in dirt came to the edge of the yard and watched me pass as she sucked her thumb. She was holding a small doll with a dirty pink dress. Not far down the street, a man wearing a dingy white undershirt sat on his front steps tipping back a beer can. A large roll of his white belly bulged out from the bottom of his undershirt. I had never seen anyone drink beer so early in the morning. The yards were littered with trash, junk car parts, and broken toys. There wasn't an ounce of shade, a creek, or a park in sight.

I'd ridden past a few trailers when I heard a voice shouting. I stopped and dismounted my bike for a moment. The noise was coming from a woman sitting in a red plastic lawn chair who was holding down a small boy across her lap. He couldn't have been older than three.

She was whacking him on his bare behind and screaming, "You're just like your good-for-nothing daddy!" She swore at him as he tried to squirm loose and called him awful names.

With every blow, his wailing filled the air like a wild cat.

"I be good! Please, Mama!"

This only seemed to make her angrier. Little goosebumps rose up on my arms. I wanted to stand up to her. I imagined myself running over and knocking her out of that chair and taking the little boy away with me, but I just stood there in the road, failing again to do the right thing. I was relieved when he finally escaped her grasp.

She noticed me there and yelled, "What are you looking at?"

She stormed into her trailer as the little boy ran screaming away from her, his shorts still around his ankles. I thought to myself, *Oh, God. Please help that little boy to get away from her.* But how could he ever?

I wasn't the only person in this place who needed God to intervene. I got back on my bike, wincing as the seat burned my legs, so I pedaled standing up. Any joy I had ever felt seemed lost to me, as though I had ridden into the lair of the devil. It was ironic that I had to come to hell to get a heavenly miracle.

I searched for the right trailer, squinting against the sun. I pulled my green bike up to a rusty single-wide at the end of Polk Street. There was a faded gold Chevy Impala parked in front. My hands were shaking, and I thought I might have to throw up.

The wooden front steps were wobbly and missing a few nails. I took a deep breath and knocked on the door. I noticed a flash of blond hair from a bedroom window but heard only silence. I knocked again, this time a little harder. I could hear the rumble of voices inside. The door opened slowly, and a pair of beady eyes beneath greasy black hair peeked out from behind.

It was the father of the Golden-Haired Miracle Boy; he wore a short-sleeved button-down white shirt but had left several buttons undone. He was in his bare feet, and his long yellow toenails made me cringe. The trailer smelled of cigarette smoke and bacon. I guess I had come during their breakfast and morning smoke.

"I came about my brother."

He stood there in a daze, trying to make sense of who I was and what I was saying. He just kept standing there at the door.

Finally I asked, "Can I come in?"

"I'm not sure . . ." He paused in the awkward silence. Almost against his will, it seemed, he opened the door. He seemed put out with me.

There was an orange couch and a mismatched green chair in the corner of the living room, with a small TV sitting on top of a TV tray up against the wall. In the kitchen they had a little card table and three chrome chairs with orange cushions. It looked like the furniture that I saw for sale at Nickel Thrift. The air conditioner in the corner was doing its best but failing to keep up with the ninety degrees outside. The air was stale and hot. I could barely breathe.

Golden Boy's daddy called out, "We got company if you can come in here please, Mary."

A voice, sharp and annoyed, came from the back. "In just a *minute*. I wasn't prepared for company."

"Have a seat." He pointed toward the seating area. I sat on the couch at the very end, trying to take up as little room as possible. I stared at the floor and finally heard a door open from the back hallway. The Miracle Boy walked in. He did not smile but simply nodded to me and met my eyes with his. Miss Mary came soon after. She wore a long denim skirt and a white blouse, with her hair up in a bun like before. The man sat in the one extra chair in the living room. There was plenty of room on the couch, but the mom and Golden pulled kitchen chairs the short distance from the linoleum to the carpeted living room. She centered all of her attention on me, like she was a waiting queen on a throne.

"How did you come to find our residence?"

"Well, Miss Mary—"

"Sister Mary. You will address me as Sister Mary and my husband as Brother Joseph."

I leaned away from the cold smack of her reprimand. "Yes, ma'am. Sorry. Miss—I mean Sister Mary."

I swallowed, trying to lather up some spit to moisten the feeling of cotton balls in my mouth.

"Oh . . . well, I was talking to the waitress at the Green Parrot Café, I think her name is Lila—"

Sister Mary cut me off. "And how did Lila know where we were staying?"

I shrugged. "I'm not sure how she knew, but she mentioned it that day at the diner."

"Really!" Cutting me off again, Sister Mary huffed out a quick breath before continuing.

I had a feeling there was a hot head under the holy-roller hairdo.

"First of all, she should mind her own business and not go spreading gossip about us!"

I didn't want to get the waitress in trouble, so I quickly added, "Miss Lila is a big admirer of Golden and your family—she said you guys were the biggest celebrities she'd ever met."

This triggered a strange event on Sister Mary's face: her lips spread upward in an odd shape that was the closest thing to a smile she could muster. She smoothed the back of her hair down and let a small giggle escape. "We are simply humble servants for the Lord."

I thought I saw Golden suppress the beginning of an eye roll, but I couldn't be sure. Then she kept going. "Also, we are only renting here temporarily since we travel so much. Our main residence is in Alabama. As you can imagine, our privacy is very important to us since we are in the public eye with our healing revivals."

"Oh, I understand that. I will not be spreading it around. I will keep it to myself."

"Thank you," Sister Mary said. "Now, may I ask why you are here?"

What I really wanted to do was run as far away from there as I could, but there was too much at stake, so I pushed through my fear. "Like I told you, sir—" I pointed to the dad—"it's about my brother, Isaac."

I went on to explain the seriousness of his condition, the tumor they had removed and the fever he was running. I couldn't help but occasionally look over at the Golden-Haired Miracle Boy. He was beautiful in the way pictures of angels are beautiful. His hair was catching the sunlight pouring in from the window behind him, and it was as if it was spun from gold. There were little curls around his face and little dots of sweat on his forehead that kind of sparkled. His skin was tanned a light brown and his eyes were the most piercing blue I had ever seen—sad and piercing. He caught me staring, and I smiled without really meaning to, which seemed to surprise him. I think he was just about to smile too when Sister Mary broke in.

"Golden, are you listening?"

He looked away from me. She stood guard over everything he did. I swam in a trance looking at him. I imagined myself reaching out and touching a lock of his golden hair.

"Hello, hello, young lady?"

I snapped out of my daydream. "Yes, ma'am."

"So what exactly do you want from us? Get to the point, please."

"I'm sorry. I just wanted to ask if Golden might be able to visit Isaac? Since my brother can't leave the hospital to come to a revival."

"Yes, I understand." Sister Mary drilled her dark eyes into mine. I noticed Brother Joseph, who had been preoccupied with chewing his fingernails and spitting them out onto the carpet, was now paying attention. It was clear who was running this show, and it wasn't Brother Joseph or Golden.

Sister Mary continued. "Of course, I am sure something could be arranged." She cleared her throat. "Joseph and myself have dedicated our lives to the work of the Lord. You can think of us like missionaries, and all missionaries, of course, have to depend on the support of the church."

She paused, attempting an awkward, plastic smile, waiting for me to respond. I wasn't exactly sure what she was saying. Then she clarified.

"If we drove to the hospital in Memphis, certainly there would be additional expenses than if we visit him here in Jubilee. Either way, we would ask that you make a donation to our ministry to help us carry on the work of the Lord."

"Donation?"

Sister Mary was only too happy to clarify. "A contribution, an offering." I must have still looked confused. "Money. We need money for . . . our ministry."

I didn't remember Jesus charging for miracles.

"We do have a recommended amount so that you don't have to be embarrassed by offering an amount . . . that might not be appropriate." She smiled, waiting for my reaction while her words hung there in the air like in a Sunday paper cartoon.

"How much does a miracle cost?"

"Oh, silly child. You are not paying for the miracle, heavens no! We simply ask for help with our ministry needs. That's all."

Sister Mary got up quickly, dashing into the kitchen for a piece of paper. She stood at the kitchen counter writing something down and remained standing as she held it out to me, sending the message that our visit was over.

"I have taken the liberty of writing down the suggested amount and our telephone number, so you won't have to inconvenience yourself coming over again."

I stood and silently took the piece of paper from her, quickly unfolding it to read the amount she had written: *$100 for ministry support with no travel. Driving to Memphis, additional $20 for gas and expenses.*

My eyes must have been saucers. The thought of giving her that much money seemed outrageous. I felt stunned by the amount.

Then Sister Mary said, "If there isn't anything else, you can be on your way?"

I walked to the door and then down the broken stairs and back out into the oven of summer heat.

While I made my way to my bike, I saw Golden standing in a window, looking sorrowfully through the brown curtains. I stood at my bike, meeting his gaze. We were locked there in a moment of shared misery. I raised my hand to give a small wave. Slowly, he lifted up his hand and waved goodbye, never taking his eyes off me.

I was pedaling as fast as I could out of hell's trailer park when I saw the first good thing in this place: Cooter Conley walking down the steps of a little yellow trailer that had clothes hanging on the line beside a small green patch of grass. He waved me down. I slowed my bike to a stop beside him and his old blue truck.

"Hey, Cooter."

"Well, hey, Miss Gracie Lou. What are you doing here all by yourself?" Cooter covered his eyes against the sun. "Did you ride your bike all this way?"

I sweated out an answer that wasn't a total lie. "Yes . . . I . . . I was visiting a friend."

He looked at me, obviously trying to work out who I had been visiting. I wanted to distract him from thinking too long about it.

"Is this where you live?" I said, pointing to the trailer.

"No, I'm living in the back of Danny Chumley's carpenter shop. Mama lives here. I stop by every day for coffee and cathead biscuits. No one can make 'em like she can."

Cooter smiled with his eyes, pulling little lines back from them. "Gracie, I have been meaning to tell y'all how sorry I am to hear about little Isaac being sick." He was silent for a minute. "You think I could stop by sometime to visit him when he gets back home? I hear your aunt June is staying with you."

"I'm not sure when they're coming home, but I know Isaac would love to see you when he's back."

"How is Sissy doing these days?"

I was saved from answering that question when Cooter's mama came out with an empty basket to take down clothes from the line. She waved at me and smiled. She was a thin woman with happiness in her eyes despite the dark circles under them. She hollered over to us. "Hey, Grace. Would you like to come in for some sweet tea, darlin'? It's so hot out, I'm sure you could use it."

"Thank you for the offer, but I better be getting home." The thought of the iced tea was so enticing, but I was getting nervous about how long it would take me to get back.

Cooter cut in. "Well, that's quite a ways to bike, and the road isn't very safe. How about I throw your bike in the back of my truck and give you a ride home?"

"Well, I kind of wanted to stop downtown. Maybe you could give me a ride as far as Main Street?" I was relieved at the thought of not riding my bike all the way home.

Cooter's mama insisted I come in for an iced tea before we left. Her house was cozy with pictures of yellow daisies on the walls and fresh daisies in a vase on the table. You could still smell the biscuits. I commented on how good they smelled and the next thing you know Mrs. Conley reached into the oven and pulled out a large cast-iron skillet with a few biscuits still in it.

She sliced a biscuit in half, slathering one side with warm butter from a covered dish on the counter and then drizzling honey on it. She slid a sausage patty onto the other half with a slice of cheese, put it on a plate printed with daisies, and placed it in front of me. "You enjoy, sweetie."

As I sat there, I couldn't help but think about the famous story of her husband getting hit in the head with a cast-iron skillet. I wondered if the same skillet that baked up these biscuits was the one that did him in. She was such a nice lady. Anyone who would be mean to a woman as kind as her deserved a skillet in the head. Daddy and I sometimes speculated about whether Jack Conley was dead or still alive somewhere. It was one of those mysteries that the locals loved to ponder.

As Cooter and I drove away, his mama stood waving at us in the bright sunshine against the cozy yellow trailer with the white sheets blowing in the breeze behind her. I thought, *Maybe you can find yourself a little piece of heaven, even in the middle of hell.*

19

MR. FARRIS

I pedaled down the few blocks from where Cooter dropped me off to Mr. Farris's house to see if there actually was a summer job he could offer me so my trip would seem legitimate. As I rode, I kept thinking there was no way I could make a hundred dollars. It was simply impossible.

When the house came into view, sitting on the porch was a head of flaming red hair talking to Mr. Farris. I wondered if I should keep on pedaling, run away, hop a train maybe. But instead I biked up to them and stopped. I waited in the middle of the sidewalk with my foot frozen on the pedal. Aunt June looked up and stared a hole right through me. I knew my chickens had come home to roost. Caught red-handed in the lie.

Aunt June and Mr. Farris had decided before I arrived that the appropriate punishment for my lie would be to actually have me do a job for him.

"I've been meaning to clean out the shed in the back for ages."

Mr. Farris said I could start tomorrow morning and that he would be happy to pay me a little something but did not mention how much.

I accepted their punishment with a certain amount of relief, considering the punishment I would receive from Virginia if she ever found out. I would wait for the right moment to beg Aunt June to keep the lie between us.

No matter how understanding June could be, biking three miles to one of the worst parts of town was not something she could keep from Virginia or Daddy. I could say I went swimming with some friends from school . . . but I wasn't wearing a bathing suit and my clothes and hair were dry.

We walked home as I pushed my bike alongside June in the agony of silence. I kept waiting for her to ask. My stomach churned. Should I keep my secret? Would June understand what I had done? Would she be willing to help with the money? After all, she had met and talked to the Miracle Boy and his parents that day at the café.

These thoughts comforted me at least a little. When we were almost to the door, we heard the phone ringing. June leapt up the steps to answer it. Nobody could bear to miss a phone call, especially not Aunt June.

I parked my bike outside and walked into the kitchen behind June, who reached the phone before it stopped ringing. It was her friend Betty from back home who'd called to tell June the latest town gossip.

"Oh, hey, Betty!" The voice on the other end launched into a stream of jabber. "Hold on a second. Gracie, there is some tuna salad and cold chicken in the icebox if you want to help yourself."

She turned toward the window, leaning against the counter, as I retrieved the sandwich and poured myself a glass of tea. I took it into the living room to eat it.

Aunt June was on the phone so long I went to retrieve my journal from under my bed and took it to the backyard. I sat in my usual spot against the trunk of the shade tree. I wrote about this morning and about all the things Miss Adams had told me when I visited. Sometimes I wrote to God, other times to some person inside of me that was struggling to be loosed. There was something about the feel of the smooth paper against my hand as the words poured from my mind. It was the closest thing to freedom I'd ever felt. Rojo pecked the ground nearby, occasionally looking up at me. I went in to use the bathroom and heard Aunt June still on the phone. I crept into the kitchen, June's back to me. I opened the door to the icebox slowly and saw some cold fried chicken. I lifted a couple pieces and crept out the screen door to the backyard to eat it. I considered giving Rojo a piece but then it dawned on me how weird that would be. "No chicken for you, pal!"

I went back into the kitchen and waited for a pause in the endless stream of talking.

"Yes, Gracie?"

"I am gonna ride my bike around the block a few times."

"Okay, sounds good. Be careful."

I rode my bike slowly, pausing under trees to feel the occasional shade. I stopped at a yard sale a few streets over and rummaged through some old albums and dusty knickknacks. When I returned, June wasn't on the phone anymore. The house was still and lonesome. I looked in the backyard but didn't see her there. I felt sweaty and exhausted, so I gave myself a jaybird's bath, as Aunt June called it, and got into bed thinking if I could fake being asleep, I could avoid her questioning. As I was pulling my nightgown over my head, I heard June coming.

I leapt into bed just in time. She knocked and then opened the door.

"Grace? Gracie, are you in bed already? I hope you didn't worry. Miss Faye a couple doors down slipped and fell, poor thing. I went over to help her get settled into bed."

"It's okay." I slurred my words, as though she had roused me from a deep sleep.

"Gracie, I feel just terrible. You haven't even had dinner yet."

"Mmmmm," I moaned.

"Well, okay. I guess you are plumb worn out. Get some rest." I felt her warm lips and a tiny dot of spit on my forehead from her kiss.

"Sweet dreams, my girl."

She eased the door closed behind her.

My eyes filled with unexpected moisture. The comfort of her mothering made me wish that I could've been the daughter she had always longed for. I was so exhausted I could have slept for a week, and I barely remembered before I drifted off that I had avoided questioning. At least for tonight.

*   *   *

The next morning, I ate my oatmeal while rehearsing a new lie, but to my surprise June never brought it up. She walked me to the Farrises' house in silence. As we walked, I thought I would fill the quiet. "I couldn't help but overhear some of your phone call. Sounds like some exciting things going on back home. What exactly happened?"

June stopped and looked into my eyes. "Do you think I don't know what you're doing? Going to bed at six o'clock and now trying to distract me with questions, to keep me from asking you where you went yesterday? Well, you ain't fooling me. But . . . I decided you can tell me when you're ready. I figure if you were willing to lie about where you went, it must be something important. I just don't want you to get hurt, Grace. Your parents couldn't bear it, and neither could I. What's done is done, but please, please don't do anything dangerous. Would you at least promise me that?"

I searched June's eyes, hoping I could keep this promise, but I wasn't sure.

"Well, do you promise?"

"Yes, June. I promise."

When we reached the Farrises', we walked up the steps and knocked on the door.

Mrs. Farris peered out around the chain and then opened it completely. Her voice had a slight wobble. "Can I help you?"

"Good morning. I'm June, Grace's aunt. I'm looking after her while her folks are . . . out of town."

"Yes, I heard about that."

Her face didn't register even an ounce of compassion. She looked down through her black bifocals, her red lipstick smudged with a generous line across her teeth. Her brown wig sat askew, with the middle part just off-center, while the bottom of the wig exposed the gray sprigs of her natural hair beneath. The smell of fried onions wafted through the open doorway and curdled my stomach.

"Grace is here to help clean out the shed."

Mrs. Farris nodded, wished June a good day, then showed me to the backyard.

Mr. Farris was sitting under a shade tree beside the shed, whittling away on something. He was leaning over his round belly with a single drop of sweat hanging down from the end of his nose. His rosy cheeks were even brighter in the heat. His silvery hair was almost white and looked soft like waves of snow. He wore round glasses, and when he smiled, his eyes disappeared into his face. Add a long white beard and he'd make an excellent Santa for the Jubilee Christmas Parade.

"Good morning, Miss Grace."

"Good morning, Mr. Farris."

Mrs. Farris turned without another word and disappeared into the house. I was glad to see her go.

"What are you making?"

"I'm not exactly sure, but I have a feeling for what it could be." A circle on one end was all I could make out.

"I'm sorry about yesterday and all."

He looked up at me and grinned. "Oh, that's all right. To be honest, Grace, I think it worked out. I really could use your help."

I nodded. "Well, what would you like me to do first?"

I followed him toward the open door of the shed and blew out a long breath. I had never seen so much stuff in all my life. Boxes and boxes. Records and Christmas ornaments and old furniture and dishes and you name it.

"It's quite a mess, isn't it? These are the things I have kept over the years. My family, we were sentimental. Collectors, you might even say. Mrs. Farris likes a tidy house with a few nice knickknacks and china dolls. I guess I like old things. Most of this was what was left at my parents' house when they both passed."

I walked over to a corner in the back and found an old phonograph, the kind that played records by cranking a handle. "Wow, would you look at that."

"That was my grandfather's. I have always wanted to find someone who could fix it. I have all these old records too."

I walked over and skimmed through the box. People and songs I had never heard of.

"My dad is a mechanic. Maybe he could fix it for you someday." I wondered why Mrs. Farris wouldn't let Mr. Farris have any of his family treasures in the house. It didn't seem fair.

"Well, maybe so. That's a good idea, Grace."

We stared ahead, wondering where to begin.

"Where would you start?"

I was surprised to be asked, as though my opinion had weight.

"Well . . . maybe we should figure out if there's anything you want to get rid of?"

He turned his head to the side, considering this.

"Maybe a pile for anything you don't want to keep and then a pile of the things you do want to keep?"

Mr. Farris ruffled my hair and smiled admiringly at my idea, and then we proceeded to do exactly what I had suggested.

There were a lot of old broken toys and things the mice had gotten into that we stacked up for a burn pile. While we worked, I told him again how I had been collecting his little wooden figures and how much I liked them. Mr. Farris was older than Virginia's father, but the kind of man a kid would love to have as a grandfather. Mrs. Farris was another story. They had never had any children. I had heard from my secret spot in the hallway that Mrs. Farris was told by her doctor that she was barren. I looked up that word in the dictionary and it said, "a woman who is unable to have children."

At noon, we had made a small dent in the pile. Mr. Farris told me I had worked enough for one day and if I was okay with it, we could continue tomorrow. I walked home slowly, squinting in the bright sun, thinking about how good a glass of lemonade would taste with lunch.

When I came up the steps, I heard June on the phone through the open kitchen window. Her voice was different. I listened for a few seconds before going in; then I eased the kitchen door open so she wouldn't hear me. She was crying.

"How long do they say it will be, John?" She sniffled and blew into a tissue as she stood at the counter and listened to the answer on the other end.

"I'll tell Grace and Sissy. They deserve to know what's happening."

Then the worst possible thought entered my mind. I couldn't bring myself to ask. I ran into the kitchen and she turned to see me as she placed the receiver back on the wall. My face was burning from the heat and the sudden outburst of tears. She bent down to my eye level.

"Oh, Grace. Shhh," she said, using the hem of her dress to wipe the tears that were slowly streaming down my face. "Isaac just isn't doing as well as they'd hoped he would be by now. He still has a fever. He's weak. They can't bring him home until he starts showing signs of improvement. He's just got to get his strength back. Your daddy says he's been asking for you and Rojo."

"Oh, June, couldn't we go and see him? Please?"

"Well, I guess that is something to consider, for certain. Let me ask your daddy about it the next time he calls. Your daddy says he reads to

Isaac all day while your mama just paces the floor and prays. He said she got this crazy idea to break Isaac out of the hospital to attend a healing revival, but the doctors stopped her."

"Well, maybe that wasn't such a crazy idea if it could help?"

June nodded in understanding as she blew her nose. "Except the doctors said Isaac's immune system is so weak that he could have caught all kinds of germs going to a revival. I know your mama was trying to help. So frustrating to feel so powerless, but when he's a little stronger . . . who knows."

I found it ironic that Virginia and I had the same idea. But it was too soon to risk June finding out what I'd been up to.

"You must be starved. Are you just home for lunch?"

"No . . . Mr. Farris said we'd done enough for today and wanted me to come back in a couple days."

"Well, it is hot as blazes out there. I'll make some lunch. How about leftover goulash?"

"I'm not feeling so good, June."

"But, Gracie, you need to eat to keep your strength up."

"I'm sorry. Maybe I'll be hungry later."

"I can keep the goulash warm in the oven."

I was sometimes amazed that she had not figured out that the only person who liked June's goulash was June. But it really would not have mattered what she had made for lunch. I couldn't eat. My stomach was in knots. How could we get Isaac home so Golden could cure him? I ran back to my room to find the shorts I'd worn the day before. They weren't in my room. I panicked and went to the laundry room, which doubled as a spare bedroom for Aunt June. There they were, still in the dirty clothes basket. I was relieved.

I felt around in the pockets for the piece of paper Sister Mary had given me the day before. I found it at the very bottom. Crumpled and sweaty. I hadn't lost it. I took the paper and put it inside my journal under my mattress, where it would be safe.

I walked back into the living room in time to see Sissy come through the door in a short skirt and a tight top that didn't leave much to the imagination.

Sissy sneered at me and said, "What are you looking at?"

I was so distraught and angry about Isaac. The rage I had buried came bursting to the surface. The words were out of my mouth before I could stop them.

"No wonder people talk about you! Isaac is laying in a hospital bed and you're running around acting like a . . . like a *whore*!"

Her face exploded into a hot rage. Closing the gap between us, she got right up in my face till I could smell her cigarette breath and Juicy Fruit.

"What did you call me?"

"What, you didn't hear it the first time?"

The sarcasm in my voice pushed her over the edge. She jumped on me, pinning me to the living room floor. I felt her long nails jab into me as I kicked and flailed.

"Get off me! Get off me!"

"You shut up, you little brat. I hate you!"

June reached down, trying to get between us, but Sissy almost back-handed her accidentally with her arms flailing and trying to pin me down. I was fighting with everything I had in me.

Sissy screamed at June, "Back off; this is between us!"

"Girls, girls, stop this now! Stop! Don't do this. You are sisters!"

Finally we ran out of steam. I felt some regret for what I had said, even if it was true. June reached out a hand to help Sissy up, but she rejected it. Sissy stood, went to the door, opened it, and looked back at me.

"Which is a worse sin, Grace: lust or lying?"

She slammed the screen door behind her, and we heard her Volkswagen drive away. My heart dropped. How did she know I had lied? Had she seen me biking to Golden's without me realizing it?

"Gracie Lou Mockingbird!" June picked me up by the collar of my shirt. "I have a good mind to wash your mouth out with lye soap! Where in the world have you heard that kind of language?"

"I've heard things about Sissy. She has a reputation."

June shook her head. "Things are rarely so simple, Grace."

I shrugged my shoulders and looked down at the scratches on my arms.

"Oh, Lordy, we better put some alcohol on there."

I didn't care about the scratches and I didn't want to talk about Sissy anymore. I would have to be more careful from now on. All that mattered was finding a way to help Isaac. A hundred dollars . . . it seemed impossible.

I went to my room, exhausted, and fell back on the bed. When I woke up, I could tell by the light outside that I had been asleep for a while. I reached under the mattress for my journal. I eased the back door open and sat down in the chair under the old tree, with a memory nagging at me. I clutched my journal, feeling the pressure of the pen digging into the knuckle of my finger as I drilled words onto the page. At first gibberish, then slowly the nonsense formed a lump in the back of my throat and became tears pouring from my pen.

No footsteps and no fingerprints
To lead me through this dark
Do You hide the light I crave?
Do You smother out the spark?
Of a beating heart, pure and good
Would heaven's treasure take?
Tiny casket—earth and wood
Is it Thy will to bruise and break?

I sat lost in the helpless feeling, watching the last bit of sunlight fade into a tiny bright dot, then disappear. I decided to call my poem "Thy Will," which I wrote at the top of the page.

"Gracie! Dinner's ready. I made your favorite—meatloaf and mashed potatoes."

Aunt June came and knelt beside me in the silence for a moment. I felt reluctant to break out of the spell dusk had put me into.

"Come on in, my girl. Everything's gonna be okay." She put her arm around my shoulder, and we walked back into the house. "How about we eat while we watch TV?"

I excused myself to return my journal to its spot under the mattress, then met her in the living room, where she had everything ready. There was nothing on but the news, and we watched in silence. After dinner, exhausted from the day, we both went to bed.

I heard Sissy's footsteps, sneaking in as I lay in my bed.

My stomach churned as I thought about Golden. He was famous for a reason. He could heal Isaac—that's what everyone said. I searched every corner of my mind. There was something I wasn't thinking of . . .

I stared out the window, comforted by the sound of Rojo's cooing. Then I shot straight up in bed. Like a lightning strike, the solution to the needed hundred dollars was here, in my very backyard. A secret I had tried to bury so deep that I would never be tempted to betray it. I offered a prayer of thanks as I drifted into a deep sleep.

20

TREASURE

The next morning June sent me looking for a shovel to dig up another bed for the herb garden. I went out the back door to grab it from the shed. Rojo was waiting there clucking and pecking in the dirt.

As I walked inside the shed, I saw where Daddy had started building a large birdhouse for the backyard. The smell of sawdust and wood stain made me ache for him. His old radio with the coat hanger antenna sat on top of a stack of books. I saw a cup with coffee grounds left in the bottom. Rojo had followed me in and pecked at little bugs that crawled along the floor. I looked around but didn't see the shovel.

"Come on, Rojo."

He pecked and scratched right behind me around to the back of the shed.

"Grace! Where are you?"

I heard June holler from the front yard where she was getting more flowers and herbs ready to plant, loosening the roots. I scanned the yard for any spot with uneven ground. For years it had been just a game, to pass the time when I was bored. Now, it was different. Now, I had to find it.

"Gracie! You there?"

"Sorry! Still looking for the shovel. Here it is!"

The shovel was leaning against the back side of the shed, but Rojo passed up the shovel and walked over to a patch of grass, pecking at worms. I noticed the ground was sunken down.

I stepped toward Rojo and put my foot in the sunken spot.

"Rojo!" I whispered. "You're a genius."

He looked up at me and clucked a bit.

Our house had been built during World War I, and the bathroom used to be so old and moldy, we could hardly stand to go in there. Back when I was still in elementary school, Virginia had taken us all to Aunt June's house for the weekend, while Daddy remodeled the bathroom. When we returned home, we all marveled at the shiny new toilet and sink and the black-and-white checkerboard linoleum floor.

Later that night, I got up to use that shiny new toilet. I thought everyone was in bed. As I tiptoed down the hall, I heard the rumble of low voices in the kitchen. It was Daddy and Virginia talking. I crouched down in my nightgown and leaned up against the wall and listened.

I heard Daddy say, "Virginia, you can't tell anyone about this, and I mean nobody. This has to be kept quiet."

"John, what is it? You are scaring me. Is something wrong?"

"No, actually, it might be good news; but we can't tell anyone just in case."

"Land sakes, John. Please just tell me."

"I will, but you have to promise me first."

Virginia let out a sharp, frustrated breath, then finally said, "I promise. I promise. Now would you just tell me!"

"While I was fixing the bathroom, I needed to take out a piece of the wall behind the toilet. I took a hammer and broke through the wall. When I did, I heard something metal. I scraped away the plaster, and inside was an old green metal box with a handle on it. I wrestled with it, and when I finally got it out, inside that metal box was another smaller metal box. When I opened up the smaller box, inside were stacks of twenties, fifties, and hundred-dollar bills tied up with brown twine. I counted it. Five thousand dollars."

I worked hard to quiet the gasp that escaped my throat.

"This is an answer to prayer, John! This could change everything!"

"Hold on now, Virginia. This doesn't change anything. Not yet, at least. We have to keep this quiet. No one can know about this."

"But John, why? This is our chance to have a better life."

"Now, you just made me a promise, Virginia. We've got to keep this a secret."

"Why in the world would anyone leave such a fortune?"

"I did some asking around. The old man who owned the house before us died a few years back. He was an only child, never had any children, and his wife died years before. Folks said he had gotten kind of senile in his old age. The only thing I can figure is that he forgot about the money hidden in the wall."

"Why in the world can't we spend some of it then?"

"Virginia!"

It was a loud whisper with more sternness than I'd ever heard him use with her before.

"Like I told you, we just can't. If no one comes looking for it by the time the kids graduate from high school, that money can send them all to college."

"But, John! Why should we struggle so much if we don't have to?"

"Virginia, if someone comes looking for that money, we want to make sure it's all there. Second, everybody knows we don't have that kind of money to be throwing around. If we up and bought a new car or a new house, people would wonder how in the world we could afford it. Besides, you and me, we never went to college. I want our kids to be able to go if they want to."

Virginia let out a weighty sigh from across the kitchen table. "Well, where is it?"

He took his time answering. "It's buried out in the yard, where no one will ever find it."

What Daddy didn't know was that later that same night, I heard the small squeak the back screen made when it opened. My room was right beside the back door so I could hear even the smallest noise. I stood up in my bed so I could see out my window into the backyard. I saw Daddy disappear around the back of the shed and return just a few minutes later. I ducked down quickly and tried not to breathe too loud. That must have been where it was.

How else would I ever be able to pay the hundred dollars to Sister Mary?

"Gracie!" June called from the garden. "Where are you with that shovel? Let's do our digging before it gets too hot."

"Coming!" I walked toward June, consumed with how I would manage to dig up the money. Guilt washed over me at the betrayal of Daddy's trust, but what choice did I have? It was for Isaac. Isaac.

All day I kept looking at the clock, trying to pass the time.

"Gracie, you're so jittery. You're making me a nervous wreck."

"I'm sorry, June. I'm just tired." I faked a yawn, then said, "I think I might turn in early."

June looked at me suspiciously. "Are you feeling okay, Grace?"

"Oh yeah. Just sleepy, I guess."

After dinner I came into the living room, exaggerating a yawn. "I think I'll head to bed."

Aunt June looked up and stretched her arms over her head, mirroring me. "Now you're making me yawn! Hey, girly, I wasn't sure if you knew that they are having a little Independence Day festival in town tomorrow evening. We're supposed to get some rain in the morning, but it's supposed to clear up by lunchtime—might cool things off. Lordy, I hope so!" She said this while cooling herself with a fan that read *ERNEST J. BELCHER Funeral Home, No extra charge for distance, AMBULANCE.*

She continued, "We could have a hot dog, watch some fireworks . . . How does that sound?"

"That sounds fun!" Daddy had taken us all to this festival the year before; the fireworks were pretty impressive for a small town like Jubilee. Not to mention getting to eat a hot dog instead of June's cooking. I headed to bed, my thoughts returning to the task before me. A few minutes later, I heard June close the door to her room.

I drifted off thinking of fireworks and hot dogs.

Then . . . I was running with Isaac. It was a misty golden summer day like the ones we loved best. We were in an open field with buttercups and lady's slippers up to our knees. The red wagon flew behind him. Rojo raised his wings as if he was about to take off. Then Isaac stopped, turned to face me, and said, "Wake up, Grace. It's time."

My breath caught in my chest and I sat bolt upright in bed. I could tell it was the middle of the night by where the moon hung, centered in the top-right-corner pane of my bedroom window. My feet grazed the bare floor, feeling bits of sand and dirt. I tiptoed down the hallway, eased the back door open and slipped out the screen door, careful not to let it slam behind me.

Rojo was sleeping beneath the big tree but raised his head up from his chest when he heard me.

"Come on, boy," I whispered.

We slunk like robbers to the back of the shed where I had seen the uneven ground. He clucked in a circle and stopped. Then without a warning he threw back his head and crowed as loud as he could. I nearly tripped and fell on my face.

"Shhhhhhh. Rojo, you got to be *quiet*."

A small cluck escaped his throat as if acknowledging what I'd said. I grabbed him in my arms and peeked around the corner of the shed to see if the house lights came on. They did.

Aunt June appeared in the back door, her hair pinned by bobby pins in small circles around her head. Light from a flashlight darted around the backyard. She called out in a loud whisper, "Rojo! You hush now. You'll wake up the whole neighborhood!" After looking around, she shut the flashlight off, and she and her bobby pins retreated into the house.

I crept around into the shed and grabbed the shovel. I let Rojo down and he moved back to the sunken-down place in the ground. I started digging. Whenever I saw Daddy or Aunt June digging up the ground for the garden, they made it look easy. It wasn't. The first time I tried, I barely even broke through the grass. I tried hopping up on top of the back of the shovel, but I just fell off when the ground didn't give way. It was like it was made of stone. I wiped some sweat from my forehead onto my nightgown sleeve. It had been such a dry summer the ground was baked into bricks. I didn't want to make any noise for fear of waking June again. She'd said it was supposed to rain tomorrow morning. I hoped the rain would make the ground softer. Rojo and I would have to try again.

"Good night, Rojo."

I crept slowly back inside, terrified of making the floorboards creak. I lay in my bed with grass and dirt between my toes, praying for rain.

21

DRY GROUND

The weatherman lied.

It didn't rain. It was as hot as it had been the days before, if not hotter, and the humidity dripped down our backs like blackstrap molasses.

I went to help Mr. Farris again, but we didn't last long. Mr. Farris said it was just too blasted hot.

I came home, turned on the hose, and let the water run down the driveway until it got cold. I held my thumb over the mouth of it the way Daddy always did, raised it as far up as my arms could reach, and the water came out in spurts and mist and soaked me, clothes and all.

June came out on the porch and laughed at me. "Gracie, that is an excellent idea!" She got close enough to feel the mist but did a dance when I threatened to spray her.

She had sliced up some watermelon that morning and had been letting it chill in the icebox. We ate a few slices on the porch, spitting the black seeds into the yard for the birds.

"Hey, I hear there are a bunch of activities going on for the festival this afternoon before the fireworks. Wanna put on some dry clothes and head on to town?"

"Sounds good."

Thirty minutes later we were rounding the corner to Main Street. Everyone in town must have been there. We stood in front of Nickel Thrift surveying the town-turned-carnival. One of the boys from my class threw a ball at the red-and-white target, making the bell ring and dropping a girl about Sissy's age wearing a red, white, and blue bathing suit down into the water tank of the dunking booth. I thought she had chosen a good job for today. We heard the rumble of drums and craned our necks to see. June clapped her hands and swayed to the music of the Jubilee High School marching band. Next came Ellie Day Castle, who was in Sissy's class, riding on the back of a white convertible, wearing an evening gown made to look like the American flag with *Miss Jubilee* splashed across a white sash.

I shouldn't have been surprised to see Rank Gunner and a few of his hoodless cronies competing in the greased pig contest in a makeshift barnyard set up behind the barbershop. June and I rolled our eyes and moved on. June saw the hot dog stand in front of Handy Hardware. We crossed the street and decided on two corn dogs, slathered in mustard and ketchup. As we turned to find a place in the shade to eat them, I saw Golden with his parents, ordering a snow cone a few booths down. He was in a short-sleeved button-down shirt and those church pants that I figured his mom always made him wear. I couldn't imagine how hot he must be. He turned and caught me staring. Our eyes locked for a moment until he turned sharply toward his mother. She shot bullets out of her beady eyes, then pulled him away, pinching the crook of his arm as he tried to pull away from her grasp. June and I ordered some fresh-squeezed lemonade and sat under a shade tree by the courthouse and ate our corn dogs.

June was waving and smiling at someone. Lo and behold, it was Mr. Walter.

I nudged her elbow.

"Oh, he's just being friendly!"

"Mm-hmm," I said, raising my eyebrows.

She giggled like a high school girl.

After a bit, it was just so hot, we decided to pick up a half gallon of ice cream from Puckett's Grocery and go home and watch the fireworks from the front porch.

June scooped out two generous bowls of maple walnut ice cream. We let the creamy goodness slide down our throats. The sounds of life filled the air, with neighborhood kids setting off jumping crackers and spraying each other with water pistols. When it was dark enough, we licked our bowls and watched the rockets and bombshells erupt in the sky, then went to bed feeling satisfied.

* * *

The next day I told Mr. Farris all about the festival. He listened as he whittled, the early morning dew still diamonds on the grass. We talked awhile, wanting to ease into the chore ahead. When there was no more stalling, we got to work.

The pile for Nickel Thrift was growing almost as high as the burn pile. Mr. Farris sat on a stool, low to the ground, to sort through everything I brought him for inspection. I came to an old red suitcase at the bottom of a pile of dusty boxes. When I carried it out to him, his Santa eyes twinkled behind his round glasses.

"I have been looking for that suitcase for years."

He bent over to undo the latches. Inside were pictures. Old family photos, yellow and brown. The kind that people never smiled in. A few of a little boy with his parents, one of a little boy in an old-fashioned bathing suit on the beach. There was a picture of a young couple, the man in a Navy uniform and the woman with dark hair and pearls.

"My dad was in the Navy too!"

"Yes, I think I knew that. Your dad's a fine man, Grace."

"Yeah. I think he is too." I looked closely at the picture. "Who is this?"

"That is me and the missus."

"Wow! You look so young."

"We were newlyweds in that photo."

"Mrs. Farris was a pretty lady back then . . . Oh . . . I'm sorry."

"She was very beautiful—I'm no prize myself anymore." He gave a little chuckle, making me feel better.

We came to a photo taken in a living room with a little boy in a Sunday suit, and right behind him was the old Victrola.

"Is that you? There's the old record player."

He smiled. "Yep. Believe it or not, I was once that small." He patted his belly. "Not anymore!"

Near the bottom of the suitcase was a picture in a frame. The minute he saw it, his face froze and he reached down, picking it up carefully as if it might break.

"Who is that?"

A little girl with dark curls in a frilly dress stared out of the old frame with a soft smile. She looked to be around five years old.

"Sarah. She was my sister."

"She was real pretty."

He took out his handkerchief and wiped the corners of his eyes.

"Are you okay?"

"I haven't seen a picture of her in years, and I guess it brought back memories. She died the year after this was taken. Pneumonia. A lot of kids died from it back then."

He wiped his eyes again, then closed the suitcase and set it beside him. "Grace, I guess I understand a little what you're going through with Isaac." He paused, wiping his eyes one more time. "And if there's anything you need, anything I can ever do, just ask."

I couldn't help myself. I reached my arms out and hugged him.

When I did, he started to cry, and so did I. We stood there dripping our tears into the dry ground.

"What are you doing!" Mrs. Farris appeared right in front of us. "What are you two doing?"

Mr. Farris ignored her and looked at me with a hand on each of my shoulders. "Thank you, Grace. You are a special girl. Thank you for caring about an old man like me. You run on home now."

Mrs. Farris stood with her arms crossed, and as I ran out of the backyard I heard her telling him, "How foolish to cry in front of her!" I hid behind the bushes, wanting so badly to defend Mr. Farris, who sat on the folding chair with his eyes closed, feeling the verbal blows of the old bag's attack. "She will tell the neighbors all our business; you just wait!"

She was wrong. I would never say or do anything to hurt Mr. Farris.

That night, after dinner, Mrs. Farris called Aunt June to say they would not be needing my help anymore. As June hung up the phone she said, "She is such an old grump! That poor man!"

I had bad thoughts about what I'd like to do to the old onion lady, and I didn't even stop to ask forgiveness. I wondered why the nicest people ended up with the meanest ones. It just didn't seem fair.

As I lay in my bed with so many thoughts running through my mind, the sound of salvation came. A single raindrop splashed on our old tin roof, then another, followed by a hard rain that was a steady rhythm to my dreams all through the night. I dreamed, knowing that I was getting closer to helping Isaac. If I could help him be healed, maybe it would fix everything. Maybe it could make up for the terrible wrong I did to Virginia. The weight of that guilt was always there in Virginia's eyes—unforgiveness. I understood since I could not forgive myself either.

Seeing that picture of Mr. Farris's little sister and the sound of the rain made me remember that day. It had all started with rain.

22

HOMECOMING

Early the next morning I looked out the back door and saw Rojo sitting still in the roost of the chicken coop, waiting like I was. It had rained all night. I could see a few mud puddles in the backyard. I imagined how soft the ground would be. Now it would be easy to dig up the treasure and get the money for Sister Mary.

The phone rang in the kitchen. It was too early for someone to be calling. Calls late at night or early in the morning usually meant bad news. June answered it. There was news, but it wasn't what I thought.

Isaac's fever had broken. They were coming home. I ran out the back door, straight through a mud puddle, splashing brown droplets all over my white nightgown. "Rojo! He's coming home! He's coming home!" Rojo looked down at me from the chicken coop. I let out a loud howl, thinking he might join in and crow. June stuck her head out the back door and laughed at me. I was flooded with relief. Everything was going to be okay. Sissy somehow kept sleeping through all of this.

June said the doctors in Memphis had given Isaac all the treatments

he needed and were sending him back to rest and make sure he continued to improve. June woke up Sissy and told her the good news.

"Come on now, lots to do; we can't sleep the day away!"

Sissy was subdued in her reaction, compared to us, but I could tell
she was glad. The three of us spent the entire Saturday getting everything ready for their arrival. Sissy ignored me all day long. June tried to
be cheerful, trying to make peace between us, but it didn't seem to make
any difference. She was determined to attend church Sunday morning,
aiming to be home before they arrived. Everything was cleaned and ready
by the time we fell into our beds that night. I didn't need to dig up the
money anymore for that wretched Sister Mary. Isaac was going to be okay.

June had breakfast ready early the next morning. We went to church,
sitting by the back door so we could slip out after the *amen*. Emoline
walked by us in the sanctuary. I turned away from her as if I had spotted
something fascinating inside the stained-glass window. When I looked
back, she was approaching us.

"Grace . . ." She twisted her Mary Janes in the carpet. "I heard about
Isaac. I just wanted you to know that I've been praying for him every
night."

I couldn't find words.

June must have noticed my frozen expression and rescued me. "Thank
you so much, darling. He's coming home today! Isn't that wonderful?"

I jabbed Aunt June with my elbow.

"Ouch, Grace."

"I'm so glad to hear that. Maybe I could . . . come visit?"

"I'm sure he'd love that. A visit from such a pretty girl like you."

I jabbed her again.

"Grace!"

Emoline gave me a knowing look. "Well, I hope you'll give him my
best?"

"I sure will, sweetie."

Emoline walked away.

June turned and looked at me. "Grace, what in tarnation is wrong with you? Why did you keep jabbing me?"

"June, I can't believe you are being so nice to her. 'Darling'? 'Sweetie'? And why did you tell her Isaac was coming home? That wasn't any of her business."

"I guess I'm just so happy he's coming home, it seems like the right thing to extend some kindness. Besides, sometimes I think she seems kind of . . . lonely."

I did not tell her that I'd thought the same thing. And now finding out that Emoline said daily prayers? This was drying up my well-watered hatred for her. Isaac had a way of bringing out the best in even the worst people.

At the end of the service, we raced through the smoking men on the church steps and pushed the speed limit all the way home, hoping to arrive before they did, but as we turned the corner onto our street, Daddy's VW was already in the driveway.

He was standing on the porch waving as Beauty pulled up. I couldn't get out of the car fast enough. I ran to him like my legs had wings. It wasn't till that moment that I realized how much I had missed him. He smelled like sunshine and coffee grounds. That was the smell of my father. I didn't think I would be able to let go of him. He gave me a good squeeze, then reached an arm to Sissy. She stepped into his embrace, his warmth and strength bonding us together.

"Is Virginia in the house with Isaac?" June asked.

"No." He looked down at us. "Your mama's at the hospital getting Isaac settled into his room."

I was confused. "Why is he at the hospital? I thought he was coming home."

He turned his face from us. "Isaac will want to see you all. We'll go visit him."

Aunt June said, "I've got sandwiches ready in the fridge. We should eat something before we go."

But no one felt like eating so we piled into the VW and headed off to see Isaac . . . and Virginia.

Daddy said that the Middlesboro hospital was tiny compared to the one in Memphis. "We have insurance, but even still, there were things it doesn't cover." He lifted one hand off the steering wheel and massaged the muscles on the back of his neck. "It's so expensive to treat a person with cancer that nobody but a millionaire could afford to pay for it outright."

I felt my stomach lurch as we rolled into the hospital parking lot. Memories of another visit here, years ago, boiled into my throat, but I fought to keep them down. That awful moment when all the love and kindness Virginia had ever felt for me was pulled up by the roots, leaving only jagged edges behind.

I took breaths to calm myself as I walked through the front lobby. Aunt June seemed to notice and reached back for my hand with a look that said, *"I'm nervous too."* We checked in at the nurses' station. They told us we would all need to scrub our hands and arms and wear gloves and masks to make sure we didn't give Isaac any of our germs.

The first thing I saw when we walked into Isaac's hospital room was the little Navajo cross that always hung over his bed at home. It was on the ledge of the large window in his room. Virginia was tucking the sheets around him. She heard us and turned around.

"Hey, June . . . kids." She walked over and gave June, me, and Sissy each a half-hearted hug.

She had lost weight from her already trim figure. Isaac looked over at us with a sleepy smile. Virginia ran her hand along his arm.

"The doctors have given Isaac a sedative and he is getting sleepy, so you should come over and say hello before he falls asleep."

Daddy spoke up. "I reckon that ambulance drive just about wore him out."

June walked to his bedside, taking his hand in hers. "Oh, Isaac. I am so proud of you. You have been so brave. Now we are going to take such good care of you." She cupped his cheek in her large, gloved hand. "I love you."

"I love you too, Aunt June."

June motioned for me and Sissy to come closer. We were afraid. I walked over first, taking his small hand in mine. I hated the gloves. Sissy stood on the side of the bed opposite me. Virginia stared out the window.

"Hey, baby brother," Sissy said.

"Hey, big sis." He attempted a smile.

"I have been missing our nightly card games."

I cocked my head to the side. I never knew he played card games with Sissy. I thought he only played cards with me.

"Yeah, I've missed that too. I can still beat you though . . ."

"I love you, little brother. I'm sure glad you're back." Then she gave him a kiss on his head, even though she had a mask on, and moved back beside Aunt June.

I sat down in the chair beside him, trying to pretend we weren't really in a hospital room. "You been reading any good books?"

"Yeah, I read a book about deep-sea exploration." His speech was slow from the sedative, but I could make it out. "Did you know there's more mysteries in the ocean than there is in outer space?"

"No kidding?"

His eyes lit up for that moment, as if forgetting where we were and why.

He reached out and took my hand and motioned me to come close so I could hear.

"I missed you the most, Grace."

His eyes were heavy and his words were starting to slur. As he drifted off to sleep and we made our way to the door, he said, "Tell that ole rooster I miss him, too."

"He's waiting for you to come back home."

He was already asleep.

Virginia stood, moving toward us. "We better let him rest. Y'all go on home now."

Daddy had slipped out of the room but we found him standing in the hall talking to Dr. Clarke. He went back inside and kissed Virginia and Isaac both on the forehead, standing there under the dark cloud of this life they had been living for the past few weeks.

On the way out we passed Cordelia's brother, Dr. Oden, in his white coat. He was short, with acne scars on his face and unusually broad hips for a man. He told one of the nurses an off-color joke. Her laughter seemed forced. Who could laugh on such a day?

I burst through the hospital doors ahead of Sissy and Daddy. The sky overhead was clear and bright. It would have been better if it had been raining. The world had turned gray for me. Beads of sweat and fear dripped down my back, finding their way down into my bones.

I ran across the parking lot and threw up under a large oak tree. The present blending with memories of the past. Daddy came to me. He knelt beside me and held my hair back while I gagged and spewed bitter acid and tears onto the roots of that tree.

June came running out of the hospital doors with a Sprite and a cold washcloth the nurses had given her. "This might help. Poor baby."

I couldn't look up.

"Me and Sissy will wait in the car."

I was grateful she had given us privacy. Daddy gave me a drink of Sprite. It burned my throat and I was glad it did. It was something to feel, other than the presence of this despair that Isaac was not coming home, maybe ever.

"Oh, Daddy. I'm scared."

He dabbed the cold cloth against my face and forehead. "I know, Grace."

He held me, not needing to say anything else. There was nothing else to say. As we rode home, one thought replayed in my mind.

We have to save Isaac.

23

LIES AND CIGARETTES

We fell into a rhythm the first week Isaac was back. Virginia slept on a cot at the hospital most nights, only coming home for a little while in the afternoons while Isaac napped, to bathe and wash her hair. Daddy went to see Isaac every night after work and offered to sleep in Isaac's room on Saturday and Sunday nights to give Virginia a break, but Virginia said no.

When she was home, Virginia wandered through the house like a ghost. Sometimes I heard her crying over the sound of the water filling the bathtub. I didn't know what to say to her, so I didn't say anything. June told me Cordelia had the audacity to call Virginia to see if she'd be able to help the SWS ladies serve at the Spaghetti Supper.

"Your daddy told Virginia to tell Cordelia to take a flying leap!"

Sissy steered clear of Virginia, picking up extra shifts at Tri-Way.

On that first night after Isaac's return, I'd sat exhausted and numb in the hallway while Daddy told June about the hospital bill he'd been given before they left Memphis that the insurance wouldn't cover.

"I will just have to pay it off a little at a time. I'll need to start working

Saturdays and maybe even Sundays to make extra. I imagine it will take years, but they can wait for it. I'll just do the best I can to pay it."

June was outraged. "As if you didn't have enough on you already. There's a special corner in hell for those bloodsucking insurance people."

Daddy chuckled at June, which made them both laugh. He didn't believe in credit. He told June he'd been making extra payments and was one year shy of having the house paid off. Now any extra money would go to the insurance bill.

I thought of all that money buried in the backyard. He could make all of this stress go away. I wondered why he didn't.

I had attempted to dig up the treasure again the second night they were back but was almost caught by Daddy, who'd come outside late, after I thought he'd gone to bed, to do something I'd never seen him do before—smoke.

I held my breath in the backyard until he finally went back inside. Terrified he might look in on me in my room, I slowly crept to the screen door, shaking and waiting until he went back to bed. The sun had been baking the ground rock solid every day since.

I went to see Isaac every other day. We played card games when he felt up to it, and other days I would read to him. At night I prayed for it to rain, but still nothing. Daddy had worked so hard to keep it a secret. What if I dug it up and someone saw me and tried to steal the rest? My stomach lurched at the thought of it.

What June said kept nagging me—that Virginia had wanted to sneak Isaac out of the hospital to go to a healing revival. If he could build his strength back, and we could take him to see Golden at one of his revivals, it would solve everything. I could stop praying for rain and Daddy's treasure could stay a secret.

June had complained that morning while she read the paper, "I've been looking every day for Golden's list of revivals, but I still haven't found anything about it."

I decided now that Isaac was back, the next thing to do was to call and ask if there was a revival close enough for us to drive Isaac to. June came out the back door carrying a basket of wet laundry to hang on the line. I got up to help her.

I stretched out the long white tablecloth and pinned it on my end and then asked, "Aunt June, are you going anywhere today?"

"I just need to pop over to Miss Faye's. Thought I would check on her and visit for a spell. Poor old soul. Just as lonesome as can be. Why? Would you like to come?"

"Actually, I wondered about seeing if Sissy could take me for a swim?"

"Well, you won't catch these thighs in a bathing suit, and I think it would be good for you sisters to spend some time together."

"Okay. I think she's still sleeping."

"Well, ask her when she wakes up, and if she says no, then I can take you as long as you don't try and throw me in!" She giggled, which made me giggle.

After June and I finished hanging the clothes on the line, she said, "I think I'll just go on over to Miss Faye's now. I could brew us a pot of coffee."

I waited till June was walking down the sidewalk before I went to the kitchen and retrieved the number from the front pocket of my shorts. I dialed quietly, nervous of waking up Sissy. I had a feeling she had some sort of sixth sense about when I was being sneaky. It rang about ten times, but no one answered. I hung up and dialed again but it just rang and rang. Maybe they were in town? June had just left. I could quickly bike to town and be back before she returned from the neighbor's. I flew out the door and jumped on my bike, my legs burning as I pedaled as hard as I could. In a matter of minutes, I rounded the corner and parked my bike against a tree behind Handy Hardware.

I darted around corners, trying not to be seen. I took a risk and went into the Green Parrot to ask the waitress, Miss Lila, who had originally told me where they lived, if she'd seen them around, but a waitress I didn't know said that Lila had the day off. I peered into shop windows, but there was no sign of Golden or his parents. I hopped back on my bike and pedaled home, my heart racing with excitement and nerves, hoping I'd make it back before June. It was already so hot. I thought of just biking to the trailer park but I thought I would pass out from heat stroke, besides the fact that it would take far too long to get there and back without a cover.

I thought I might go crazy if I didn't do something to help Isaac. I had to take action. There was only one person I could ask for help who wouldn't rat me out, since I happened to have some serious dirt on her.

I climbed onto her bed and straddled her to get a good hold before I clamped my hand over her mouth. Her eyes bugged out of her head and she started thrashing around, but I managed to keep my grip.

I stared down at her as she tried to buck me off. "I need you to calm down and listen. I need your help and if you don't help me, I won't think twice about telling Virginia what I saw you doing at the skating rink."

Her disgust for me was clear in her eyes, but my determination played perfectly against her fear of being found out.

"Deal?"

Finally she stopped fighting me and nodded her head.

"Okay. I'm gonna take my hand off."

I lifted my hand and she flung me off her and off the bed. I landed with a loud thud and suppressed a yelp.

"This better be important or you're gonna get it!" She hissed the words as she held up her fist at me.

"It's about Isaac." I sat rubbing the elbow that I had landed on.

She took a deep breath and fell back on the bed.

I told her my idea and the story we would have to tell June for her to let me go. Sissy lay in bed listening. I kept waiting in dread for her response. I knew I had threatened her, but I also knew that she loved Isaac and might even be glad for a way to help. As it turned out, she was.

Once June returned from the neighbor's, I gave June a kiss on the cheek.

"Now what is all this?"

"I'm just glad you're here," I said, smiling with as much charm as I could muster.

"Okay. Tell me what you want!" She laughed.

"Sissy said she'd take me swimming."

Sissy nodded, looking much less enthusiastic than I would've liked.

June's eyes showed equal amounts of shock and happiness. "Well, ain't that a nice thing for you to offer, Sissy! What a sweet big sister. I absolutely approve."

I gave her one last hug for good measure, then elbowed Sissy, who gave her a side hug on the way out. We ran and put our bathing suits on underneath our clothes to make our whole act convincing. June stood on the porch, smiling and waving as we backed out of the driveway.

"Have fun!"

As soon as we were out of the neighborhood, Sissy reached into the glove box, grabbed a cigarette from her pack of Camel Lights, and lit up. I stared at her.

"What are you looking at?"

"What is smoking like?" I asked her.

"Wanna try?" She gave me a playful look and held the cigarette over to me. I reached for it, trying to copy what I had seen her do. I took a deep breath, then coughed and gagged. She laughed.

"What are you trying to do to me? Are you crazy?"

"You breathed too deep. You start off with just a little puff, like this." She demonstrated.

I was still trying to catch my breath, but managed to get out, "No thanks!"

"Suit yourself." She blew a long puff of smoke from her pink lips. "All right, brat, where does this Golden boy live?"

"The Shady Creek Trailer Park." I left out the part about me already coming to Shady Creek.

She took a long drag off her cigarette. "What's so special about him?"

I looked at her as if she had been living under a rock. "He is only the most famous child healer anybody's ever heard of. The parents are a little creepy . . . Anyway, Sissy, we've got to do something."

"This sounds a little out there, Grace. Don't get your hopes up in case it doesn't work."

She drove with one arm flung over the steering wheel, taking in long puffs off her cigarette and flicking the ashes out the window. She made the turn into the trailer park.

The fat man in an undershirt was outside on his porch steps drinking his morning beer. The little boy I saw getting a whipping was standing at the edge of his yard staring as we drove by.

Sissy tossed her cigarette out the window, scanning the trailer park wide-eyed. "I guess this is quintessential white trash. What a depressing place to live."

I nodded in agreement but couldn't muster any words. I was too nervous about seeing Golden again.

I directed Sissy to their trailer.

"So the most famous child healer in the world lives in a run-down trailer park?"

"They are always moving around, and I'm guessing they don't make much money."

"Grace, this feels—"

I cut her off. "That's it. That's their trailer." She parked in front of the stairs.

"I'll be right back," I told her.

"Wait. Don't you want me to . . . come in?"

"No. It's okay. I won't be long. Just wait here."

She let out more smoke. "Be careful."

I walked up the rickety steps, steadied my nerves, and knocked, but no one came. I knocked again, a little harder. Nothing. All that for nothing.

"Oh well," Sissy said. "Now look who's got dirt." She smiled a wicked smile. How could I have been so stupid?

As we left, we drove by the yellow trailer. Without thinking, I said, "That's where Cooter's mama lives." The minute I said it, I knew I'd made a huge mistake.

Sissy stopped cold right in front. "And how do you know that?"

They say it's easy to slip up when you lie. That one lie always leads to more. Here was the proof.

"Hey, y'all!" Cooter was standing in the front yard. Sissy's demeanor changed; she brushed back her hair and put out the cigarette in the ashtray. Cooter made his way over to the car window on Sissy's side.

"What are you two doing over here? Good to see you again, Grace." Cooter's eyes rested on Sissy's face like they were ready for a long nap. Not dozy . . . dreamy.

"Grace says your mama lives here?"

"Yes ma'am. I come over every day for biscuits. She ain't feeling too good today. I just came to check on her." They stared at each other like I wasn't there. "I been praying for Isaac. How's he doing down in Memphis?"

I spoke up. "He's back. At Middlesboro General."

"Could I stop by to visit him?"

We both nodded. "He would really like that, Cooter," I said.

Sissy was nervous, especially compared to her usual dominating personality. She blushed as Cooter waved and watched us drive away.

I wasn't any closer to helping Isaac, and now Sissy knew that I had lied to June.

"How are we gonna explain to Aunt June why we didn't go swimming?" I asked her.

"That's easy." She took a hard turn down onto a dirt road that led to the river. She drove her Bug right to the edge of the water and turned the car off. "Get in. You can jump in, get wet, and then I'll drive you home."

I got out, stripped down to my bathing suit, and waded in. Sissy was on my heels. "There is a part up ahead that gets deeper."

A few minutes later, I felt Sissy's hand on my arm and then I was underwater. I struggled and fought until finally she let me up.

"What are you *doing*?"

She stood leaning over and laughing. It was a real laugh, like we were having fun. I splashed back at her with a vengeance. The water was only up to my waist, but it was deep enough to get us both wet. We did that for a few minutes and then she turned back to the car.

"Let's go!"

I was sad the fun had ended. It was the first time we had laughed together in years.

When we pulled up to our house, she reached over and grabbed my wrist. "Just remember, I know you've been riding over to that hellhole trailer park, and I bet Mama and Daddy would just loooooove to know that. As well as the fact that you were smoking!"

"What? I only took one puff!"

"Smoking is smoking. So don't even think of telling them about the skating rink or the black eye. Got it?"

She looked at me with her smug teenage face and I knew she had me. Any leverage I had was lost.

"Oh, and tell Aunt June you got tired of swimming and that I'm going to pick up Tina and swim some more."

"Wow. You are really good at lying."

"Look who's talking?" I saw a trace of disappointment in her eyes.

I got out of the car and watched her back out of the driveway in the little red Bug Daddy had fixed up for her. I usually thought it was red to match her devilish heart, but strangely, there was a sudden bond. Built over lies and cigarettes.

Today's plan had failed. After running into Cooter a second time, I was afraid of going back. If he kept seeing me there, he might feel the need to tell Daddy out of concern. Sissy wouldn't help me again, that was for sure. I would have to keep calling. I prayed for Golden, and not Sister Mary, to answer. If that didn't work, I would have no choice but to dig up the money. I knew Sissy would be keeping an even closer eye on me now. I would have to be careful.

24

SILVER BIRD

I finished my oatmeal and was out the door by 8 a.m. to get a jump on the sun. Mr. Farris was on the front step drinking his coffee and reading the paper when I got there.

"Well, Grace, you're an early bird today."

"I need to run an errand for Aunt June later this morning."

"I was glad when you called yesterday. Mrs. Farris will be out of town for a few days visiting her sister. This will give us a chance to get that shed all cleaned and organized by the time she's back. That will please her very much."

What June didn't know was that, before I called Mr. Farris, I had called the number on the crumpled piece of paper again when Sissy and Daddy were both at work. June had run to the store and Virginia was at the hospital with Isaac. The phone rang only once.

"Hello?"

"Hello . . . This is Grace . . . Mockingbird? I came to see you about my brother, Isaac."

"I remember. Can I help you?"

"Isaac is back from Memphis and—"

Golden cut me off short. "How about we meet and talk it over?"

"But I could just ask you over the phone."

"I'm alone here now, but I don't have much time."

"It's just a quick question."

"If it's all the same to you, it would be better if you asked me in person. There's actually something I wanted to tell you . . . but not over the phone."

My curiosity was in overdrive. What could *he* want to tell me?

"I guess I could do that. Where should we meet?"

He gave me the details and I heard myself agreeing to the rendezvous, knowing how much trouble I'd be in if anyone found out. But if we could bring Isaac to one of his healing services, the risk was worth it.

I hated lying to Mr. Farris, but neither he nor Aunt June would approve of me meeting up with some boy I didn't know, even if he was a famous evangelist. If there were no revivals nearby, I'd brought the five dollars I'd saved from my last birthday as a down payment. I figured having some of the money with me would show him I was serious.

Mr. Farris and I worked fast. We had our system down of separating things into piles. I came across a cardboard box that had something wrapped in old newspapers. When I peeled off the newspaper, I found another smaller cardboard box. It was heavy. I didn't want to take any chances opening it in case it was breakable. I placed it gingerly in front of Mr. Farris. He stared at it, wiping his forehead on his sleeve before picking it up. He opened the cardboard box and carefully lifted out a small silver box. He used his hand to wipe the dirt from it. It shone, almost like a mirror. He reached under the bottom and cranked a small lever several times, then opened it.

The silver box was lined with red velvet and had small compartments for rings. Another compartment rose from inside the box and revealed a tiny silver bird spinning slowly to a song.

The melody was familiar, but I couldn't place it.

"It's so beautiful."

"It was my sister's. A gift from our great-aunt Katharine. Came all the way from New Orleans. Sarah loved it."

I thought of the photograph of his sister—the one he had cried about that made Mrs. Farris so upset. Cleaning out this shed had unlocked so many memories. It was as if a part of him had been packed away with all these things.

"I always thought I would give it to my little girl one day . . ." He closed the lid and looked at it, then he placed it in my hands. "I want you to have it."

"But it was your sister's."

"Grace, you're like a beautiful bird that has flown into my life. I'd love to give it to you as a way of thanking you for being kind to an old man."

"Are you sure?"

"Yes. I'm sure."

"Oh, Mr. Farris, thank you!" I watched the spinning bird, mesmerized. He chuckled, but his eyes were moist and some life had returned to them.

"Mr. Farris, if I ever have a little girl, I will give it to her in honor of you and your sister, Sarah."

He placed his hand on my cheek and smiled. It was a warm, soul-quenching smile that seeped into my heart.

"Now, how about some lemonade?"

When we walked into the kitchen, I looked up to see the cuckoo clock. It was 9:50. I panicked.

"I didn't realize what time it was. I'm sorry, I almost forgot I've got to go run that errand for Aunt June."

"So soon?"

"Yes. It's something she needs done this morning, but I'll come back as soon as I can. It shouldn't take long."

"Grace, is everything okay?"

"Yes, sir."

My hands were sweating and my throat went dry. Lying to Mr. Farris after he'd given me such a wonderful gift was a terrible thing to do. He nodded, letting a small, worried look crawl across his face.

"When I get back, I'll stay as long as you need me to finish the shed."

"That's fine, Grace."

"Oh, and could I leave the music box here until then?"

"Of course."

I walked away from him and he called behind me, "Please be careful."

"Yes, sir. I will."

I took off, pedaling my green bike as fast as I could. I had no idea how long my visit with Golden would take. I had a feeling Mr. Farris had not believed my story. But knowing what I did about his sister, I thought he would understand. I wanted to believe that I would do whatever it took to save Isaac. I guess time would prove whether that was true or not.

I finally arrived at Handy Hardware and parked my bike against the old tree behind the store. I took a minute to straighten my shorts and smooth down my hair, then walked toward the water. I came around the corner and saw his halo of golden curls in the light of the morning sun as he sat quietly on a large rock by the riverbank.

I crept behind him, but he heard me.

"Hey, Grace."

He stood and nodded in my direction. I could feel my palms beginning to sweat. He wore a white button-down shirt and had rolled up his trousers to his ankles. I thought he must have been burning up. I felt underdressed in cut-off shorts and a tank top.

We stood there a few feet apart, not speaking, the smells and sounds of the creek all around us. A tiny bird, no bigger than a half dollar, flew into some honeysuckle that was growing by the water—a hummingbird. We marveled at its wings, how fast they moved, allowing it to remain still as it drank the nectar from the plant. He pointed to the large rock, and we sat down beside each other.

"Tell me about Isaac."

I told him about the tumor and the radiation treatments and how Isaac's immune system was weak. "I was thinking if you were having any revivals close by that I could bring him to one of them?" I took a breath, relieved to have finally gotten that question out.

"Our summer revivals are all a few hours' drive away. It doesn't sound like he's in any condition to drive that far."

"Well, in that case, could you come and see him at the hospital?"

He listened while he held a stick in his hand, tracing an outline in the gravel beneath the water. He had removed his shoes and socks and his feet were a golden brown like the rest of him.

"Oh, and before I forget, when I came to visit you, there was this little boy . . . a few trailers down from you. His mother—"

"Beats him? I know exactly who you're talking about."

"I just hoped maybe if someone could do something . . ."

"Everyone in the trailer park has seen her do it. She's a lunatic. He plays out in the street. I think she gets drunk a lot. People in the neighborhood try to look out for him. Sometimes I play catch with him."

"I felt so awful that I couldn't do anything. I'm glad you and the neighbors are looking out for him."

He lifted his head and bent his neck from side to side the way Daddy did when his muscles were tense.

"Grace . . . there's something you oughta know . . ."

"Golden Shepherd!"

We both jumped, startled by the angry voice breaking into our quiet moment. Sister Mary was stomping up the edge of the trail a stone's throw away from us.

"What are you doing, and why are you here with *her*?"

I took the lead. "I . . . I'm sorry, Sister Mary. That's my fault. I was riding by on my way to do an errand for my aunt June, and I saw Golden sitting back here and I thought I'd ask him about my brother. He's back from Memphis now, but he's not doing so good. If you think Golden could still come to visit him in the hospital, I have some of the money that you asked for right here."

I took a deep breath, exhausted from my improvised speech that was mostly lies.

I reached down in my pocket and pulled out the sweaty five-dollar bill. "It's just a down payment."

Sister Mary's demeanor changed. Her eyes settled on the sweaty bill, looking offended by it. "I heard that your brother is back in town. Talk certainly does get around."

"Yes, ma'am, he's at Middlesboro General."

"We will be on the road for a few days, but I'm sure something could be arranged. We will be returning Monday night and could come Tuesday morning. Would that work?"

I sat there panicking, giving her a deer-in-the-headlights stare, thinking, what if I couldn't dig up the money by Tuesday? What if Virginia said no? What would I do then? It was crazy to say yes, but what else could I do?

"I can run home and call Virginia—I mean, my mother—at the hospital to ask her about it."

Sister Mary eyed me suspiciously but nodded in agreement. Golden held his heavy black shoes in his hands, saying nothing.

"We will plan on Tuesday. It will give Golden time to prepare for the healing. You can bring your donation with you then."

"You don't want my five dollars?"

"No, child." She smiled, as if feeling sorry for me and my sweaty five-dollar bill. "Just bring the full amount when we come to the hospital. Let's say if we don't hear from you on Monday, we will assume it's confirmed. We will meet at the hospital at ten o'clock sharp Tuesday morning."

She turned on her heels, done with our conversation. Golden glanced over at me, trying to send me a message with his eyes so deep and sad that I could go swimming in them. He followed Sister Mary back to the street. I stood listening to the water. The next thing would be the hardest thing of all. What if Virginia said no? What if that sunken place Rojo found was just that?

I raced into Handy Hardware and bought a pack of wildflower seeds that I had heard June mention she'd love to plant along the fence of the backyard, then I rode my bike back to Mr. Farris's house like it had wings, my heart pounding. I would have to tell June that Mr. Farris offered me the pack of wildflower seeds. Lies, lies, lies.

Mr. Farris and I kept working, but I was distracted.

"Grace, you seem very quiet. Is everything all right?"

I wanted to tell him so badly. "Yep. Just a little tired."

I was glad he didn't press me. We finished the shed. It was swept clean with only a few boxes neatly lined up on the shelves, leaving the floor clear for him to park his lawn mower and some other garden supplies inside. Under normal circumstances, I would have felt proud of myself for completing such a job, but all I could think of was what I had just set in motion. What if I got caught digging up the money? Was I at risk of driving an even bigger wedge between Virginia and me?

"Grace, you seem worried."

"I . . . I guess I'm just thinking about Isaac."

His knees made a popping sound as he strained to crouch on the ground, eye to eye with me. "If there's anything I can do, just ask."

"Thank you," I croaked. I couldn't risk another word for fear of blurting out the truth. Then he would know that I wasn't a wonderful girl. I was a girl who told lies to sweet old men and took gifts from them while I was doing it.

He wrapped the silver box in a towel to protect it, then put it inside a cloth bag with handles so that I could hang it from my handlebars while I rode home.

As I rode up to the house, June was sitting on the porch step with Rojo, breaking beans for dinner. I swallowed the giant lump in my throat. It was time to come clean.

25

THE SEED

We each had our own way of dealing with Isaac's illness. June cooked, cleaned, and gardened. Virginia sat by Isaac's bed. Sissy smoked and terrorized me. Daddy worked. My way was to find a way to fix it, so I schemed.

I decided I would tell June about everything except the money. If I pulled that thread, I feared the plan would unravel. June would think there was no possible way for us to pay the money, because she didn't know about the treasure. There were too many questions I could not answer without revealing my constant eavesdropping. The tangled web of lies and secrets was getting more and more difficult not to trip over, but I needed her help. If anyone could persuade Virginia, it was June.

I fearfully placed one foot in front of the other and climbed the porch steps.

"Gracie, is there something wrong?"

I nodded. "I have something important to tell you, June."

She stopped breaking beans. I sat down on the steps beside her and began. I told her about riding my bike to hell's trailer park, and Sissy taking me back a second time. June kept bringing her hands up to her face, shaking her head as if she couldn't believe I had fooled her so many times. I even told her about meeting Golden by the riverbank.

"Gracie, Gracie, Gracie. What if you'd been kidnapped or run over? I swear it makes me sick at my stomach."

"But I'm okay, Aunt June! I'm sorry I lied, but I had to do something. I am telling you all of this because I need you to convince Virginia to let Golden come to the hospital. If he can do miracles like they say . . . then he can heal Isaac."

She reached out her long arms and buried me in the pillow of her ample bosom. I could barely breathe. "Gracie, I'm not gonna deny that I'm a little upset, but I want you to know that I think you are the most amazing girl. I can't believe you have done all this for your brother."

I felt the weight roll off my shoulders. I had no idea how tight they had been from carrying around those lies until I released them into the air. Aunt June hugged me again, but with the heat, I felt queasy from the smell of ginseng that clung to her clothes.

She let go, raised her hands to heaven, and said, "Thank You, Jesus! Why would we *not* want that sweet Golden boy to come pray for our Isaac? Gracie, what if this works? What a story to tell."

She hugged me again and I felt, for the first time, something besides that feeling of dread.

A tiny seed of hope.

I made myself scarce when Virginia came home. I rode my bike around the neighborhood, poked around at a yard sale a few streets over. After a couple hours, as I turned the corner past Mr. Farris's house, heading home, it felt like I was pedaling through mud. The harder I pedaled the slower I went. I stopped and saw the problem—a flat tire. A nail had torn a hole in it.

I got off and pushed it back home. June's car was gone. She had been letting Virginia drive Beauty to and from the hospital. I dropped the bike and flew up the driveway.

June was sitting on the porch. I sat on the front steps again, tired from all of my pedaling. My stomach lurched and my mouth was so dry that my tongue stuck to the roof of my mouth as I gathered my nerve to ask the hundred-dollar question. "What did she say?"

June swung softly in the swing as she told me. "At first she was quiet, like she was studying on it. Then, as if something shifted inside her, she said, 'Tell them to come. Maybe this is the miracle we've been waiting for!'" June threw her hands up in the air, giving herself a giant push on the swing.

"Are you serious?" I danced around the yard while June giggled at me. "I can't believe she said yes!"

"I can hardly believe it myself, but I think she was shocked that someone of his notoriety would be willing to come, out of the goodness of his heart, to pray for Isaac. She seemed relieved. Especially now . . ."

"What do you mean 'especially now'?"

"Oh, nothing! I don't know why I said that, Grace. I'm just plumb worn out by all of this. Don't pay me any mind."

Those words wafted into the air as she got up and disappeared into the house. I had gone from euphoric to having the sick feeling that there was something June wasn't telling me. I was glad I had not told June about the money. Whatever the risk, it would all be worth it when Isaac was healed.

* * *

We waited for Tuesday. Counting the hours, minutes, and seconds. I prayed for rain. It had to rain before Tuesday or I wouldn't have the money. If I didn't have the money, would Sister Mary allow Golden to heal Isaac? I couldn't take the chance and show up without it. If I had to shovel through solid rock, I would do just that.

I avoided Virginia as much as possible, though she barely noticed me. She was rail thin from not eating and worrying over Isaac. Daddy worked constantly but came home in the evenings to eat dinner. A few nights before Golden's visit, Daddy invited me to sit on the porch with him. The porch had always been the place where he told me the stories of his younger years and his days in the Navy. I sat beside him on the swing. He pulled a photo out of his wallet and handed it to me. A seventeen-year-old version of him stood in front of a massive ship. The name on the side of the ship read USS *Cony*. It was white and looked as long as a football field.

"That class of ship is called a destroyer escort."

"That's an interesting name. Like they were carrying destruction?"

He nodded, but his eyes seemed to be watching a scene from another time. "I remember we were out in the middle of the ocean, a big storm hit—it could be calm one minute and seconds later we were holding on for our lives. During that storm, we saw a Navy ship bigger than ours out in the distance. The massive waves swelled and our ship rose up so high on the top that the other ship at the bottom looked like a toy boat."

"Were you scared?" I asked him.

"Terrified. Any man would have been a fool not to be . . . but we also stood in awe of such power. Sometimes I still can't believe I survived it."

I was glad to be on dry land. The sea was mysterious like Isaac had said. Surely the mysterious God who had made the oceans and the dinosaurs had the power to heal Isaac, if the right person asked.

"Grace, I wanted to talk to you about this Golden that's coming to see Isaac. I don't think you should put too much faith in this boy."

I looked at him, afraid to speak. If he didn't believe, how could I?

"Don't you believe in healing, Daddy?"

"Yes . . . I believe Jesus healed people in the Bible, and I've even heard stories of healings in our time. I just don't want you to count on this."

"But, Daddy, all those people at revivals who have seen him heal people with their own eyes—isn't that reason enough to believe?"

He seemed to be weighing his response carefully. "You see those stars, Grace?"

I craned my neck up toward the black, silky sky. It was as if a great hand had scattered millions of diamonds onto a black cloth.

He continued, "We look up and think, *this is all there is,* but there's a telescope that allows astronomers to see out past our galaxy, and they have seen thousands of other galaxies, millions of light years away."

I drank his words in with disbelief and wonder and thought of how much Isaac would have loved this conversation.

"But for me, staring out across fathoms of that deep, ancient ocean taught me something important about the Creator of all this."

"What's that?"

"He doesn't dangle from the end of anybody's string. No matter what you or I or a fourteen-year-old boy prays for, God serves a greater justice that may not look like justice at all to you and me." He sighed gravely. "I know you want to help Isaac, Grace. We just don't know what's gonna happen." He slipped his arm around my shoulder and kissed the top of my head. "I'm headed to bed."

I sat there looking up at the stars for a while. Could a Being so supreme even care about the prayers of a teenage girl? A lying teenage girl at that. I sent out a prayer into those galaxies and finally went to bed.

I crammed down all the doubt that Daddy's words dredged up from my heart and steeled my determination for the job ahead. There would be no healing without rain. What was one more prayer in a symphony of prayers that went up every second of every hour of every day? I prayed for rain. The next morning was as hot and dry as it had ever been.

* * *

On Monday morning, Aunt June and Virginia made a big breakfast. We ate and quickly packed a breakfast basket for Isaac, then headed to the hospital to see him. Over the last few days, our visiting time with him had been limited because he'd had a fever. Dr. Clarke had called Virginia last night to say his fever broke and we could all come.

We scrubbed our hands and up to our elbows like always to get rid of any germs, then put on our gloves and masks. Dr. Clarke told us maybe we should go in two at a time so we didn't overwhelm him.

Daddy spoke up. "How about if we let Grace go in first. Grace, take the basket."

I nodded a thank-you to Daddy and followed Dr. Clarke into the room. "Isaac, you have a visitor . . . I'll let y'all visit."

Isaac sat up in bed.

"We brought you some breakfast." I held up the basket.

"Did you cook it? I don't want to get poisoned."

It had been a while since he'd roasted me. The weak smile that tried to overtake his tiny face ignited a tiny spark of hope. I tried not to notice his gaunt cheeks and the dark circles like half-moons under his deep-set eyes. It wasn't until now that I saw how much Isaac's appearance had changed.

"Don't worry, I didn't make it."

I set the basket in front of him. He lifted the lid, reaching his small hand in to bring out a biscuit. He nibbled along the edges of it. I moved the basket to the table beside his bed.

"How's Rojo?"

"He's all right. He sits by the back door and waits for me and June to come out in the morning and water the garden . . . I'm sorry, Isaac."

"Why are you sorry, Grace?"

I burst into tears. "Because I feel awful that you have to lay here all day and can't leave. I wish I could just stay here with you."

He laid the biscuit down on the sheet in front of him and reached out for my hand. "There's a girl here in the hospital. She's about my age. She visits me sometimes. The nurses are real nice, and I get to read a lot. I don't want you to feel bad. It isn't your fault."

Somehow it always felt like it was.

"So, what have you been doing? Tell me all of your summer adventures."

I told him about helping Mr. Farris and about the picture of his little sister and the music box he gave me.

"Think you could bring the music box and play it for me?"

"Sure. I'll bring it tomorrow!"

"Grace, I don't want you to worry."

"Isaac, I just want you to come home. For every birthday and Christmas present for the rest of my life—I just want you to come home."

"I have a lot of time to think and pray . . . Mama prays all the time. Her prayers . . . I know she means well, but they make me feel so bad. I know she wants me to get well, but, Grace, I feel like everything's gonna be okay. No matter what happens."

Against my will, the tears kept coming. "What do you mean, 'no matter what happens'?"

He lifted his tiny hand to wipe away a tear from my face. "Late at night I talk to God when everything is quiet. A hospital is a strange place at night. I can hear people talking to themselves or crying. Some older folks don't get a single visitor, from what the nurses tell me. What I've realized is that there's worse things than dying."

"Isaac, don't say that. There wouldn't be anything worse than you dying."

"You're a good sister, Grace."

There was a knock at the door.

"Hello, are you ready for your next visitors?" It was June's cheery voice.

I grabbed a tissue from the table to wipe off the tears that were seeping under my mask. Isaac and I shared one last glance; then I hugged him and told him that I'd bring the music box for him to see.

My heart felt like it might beat out of my chest. Was he giving up? I had to give him a reason to believe he would get better. A reason to fight. I wandered down the hallway. I passed an office where Daddy and

Virginia and Dr. Clarke were talking. Looking at them from this angle, they looked older. Worry lines creased their faces.

There would be no turning back now. Tonight was the night. Rain or not, I was digging it up. But maybe God had been listening to at least one prayer from my lying lips. The clouds started to gather that afternoon, and then it started to rain. It rained all afternoon and into the evening. Daddy had stopped for a bucket of chicken on the way home. We ate the chicken out on the porch, watching the drops of rain soak into the ground.

In the middle of the night, I eased out of bed, grabbed the flashlight I had brought into my room, and inched softly like a burglar to the back door, but I was breaking out, not in. I eased the door open, praying it wouldn't make any noise. A sudden squeak from the screen door made my heart stop, but the house slept on. I slipped out the door. Rojo was under the awning. Maybe his sixth sense told him I was coming.

"Thanks for waiting for me, buddy," I said as though he could understand.

We crept silently over the soft ground to the sunken spot behind the shed. The shovel slid into the ground like it was butter. After a few shovelfuls, I heard a clink. Metal. After a few more scoops I saw the old black box. It had been wrapped in plastic and was coated in brown mud. I could hardly believe my eyes. I felt dizzy with excitement. It creaked open. I winced, afraid of the noise it made. But like a miracle, there were the wads and wads of tens, twenties, even a few hundred-dollar bills. It was more than I ever thought I'd see in a lifetime, and I was suddenly struck by the amount of self-control Daddy must have had to simply put it in the ground and not be tempted to spend it.

I crammed five twenties into the waistband of my underwear, wrapped the plastic back around the box, and put it back in the ground the way I had found it. I shoveled the dirt into the hole and then the layer of sod over the top. For good measure, I decided to park the wheelbarrow, leaning up against the fence, over top of it. Just in case someone was to come see that the ground had been dug up.

I turned on the hose on the side of the house and quietly washed the mud off my bare feet. Rojo never made a peep. He followed me around as quiet as a praying mantis. It was sad that some folks didn't believe that animals went to heaven. I thought Rojo had definitely earned his spot. Could it really be heaven without the songbirds and dogs and even ole Rojo? Maybe I would ask Isaac about it the next time I saw him.

I did my burglar routine in reverse, exhausted as I slipped under the sheets of my bed and drifted off into a deep sleep for the first time in a while. Maybe everything would be all right.

26

THE HEALER

As soon as we walked into the small waiting room at the front of the hospital, we saw the hell's trailer park trinity dressed in their finest Sunday clothes. The buttons of Brother Joseph's lavender dress shirt were straining against the girth of his bulging belly. The fat of his neck gathered around the small knot in his tie and looked as though it was attempting to strangle him. Golden wore a dark-blue suit two sizes too big for him. He had rolled the cuffs up twice at the bottom. He avoided looking at me. Sister Mary wore a stiff gray dress with her hair in a bun so tight that it made her eyes pull back on the sides.

June rushed forward. "So happy to see y'all." She stuck her hand out and pumped each of their hands vigorously. "I can't thank you enough for coming. It means the world to all of us."

Sister Mary took charge. "Thank you. We are glad we could fit it into our schedule."

Golden stood and finally looked at me. Why did he look so sad?

Sister Mary said, "I wonder if we could step outside and discuss a few things so you can understand . . . what to . . . expect?"

"Absolutely," June said. I followed June and Sister Mary outside. I had the money in my hand and was dreading the moment I had to hand it to her, because that was the moment June would know that I hadn't completely come clean. As we stood outside in the early light, I could see for the first time that Sister Mary's two front teeth had a gray undertone and caved into each other, as if they were rotting. She noticed me looking at her teeth and closed her lips tight, turning away from me to face June.

"First, there is the matter of the contribution to the ministry?"

"The what?" June looked at me, confused.

"I have it!" I spoke up quickly, handing it to Sister Mary. I had wrapped the money in a piece of notebook paper so that no one could see how much it was.

June watched me hand over the money. Sister Mary took it and quickly put it away in her purse.

"All for the work of the Lord, I assure you."

My heart hammered in my ears. Would June tell Virginia and call the whole thing off? She gave Sister Mary the most drop-dead threatening look I had ever seen any woman give another. *Please, June, we have to let Golden try.* I willed June to read my thoughts as I looked up at her.

"Now, we want you to understand that Brother Golden needs absolute silence when he begins to let the healing power flow. What I am about to tell you is of the utmost importance: Everyone in the room must have total and complete faith. You see, healing is an act of faith, and if the parties involved do not believe in Brother Golden's power to heal, well, many times, the healing does not happen."

June looked over at me and then back at Sister Mary. Her voice was ice-cold. "We believe."

"Wonderful," said Sister Mary. "I just wanted to make everything clear. Shall we go?"

June robotically introduced Sister Mary, Golden, and Brother Joseph to the nurse on duty, who Aunt June had become friends with from her frequent visits over the last few weeks. Virginia had already explained to the staff that they would be coming.

The nurse seemed nervous and almost giddy to meet them. She gushed, "It's an honor to have y'all here. I traveled three hours to your crusade in Knoxville, Brother Golden."

Sister Mary's face beamed, taking it in. Golden nodded at her, barely looking up. Nervous. Brother Joseph told the nurse he had been feeling a little under the weather, so he thought it best for him to wait in the lounge area while we went in.

"Yes, sir. That is definitely for the best. There are magazines, and I just made a pot of coffee, so help yourself."

Sister Mary looked at him disapprovingly.

The nurse led us all to the sink to wash our hands and arms thoroughly and put on the gloves and white face masks. When we reached Isaac's room, I saw Virginia through the small window in the door, sitting where she always did, in the white chair beside Isaac's bed.

June knocked lightly and whispered through the opening, "Hello. We are all here."

I was hoping that Daddy had decided to come, but as the door opened, we saw Virginia motioning for us to come in. Isaac was lying in his bed. He waved to us, looking so fragile. Daddy's absence left me with a sinking feeling.

Sister Mary began explaining what Golden would be doing. Virginia stared intently at Sister Mary and Golden, listening. Then as Golden stepped forward to begin, Virginia's eyes closed and her lips moved silently in prayer. June stood against the wall, looking stoic. I kept trying to catch her eye, but she wouldn't look at me. Was she mad? At least Golden was here. If this worked, I figured nobody would care about the missing hundred dollars.

Golden stood at the foot of the bed. The mask over his mouth and nose made his enormous blue eyes seem even larger and sadder. He and Isaac looked at each other as if squaring off for a fight. Finally, he extended both arms stiffly toward Isaac and started to pray. The oversize suit jacket jutted out past the sleeves of the gown Dr. Clarke had insisted he wear. He started off quiet at first, his lips moving in a whisper. Then his blond cascade of curls started to shiver around his head, his voice rising. Sister Mary, who hovered a few feet away, repeated parts of what he said, like an echo chamber.

Suddenly it was as if we were all underwater, watching it happen in slow motion.

Golden took a deep, exaggerated breath and walked around to Isaac's bedside opposite Virginia. He moved carefully, avoiding the clear tubes running into Isaac's arm. He put his hand on Isaac's head very softly, but his voice boomed in my ears.

"O Lord, send Your healing power down and give us faith so that we will receive a miracle! Please, Lord. Please! We believe You can do this!"

His words were slurred through my underwater version of it all. There was a rhythm and cadence almost like an auctioneer. He kept going.

"Lord, You said if we had the faith of a mustard seed that we could move mountains, and so we are asking You not to move a mountain but to move this cancer out of Isaac's body. Move, I said!"

Isaac, wide-awake now, looked over at me then back at Golden, as if peering right through him. Then he motioned his hand slowly, asking for him to lean down. Golden looked surprised but carefully bent down. Isaac whispered something in his ear. I saw a strange look in Golden's eyes. As he rose up from Isaac, he took his hand off him and just stood there, looking down at him, not saying anything.

Sister Mary stepped forward, then backed away as Golden knelt down on that cold hospital floor and took hold of Isaac's hand with his gloved one and prayed. I couldn't make out what he said, but there was something electric about the moment. I felt all the little hairs on the back of my neck stand up.

Sister Mary squeezed her eyes, focusing on the back of Golden's head, pursing her lips. Golden stood and backed away from Isaac. She reached her hand into the crook of his arm. Like a falling star burning out, it was over. He turned to Sister Mary, and she took charge. Her razor-sharp voice broke the underwater trance, and I resurfaced again to hear her words in real time. "The healing prayer is complete."

As she and Golden left the room, he looked at me, both of us peeking out over our masks, a pleading in his eyes.

I wanted to believe. I kept repeating to myself over and over again, *Believe, believe.* Like trying to talk yourself into believing Santa is real after you've seen your dad sneak into the living room to eat the cookies and drink the milk.

It felt hollow, but I tried to convince myself that something real had happened. The moment when Isaac whispered into Golden's ear had rattled him. But I had to believe that the Miracle Boy really could bring a miracle. Daddy's words rushed back, but I blocked them out of my mind. Golden was famous; there must be some truth to his gift.

I went to use the bathroom, and when I came back, Isaac was already asleep. All the excitement had worn him out. I asked June if we could stay awhile in case he woke up. I wanted so badly to know what he'd said to Golden and if he felt anything . . . different.

We stayed for a bit, but he was in a deep sleep, which June said was a good sign. "Our bodies heal when we sleep."

Virginia finally said, "June, I guess you'd better take Grace home."

Before we left, I slipped the music box from June's purse. I'd asked her to carry it to the hospital for me that morning. I laid it on Isaac's bedside table and asked for a pen and paper to leave him a note.

Hey, Isaac, I wanted to stay, but you were sleeping. Here's that music box. I thought you could enjoy the music. I can't remember the name of the song, but it sounds familiar. Oh, and I've got a question—do you think roosters (and other animals) go to heaven? I'll come back soon.

Your favorite sister, Grace

June didn't say much on the ride home. There was so much tension, my stomach tightened and my shoulders ached. I didn't want her to be mad at me, but I also didn't know how to explain the money. She started to speak several times and then stopped herself midsentence. She rested her arm on the window frame and ran her fingers through her red hair, the soft skin on the underside of her arm jiggling as she raised it into the wind. She forced out long breaths as if she was letting off steam. Silence seemed safest for now. The awkwardness lingered between us. The air was thick with all we were not saying. But I could not risk Daddy finding out about paying Sister Mary. June would just have to be mad at me until something changed.

As I lay in bed that night, I kept thinking about Golden. The way his eyes looked translucent when the light hit them. How his mother hovered over him. I was dying to know what Isaac had said to him. I felt strangely at ease with him, and I wasn't sure why. Like a force or a magnet drawing me to him. I had heard of soulmates . . .

I lay there thinking of his eyes. The entire experience had fused us together. How could I see him again when Sister Mary stood watch over him constantly? And with my bike still out of commission?

There was something else. The moment by the creek. He told me there was something important I should know. I had forgotten he'd even said that until now.

The train whistle blew in the distance, and Billy Raines's story from Sunday school all those weeks ago came back to me like a prayer. Was the Starmaker sending me yet another sign? I replayed Billy's story in my mind and moved each puzzle piece around. It was insane, but it could work. I would just need a ride to the hospital.

27

THE GARDENER

Two mornings later, Daddy and June sat quietly in the kitchen drinking coffee. The normal morning chatter was absent. Virginia was up early as usual and back at Isaac's bedside. The healing was working. Isaac's appetite had improved, and his fever had not returned, so that was positive. Isaac had needed extra rest after the ordeal of having a "circus act," as Dr. Clarke called it, in his room, but now he said it was okay to visit. Listening from my normal spot in the hallway the night before, I had not heard June say anything to Daddy about the money. I was beginning to believe that my plan had worked. Maybe I could even find a way to replace the money.

As Daddy left for work through the screen door, I dialed the phone and hung up when I heard the voice on the other end. I ran to catch up with Daddy at his car.

"Hey, Daddy, do you think you could give me a ride to the hospital? June says it's fine with her. She's happy to pick me up since I haven't seen Isaac in a couple days."

"I guess that would be okay."

"I'll tell June! Be right back."

I said this while looking him square in the eyes. It worried me, how good I was getting at lying.

Daddy put his hand gently on my face and said, "You sure love him, don't you?" He hugged me.

I raced back into the house, the fragility of my plan making my heart race. If even one part didn't work, I was in massive trouble.

"June, Daddy says I can go to the shop with him if you don't need me for anything?"

"Okay. Whatever your daddy says is fine with me."

"Thanks, Aunt June!"

Her eyes followed me out the door as I got into the car.

I knew this could all go terribly wrong, but somehow I didn't care. There was a magnet pulling me to Golden.

When we got to the hospital, Daddy asked if I could walk in by myself. He had a customer waiting at the shop.

"No problem. I know the way." I made my voice especially chipper.

"I guess you do. You're growing up to be quite a remarkable young lady, Grace."

I leaned over and gave him a hug, feeling sick to my stomach. How disappointed he would be if he knew the truth. There was a part of me that wanted to tell him everything, but if I did, I might never see Golden again. My heart was driving me with a gale-force wind, and I couldn't stop from walking right into the storm.

I brushed away the fear and guilt and waved goodbye as he drove away. As soon as he was out of sight, I ran around to the back of the hospital. The train cars were all being loaded.

During some of my visits, the hospital shook as the train thundered past, the whistle blaring. I had asked one of the nurses about it and she told me, "It loads up every morning by nine and takes off to pick up loads down the line. You can set your watch by it."

I remembered waiting at the tracks as the train made the stop at the old shoe factory. If the boys in Sunday school could see me now. And it was just a few miles from the hospital to the trailer park.

It was nearly eight thirty, so I had to hide for thirty minutes before the train took off. I didn't see anyone, so I crept to the end of the train and climbed onto the caboose. I sat on the metal floor behind the railing, hunkered down so no one would see me. As the whistle blew a short blast to depart, I clamped my hands over my ears. It was so loud I thought my eardrums would burst. The train picked up speed and we wound through the countryside. I slowly stood up, gripping the railing. It was exhilarating. Like I was flying. Before long the whistle blew again, and I saw the old shoe factory up ahead. The tricky part would be getting off without being seen. I saw the workers standing on the platform, waiting to load the boxes onto the train. I squeezed down behind the railing again. They walked toward the train with arms full of boxes. When they started loading, I jumped off.

"Hey! What are you doing!"

I looked back to see a man in a conductor's uniform behind me.

"Get back here!" He sprinted toward me.

I ran harder than I ever had before. My legs burned and my side ached, but the adrenaline pushed me on. He gave up after a while. I looked behind me and saw him take off his hat and throw it on the ground. I laughed. *What am I doing?*

It was as though something inside me had cracked open.

I came to the road and slipped under some trees, grateful for the shade. I was walking slowly, trying to catch my breath, when I heard the crunch of gravel beside me. A car slowed down. A middle-aged man rolled down his window. I had never seen him before.

"Hey, pretty girl, do you need a ride?"

"No thanks—"

"You sure? It's awfully hot out. I could take you to your house." He smiled.

My skin tingled, like a warning signal. I had once heard of a high-school girl in Middlesboro disappearing. I shook my head and kept walking.

"I've got some music I bet you'd like. I have a whole stack of records. They're all right here in the car." He opened the passenger door, welcoming me to get in. I stood frozen, wondering about those records. An old truck pulled up behind him and honked. He reached across, slamming the door shut, squealed his tires, and took off.

The truck pulled over and an older man asked, "You okay?"

I nodded.

"You need a ride somewhere, sweetheart?"

"No thanks. I'm almost home." I pointed to the entrance of Shady Creek.

"Be careful. It ain't safe for you to be out here walking."

"Yes, sir. Thanks." I took off running toward the entrance.

And there by the sign to Shady Creek was Miss Pearl's peach stand. She stood up and shaded her eyes. "Is that Miss Grace a-walking?"

"Hi, Miss Pearl. Hi, Theo." Theo gave me a shy smile and I noticed dimples in his cheeks and how beautiful his teeth were.

"Child, it ain't safe for you to be out here by yo'self. You could get picked up by some lowly sort."

"Yes, ma'am. I'm visiting a friend."

"Well, you best tell yo' friend to give you a ride back to town. If your friend can't, me and Theo would be happy to give you a ride home."

"Thanks, Miss Pearl."

"Come back for a peach on your way out!"

"Yes, ma'am!" I waved as I ran into the entrance of Shady Creek.

I walked quickly, the place becoming strangely familiar. I didn't see the beer-drinking man or the little boy. It was too hot to be outside. I looked for the gold car parked in front of the trailer. I saw it up ahead. It looked as dismal as always. I was relieved to see them home. When I had dialed their number that morning while June was in the bathroom,

220

Golden's dad had answered, and I quickly hung up. I had taken my chances that they would still be home by the time I got there.

When I was here the first time, I remembered Golden walking back to the far left end of the trailer and waving at me from that window. I assumed his bedroom was on that side. It was a risk . . .

I took a deep breath and picked up a small rock and threw it at the window. I waited a minute, got no response, and then found another rock, small enough not to do any damage but big enough to be heard, and threw it right in the center. If he was in the kitchen or living room, he probably wouldn't hear it. If I remembered wrong, I could be throwing a rock at Sister Mary's window. I was about to throw a third rock when the white curtain opened and there he was, filling the window with his curls and those eyes.

He looked at me and raised the window. He whispered, "Grace, what are you doing here?"

"I wanted to talk."

He stared at me and pointed toward the woods behind their trailer. "Back over there is a path that leads to a park. There are picnic tables and an old swing set. Give me a few minutes and I'll meet you there."

He held his finger over his lips.

I wanted to throw up, but my heart was racing with excitement at the same time.

I found the path through the trees. There was a small clearing up ahead with the picnic table and the swing set.

"Hey."

I turned around. My mouth was so dry my words were stuck to the back of my throat. "How did you get away?"

"I'm allowed to come down here to . . . pray and meditate. At least that's what I tell them so I can get away, have some time alone."

For the first time he was dressed like a normal teenager, in a white cotton T-shirt and a pair of cut-off jeans and bare feet.

"It's hot." After everything it took to get here, those were the only words I could get out? Then I thought of something else to say. "I should have brought peaches."

"From the lady at the entrance?"

"Yes, that's Miss Pearl. Her truck stays parked by my school in the spring. Sometimes she gives me a free peach." My mouth watered at the thought of it. I was suddenly very thirsty for some peach juice dribbling down my chin.

"I have always wanted to stop, but Mary is allergic to peaches."

"Oh." He called her "Mary" instead of "Mother." I could relate.

He pointed. "The path keeps going up ahead. It's cooler back there."

I followed him through the trees. As we got farther back, we came to an old, run-down farmhouse, and behind it was an enormous overgrown garden. You could tell the house had once been beautiful.

"An older man who lives a few trailers down told me the history of this place. A few decades ago this was farmland. A banker from Louisville bought it, moved here, and built this house and planted the garden for his wife, who was from England, called it her English garden. Something to remind her of home. She got sick one winter and died of consumption. He was so heartbroken by her death that he became a recluse. Paid a Negro lady to come and deliver food and cook for him. After a while, she stopped coming. Said he scared her. He went out of his mind. People just kind of forgot about him. He was behind on land taxes, so someone from the county came back here and found him in the house nearly a year after he had died. No next of kin. The whole place went into foreclosure. A developer bought it and made it a trailer park."

He led me deep into the overgrown bramble and cobblestone and pointed to a small sign that read *Shady Creek Garden*. "It's so tragic, you can almost feel his desperation." I could see a struggling blossom here and there poking out from the vines and weeds.

It felt as though Jubilee and the rest of the world didn't exist. My spine tingled being in this strange place, standing so close to him.

"I want to show you something." He walked through the maze of the garden, and in the very back by a large shade tree was a small bench. You could hear the trickle of water, and around the bench rosebushes and lilacs were blooming in lavender and bright pink.

"It's so beautiful, but why is this not covered up in weeds?"

"It used to be." He reached into a wheelbarrow that held gardening supplies and started snipping away on another rosebush you could tell he had been working on.

"You cleared this away?"

He nodded. "I come here a lot to think. You see, the vines and weeds are so aggressive that, once they get hold, they overtake everything in their path. They rob them of all the nutrients they need to grow. They smother them till they shrivel and die, destroying everything that was once beautiful. I hate them—the vines and weeds."

I looked around and could see what a wasteland the weeds and vines had made of it.

"But there's something about returning life to what was left for dead. That seems . . . sacred."

"Looks like your calling is to heal in more ways than one. That's why I came, to thank you . . . for coming for Isaac."

His face darkened. "You don't need to thank me."

"Of course I need to thank you. Isaac . . . he's not only my brother, he is my best friend in the world." I stepped up beside him and reached out to deadhead a few roses, which calmed my nerves. "What did he say to you, when he whispered in your ear?"

He stopped snipping off dead limbs. "He's special, you know. Something about him is different. Like he's old. I mean he has a kind of old wisdom."

"I know what you mean."

A leaf fell from above us and landed in my hair. It was in that moment that the air shifted and something between us changed. He reached out to take the leaf from my hair, and we stood locked in each other's gaze. A light breeze blew around us. He traced my face with his finger. I closed my eyes.

Then I felt a stabbing pain like an ice pick. I screamed and opened my eyes to see the huge snake that had its fangs stuck in my ankle.

Golden quickly moved me back. He grabbed a hoe from the wheelbarrow and killed the copperhead that was coiled and ready to strike again. Two red bite marks pulsed in my ankle. I remember the sound of water and the feeling of being carried before the world disappeared.

28

HEZEKIAH

When I woke up, I was in a familiar place. It was white and smelled of disinfectant. I had a needle with a tube, like Isaac's, stretching from my arm into a bag of clear liquid beside the bed on a tall silver stand. Daddy's face was the first thing that came into focus. He was holding my hand and smiling.

Behind him were Cooter and Golden, bare feet and all.

"You gave us quite a scare, Miss Grace." Cooter's smile was as dazzling as always.

I tried to understand what they were saying, but I was still a little dazed.

Cooter hitched a thumb in Golden's direction. "You should thank this guy here, who carried you to Miss Pearl's peach stand where I was buying peaches for Mama. I drove like a bat out of hades all the way to the hospital."

It was so strange to hear about all of this happening to me and not remember any of it.

Cooter continued, "Dr. Clarke was walking out of the hospital to grab lunch when we pulled in. The doc looked at the bite and Golden confirmed it was a copperhead. Dr. Clarke said it looked like it hadn't gotten its fangs in too deep and that was good. Probably thanks to Golden, who I hear bested that snake with a hoe."

Cooter draped his arm over Golden like a proud big brother.

Daddy smiled at Cooter, then added, "Dr. Clarke gave you some antivenom to be on the safe side."

"I'm sorry, Daddy . . ."

There was much to be sorry for. I stopped counting the lies, there were so many. He was probably waiting to ask the hard questions when we were alone. At least I was back at the hospital where I started this morning.

Daddy sat looking down at me, all those questions passing through his eyes, and still, behind those questions was relief. I guess it could have been worse.

Cooter spoke up, maybe sensing our need for privacy. "Well, me and Golden are gonna take off. Hey, John, do you think we could stop in to see Isaac while we're here?"

"He's next door. I'm sure he'd love a visit, but the nurses will probably make you wash up before you go in there."

I could see the anxiousness on Golden's face. He looked freezing in his bare feet and shorts, or maybe it was just nerves. He was a different person now than his last visit. I wondered if the nurses would even recognize him. I sat there shivering under the sterile blankets. I didn't know if it was because of the air conditioning or the fact that I knew how much trouble I was in.

Cooter patted my feet through the white sheets and blankets. "You look after yourself. No more snake charming for you."

Daddy stood and thanked them both again.

Golden nodded to me, and they left.

"All right, Grace, let's have it. You know you gave us the scare of our lives. First, how in the world did you get out to Shady Creek?"

I told him that I just wanted to thank Golden. He was my age, and I knew he didn't have any friends. I described my whole adventure on the train, which, in retelling it, really was one of the best adventures of my life.

Daddy listened, asking questions for clarification along the way. "I wish you had just asked me to drive you out there. And that leads me to my next question—how did you know where he lived?"

"Oh, Miss Lila at the diner told me."

"Well, I can tell you that I'm not at all happy with you lying, Grace. It's never just one lie; they domino into more and more lies."

He had no idea how right he was. There were so many other lies I wasn't telling him about.

"I will say that Golden seems like a decent boy. Cooter said he was very brave," Daddy said. "I asked Cooter why Golden hadn't asked his parents to bring you to the hospital instead of him."

"What did he say?"

"Cooter said he was afraid for them to know y'all had been together in the woods."

I nodded, feeling the gut punch of fear at the thought of what Golden would be facing when he went home. He must have been gone for hours. Wouldn't Sister Mary or Brother Joseph go looking for him? Why was Golden so afraid? Not that I blamed him—I was terrified of Sister Mary myself. Questions I wanted answers to, but I thought I should focus on surviving my current troubles.

"I don't approve of you wandering around in the woods with a boy, and especially a boy we don't know—even if he is a famous healer. It was a dangerous thing to do, Grace."

"I'm sorry, Daddy."

"You're lucky your mother doesn't know. She had just left when you arrived. I was able to call June and let her know not to say anything and to keep her home awhile. I didn't want to give your mama anything more to worry about. She will find out soon enough, though. You can't hide much in this town."

"I just felt like I would die if I didn't see him."

He looked at me strangely, letting my sudden confession sink in. "Well, I'm glad you're okay, Grace. Something could have gone very wrong."

I thought of the man who tried to give me a ride. The train conductor who had chased me.

I nodded, feeling tears threatening at the corners of my eyes at having disappointed him.

Dr. Clarke knocked. "Hey, there. I have a friend here who wanted to stop in and say hi."

I quickly dried off my face with the bedsheet and grabbed a tissue to blow my nose.

"Well, look who's here." Daddy stood and shook the man's hand warmly as he and Dr. Clarke walked into the room. "Grace, this is Reverend Hezekiah Washington."

I remembered reading his name on the church billboard when Daddy, Isaac, and I sat outside his church one night last summer, listening from the car with the windows down. We were bored and out for a drive. Daddy said he'd heard from Hutch what a powerful preacher Reverend Hezekiah was. We listened to the choir sing and then the sermon, mixed with the croaking of the frogs and the buzz of the June bugs. It was kind of magical. I remembered thinking how exciting his sermon was, especially compared to the long and dull muttering of Pastor Bluin.

I didn't mean to stare, but I had never seen a Negro in the hospital before. Reverend Hezekiah looked to be about Daddy's age and wore a white short-sleeved dress shirt and a brown striped tie. He was handsome with an easy smile. He was the kind of person you liked right away. I seemed to remember him standing close to Hutch at the rally. He had a presence that you didn't forget.

"I was here visiting some of the patients, and Dr. Clarke told me Miss Grace might need a word of prayer. I wanted to drop by to see how you were doing."

Dr. Clarke checked the bite, which he said looked good, then took my blood pressure and listened to my heart. He said he thought I'd be out of there by dinnertime. He shook Reverend Hezekiah's hand before he left.

The reverend came to my bedside. "Little sister, could I say a word of prayer for you?"

I nodded.

He spoke words of love and blessing and angels on my left and on my right. His voice was rich and alive, and I felt the love of something greater than me pouring into each word. "Amen. All right, then. God bless you, little one."

Daddy walked him out of the room. I could see their faces through the window in the door to my room. They spoke comfortably and laughed a bit. Maybe Daddy was telling him about my train-hopping adventures. They seemed like friends. Dr. Clarke invited him to pray for patients in the hospital—maybe the people Isaac said never had visitors? Had he prayed for Isaac? I wondered if Dr. Clarke was determined to adhere to the integration laws, despite the threats of Rank Gunner and the rest of the ridiculous Klan. I wondered if Miss Adams was rubbing off on Dr. Clarke. He did seem to be sweet on her, and who could blame him? For a moment, it felt like the rest of the world was mad and things only made sense here, where Daddy and Reverend Hezekiah seemed like old friends. I was afraid the rest of the world would come crashing in and this beautiful moment would be shattered.

29

THE MIRACLE

We held our breath.

Waiting for Isaac's miracle while June and I cooked and cleaned and Sissy ran around sowing her wild oats. Virginia kept sitting by Isaac's bed and Daddy kept working long hours. Isaac's fever had returned. I would hear June in her room folding laundry, fussing at God about why Isaac wasn't getting better.

When a change seemed hopeless, Dr. Clarke called to say that Isaac's fever had broken again and he woke up hungry. We had been down this road before, but maybe this time it would be different. The doctor thought a visit from me might be good medicine.

I walked into Isaac's room and found him sitting up in bed, eating lunch and reading the paper—I could see today's date, July 22, 1963, on the front page. Virginia had gone home for a nap.

We had barely said hello when he started telling me all about what he was reading.

"Dr. Clarke thought I'd like this article about NASA sending up a civilian test pilot, Joe Walker, in an X-15. He reached 105 kilometers."

Excited, he reached to his bedside table for a *Space World* magazine and opened it to a page he had saved with a small candy wrapper. "And, Grace, the Russians have sent up the first woman into space!"

His eyes were wide with excitement; his cheeks had color in them. It was the first time since he'd returned that he seemed like his old self. I reached to give him a hug, careful not to squeeze him too tight.

After he told me all about space travel, he took a drink from a can on his bedside table, then said, "I heard you got bit by a snake?"

"Yep, copperhead." I lifted my ankle and showed him the two puncture wounds that were healing over.

Wheeeeeew. He whistled the way Daddy did. "How did it happen?"

I wrestled with whether or not I should tell him the whole story, but then I thought he might enjoy hearing about my adventure, so I gave him the nuts and bolts, leaving out plenty of details but including the most exciting parts.

His eyes were huge as he listened. "You hopped a train?"

"Not exactly, I got on and off while it was stopped."

He continued to eat as I kept talking and ended the story where I woke up in the hospital.

"Did you get in trouble?"

I nodded. "Daddy grounded me from TV for a week and I have to do extra chores around the house."

"What about Mama?"

"Well, that's what's strange. I thought for sure she would ground me for a year and give me the switch, but she never even acknowledged it."

"Grace, your face just got sad."

It wasn't until that moment that the strange disappointment settled on me.

"I guess as relieved as I am that she didn't get mad, it makes me wish she had been a little worried at least for my safety."

"Are you sure she knows?"

"I know she must have heard about it from somebody—maybe Daddy never told her, but I can't imagine the nurses not saying anything."

"The nurses told me, said that the Miracle Boy rescued you."

My face turned red.

He pinched my leg. "Is he your boyfriend now?"

"Ouch! What? No!"

"Why did you do all that to go see him?"

"I wanted to thank him for coming to pray for you and I also wanted to ask him . . . what it was you whispered in his ear."

He looked at me, considering this, then said, "That's his to tell."

I rolled my eyes, and he kept talking.

"He and Cooter came and prayed for me . . . I was glad to see Cooter."

"Yeah, Cooter's great. His mom lives over where Golden does at Shady Creek." I told him all about the history of Shady Creek and the English garden.

"Weren't you scared to hop the train?"

"Yeah . . . but it was also exciting."

Isaac's eyes drifted and gazed out the window, his thoughts somewhere else. "I think about space travel or deep-sea diving, exploring the mysteries of the universe."

"Well, you're getting better now. I figure you're smart enough that you can do whatever you want, little brother."

His eyes squinted as if he was trying to bring something into focus. "What is it?"

"I was just remembering something."

A nurse with a round body and short skinny legs came in. "I'm sorry to cut your visit short, darlin', but it's time for his bath."

I looked at Isaac, my face showing my dread for him.

He bounced his head onto his pillows, his eyes rolled back, and he let out a sigh. We giggled.

"I'll come back tomorrow if that's okay?"

"Okay. See you, Grace." I gave him a hug and made a face behind the nurse so that he would laugh. He did.

June was waiting for me in the lobby, reading a magazine and drinking a Tab. The nurses were watching a small TV that had been placed in the waiting area. The big news was about the growing number of people from around the country who were planning to be a part of the March on Washington next month. The nurses shook their heads, obviously not in favor.

June burst out as she rose and stood in front of them, "I think that is just great." She turned to me. "Gracie, maybe you and me ought to go!"

The nurses looked at her with open mouths. June reached for my hand and smiled and started to sing, "Jesus loves the little children . . . red and yellow—" then very loudly—"*black* and white . . ."

Even though Aunt June did embarrass me sometimes, she was pretty cool.

* * *

A few days later, Dr. Clarke told Daddy that Isaac wasn't out of the woods, but that if his vitals and immune system continued to improve, they could see the possibility of sending him home in a few weeks. It was a restrained optimism but cause for hope, and the mood in our house was a little lighter because of it. I was afraid to believe that I had succeeded in helping to find a miracle for Isaac, but I wondered if it had at least been a part of the reason he was getting better.

Over the next few days, there was continued improvement. We would go see Isaac at lunchtime and then let him rest.

One night, Sissy crept in late, like she always did, but Virginia was home and had waited up for her. I was still awake when I heard the front screen door screech on its hinges and then Virginia's voice from the living room.

"Home so soon?"

"I had to work late. I'm going to bed."

"Is that so?"

"Look, I'm tired, and I don't feel like talking, all right?"

"What do I smell? Cigarette smoke?"

"Everybody smokes at Tri-Way, and plenty of people smoke while they eat. I can't do nothing about that."

I cracked the door of my room to see what was about to go down. I could see them at the end of the hallway, Virginia blocking Sissy from going to her room.

Virginia leaned in closer. "Blow."

"What?"

"I said *blow*. I want to see if your breath smells like hamburgers or cigarettes."

"Get out of my face."

By the time Sissy said this Daddy and I had stepped out of our bedrooms into the hallway.

Virginia got up in Sissy's face and grabbed her chin in a vise grip with one hand. Sissy swung her arm to get loose and hit Virginia in the face. She ran out the back door, slamming it behind her. Virginia started to take off after her, but Daddy held her by the shoulders.

"Let her cool down a minute," Daddy said, his voice calm and steady. "I don't think she meant to hit you. Are you okay?"

He touched his fingers gently to the red spot on Virginia's eye.

"No, John. I am *not* okay."

Why couldn't Sissy just act respectable? Why did she have to bring all this drama in on us? We had enough to deal with already.

I decided it was time to let her have it.

I slipped to the back door, twisted the handle quietly, and slipped out to the yard. Sissy stood behind the shed, drawing a deep drag from her cigarette.

My words were sharp and full of venom. "Don't you think Virginia and Daddy are dealing with enough without you making it worse?"

She turned abruptly. "Well, isn't that rich. You, who has lied, snuck around, hopped a train, and got caught with a strange boy and hospitalized with a snakebite. You justify it all in the name of helping Isaac. But I don't buy it, Grace. You need to stop pointing the finger and take a look in the mirror."

She blew a thick cloud of cigarette smoke in my face and walked out the gate.

I felt exposed and furious. How could she compare herself to me? I stuffed down the truth of it and crept in the back door. I twisted in my sheets, wrestling with her words till my body gave in to sleep.

We were in the garden again. Golden traced my face with his finger. Just as he was leaning in to kiss me, a giant snake with Sister Mary's head hovered over us and reared up to strike. With her forked tongue she said, "You sssssinners. Evil little sssssinners. The devil's gonna get you." She lurched out to bite me.

30

POLAROID

A small mercy appeared like sun in the heavens in the form of Miss Adams, who knocked on our door the next morning.

June opened the door wide and said, "Won't you come in?"

"Thank you, but I can only stay a minute. I'm on my way to a birthday party and wanted to invite Grace. Hutch's daughter, Yully, is turning thirteen, and she asked me to invite Grace to her party."

"Well, isn't that the sweetest thing. And who is Hutch?"

I broke in with a frantic explanation. "He is a friend of Daddy's. He works at the gas station in town."

"That sounds fine, as long as your daddy knows him. I think a party would be wonderful. There has been way too much seriousness. You need to go and have some fun."

I hugged June and thanked Miss Adams.

June insisted on bringing Miss Adams a glass of sweet tea while I ran and got dressed.

Sissy's accusation stared back at me as I looked in the mirror, thinking about returning to Miss Adams's neighborhood without telling June that I had been forbidden to see her. June stood on the porch smiling and waving us away. She had no idea who the real snake was.

* * *

I followed Miss Adams into Mr. Hutch and Miss Hazel's backyard; people from the neighborhood were streaming in. They had decorated with balloons and flowers. There was a picnic table with a pink table-cloth over it and everybody brought a dish of food. Catfish and coleslaw. Fried okra and garden tomatoes. Corn cakes and fried potatoes. But there were other foods I had never seen before—fried hog jowls, which were the cheeks of a hog, and chitlins, which were deep-fried pig intes-tines. Miss Adams assured me both were delicious. It all looked tasty, though I was pretty sure I'd pass on the pig guts.

Yully introduced me to her other friends. One girl named Ida, who towered over me and Yully, looked at me sternly and said, "Why you want to be coming to Yully's party?"

Yully rolled her eyes and said, "Shut up, Ida. It ain't your party, it's mine, and I can invite whoever I want."

Ida squished her nose, as though she smelled something unpleasant, and fell back into a game of jump rope.

Another girl, Bri, whose face was set in a permanent smile, flicked her hand back as Ida walked away. "Don't pay her any attention. She was born with that attitude. You are very welcome here."

I smiled back nervously and said, "Thank you."

She left us and joined a game of tag. Walking up behind Yully was a familiar face, with eyes like green marbles.

"Hi, Grace."

"Hi, Theo."

"You two know each other?" Yully seemed more than a little surprised.

"Yes, we do. She comes to my granny's peach stand. Granny thinks the world of Miss Grace."

I blushed, embarrassed by the compliment. "Is she here?"

"No. She decided to work the peach stand since she has so many ripe ones. She's afraid they'll go bad if she doesn't sell them today."

The sound of a dinner bell rang, and we headed off to the line.

"Elders and children first!" yelled Miss Hazel.

The ladies ushered me, Yully, and Theo to the front of the line, putting a hand on my shoulder and calling me "baby." Yully insisted that her grandmother go first, which I thought was very nice.

We filled plates and found a spot on a blanket in the grass under a large shade tree, where we ate our fill and drank sweet tea and lemonade till I thought I'd bust. After we ate, Yully opened her presents; then we moved on to cake and ice cream.

Theo decided he would help Yully entertain me. Miss Hazel suggested that Theo, Yully, and I take Miss Adams's dog, Maggie, to play fetch. Maggie, who had wandered over from next door, begged us with sad brown eyes, thumping her stub of a tail. She chased us through the woods behind Miss Adams's property. It was cool under the canopy of trees.

Theo was the best at throwing the stick, so we let him. Yully and I swayed in an awkward silence watching Theo. I strained to think of a question, feeling unsure of what to talk about. "Do you have a dog?" I asked.

"No. I got a pet mouse, though."

"One from a store?"

"Naw. I found it as a baby. Its mama and brothers and sister got eaten by our cat, Rusty. Stupid cat. It didn't seem right to leave it to die, so I fed it milk from the tip of my finger till it was old enough to eat. That mouse think I his mama."

"Wow. I would love to see your mouse sometime. What's his name?"

"His name is Squeaks. 'Cause when I found him, he squeak and squeak till none of us could sleep. That little mouse drove us all crazy. I think it was just 'cause he was hongry."

I must have asked the right question, because once the silence was broken, Yully could, as Grandma Josie used to say, talk the hind leg off a mule.

I liked how her eyes darted back and forth when she explained things and how she used her hands to express herself. She didn't smile much, but her talking made up for it.

"What about you? You got any pets?"

"Well, yes. We have a rooster named Rojo, which is Spanish for *red*. He is really Isaac's pet."

"You got a pet rooster?"

This caused Yully's mouth to crack open, and she started to laugh. When she couldn't stop, I started to laugh too, and we both lay down in the grass with that good feeling in our chests.

Theo came over. "What are you crazy girls laughing at?"

We caught our breath and waved off his question.

"I'm tired a' throwing this stick. I need to cool off." Theo walked Maggie to Miss Adams and came back. "Let's go to the creek, y'all."

When we got to the creek, Theo took off his shirt and rolled up his pants and got into the water.

Yully noticed me looking at him and punched me in the arm. "What you looking at, Grace? Ain't you never seen a boy with his shirt off?"

She threw her head back, laughing. I swept my hand through the water and sprayed her in the face.

"Oh, that's how it is!" She went in with both hands and drenched me. We fell down splashing and laughing, not caring that we were now completely soaked.

We decided to walk a little farther upstream to catch some crawdads since all our splashing had scared them off where we'd been. We talked about all the things we liked best about summer. About the best kind of ice cream and how good an ice-cold Coca-Cola would taste about now.

"Hey, Grace, can you show me and Yully your scar from the snake-bite?"

I had almost forgotten that Theo had been at the peach stand when Golden brought me there for help. I lifted my leg to show them my ankle with the two small marks that would someday be scars.

"Did it hurt?"

"Yeah, but I don't remember much. I passed out."

"That Golden. He ran out yelling, 'Help, help.' He's the healer who helped your brother, right?"

"Yes. That's him."

"Did it work?"

"I think so. He seems to be getting better."

"Well, hallelujah!" Theo seemed sincere. "My father is a preacher. That's what I'm gonna be one day."

"Is your daddy Reverend Hezekiah?"

"One and the same."

"I met him at the hospital. He was very nice. He prayed for me."

He smiled, obviously proud of his father.

"Kids!" We heard Miss Adams's voice.

It was time to go.

This was the first time I could remember that I had played with kids other than Isaac or Sissy. I suddenly felt lonely at the thought of this being the only time I would be with them. Miss Adams was off-limits. There was no way Virginia would let me come play with Yully and Theo.

Even Daddy would be concerned because of the Klan.

I stood there looking at Theo and Yully. "I just wanted to say that I had a great time with y'all today."

Yully grabbed one of my hands, patting it as she smiled at me. Theo put a hand on my shoulder and said, "You're all right, Grace."

Miss Adams came outside and saw us gathered there. "Well, isn't this a wonderful picture. Wait right here!" She ran inside and then came back out with a camera. "Now smile like you mean it!"

We stood close together, connected in a way I had never imagined possible. She snapped, and the small photo rolled out. That moment, frozen in time.

"It will take a few minutes to develop. Grace, we better be going."

As Miss Adams drove me home, she squeezed the steering wheel nervously and seemed lost in thought.

"Is everything okay?"

"Grace, did you happen to mention to your parents where I lived?"

Acid boiled up from my stomach into the back of my throat.

"No, ma'am."

She let out a long breath. "Oh, well, I assumed you had, which I shouldn't have. I'm just a little concerned . . ."

I nodded, trying to swallow the lump in my throat. "I'm sorry; I should have told June."

"Well, maybe it will be okay. Let's agree that before you visit again, you will let your parents know?"

"Yes, ma'am." But she had no idea what she was asking.

When I walked into the house, June asked me a dozen questions about the party. I answered them as truthfully as I could without revealing the whole truth. How long could this go on?

Daddy and Virginia arrived home later than June expected—we had already eaten. I hung out in the backyard and thought about Theo and Yully.

I took a bath and then went to bed, feeling exhausted. Daddy poked his head into my room, but I pretended to already be asleep. He stood there watching me, then sighed and walked quietly out of my room. I melted into the bed.

A bright light and shouting broke into my dreams. I shot straight up in bed and saw lights out of my bedroom window. I ran to the living room and saw that the light came from a cross. Burning.

"John! John Mockingbird! Come on out!"

One of the men heaved an arm back and threw a rock that shattered one of the windows. Daddy ran straight for the rifle he kept locked up in the gun cabinet in the back room where June slept. Sissy, June, Virginia, and I stood in the living room in our nightgowns.

"June! Call the sheriff."

We could see a crescent moon of men in white robes and white hoods around the burning cross. I could not make out their shoes. I was afraid to linger too long in front of the window for a closer look.

Daddy turned to us swiftly. "I want all of you to go to the back of the house away from all the windows." When he stepped out on the porch, we returned to the safest window in the living room to watch what was happening.

He stood with his rifle aimed straight at them and said, "Y'all are on private property." His voice was calm and steady.

By now the entire neighborhood was watching and listening from corners of windows, while some were bold enough to stand on their front porches, smoking cigarettes and watching.

The first hood to speak had tiny arms and stood three heads lower than the burning cross as he spoke in a high, nasal voice. "We been leaving you alone, John! We knew yo' boy was sick, but we can't turn a blind eye no mo'. We heard all about your little girl going where you ought to have taught her not to go. Joining the ranks of that smart-mouthin' teacher."

A look of confusion passed over Daddy's face. He was the last to know. I wondered who had told.

From the back row, a red hood moved to the front. His voice was low and raspy, but it seemed too dramatic to be natural.

"This is a warning: you tell that girl of yours she better find some new friends if she knows what's good fer her."

June's head went in her hands and Virginia stared at me with contempt, then asked June, "What is he talking about?"

June was squinting her eyes, which looked teary. "I'm so sorry . . . I let her go. It's all my fault."

In the distance, a siren rang out. The sound of the cavalry coming too late. The Klansmen got back in their trucks and drove off with rebel yells echoing through the night air and rebel flags whipping in the breeze from the back of the pickups. They disappeared from sight as Sheriff Teeton made his way into our driveway.

The sheriff took the report but seemed agitated. I wondered why in the world he would be irritated with Daddy when we were the victims.

"John, I feel awful for what you're going through with Isaac. I will do everything I can to protect you all, but if I was you, I'd get that daughter of yours under control."

My face burned red with embarrassment. I could read Sissy's expression: *Look who is the black sheep now.* I had always been the good girl. What had happened to me? The thread holding our family together was beginning to unravel. Yully and Theo could never be my friends.

I looked around, noticing Virginia had disappeared. June stood beside me with her hands on her head, rocking side to side as if to comfort herself.

Daddy stood with the hose in his hand, putting out the burning cross. The sheriff looked on and kept talking.

"I can have a deputy cruise by here now and then." He paused and leaned his head over the grass to spit out the dark tobacco juice gathering from the snuff in his lip. "You never heard it from me, but there are some higher-ups in the local government that might be members of the Klan. I'm not sure I can protect you if you continue to ask for trouble, John. It's just how things is. Now smarten up. This ain't nothing to mess around with."

Daddy shot a harsh look at him, picked up a piece of the charred cross, and threw it into the street.

Sheriff Teeton backed out of the way and watched it land. "I'm sorry, John. It is what it is."

He headed back to his police car. Daddy stood on the porch, staring at the remains of the burned cross.

For as long as I live, I will never forget Daddy's eyes when he came back in and looked at me, not with anger, but with disappointment. I had let him down. Deceived him. Of all people.

June interjected, "It's all my fault. I let her go. I thought it would be okay . . ."

Daddy looked at June, then at me. "What do you have to say, Grace? Are you gonna let June take the blame?" His words were measured, short and jagged.

"It's my fault. I never told June I wasn't supposed to see Miss Adams. She had no idea." I turned to look at her. "I'm so s-s-sorry, June! I just wanted to go so bad . . . it was s-s-stupid." My words came out choppy because of my out-of-control sobbing. My breathing was erratic, and suddenly I was freezing and my entire body was shaking.

"Did you know where she lived?" Daddy asked me.

"I didn't the first time I went to her house. I didn't think I'd ever get to go back. But today, going to the party sounded like fun. I never told June where she lived."

I was devastated by the break between me and Daddy. He had always treated me as an equal and I had betrayed that again and again over the last few weeks. As terrible as that moment was, a weight was lifted from my chest—coming clean for June's sake and for mine. But the look of disappointment in Daddy's eyes replaced it with an ache much deeper than guilt. I had broken his trust.

Sissy was silent. I dreaded facing her, because she was going to give me the big "I told you so" attitude, but when I could no longer avoid looking at her, I saw something in her face that could not have surprised me more. Compassion.

Virginia charged into the living room, her hand behind her back, as if she was hiding something. The rage in her eyes was throwing sparks that would have burned me if I'd stepped any closer.

"I guess you figured we didn't have enough to deal with, Grace?" Her words sliced through me. "Did you figure me trying to take care of Isaac and your daddy working himself into an early grave wasn't enough?

Oh no! You had to go running around with that woman! That trouble-maker that we expressly told you not to associate with. You not only go with her, but you hide where she lives, and you go playing with colored children? What kind of stupidity possessed you? Or maybe it wasn't stupidity. Maybe it was that devil in you. That same devil. You remember, don't you, Grace? Or have you forgotten what that devil made you do the last time?"

June let out a gasp. The other shoe had finally dropped. What Virginia had been holding in all these years finally spewed out.

The guilt and shame of it all covered me like a mudslide. I could barely breathe or speak. Then she brought out what had been behind her back and held it up. It was my red journal.

"I know what goes on in my house, Grace. I've seen you hiding this under your mattress. I'm surprised at you. Questioning God's will! Almost blasphemous!"

My breath caught in my chest, knowing that she was referencing the poem I had written.

"I also know who gave it to you. The woman who is responsible for all of this!" She swept her hand toward where the burned cross was still smoldering. "I can tell you where this belongs!"

She blew past me through the front door and threw the journal into the smoldering pile of fire and ash.

"No! Stop it! That isn't yours! You have no right!"

I was trying to run to grab it from the pile of ashes, but she stopped me.

"I have *every* right! You have no privacy under this roof! Everything you do is under *my* permission."

I tried again to get past her. She pushed me back and then her hand came hard across my face. It felt like a hundred beestings.

"Virginia! Stop!"

She was about to strike me again, but Daddy held her hand as she brought it over her head. She stood there shaking, her arm frozen in the air. I ran to retrieve my journal from the ashes. I was able to clean most of the ash from it but there was a black mark across the wing of the bird on the cover. It was exactly how I felt. Marked.

In that moment, any chance of Virginia and me having a real relationship died. Bitterness spread through my heart like a slow fire, burning away the small fragments of hope.

June came out into the yard and hugged me. Sissy stared from the porch.

I buried myself in June's arms. There were no words to make this better. It could only get worse.

And it did.

31

RED

I wrestled with nightmares of burning crosses and biting snakes through-out the night, but this time, instead of Sister Mary's head on the snake, it was Virginia's. What a fool I had been to think everything would be okay. Some people never got the happy ending. How could I have thought there would be no consequences? I lay there, watching the pale light of the sun erase the shadows I had traced on my walls. I had drifted back to sleep for a few moments when I heard the phone ring in the kitchen.

June's door opened, her bare feet scurrying down the hallway to answer it. I heard a small knock, then her voice. "John . . . it's Hutch."

I wondered why he would be calling. And so early.

Feeling almost numb, I lay in bed, waiting for whatever the news was. I heard the soft pad of bare feet on the hardwood floor.

June knocked softly and poked her head into my room. "Your mama is already gone to the hospital, thank the Lord."

"What's wrong, June? Why is Mr. Hutch calling?"

"I don't know yet, but it doesn't sound good."

I threw my legs over the side of the bed and followed June into the kitchen. Daddy had just hung up the phone. I was glad June asked the next question because I was too afraid.

"What's happened, John?"

He looked at June and then said to me, "Get dressed. We are going to the hospital."

On the ride to the hospital, Daddy was silent, with the exception of an occasional sigh as he raked his fingers through his dark hair.

"Do you know what happened?" My voice broke on the last word.

He reached across and took my hand. I clung to the comfort of his rough mechanic's hands with the faint smell of grease and lemon hand soap that he used at the garage, now a permanent part of his skin. I brought his hand to my face and held it there. Did this mean he had forgiven me?

"I think it will be best coming from Hutch. He will tell us the whole story when we see him."

I nodded. Just grateful to be near him.

"And, Grace, what your mama said last night . . . that wasn't right. I mean, you have done a lot of dishonest things over the last few weeks, but I think I can understand why you did those things, even though it was stupid and unsafe. Anytime you want to keep something from your parents, it usually means you shouldn't do it.

"But what she said about Josie . . ." His voice cracked. "You were just being a kid. She should never have said that."

I squeezed his hand, feeling a cold sweat. I didn't want to see Virginia at the hospital. I needed to do whatever I could to avoid her. I had no idea what was coming from Hutch. Was I responsible? Was that why Daddy and I had been summoned? After last night, I knew God must hate me. There was no magic healing for this. Just the consequences of my actions. The ones I'd felt so justified in. I laid my head against the window and moved my lips, mumbling a silent prayer. The sick feeling I had lived with daily dulled into despair.

* * *

Miss Adams looked more girl than woman in the hospital bed. Smudges of mascara created dark shadows under her eyes. Her usually perfectly coiffed hair fell wildly around her face. Dr. Clarke held her porcelain arm gently, like a doll's. He took her blood pressure while he gazed at her warmly.

"It's 115 over 71. Perfect."

She coughed into the sheets that she held up to her face.

"That coughing is normal. The smoke you inhaled during the fire has created some inflammation in your bronchial passages. I will give you something to calm it, but it will take a few days to be back to normal."

"What fire?" I asked.

Hutch wiped his face with a washcloth that was now smudged with black char. "We were all in bed asleep when I heard sounds outside. Men's voices. I got my shotgun and went to the window to see. There in Miss Adams's front yard by her prize rosebush was a cross burning. There was a straight line of fire from the cross to the porch. I knew they had poured gasoline so that the fire would trail to her house. I couldn't believe it, but then again, I guess I could. I snuck out my back door and planned to get Miss Adams out through her back porch before they saw me. I was on the steps when I heard screaming. Raised the hair on the back of my neck. I ran around the side of the house toward the screaming, and there was Rank Gunner, on fire. Red flames on a red robe and red boots. A little gasoline had spilled on his leg and he was trying to run to put out the flames. I saw the hose there on the side of the house. I grabbed it, turned the water on and ran as close as I could and sprayed him down. By now, Miss Adams was out on the porch. The other Klan boys just stood there watching with their mouths open.

"Miss Adams called an ambulance. I was able to put out the fire before it did much damage. Just burned up the steps up to her porch.

The Klan boys took off and left Rank Gunner there like a burned piece of wood in the yard."

"So much for loyalty," chimed in Dr. Clarke.

Daddy spoke up. "They must have come straight from our house to yours." He told them about the burned cross in our yard.

"Teeton came last night, but too little too late, I'm afraid." Hutch set his mouth in a straight line then said a little too loudly for the small room, "Does this come as a shock? Do you all think it's a coincidence the law shows up after the damage has been done?"

Daddy and Dr. Clarke nodded, understanding landing in their eyes.

"No, sir! It's the same as it's always been."

Dr. Clarke nodded again in agreement. "We are just getting a small glimpse into what you and your family have been dealing with for years."

Hutch inhaled a deep breath. "I didn't mean to take it out on you here. Miss Adams, Miss Grace, I'm sorry I raised my voice in your presence."

"Oh, dear Hutch," Miss Adams said as she reached for his hand, looking so frail. "We bear witness to your pain and the injustice you have weathered all of these years." She started to say more but began coughing.

I stepped toward Hutch and took his other hand silently in mine.

Daddy spoke casually as if to ease the tension. "Does Teeton know what happened with Rank yet?"

Dr. Clarke answered, "I just called him a few minutes ago. He's headed this way."

"What about Rank?"

"Intensive care. Burned pretty bad. He might lose the leg. But our friend Hutch here is a hero of the highest order."

Hutch lowered his head, obviously embarrassed by such praise.

Miss Adams spoke up. "There was another cross, lying down in Hutch's yard. Probably planned to burn both our houses."

Was it wrong that I felt satisfaction knowing that Rank had gotten what he deserved? What if Miss Adams had been trapped in that fire? She could have died.

I looked up at Daddy, Hutch, and Miss Adams. "This is my fault. If I hadn't come—"

Miss Adams interrupted. "If you hadn't come, then you would have never made such good friends with Yully and Theo. And if you hadn't come, the Klan still would have because they were after me. I was foolish. I have put you all in danger. I'm so terribly sorry."

"The people to blame are those terrorizing the innocent," said Dr. Clarke.

Hutch looked at me warmly. "I know Yully and Theo were mighty glad you came."

Miss Adams's voice wafted into the air. "Mr. Mockingbird, I had a feeling that you must not have known. I should have cleared it with you first. I was just so sick of those wicked buffoons dictating what we could or couldn't do."

Dr. Clarke took her hand in his to comfort her.

Daddy spoke up. "I've been working so much, I didn't even know what was going on in my own household. And the people most responsible seem untouchable. Do you have a clue as to how they found out that Grace was over there?"

"Well . . . I think it was Miss Pearl," Hutch said. "She was so pleased for Grace to come and be with Theo and Yully and the other children. Said things are changing, and see how even a white teacher living in the neighborhood and a nice girl like Grace be coming to the birthday party of a Negro girl. I think she bragged about it at the peach stand and someone overheard her. Word gets around this town fast. She didn't mean no harm."

Gold-hearted Miss Pearl. She would feel awful if she thought she was the cause. But she wasn't. If I had obeyed and stayed home, none of this would have happened.

Miss Adams let out a deep sigh. "Well, there is only one thing to do. I have decided that I am leaving Jubilee."

Dr. Clarke gazed at Miss Adams calmly, as if this wasn't news to him.

"No! Please don't go!" I blurted out before I could stop myself.

"Grace, there's something I didn't tell you. I got a call from the principal after the rally. He said that my services were no longer needed or wanted as a teacher at your school."

"But you can't. Not *now*. If you leave, it's like they have won." I felt Daddy's hand on my back. I thought I noticed a trace of relief on Hutch's face.

I knew one person who would be thrilled with the news—Virginia. But after what she'd done last night, I had a good mind to hide away in Miss Adams's suitcase, if for no other reason than to spite Virginia.

Miss Adams wiped a tear running down her cheek with the white sheet she had pulled up closer to her face. "College makes you believe anything is possible. I was so focused and maybe even a bit overconfident about what I could accomplish. I'm starting to realize it's not nearly as simple as I imagined it would be. I just don't want to mess up anything else!"

"Are you going back to yo' people in Mississippi?"

"Not yet."

She squeezed Dr. Clarke's hand, then released it to reach for a tissue from a box beside the bed and wiped the corners of her eyes. "Whatever injustice has been suffered by Negroes in Kentucky, Mississippi is worse."

Hutch nodded in agreement. "I got people down there. They say it's real bad."

"The irony is, the people I know are so good at presenting a picture-perfect life, hiding what's really going on. I obviously have a lot to learn. I have decided I am going to try to join up with Dr. King. See if he could use a schoolteacher in his ranks."

Hutch's eyes seemed to bulge and then settle into something that read like doubt. Maybe after the world has dragged you around behind it for long enough, it's hard to believe in the possibility of real change. Maybe the odds were against it.

"Couldn't you wait at least till the end of summer?" I asked Miss Adams, almost pleading.

"I'm not leaving immediately. I need some time to pack my things, figure out where I go next. At least till I leave for the March on Washington, which I plan to attend."

I told her about what June had said to the nurses. Dr. Clarke seemed especially pleased by this. We laughed, feeling better for a moment.

I was relieved that Miss Adams and Hutch and their houses were okay. Maybe it was all I could ask for right now.

"We better be going," Daddy finally said. "We'll stop in to see Isaac while we're here."

We said goodbye and walked down the hallway toward Isaac's room. I saw a boy and a woman come out of the room in the hallway ahead of us. They looked as though the world had caved in on them. The boy turned to see us, and my breath caught. Eli Gunner. I had totally failed to think of how this would impact him and his mother.

He saw me and immediately quickened his pace toward the hospital lobby.

"This can't be an easy time for them," Daddy whispered.

As we passed the door, I could hear Rank talking to the nurse, his voice bitter and hateful.

I wanted to run out of there. I could not handle seeing Virginia.

"Daddy, could I wait outside while you go to see Isaac?"

He slipped his arm around my shoulder. "Yes. That's fine."

I walked quickly past Isaac's door, hoping not to be seen by either of them.

32

WILLY

A couple days later I was in the backyard playing with Rojo and watering the wildflowers June and I had planted along the back fence. The lies I had sown this summer had definitely caused a harvest; at least these seeds were growing something good. Little sprouts of daisies and echinacea were bursting through the rich dirt and it gave me a feeling of hopefulness. I had been trying to lie low since the town's gossip had been brewing with the news of the cross burnings. I heard someone knock on the front door, so I came around behind the bushes at the side gate to see who it was. A man with glistening dark hair—so much so, it looked wet. He shifted back and forth waiting for someone to answer. It was Willy, Virginia's father.

I had come across an old family album with pictures of him holding Virginia when she was a little girl. He had been handsome then. We had never called him "Grandpa." He was lucky we didn't call him something much worse.

Virginia had come home from the hospital to take a nap. I saw the shock on her face when she opened the screen door. I didn't want to miss anything they said, so I snuck in through the back door and crouched down at the end of the hallway where I could listen to what was happening on the porch.

"Ginny, I was sent down to tell you, you better come quick to see your maw. She's took a turn for the worse since her fall."

"I sent up a doctor to examine her after I went to visit. I know he recommended that she be hospitalized, but Thomas said no. She hasn't improved?"

"Naw. Retha said she looks real pale and her breathing ain't too good. That disgusting SOB Thomas. I'd like to shoot him right here." He pointed a long index finger right between his eyes.

I didn't think he'd get any argument from the family on that one.

"Well, anyhow, Ginny, I thought you ought to know."

"How did you get down here?"

He stuck out his thumb into the air. "Hitched a ride. Thought it would be nice to see you."

Virginia had more questions. "How are you getting back up to the hills? Do you want me to drive you back?"

"I was wanting to stay in town for a couple nights so I could see how little Isaac's doing. Is he here?"

"Isaac is at the hospital in Middlesboro."

"The hospital, is he? I ain't got a car, but I'll sure try and get over there to see him. But, uh, Ginny, it sure would be nice if you could do your old dad a favor and lend me a few bucks. I promise I'll pay it back. Just a little money for food."

"You could come eat with us."

"Oh, I wouldn't want to disrupt you. I just need a few dollars . . ."

Virginia turned around, and I quickly scooted down the hallway out of sight. I heard her open the kitchen door and lift the lid off the Maxwell House can where Daddy kept a little extra money for emergencies. She came back out onto the porch with a small wad of cash that she placed in his hand.

"Want to come in for a glass of tea?"

"I'd like to, Ginny Sue, but I really need to get going down the road. I'll do my best to go see Isaac. Next time we'll have a good long visit."

Ginny Sue. I had never heard anyone call her that before. It was a little girl's name. Nothing about Virginia had ever seemed like a little girl to me.

He leaned in awkwardly to hug her, but she backed away and offered a handshake instead. He shrugged his shoulders.

Virginia stood in the doorway, slowly rocking back and forth as Willy walked away without looking back. She was a girl again, wounded and abandoned. The hand that held the doorknob began to shake. Her body testified to her long-buried pain. I thought of how Daddy described the first time he saw her in an old dime store in Middlesboro. He said her eyes drew him in like a great sad moon.

I crept to my room, fighting against the small sliver of pity that nearly moved me to tears before I remembered how wretched she had been to me, throwing my journal in the ashes.

That night I listened as she told Daddy about Willy's visit and what he had said about Granny Bee. She would leave in the morning.

* * *

Early the next morning I heard Virginia's heels clicking down the hallway. Some instinct told me to say something nice to her before she left, but I carefully told my instinct to go suck eggs.

Aunt June came out of the kitchen. "You almost ready to go, Virginia?"

"Yes. Just about."

June turned and looked at me, probably feeling the tension between me and Virginia. "Grace, why don't you go have some breakfast with your daddy; then we'll get ready to go see Isaac. Sound good?"

"Yes." I gladly went into the kitchen, relieved that Virginia was leaving.

* * *

Isaac was awake when we got to the hospital. Sitting up in bed eating a little breakfast.

The smell of the hospital always filled me with dread. It was sickness and death and strong cleaning solutions. No matter how many times I walked into this place, I never got used to it.

"Hey, Grace." His voice was low and raspy.

"Hey, little brother."

His tangle of white sheets made a bland backdrop for his blue pajamas. I looked past him to the blaring sunshine and the small patch of grass below the window.

Aunt June chimed in, a little cheerier than what was believable. "Hello, my little man. I'm so glad to see you."

He tried to muster a smile back, offering a small, "Me too."

"How is breakfast?" June asked.

"It's okay." He hadn't eaten much. "What have y'all been up to?"

June produced a brown bag and pulled from it a loaf. "We brought you your favorite bread—banana bread with walnuts and chocolate chips."

"Thank you. Sure looks better than this," he said, pointing toward the dreary bowl of oatmeal.

He nibbled on the bread while June and I told him about the herbs in the garden and Rojo trying to eat corn right off the ears that we had laid on the ground. We left out everything about the cross burning and the huge fight between Virginia and me. He told us that he had heard about Rank Gunner and the fire.

"Isn't it a sad story all the way around?" June said this as she lifted his breakfast tray off his lap and set it on the table beside the bed.

I wanted desperately to change the subject and bury all the terrible feelings it gave me.

"I think Cooter's gonna come visit you today!" June said.

Isaac smiled. "I like Cooter. He makes me laugh."

I spoke up. "He ain't bad to look at either." I lifted my eyebrows, and Isaac laughed. It was so good to hear him laugh. He still seemed tired. He mostly listened and didn't talk as much as he had the week before.

June went to the bathroom, and that's when I thought to ask him about the note I'd left him awhile back.

"So, did you get my note I left with the music box?"

He nodded. "Yep. I got it." He stretched to yawn.

"Well, what do you think about Rojo and other animals being in heaven?"

Isaac reached over and touched the music box, then opened it and let the tune play for a minute. "Well, in the Bible, Isaiah says, 'The wolf also shall dwell with the lamb, the leopard shall lie down with the young goat, the calf and the young lion and the fatling together; and a little child shall lead them.' I would think if they let in lions, wolves, leopards, and lambs, it makes sense to assume that Rojo and other animals are getting in too." He paused for a moment. "Especially birds. Can you imagine heaven without birds?"

I nodded to let him know I agreed, but all this talk of heaven seemed too real.

Then Isaac asked, "Have you seen your *boyfriend* anymore?"

I punched him softly on the arm through the blankets. "Cut it out!"

I did tell him that I had heard from Aunt June, who heard from the waitress Lila, that Sister Mary, Brother Joseph, and Golden the Miracle Boy had come into the Green Parrot a few days ago. I was glad to hear they hadn't left town yet. I thought maybe I would call and risk Sister Mary answering the phone.

June came back in and entertained us with a story from her younger days. After a while, Isaac started yawning.

"Isaac, I'm thinking we should let you rest since Cooter plans to come visit after lunch."

Isaac nodded. I didn't want to go.

As we left the hospital, my thoughts went to Golden. I wondered how long before they left for the next town. Would I ever see him again?

When I got home, I went looking for the little scrap of paper I'd hidden inside my Bible in case Virginia got any more ideas about snooping through my things. When June went to visit the elderly woman next door, I ran to the kitchen to dial the number, watching out the window for June. If Sister Mary answered, I would hang up.

"Hello?" It was him.

"Hey. It's me, Grace . . ."

"Hey . . ." He spoke in a low whisper. "I only have a minute to talk. Is everything okay? Is Isaac okay?"

I watched the yard next door for June's return. "He's okay. I was just wanting to . . . talk."

He answered quickly, his voice a bit muffled. "Can you meet?"

"I'm not sure . . ."

"Look, there's something I need to tell you. It's about Isaac."

"Okay. I'll come."

"How about tomorrow at ten, by the creek where we met before?" It sounded like he'd cupped his hand over the mouthpiece.

"I'll do my best. Are you okay?"

There was silence on his end. "I'll see you tomorrow, Grace."

I couldn't sleep that night. I lay there thinking about everything. About Isaac, about Golden, about Miss Adams moving, about the fire and Rank Gunner. About Virginia. So much sadness and hurt. I felt the weight of it. My shoulders ached and my heart felt raw and open. Isaac had looked tired today. Maybe he just needed more rest.

33

BIRDS

I got up after I heard Rojo's daily alarm to the neighborhood. I wanted to talk to Daddy before he left for work. I smelled coffee, feeling strangely comforted by the sound of the percolator gurgling. Then I smelled biscuits and bacon. I used the bathroom and made my way quietly down the hallway to the kitchen.

Daddy was leaning back against the counter, staring out the window over the sink at the sunrise, which was filling the pale-blue sky with shards of orange and pink.

He turned his head, surprised to see me. "Grace, why are you awake?"

I walked over to him. "Are you okay, Daddy?"

He drew in a long breath and opened his arms to me, and I leaned into him. "I watch the sunrise every morning. Whatever else is wrong, the sun still rises. There is something comforting in that steadiness. Knowing that you can count on it."

I nodded, feeling his rough hands on my bare arms. "I have something to tell you . . . or to ask you, I mean."

His eyes were watery and tired. He seemed to brace himself for whatever bombshell I was about to drop.

"I want to go talk to Golden."

His shoulders relaxed. "And what do you want to talk about?"

"I . . . thought I could tell him how Isaac is doing."

"Let's sit down, Grace. I'll pour some coffee. Would you like some juice?"

I nodded. He went to the cupboard and pulled out a small jelly jar, then grabbed the orange juice out of the icebox.

"It's just that I thought he might be worried if he heard about the cross burnings."

He nodded and set my juice in front of me as well as a plate of biscuits with bacon. He poured his coffee and pulled out the chair to sit across from me.

"He also said there was something he needed to tell me . . . about Isaac."

His eyebrows gathered in the middle. He inhaled deeply, then asked, "When and where?"

I swallowed my juice along with the lump in my throat and told him where Golden had suggested. He blew on his coffee and took a small sip. "Does his mother know?"

"I'm not sure. I think they would have to give him a ride to town unless he found another way." I reached for a biscuit.

"I met him that day when he brought you in to the hospital. I don't think he would harm you. He did, after all, save your life." He smiled and took a bite of the biscuit. "How do you plan to get there?"

"I could ride my bike, but it has a flat."

He took another drink from his coffee, looked up at me. He must have seen how nervous I was because he reached his hand across the table and squeezed my hand.

"I could fix that for you." He smiled, and I noticed that the lines around his eyes creased a little deeper than they used to. "I want to thank you for asking me, Grace. I think it shows maturity and maybe that you have learned from . . . what has happened in the past few weeks."

I nodded slowly, scared to say anything.

"I'll make a deal with you."

I tried to suppress the sudden excitement I felt.

"June told me last night she was gonna suggest you help out with the church yard sale. It's in town, right by where you're gonna be. If you are willing to help out with the yard sale, then I guess it's fine for you to meet with him to talk before."

I got up and bolted around the table and hugged him. "Thank you, Daddy, for . . . trusting me."

"Trust is a fragile thing, Grace. But I want to give you a chance. Everyone deserves a second chance."

June stumbled into the kitchen, her hair sticking out in several directions. "Well, Gracie! What are you doing up with the chickens?"

Daddy and I laughed. It felt good. Daddy explained everything to June as he finished his biscuit and then went to the shed and grabbed a few tools to fix my flat tire before he left for the shop.

After he was gone, June looked at me and said, "Gracie, I think you just learned something valuable about life."

"What is that?" I asked her.

"It pays to tell the truth."

I helped June clean up the breakfast dishes. Then we stood over the patch of wildflowers that were sprouting up so quickly you could almost sit and watch them growing. After that we hung the wash out on the line. Sissy wasn't in her room when I peeked inside her open door. She always managed to be absent when there were chores to do. I had already worked up a sweat. I decided to take a shower, then pulled on a blue cotton sundress June had bought for me at Nickel Thrift.

June came into the house and spied me in my room. "Well, don't you look like an angel."

I blushed. "Thanks, June."

June walked me to my bike. "Lordy, can you ride that bike with a dress on?"

"I'll manage." I gave her a quick kiss on the cheek, the weight I'd been carrying around my shoulders gone. *"The truth will set you free"* was a perfect description of how I felt.

I biked away, trying to keep my dress from flying up. On the sidewalk up ahead, I saw Sissy and Tina walking toward me, smoking. As I got closer, I could see they had their swimsuits on underneath their shorts and tank tops. It was scorching hot already.

Sissy called out, "Hey, where are you going?"

Knowing that I could simply tell the truth was invigorating.

"I'm going to meet a friend in town; then I'm helping with the church yard sale."

Sissy took a deep drag off her cigarette and smiled a little. "Who is this *friend*?"

"Um . . . Golden."

"Oooh. Not just any friend, a *boy* friend. Is that why you're wearing a dress?"

She and her friend chuckled. I was annoyed.

She blew out a question and a small cough with her next puff. "Does Daddy know about this?"

"Yes, actually, he does."

She looked at me with surprise and sucked on her cigarette, releasing perfect rings from her lips. "Well, well, well . . . he's letting the baby bird take a little trip out of the nest."

I rolled my eyes and took off pedaling, leaving her in the middle of another drag on her cigarette.

"Be careful!"

I looked back. The beast had a heart. I nodded my agreement to do so and pedaled away.

As I rounded the corner to town, I came within a whisker of running my bike into Cordelia and Emoline Bluin. They were coming out of Handy Hardware with signs that read *Yard Sale*.

"Grace! Watch out! You nearly ran us over!" Cordelia looked around me. "Is your mother with you?"

"N-n-no," I stuttered. "She's with Isaac at the hospital."

"I thought you might be coming to help with the yard sale. We are definitely needing help."

"Yes, ma'am, I am coming over to help in just a little while. I have to meet up with a friend first."

Emoline drilled her eyes into mine, as if to say, *"What friend?"*

The sweat was running down my face as I squinted against the glaring sun. I was saved by the mayor's wife, who called to Cordelia from across the street. She forgot all about me and started waving and walking toward her.

"Come on with those signs!" she yelled back.

Emoline held my stare, then turned away from me without saying a single word. The large, round clock outside the diner read a few minutes past ten. I made sure no one was looking and pushed the bike behind Handy Hardware. I almost didn't care if Emoline thought I was lying. I knew I was telling the truth. I wasn't keen on Cordelia or Emoline knowing that I was meeting up with Golden. I had no desire to be in the center of their gossip wheel.

I parked my bike in the bushes, smoothed down my hair, and inspected the light-blue sundress. I crept back through the trees to the creek. He stood at the edge of the water, glistening in the sun, his golden curls clinging to the sweat on his face.

I was shaking as I inched carefully closer to him. "Hi."

He turned, kind of jolted. "I didn't hear you behind me."

I stopped beside him. As he turned to me, I was taken off guard by how tender his eyes were.

"I'm glad you were able to make it. I wasn't sure . . ."

"Yeah, me too. I asked my dad . . . He said since you saved my life, he figured it was okay." We laughed a little and it relieved some of the tension. "Oh, and I'm gonna help with the church yard sale after this."

He nodded. "Paying penance?"

"Something like that. Since we're on the subject, I guess I never got to thank you . . . for saving me."

"Well, it was the least I could do." His smile made my head swim. "Did you get into trouble?"

"I had to do extra chores and no TV for a week. Did you get into trouble?"

A moment of anger flashed across his face; then he looked straight into my eyes and said, "Would it sound strange if I told you it was worth it?"

He picked up a rock and threw it into the creek, then faced me again. "I heard about the cross burning. I was worried about you . . . and your family."

I closed my eyes, trying to block out the memory of Virginia throwing my journal into the fire. "Did you hear about what happened with Hutch and Rank Gunner?"

"Yep. Cooter told me. Sounds like poetic justice."

I told him about what Isaac did during the checkers game at Handy Hardware, which made him laugh.

"Isaac is pretty much the coolest kid ever. As for Hutch and what he did—to love your enemy, much less save his life . . . that's something not many people ever learn to do."

I nodded and thought of Hutch's picking up Isaac's little boot.

Golden turned back to the water. "Before you got here, I was thinking about birds. Do you like birds, Grace?"

"Yes, I love birds."

"They seem so sure of themselves. Their calling in life is simple—to gather food, build a nest, care for their young, to fly, sing. So wonderfully simple."

We both looked up into the trees as a blue jay flew from branch to branch.

"If I were a bird, I'd wake up and say, where do I feel like flying today? But I'm here with you. I guess I couldn't do that if I were a bird."

The warmth in his smile made my entire body melt. "But you're the Golden-Haired Miracle Boy. Isn't healing your calling? People come from all around to see you."

"People want to see a circus act. That's all I am really—a carnival attraction."

"You're not that to everyone . . . not to me. Isaac is getting a little better. That has to be, at least in part, because of you."

"Grace, there are many things I'm unsure about in life, but one thing I am sure about is that I have nothing to do with Isaac getting better."

"Why would you say that?"

He started walking along the creek and I followed. Words came easier as we walked.

"Mary and Joseph aren't my parents."

"What? But I thought—"

"They came into the orphanage in Montgomery, Alabama, when I was about seven years old. They told me at the orphanage that my real mom was only sixteen when she had me. Her parents made her give me up. Sometimes I dream about her and wonder if she's got yellow hair like me, and if she ever wonders where I am."

He looked so alone; I reached my hand to touch his arm. I felt a spark of electricity between us.

"Sister Mary said when she saw me standing in a row next to the other kids, it was like my golden curls were a halo around my head. On Saturdays at the orphanage they dressed us all in our nicest clothes and lined us all up for prospective parents. They would parade through to pick the one they liked. The ladies always wanted a baby so they could raise it—like it was really theirs—but Mary said I was the perfect age for them to start 'training' me. Mary said she knew my golden curls were their ticket out of the poorhouse. That's why they changed my name to Golden. They made up that story about me speaking in tongues in the bathtub. They taught me how to preach and how to say fancy prayers to impress the grown-ups."

I grabbed his arm to stop him from walking. "Wait, so you're saying none of the stories about you being some sort of spiritual prodigy are true? You and Mary and Joseph were just putting on an act?"

"Yes. That is exactly what I'm saying."

"But you lied! You all lied to me and to my family and to Isaac! Do you know how much I risked for you to come *heal* Isaac?"

He took a deep breath, feeling the shame I showered on him; then I thought of the lies I'd told and realized how easy it was to lie once you started. I felt like a hypocrite, but I was angry.

Angry that it had all been a lie and yet . . . maybe Isaac was getting better.

"I'm sorry, Grace. Everything you said is true. Every bit of it, and you have every right to be angry. I wanted to tell you in person. I was so relieved when you called."

"So what else did they do? To turn you into Golden the Miracle Boy?"

Anger flashed on his face again but also sorrow. We started to walk again down the bank.

"They would stand me in a corner for hours, making me memorize Bible verses and whole books of the Bible, teaching me how to talk 'preacher talk' and 'speak in tongues.' The whole time they held a belt or a big switch in their hands. They called it their 'God rod.' Sister Mary loved to quote, 'Spare the rod, spoil the child.' If I messed up, Sister Mary never spared the rod. When I refused to do what they asked, I paid a price . . . but I think it was my way of preserving something of myself, who I was before they came along."

I felt nervous to ask but wanted to know. "How do they punish you now?"

"Oh, lots of things." He closed his eyes. "They might hold the end of their lit cigarette on my arms and legs and say, 'You got the devil in you, boy. Maybe we oughta give you a taste of some fire.'"

I saw a small round scar on his arm. I put my finger on it. He pulled up his sleeve and showed me another round scar and one beside it, still red and just starting to scab over.

"Golden, that's awful . . . But if you would have just told someone . . ."

"My name isn't Golden. My name is Daniel Dunnigan. Their names aren't real either. They're actually Hilda and Bobby Owens from a podunk town called Sandy Rock, Alabama."

"How do you know that?"

"I found their old driver's licenses in a hidden pocket of a suitcase. They don't even know that I know."

"I won't tell anyone," I said, managing to look him in the eyes. "But why didn't you ever tell anyone?"

"Grace, you don't know what it's like being an orphan. You have no rights. No one ever believes kids over grown-ups. Especially Mary. She can lie better than just about anyone I've ever seen. She's good at charming people or intimidating them. If I had told and no one believed me, I would have been worse off than before. They would have locked me in my room all day and not let me have any freedom. Not that I have much."

We finally sat down on the creek bank. The story seemed to drain the energy out of him.

I sat close beside him and allowed my arm to brush against his. My spine tingled.

He was silent for a moment before he continued. "When you came to the trailer that day, it was the first time anyone looked at me like I was just another kid and not some miracle freak. Mary and Joseph don't let me have friends, but I . . . I guess I wished that we could be friends."

"We are friends. You saved me from a copperhead." We laughed.

"Only problem is, Mary and Joseph want to head out to Kansas to hook up with a tent revival circuit they heard about. That's how it always is. They stay in a town for two or three months, draining as much money from people as they can, and then they move on. They always leave a trail of success stories behind. They made up one here about some cripple boy up in the hills that I healed. No one will ever come forward to say it didn't happen 'cause they always make it so you don't have enough information to go looking to see whether it's true or not. They always make sure someone overhears them talking about it. Like at the Green Parrot. They told that waitress in there, and the next thing you know, it's all over town."

The muscles in his jaw flexed. He picked up a good-size rock and threw it as hard as he could, making a big splash in the water. I picked up my own rock and threw it, trying to make firm skips across the water, feeling my anger boil over at Mary and Joseph—or Hilda and Bobby. Whoever they were, they had no trouble lying, cheating, or destroying someone's faith for a few bucks.

"It's all made-up. It never happened. It's nothing but a lie," he said as his voice got loud and angry and he slammed his fist into the creek bank.

There was a question I was so afraid to ask but I had to know.

"Was your prayer for Isaac like that?"

He let out a deep breath before he answered. "It was when I started. I said the same prayers and Scriptures that I've memorized. Sister Mary was the one who always made a big deal about saying that everyone had to have enough faith for the healing. That way, when no one gets better, the blame is on the family for not believing, and Miracle Boy, Mary, and Joseph are off the hook."

I sat there, not wanting to believe that there were such wicked people in the world.

He went on. "I was just doing the same old lines that I did everywhere I go. Grace, I remember standing there looking at Isaac in his bed. He looked so thin and sick. I felt like throwing up. I knew what I was doing was wrong, taking so much money. I felt this hate for God and wondered, if He is real, why would He let this go on? Why would He let Mary and Joseph rob you people? When folks come to us, they are so desperate and get their hopes up for a miracle. But they don't know that the Miracle Boy is nothing but a fake. 'All in the name of Jesus. Amen! Hallelujah!'"

His words were bitter and mocking. It made me afraid that God might strike him dead. But He didn't. We just kept sitting in the sun, listening to the water trickle by.

"When I was praying for Isaac, he asked me to lean down so he could whisper something in my ear."

"I remember that. I wondered what he said. I even asked Isaac, but he wouldn't tell me."

Golden leaned his head sideways. "To tell you the truth, I was kind of afraid to get too close to him and even more afraid of what he was gonna say. I thought for sure he was gonna tell everyone that I was a big fake, but he ended up trying to give me what I couldn't give to him."

"What's that?"

"Healing. It was as if he could see into my soul."

"What did he say?"

He thought a moment, as if weighing whether or not he was gonna tell me. "'I have heard your prayer, I have seen your tears; surely I will heal you.'"

"What? What is that?"

He shot back, "Grace, don't you read your Bible?" I gave him a mean look in return.

He nudged me a little on the arm to let me know he was just joking, then he took a deep breath. "It's from Second Kings, when God told King Hezekiah He would heal him and give him fifteen more years to live."

"But why would Isaac say that?"

He shrugged.

"What do you think he was telling you? What did it mean?"

"I have lain awake at night wondering that. Maybe that I was gonna get a second chance, or that he knows what has been going on at home. But when he whispered in my ear, it was as if some sort of electricity ran through my body. I felt something like what people might say was a healing touch." Golden's eyes filled up with tears. "I had never felt anything like that before."

"What about in revivals when you actually have healed people? What about that?"

"It's called 'the placebo effect'. The person believes they are healed and something in their body begins to heal them. Or sometimes, it is a short burst of adrenaline that allows them to walk or stand when they couldn't before. The adrenaline doesn't last, though. When you see evangelists in these famous healing crusades, there is an art and a science to what they do. Smoke and mirrors. It's just sad that so many people get scammed."

I cut him off. "Are you saying you don't believe in healing? Ever? I mean, I've heard stories in church about people being healed back in the Bible days."

"Well, I can't speak to what did or didn't happen two thousand years ago, but I have heard a few stories of an actual miracle happening on the circuit. Freaked the evangelist out, big-time! But I've never seen it happen." His eyes were locked with mine. Then he stood and we started walking again.

"Let's go a little deeper into the woods."

I followed him. Even after he'd just told me that he and his band of robbers had ripped us off for a hundred dollars, I followed him.

We made our way through the forest until we came to a clearing where the creek opened up into a wide spot. I stumbled on a loose rock and he caught me in his arms before I could fall. We were so close I could barely breathe.

We went on a little farther. We got to a shallow spot and decided to take off our shoes and slipped our bare feet into the cold, clear water. He removed his shirt and lay right down in the river and let the water wash over him in the shallow bed of creek rocks and sand.

271

His skin was like his name, glistening in the sun. His body was lean and strong, and I tried to stop myself from staring, but it seemed he had me in a sort of trance. My heart was beating fast, and even though I still felt betrayed by him, I felt drawn in, like the pull of a beautiful dream. Could I trust him? He had lied to me, after all.

"Lay down in the water, Grace. It's as hot as hell and the water feels like heaven."

He stretched his arms out in the water. I thought my heart might beat out of my chest. I didn't lie down; instead, I knelt beside him, feeling the hem of my dress getting soaked. I was glad we were in moving water where there would be no snakes. They liked the deep, still water with tall grass. I splashed him, letting out a little of my anger at him. He smiled, unfazed by it, and looked up at the sky, which was a clear reflection in his eyes. We sat in the silence for a few minutes.

"Grace, if you could do anything, go anyplace, be anybody, do anything, what would it be?"

I caught a small crawdad behind its pincers the way Isaac and I had done so many times and thought about whether I wanted to answer. I looked up, meeting his eyes for just a moment.

"I would save Isaac."

"I know you would, Grace. You have done nothing since I met you but try to do just that. But think about yourself. Something just for you. What would you do just for you?"

I took a deep breath. "I'm not sure I know what else I really want, other than . . ." Then I stopped. I wasn't ready to answer that question.

"I can tell you what I want. I want to run away. Be free of Mary and Joseph. Maybe even go find my real mother."

"I don't blame you. My mother . . . I think she hates me. Sometimes I wonder if she wishes it were me instead of Isaac that was sick."

"What would make you think that?"

"She's said things, done things. Something happened a long time ago that she's never forgiven me for. So now, she keeps trying to hurt me, to get me back. But it just makes it worse. There are some things you do to people that they can never get over."

He sat up, looking into my eyes, my heart pounding harder the closer he came to me. The water streamed down his bare back. When he raised himself up, his face was suddenly very close to mine. He reached his hand to stroke the side of my face and leaned in, touching his warm lips to mine, flooding my body with warmth and light. He tilted his head against mine and we sat there in the breathless moment, our kiss igniting a fire inside of me. He gazed into my eyes. I couldn't speak. He kissed me once more, then stood and reached a hand down to help me up. I floated out of the water and wanted more than anything to stay there in that moment with him.

We walked hand in hand back to my bike. He watched me as I left.

I was in a daze. Trying to process everything. As soon as I came around to the street, I saw Emoline staring straight at me. She saw me come from behind the store? Had she spied? I pedaled across the street and rode past her, ignoring her stares and going straight up to Cordelia.

"Hi, Miss Cordelia. I'm here to help."

"Good. How about you come with me. I have just the job for you."

She took me to a large bag of clothing that needed to be hung on a clothesline. I got busy, replaying all the things Golden—or Daniel . . . he was Daniel—had told me and thinking of his face and the warmth of his lips on mine.

"I saw you two."

I turned around, my face a question mark, and saw Emoline.

"I saw you and that boy."

I felt enough rage to rip the lips off her face for spying on us and at the same time was terrified that she might tell someone.

"What did you see?" My words came out through my gritted teeth.

"I saw plenty, enough to get you into trouble. Getting your dress all wet."

"You were spying!" I wanted to tear into her.

"Don't worry, your secret's safe with me, but I might need a favor. And I figure I'll keep your secret if you keep mine."

My face was hot, embarrassed and angry. I hated being at her mercy.

"I take your silence as an agreement."

The deal with the devil was made. I had no idea what I had agreed to. Even though Daddy had given me permission to talk to Golden, I didn't think he would be okay with me kissing him. I couldn't win. Blasted Emoline. Her day was coming.

* * *

I lay in my bed that night replaying the moment that Golden kissed me. Feeling the warmth of the sun and the chill of the water. What happened now? Would he move away? I closed my eyes and dreamed.

We were both dressed in long, flowing clothes in colors of bright greens and blues. We ran to the train tracks just as the train pulled out. We started running behind it until we caught hold of the railing in the back. As we held on, our legs were floating behind us, and then we had wings, and then we were birds. But it started to rain, and his wings melted away in the rain and he lost his grip on the railing and dropped onto the tracks. I saw his blood trailing behind the train. I let go and flew back to him. He lay there in his blood-soaked shirt and his beautiful blond curls. I held his lifeless body and wept. Then a small hand appeared on my arm. It was a little girl. She looked like the pictures I'd seen of Virginia as a child.

She wore a cotton dress that was the color of the clouds in the sky. She put both hands on my face and said, "I'm okay, Grace."

I woke up drenched in sweat, with my heart hammering out of my chest.

Josie.

34

JOSIE

I was about to turn nine. Isaac was almost three. He imitated just about everything I did and would do anything I asked him to.

I could still hear Virginia in the kitchen talking on the phone with Cordelia Bluin, the newly elected president of the Southern Women's Society. Virginia was using her most charming voice as she tried to wheedle an invitation to a meeting. There were steps a person had to take to even be considered for membership. The first step was to be invited to a meeting as a silent observer. Virginia had been hoping for an invitation from Cordelia.

It seemed like she and Cordelia would never tire of talking. I was bored.

It had started to rain an hour earlier. There was the most wonderful rain puddle forming in our driveway where the dirt and gravel had eroded, leaving a shallow hole the size of a washtub. I could think of nothing I wanted to do more than jump in the puddle and dance around, letting the rain fall into my mouth. Virginia had made us come in when the rain started and forbid me and Isaac from going back outside to keep us from "trampling mud in everywhere."

But maybe, if I asked really nice, she might change her mind. I crept into the kitchen and tugged at her baby-blue shift dress, which hung loose like a small tent over her belly that carried our new baby brother or sister, due in only a few weeks. She gave me a stern look for interrupting and pointed for me to leave the kitchen.

I only wanted to ask her, to make sure it was okay if I went outside, so I tugged on her skirt again. "Mama, can I . . . ?"

She clamped her hand over the phone and hissed, "Out, Grace," then sent me out of the kitchen. She had been talking to Cordelia for so long. All I wanted was to ask a simple question.

It was at this moment the thought came to mind. I would slip out and be back in the house by the time Virginia was off the phone. It was no fun to play in the rain alone, though. Sissy was at drill team practice, but Isaac was in his room coloring. I went into his room.

"Isaac," I whispered. "Wanna come play in the rain?"

He nodded with enthusiasm. I told him we had to be very quiet.

We slipped out the back door and made our way around the front to the giant puddle. There was Isaac's red ball in the yard that we had been playing with before the rain started. I stood in the middle of the puddle with my eyes closed. I started to spin around, letting the rain drop into my mouth and onto my eyelids. When I opened my eyes, I saw the red ball picked up by a gust of wind and Isaac, without thinking, run after it. As soon as he got to it, he kicked it, and it lifted into the air toward the street. Isaac was squealing with delight and I was yelling his name when Virginia came racing past me. She'd seen what I had not—the car making its way down our street with the windshield wipers doing a poor job. She got to Isaac just in time to grab him from the oncoming car, but as she lifted him, she lost her balance and fell backward on the wet sidewalk with Isaac on top of her.

I ran to her side. "Mama, Mama, are you okay?"

She didn't say anything. She had hit her head. Her eyes were closed as if she was sleeping.

That's when I saw it. A red stream running down the street beneath her.

I took Isaac by the hand and ran to call Daddy at work.

Dr. Clarke looked after Virginia. She had a concussion, but the bigger concern was the baby. They did their best, but the trauma from the fall caused internal hemorrhaging. They did surgery to deliver the baby and repair any internal damage caused to Virginia. Virginia was okay. The baby did not make it.

One of the nurses handed Daddy a small white basket with a lid. I imagined it was like the one Moses had been put in when he was just a baby. They told Daddy if he and the family would like to see the baby, they would close off the small room they called the chapel for us.

The basket was lined with a white cotton blanket. The baby was a girl, so tiny with dark hair and a sweet face. One of the other nurses had gone out and bought a little white nightgown that must have been made for a doll—it flowed down over her tiny body. We sat there, staring at the little baby, so perfect, she seemed to be made of stone. It was the first time I ever saw my father cry. The tears rolled down his cheeks, belying the brave face he tried to show to me, Isaac, and Sissy.

Virginia woke later that night. Daddy told her what had happened and, when she was ready, brought in the little white basket so Virginia could see the baby. Virginia lay there in the hospital bed and cried for days. She wasn't able to come with us when we drove up to the family burial place to bury little Josie, named after Grandma Josie.

Even now, with Isaac so sick, nothing would ever feel as terrible as the moment when Daddy brought me to see Virginia that first time in the hospital.

"Virginia, there's someone here to see you."

She rolled over and looked at me. I stepped closer to her. Her hair hadn't been washed in days and her face was gaunt and pale. Her eyes looked dead. She simply rolled back over in bed and said nothing.

Daddy reached down for my hand and led me out of the hospital. There was a bench under the large shade tree, so we walked over to it and sat down. My lip was quivering and my eyes were filling with hot tears.

I sat wishing it had been me who died instead of that little baby. It was my fault. I should have waited till Virginia was off the phone. I had to say it out loud or I thought I might die.

"It's my fault. It was all my fault. I'm why little Josie is dead."

Daddy pulled me against his chest, then took my face in his hands. "Gracie, you are a child. You were doing exactly what children are supposed to do. It was a terrible accident that no one ever meant to happen. Your mama is grieving. She is on so much medication, she doesn't know how to respond right now. Just give her time."

I buried my face in his shoulder and wished I could just stay with him forever. He folded his arms around me as if he was trying to shield me from all the pain. But it didn't work. I felt every ounce of my mother's pain and the blame she knew was mine. I couldn't see my way out of it, and I figured she couldn't either.

Isaac was the one who brought her back around. Daddy brought Isaac to the hospital, and he crawled up onto the bed with Virginia. She held him for a few moments, and then he looked up at her.

"It's okay, Mama. Jesus has little Josie now."

Something broke inside Virginia. It was the beginning of her coming back to us. She even gave me a hug when she came home from the hospital, but her eyes told me something different.

Now, as I lay there thinking of Isaac and little baby Josie, it was hard to think what our family had done to deserve another dose of such misery. Maybe God knew something I didn't. Or maybe God was cruel and removed from our pain. I crawled out of bed, felt the cold, hard wood against my knees, and leaned up against my bed, folding my hands the way they teach you to in Sunday school. My throat was thick with tears. I could barely speak through my sobs.

"Oh, God. Can't You help Isaac? I'm sorry for the lies and for baby Josie. I'm sorry for all the ways I have disappointed You, but don't hold that against Isaac. He hasn't done anything wrong. Can't You see? He's someone who deserves to be saved. Do something."

I couldn't bring myself to say amen.

35

TWISTING

The next morning the phone rang. June answered.

"Grace, phone for you!"

The voice on the other end was barely above a whisper. "Are you ready to keep your end of the deal?"

My stomach churned. I had no choice.

"Yes." I kept my answer short in case June was listening from the living room.

"I need you to get me to the hospital."

"What?"

"The hospital."

"But how? And . . . why?"

"I need to see Isaac."

"Why?"

"I don't have to explain myself to you. I just need you to hold up your end of the deal, or else . . . your folks find out about your little rendezvous."

"Okay. When?"

"Today. It has to be today."

We hung up and I wondered how in the world it was even possible. There was only one person I could ask. Doing so would put me deeper into her clutches, but I had no choice.

I knocked on her door.

"Go away!"

Since her fight with Virginia, Sissy had been sowing fewer wild oats, but her mood was terrible. She slept in even later than usual, and if she ate, I never saw her.

I cracked open the door. Her room was a mess. Clothes were piled up. Gum wrappers and empty bottles of Coke. If June saw this room, she would break out in hives.

"What do you want?" Sissy covered her head with her pillow. She was not a morning person.

"I need a favor."

She sat up in bed, her blonde bob somehow looking perfect. "Oh, do you now? And what makes you think I would want to help you?"

"Nothing, except, if you do, I'll give you my allowance for the next three weeks."

"That's peanuts. You're gonna have to do better than that."

"I'll clean your room. I'll do your laundry. Whatever you need."

She eyed me, considering this. "Now we're getting warm."

She took a piece of gum from her nightstand, unwrapped it, and started to chew. "So what do I have to do?"

I came inside the room and closed the door behind me, then told her what Emoline had asked.

"That's strange. Why would that little prima donna want to have anything to do with Isaac?"

"I have no idea, but I think he kind of had a crush on her before all of this."

"Really? Poor Isaac. Even as smart as he is, he isn't immune to the allure of a hot babe."

"Gross."

She threw a pillow at me and we laughed for a moment.

Finally Sissy said, "I won't go over to her house to pick her up, but if you can get her here, I'll drive her over. *But*, in exchange you have to clean my room for the next month and give me your allowance for the next two months."

"What? That's crazy! And besides, don't you want to see Taylor?" I let my voice singsong his name, thinking that would sweeten the deal.

Her face dropped and she turned hot and angry. "Grace, you'll have to find someone else to take you. Those are my conditions, take it or leave it!"

I waited until June had gone outside to hang a basket of laundry. I watched as Rojo trailed behind her like a puppy and called Emoline back.

I told her Sissy's condition.

"Let me think . . ." She held her hand over the phone. I could just make out the muffled sound of an argument. "I can get a ride. I'll be there in an hour."

I ran to tell Sissy, who slowly rolled out of bed, taking her time getting ready.

I told June that Sissy and I were gonna take Emoline for a burger at Tri-Way, which was close to the hospital. If we stopped by Tri-Way, then it wouldn't really be a lie, right? I rationalized with my guilty conscience.

June squeezed her eyebrows together, looking confused. "Grace, isn't Emoline the one that's always been so mean to you? Didn't she humiliate you and burn your bangs? Why are you wanting to take her for burgers?"

Why had I not seen this question coming? I stalled, staring at the linoleum on the kitchen floor.

"Thing is, June, Isaac kind of made friends with her at church. We worked together the other day when I helped out with the church yard sale . . . I guess I'm trying to give her another chance."

"That's mighty Christian of you. I'm not always so good at trusting people who've burned me, but good for you, Gracie!" She patted me on the back and left the kitchen.

Whew!

An hour later Taylor pulled into our driveway. Sissy looked out the window and ran to her room, almost panicked, which made no sense, but I had no time to worry about that now.

I met Emoline out on the porch and filled her in on the plan so our stories would match up for June. Before we left, June asked Sissy to be extra careful driving with "precious cargo."

"Oh, I'll be careful, all right." No doubt, she didn't want to do anything to mess up the deal I'd made with her.

We drove in awkward silence to Middlesboro. I was relieved when we were finally there. We found a parking space behind some bushes—hidden, but with a view of the hospital door so we could see Virginia leave for her afternoon nap.

At one o'clock, she walked out, heading in the opposite direction of us, toward Beauty. A minute later, Dr. Oden walked out as well, following her. They stood by her car talking. They seemed to be arguing. Sissy and I exchanged glances.

Emoline looked from Sissy to me. "Why is my uncle talking to your mom?"

I had totally forgotten that Dr. Oden was her uncle. "He's one of Isaac's doctors. It must be about Isaac."

Her face showed the cynicism we were both feeling. "You guys have to get me in there before my uncle comes back in the hospital."

Sissy stayed in the car. Emoline and I crept along the bushes to the hospital entrance. I introduced her to the nurses, who knew me very well by now, and explained that she was a friend of Isaac's. The nurses took us both to scrub up and put on our masks and gloves. Emoline seemed terrified.

"Don't worry. They just do this to protect Isaac from our germs, not us from his."

"Oooh," she said, relieved.

I led her down the hallway to Isaac's room. When we got to the door, she stopped and turned to me.

"I want to go in alone."

"What? But—"

"This is none of your business. It's between me and Isaac."

I reluctantly returned to the waiting room, deflated and curious out of my mind about why it was so important for her to see Isaac. Dr. Oden stormed through the hospital doors and across the lobby, never even looking up. He was angry, but why would he be upset with Virginia? I sat there reading the same old magazines they'd had out all summer. I walked over and turned on the TV, but all that was on was a soap opera, so I turned it off again.

Finally Emoline came out. She had been crying.

"Let's go."

"I was gonna go see Isaac."

"He fell asleep just as we finished talking. Besides, I have to get out of here before my uncle sees me and blabs to my mother."

Sissy was snoozing when we came back. Emoline begged and tried to talk Sissy into taking her home. "No one will be there. My mother went to visit family and Taylor is at football practice."

Sissy seemed to relax knowing this. I guessed she wanted to avoid any further drama with Virginia.

We first ran by Tri-Way to order burgers and shakes, so I could honestly tell Aunt June about our visit. Emoline was very ladylike and didn't spill mayo on herself the way I did.

She broke the silence. "Did you hear they fired Miss Adams?"

I nodded.

"Serves her right."

"What do you mean? She's the best teacher I've ever had."

"She's a liberal. Probably a Communist. That's what my daddy says."

I was reminded of her ridiculous comments in class to Miss Adams and could not stay silent. "Because she thinks Negroes have rights?"

"Because she's trying to brainwash all of us to her way of thinking." Emoline took a long swig from her shake, seeming very confident in her position.

I kept going. "Her way of thinking happens to represent the law, Emoline."

Sissy laughed at this but remained silent, as if enjoying the match between us.

Emoline's turn. "I don't care. I'm not about to be forced to do something I don't believe is right. It isn't American."

Any warmth that had been building between us disappeared, and I remembered why I'd never liked her. I thought about my burned and chopped bangs and what June had said earlier.

Sissy watched me, smiling, knowing that I was close to tearing into Emoline. "Emoline," she said, "time to get you home."

She turned on the radio to ease the tension. "Twistin' the Night Away" came on, and Emoline screamed from the back seat, "I love this song! Turn it up!"

We sang along with the windows down as we sipped the last of our shakes. The radio man came on and said, "And that was 'Twistin' by the golden tones of Sam Cooke."

"His voice is dreamy!" Emoline erupted.

We arrived at her house, just three girls out for lunch and a drive on a beautiful day, barely August, but you could smell the end of summer in sight. Early fall flowers were budding on the sides of houses. Crape myrtle trees drooped with the heavy arms of a weary mother, scattering tiny baby petals onto the ground below.

Emoline waved from the porch before going inside. It was almost as if we were friends. But I knew better. I had a month of cleaning Sissy's pigsty room and two months without an allowance ahead of me, and I still didn't know why it was so important for Emoline to see Isaac. But I would find a way to get to the bottom of it. Emoline would not have the last say on anything concerning my brother.

36
THE WINDOW

Saturday afternoon, June and I went back to the hospital for a visit. Isaac's color was pale. June and Virginia and I sat in the room while he slept. His breathing was shallow, which was strange. I wanted to ask him about Emoline, but he had been sleeping since we arrived, and I couldn't ask him while June and Virginia were here anyway.

Virginia seemed distracted and edgy. June asked carefully, "Virginia, could I get you something to drink? A Tab maybe?"

"No." As she shook her head, Dr. Oden came into the room and checked Isaac's heart and his blood pressure. I wondered why he was there instead of Dr. Clarke. I couldn't stop thinking of him and Virginia arguing in the hospital parking lot. I hated the thought of him caring for Isaac.

He turned to Virginia. "Could I speak to you for a minute in the hallway?"

There weren't enough chairs, so I sat on the floor with my back against the wall. I could only make out the movement of the tops of their heads through the window in the door. June squinted, watching them.

When Virginia came back in, June asked, "Is everything okay?"

She returned to her chair, biting her nails, something she never did. She stared out the window as if she hadn't heard June's question.

Virginia looked as though she were staring into a black hole. June, who was normally a chatterbox, was silent, watching Virginia. I heard the *drip, drip* of the tubes running fluids into Isaac. A buzzing fly against the window.

The sudden rasp of Isaac's small voice took the air out of the room. "Is Grace here? Grace?"

"I'm here." I stood and took his hand, which seemed half the size of mine. "Hey, little brother."

"Hey."

Then he looked around, seeing June and Virginia. "Could I talk to Grace alone?"

Virginia came to his bedside. "Isaac, is there something you need? Can I do anything for you? Is something . . . wrong?"

What a strange question. There was so much wrong. Everything was wrong.

"Don't worry, Mama. I just want me and Grace to have a few minutes alone."

June spoke up to help. "Virginia, why don't we go get something to drink. I'm feeling kind of thirsty. Let's let the kids talk."

Virginia reluctantly and wordlessly followed June out of the room.

I sat down in the chair beside him. "What is it, Isaac?"

He reached out for me to take his hand again. "I was just dreaming about us. We were running down the sidewalk with the wagon and Rojo."

"I know Rojo can't wait for you to come home and do that again."

He looked over at me, a small smile on his tiny lips that seemed to be disappearing into his face. "I'm not sure that's gonna happen, Grace."

"What do you mean? Of course it's gonna happen. You're getting better every day."

He squeezed my hand. "I don't think so."

"Isaac, you've been doing so much better. You're just having a bad day; that's all."

He shook his head and looked at me without a word.

Tears streamed from the corners of my eyes.

"Remember the girl I used to play with down the hall?"

I nodded, my words lodged in my throat.

"I dreamed a few nights ago that I saw a man in a white gown. He was glowing. He came in and stood by my bedside and said, 'Isaac, tonight, I am going to take your friend home, but don't worry about her. She's going with me to a wonderful place. I will take care of her.'

"The next morning when I asked the nurses if I could go see her, they told me she had died in the middle of the night."

I couldn't speak.

"I'm not afraid, Grace, and I don't want you to be either."

"Afraid of what?"

"Maybe he's coming for me too. But I'm not afraid to go with him."

I leaned over, unable to stop my tears as I put my head against his.

"It's okay, Grace. It's okay."

"Knock, knock" came June's voice from the doorway. Virginia came into the room right behind her.

Isaac spoke just above a whisper, his energy seeping out of him. "Mama, could you do something for me?"

Virginia walked to him. "Anything."

He looked up at her with his brown eyes that seemed twice their size in his thin face. "Could you bring Rojo to visit me? I sure would love to see that ole rooster."

I shot a look to Aunt June, who looked at Virginia.

"I know he'd love to see you too, Isaac."

He yawned and drifted back to sleep before Virginia could even answer.

We all stood there staring at each other, knowing we couldn't refuse him but wondering how we could ever pull that off, since the hospital would never let a rooster in. Then, as if a light bulb had switched on, Virginia looked past me, toward the window, and said, "I have an idea."

* * *

June dropped me off at the shop to tell Daddy about our plan. He finished up with his customer quickly and we headed home in his little blue Bug.

As we pulled into the hospital parking lot, we looked up and saw dark clouds in the sky, hanging heavy, and the wind started picking up. Sissy had come with us. She ran into the hospital to tell Virginia and June that we were there with Isaac's visitor. We stood outside and tried to find Isaac's window.

It was a small hospital with only two floors. Luckily, Isaac was on the first floor. We had marked his window with his Navajo cross sitting up against the windowsill. It was about seven feet from the ground.

Daddy and I took Rojo out of the box. He was strangely calm. I held Rojo and Daddy bent down on his knees so I could climb up on his shoulders, then he stepped onto the large footstool made of two-by-fours he had nailed together in his shop to make sure we could reach the window. I lifted Rojo up so that Isaac could see him.

It all looked so different from this angle. The room, Isaac, and Virginia in her pale-blue dress that she always looked so pretty in. I watched Isaac's lips moving as he looked up at us, and I wondered what he was saying.

I wanted to freeze this picture in my mind. To make it last as long as I could.

Then it started to rain.

37

THE FLOOD

The devil was beating his wife again. That's what folks in the South said when the sun poked out from the clouds while it rained.

It had been raining steady for three days. The brief moment of sunshine didn't last long. The gloom returned and it rained even harder. The folks who lived close to the river had been told to clear out until the rain stopped and the waters went down. We heard stories about Danny Chumley rowing his fishing boat to his mama's house so he could paddle her to higher ground. While he was paddling down the street, he caught sight of an old woman clinging to her pots and pans on the roof of her trailer, afraid to move. Danny talked her down, and she got into the boat with him and his mama.

The hospital sat up on higher ground, but they decided to move all the patients to the second floor just in case. Isaac and Mama were safe from the floodwaters there.

The water started to rise in the little creek behind our house that was usually a dry bed in the summer. When it got about halfway to the oak tree in the backyard, Daddy said for each of us to pack up what we could. We put our clothes and family pictures and valuables in garbage bags to carry up to the attic, and then we packed a small grocery bag each with a change of clothes and our toothbrushes, as well as some blankets and pillows, to take to the church. When we were all packed, we made a run for the car.

We looked up, and there on top of the roof was Rojo. He was standing by the weather vane, with his metal likeness swinging back and forth from the force of the wind.

"Oh, Daddy! What are we gonna do? We can't leave him there."

Daddy stood in the rain, staring up at him. "Wait in the car."

Me, Sissy, and Aunt June got in, sliding our soaking wet bodies across June's slippery bench seat. Daddy had left his blue Bug at the hospital for Mama in case she needed it. Beauty had plenty of room. The windows fogged up with the humidity and the rain blurred our view. We rubbed a plate-size circle in the windshield and saw Daddy come out of the shed with a ladder, prop it against the side of the house, and climb up. He tried sweet-talking Rojo over to him first, but that didn't work. Finally, Daddy walked out on the roof and picked him up, easing himself back down onto the ladder with one hand and making his way to the ground that was now one big mud puddle.

He ran back to the shed with Rojo in his arms and came out with the same brown box we had used to take Rojo to the hospital. Rojo sat in the back seat in the box, between me and Sissy.

Daddy drove over to his friend Jerry Lawler's house, which was high enough and far enough away from the river that they were safe from the flood.

Daddy ran up with the box. I decided to go with him, running through the rain to the covering of their small porch. Jerry opened the door before we even knocked. Daddy asked Jerry if Rojo could stay in his barn for a few days.

"Why, sure. You leave him with us. John, y'all are sure welcome to stay too," Jerry said, motioning for him to come inside.

Daddy thanked him and told him we were planning to head to the church. It had been a while since I'd been to Jerry and Ann's house. It was real cozy, but tiny. The house had belonged to Jerry's grandmother. It was what the old timers called a "granny house" 'cause it was just big enough for one or two people to live in. Too small for all of us.

"Let me and Ann know if y'all need anything."

We backed out of the driveway, with a picture of Jerry holding Rojo in his arms.

As we drove toward town, an old lady looked out at us from her front porch, sweeping the water away from her top step with a broom, as if that broom or anything could hold back the water that was gushing over the bank of the Cumberland River.

When we drove across the bridge, it gave us a good view of the river and Main Street, which ran almost in a straight line downhill from the bridge. The river looked like chocolate milk, but it smelled like fish. The water was up to the sidewalk in front of the Green Parrot Café and the Nickel Thrift. All of the businesses had sandbagged their storefronts to keep the floodwaters out.

Floating along every now and then were chunks of coal. You could see a black film covering just about everything in sight. A red swing set floated by us with a little baby swing and teeter-totter bobbing up and down with the current. I wondered about the swing set and if that family had left their home in time.

I wondered where Miss Adams was. I hoped she was okay. Daddy said he had heard that folks living by the river woke straight up in their beds to water almost up to the mattress and had to climb up on the roof and wait to be rescued. The fire trucks came for some. Rowboats for others.

Our church sat at the top of a long, steep driveway that was near impossible to drive up in the winter when the roads were slick but was a safe place from the flood. They had opened the doors to those who had nowhere else to go. Some folks had relatives in the hills and went to stay with them till the waters went down. Going to the hills was something no one in our family wanted to do. We all agreed: the church was the best option we had.

When we got to the parking lot, it was packed with old Ford trucks, a few Studebakers, and Chevys. Daddy even saw the VW belonging to Miss Rachel, Old Man Drake's daughter. It was hard finding a place to park, but Daddy found a spot for ole Beauty under the trees, off the blacktop in the back. When we came to the front door, there was a handwritten sign that read *First Church of Christ Flood Relief Center*.

Lugging our blankets and our bags, the first person we saw when we came in the door was Cordelia Bluin holding a clipboard with an in-charge smile. I wondered if their house was in the flood zone. If so, Emoline's princess bedroom might get filled with muddy water like everybody else's.

Emoline walked up beside her mother, holding her own clipboard and looking at me as if we were little more than strangers.

Cordelia spoke in a very official-sounding voice. "Hello and welcome to the flood relief center. I will need to sign y'all in so we can keep a count of how many occupants are here. The fire code will only allow so many. When we are full, no more will be allowed to enter."

I was holding a pillow and a small bag that, in addition to my toothbrush and a change of clothes, held my journal from Miss Adams and the little figurines Mr. Farris made that I had bought from Nickel Thrift.

Daddy, Aunt June, and Sissy were holding blankets and pillows in their arms, along with a few things of their own. As I shifted my pillow to the other hand, my bag dropped to the floor and out came my journal.

"Oh, Grace, is that your diary?" Emoline smirked. "Have you been writing about a boy in there?"

She was reminding me that she had the power to bury me.

Aunt June broke in behind us. "Cordelia, seriously? We are exhausted!

We just want a dry place to get some rest. Just write us down on your clipboard and let us go on in, please?"

Cordelia let out a huff. "Go on through, I guess. Emoline, darlin', the Sunday school rooms and the nursery are all full, so you can take them to the sanctuary."

We followed Emoline, who told us, "Don't go there" and "The bathrooms are right down this hallway" as if we hadn't been to this church a hundred times. Give somebody a little power and it all goes to their head.

We got to the sanctuary, where a few other folks were setting up camp. Coming up the aisle in our direction was Taylor Bluin.

Sissy caught her breath, stopped cold, and grabbed my wrist. "Grace, stop. We have to turn around."

I turned and looked at her.

"Please, I . . . I have to go to the bathroom. Come on!"

Without telling Daddy and June where we were going, we practically ran down the hallway to the bathroom.

"Sissy, what is going on?"

When we got to the bathroom, Sissy pulled me inside and then checked every stall to make sure no one else was in there. When she was sure we were alone, she locked the door behind us and slid down to the floor.

I sat beside her. "Sissy, are you okay?"

"I think I'm gonna be sick."

"What is going on? You can tell me. I won't tell Virginia. I won't tell anyone."

She looked at me, weighing the decision very carefully. "You swear you won't tell anyone? Not a single soul? I'll be able to tell if you do 'cause you can't lie for squat."

I wasn't sure I agreed with her, with all the practice I'd been getting these days. "I won't. I promise."

She took a deep breath, then blurted out, "Me and Taylor—we . . . did it."

"Did what?"

"You know . . . we had sex."

I tried to wrap my head around it, forcing out the pictures in my mind that made me want to puke.

She kept going. "I thought I was pregnant because my period was late. I was so scared. Thank God I started! But I've just felt awful since . . . that night."

"What night?"

"The night that I came home with bruises and scratches, dummy."

"Wait, he did that?"

Sissy paused before she went on. "Grace, I don't want to get into any details . . . but the worst part is after doing what we did, now he looks at me smugly and keeps walking. Like now that he got what he was after, he has no use for me." She burst into tears.

"That jerk!" I felt so angry.

"Maybe I got what I deserved, putting myself in that situation with him. I guess I just thought him being a preacher's son and all . . ."

"You don't deserve being treated like that— no girl does!" My blood boiled at the thought of him doing what he had done and then ignoring her.

"Let's face it, Grace." She blew her nose before she went on. "You are the good girl in the family."

I felt a sudden rush of sisterly affection. "You're not a bad girl, Sissy. You've got a good heart and you're smart."

I ran out of other good things to say. Sissy reached over and put an arm on my shoulder. Then she stood up and ran into the stall and got more toilet paper for both of us and sat back down beside me.

"Thanks, Gracie." She blew her nose and wiped the tears from her eyes. I did the same. Then we sat there on the cold linoleum floor. The tears felt good. There was so much we'd been holding in.

"Thank you for the nice things you said. I have been pretty crummy to you." Her hands were shaking as she peeled off the skin from the corner of the nail she'd been chewing on. "But I am afraid I know myself a little better than you do."

"Maybe you don't see what I see?"

A knock, then Daddy's voice. "Girls, are you okay?"

We looked at each other with panic. Sissy spoke up. "Yeah, Daddy. We'll be out in just a minute!"

When we walked back to the sanctuary, Sissy never lifted her eyes from the carpet.

I wanted to kick in Taylor's perfect teeth. I sat down beside Sissy and blocked her view of him.

Daddy leaned over to us when we sat down. I was sure he could see we'd been crying.

"Is everything all right?"

Sissy said, "Just girl stuff and hormones . . ."

"Ahhh," Daddy said with a knowing look on his face, which implied that he understood and would ask no further questions. We settled into our pew, laying out our pillows and blankets before all the space was taken.

After us, lots of folks started arriving. Every few minutes, we would look up and see someone we knew walk in. First Mr. and Mrs. Farris arrived. Mrs. Farris's wig was a little crooked from the wind and rain, but her lips were as red as ever. Mr. Farris held a little brown paper sack with some wood sticking out of the top. They ended up camping out a few pews over from us.

Mr. Farris came to our pew to say hello.

"Mr. Farris, look what I brought along." I opened my brown bag and pulled out my collection of his little figurines. "I couldn't leave these behind."

"Grace, you make an old man feel proud."

"I also gave Isaac the music box so that he could listen to it in the hospital."

"You're a good sister. Such a thoughtful girl."

He patted me on the shoulder. I reached up and took his hand. Daddy was watching this and smiled but said nothing.

"Will Isaac be safe from the flood? Is your mama with him?"

"Yes, she is there with him. They moved him up to the second floor just in case the flooding reached the hospital."

While I talked to Mr. Farris, Aunt June went over and chatted with Mrs. Farris, whose cold heart seemed to be melting a little. After a while, I got restless and went exploring. I heard someone call my name from the nursery. It was Old Man Drake's daughter, Miss Rachel, rocking in one of the chairs with her baby in her arms.

"Hey, Grace, is the rest of your family here too?"

"Daddy and Sissy are out in the sanctuary."

I knelt down to see her little baby. I loved all her curly black hair and bright-green eyes.

"What's her name?"

"Emma."

I scrunched down close to her. "It's nice to meet you, little Emma."

"I'm sorry about your brother, Grace. I've been praying for him."

I nodded, suddenly wanting to escape the subject. "See you around."

I kept exploring to see who else I might know. When I was heading back to the sanctuary, I saw Cooter and his mother, Miss Leola, come in the front door. Cooter was holding his mama's things. Cordelia was giving them the once-over.

I ran up to them. "Miss Cordelia, can I show them where to go?"

"Yes, just one minute, Grace." Cordelia pursed her lips. "Now, Cooter, I want to make sure you aren't bringing any of the devil's brew into the house of God."

Cooter's mama locked eyes on Cordelia like she could mow her down with one punch. I was hoping she would. I wondered if maybe she'd packed her cast-iron skillet.

Cooter never flinched. "No, ma'am."

Cordelia blinked hard, maybe wondering if she should press him a little harder; then she looked at Cooter's mama and thought better. "All right, then, if you're sure. Grace, you can show them where they can go."

I wondered if Cooter's mama had a thought of where Cordelia could go as well.

I led Cooter by the hand to a pew right by ours. He smiled at June and then at Sissy and let his eyes linger there. Sissy was lying down on the pew under a blanket.

Cooter asked me in a whisper, "Is Sissy okay?"

"Yeah. She's just tired." Every time I could, I would give Taylor the stink eye.

Cooter, his mama, Daddy, and Aunt June settled into a conversation about the flood and all the stories they had heard. The rain had continued since we got to the church. Miss Leola said she heard someone say that they'd seen a whole house floating down the river. About that time, we all heard raised voices in the back of the sanctuary and looked back to see Sister Mary, Brother Joseph, and Golden. I went weak in the knees seeing him again. I prayed Emoline would keep her word. I broke out into a cold sweat.

They had brought too many things. I could see Cordelia arguing with Mary about taking up too much space. Cordelia was no match. In the end, Sister Mary was victorious, and Cordelia smiled at Golden while she personally showed him to an empty pew.

Cooter leaned over to me. "I finally figured out why you were out at the trailer park that first time. Before you got bit by the copperhead, I heard that Golden had come to the hospital to pray for Isaac."

"How'd you find that out?"

"Grace, Jubilee is a small town. Besides, those three showing up at the hospital is kind of big news." He smiled. "Your face lit up the moment you saw him."

"What? No!" I felt my face go red.

"I mean, he did save your life and all . . . You could do worse."

I punched him in the arm again and he broke out in a wide grin.

Golden saw me and Cooter and waved at us. Sister Mary grabbed hold of his arm and made sure he sat in the pew with them, a few rows behind us.

"I guess he can't come say hello?" I asked Cooter.

He shook his head. "No, they won't let him. They hardly ever let him out of their sight and certainly don't like him talking with other folks."

I nodded to let him know I understood. It was clear now why they kept him so close, under their thumb. I loathed Sister Mary for what she had done. Not only to him but to us. Cheating and deceiving our family and so many others. If June had any idea, she would go over there and lay her out cold on the baby-blue carpet.

I heard the sanctuary door open again and again with more folks seeking shelter. We were lost in conversations until a loud gasp echoed from the door and we all turned to see why. The gasp had come from Cordelia's mouth, which was gaping open. There, behind Miss Adams, were about twenty brown faces.

Cordelia looked at Miss Adams in complete shock and finally found her words. "I don't know what you are thinking. The answer, Miss Adams, is absolutely not. You all need to just go on out of here. You got your own church to go to. We don't want no trouble. You got your own people. You go there. There isn't enough room for you here!"

Miss Adams's voice, usually sure and confident, came out shaken. "Our church is flooded, Mrs. Bluin. We have nowhere else to go."

Daddy stood, and so did Cooter and Mr. Farris. They walked together toward Miss Adams while Cordelia was ranting.

Daddy spoke calm and clear but strong enough that everybody heard. "'For I was hungry and you gave Me no food; I was thirsty, and you gave Me no drink; I was a stranger and you did not take Me in, naked and you did not clothe Me, sick and in prison and you did not visit Me.' Then they also will answer Him, saying, 'Lord, when did we see You hungry or thirsty or a stranger or naked or sick or in prison, and did not minister to You?' Then He will answer them, saying, 'Assuredly, I say to you, inasmuch as you did not do it to one of the least of these, you did not do it to Me.'"

Cordelia stood with her clipboard. I wondered where Pastor Bluin was. Maybe hiding under a hood somewhere. Without asking her permission, Cooter, Daddy, and Mr. Farris led the whole group into the sanctuary.

Like the Red Sea parting, people moved and made room for them. Hutch and Miss Hazel, Yully and her little brother, Eustace, were there too. Then I saw Miss Pearl, and her face dropped when she saw me. Theo was walking beside her, holding her by her arm. Reverend Hezekiah was behind them both.

I walked to Miss Pearl and felt compelled to do something. So I did. I stepped close and put my arms around her and hugged her.

Theo, the reverend, and everyone around us seemed shocked. I guess I was too. But Miss Pearl seemed to understand immediately what I was trying to say with my hug.

"Oh, child, I'm so sorry. I love you too." She hugged me back.

Reverend Hezekiah came around and said, "Miss Grace, it sure is good to see you. Mama Pearl thinks the world of you."

I was filled with an overwhelming love inside of me for these people who seemed to like me for exactly who I was. Maybe even . . . love me.

Daddy sat with Reverend Hezekiah, Hutch, and Miss Hazel. I was aching to go talk with Golden, but I knew Sister Mary would never allow it, so I sat with Yully and Theo. I decided to go say hello to Miss Adams, who was sitting two pews up from us. A leather duffel bag sat beside her. I noticed a large photo album sticking out of the top.

"Miss Adams, what do you have in that book?" I pointed to it, hoping to see photos of her childhood.

"I decided to grab a few things that are very special to me, just in case the floodwaters did their worst. This has all my favorite trips I've taken, as well as some special drawings and poems."

She lifted it out of her bag and a loose piece of paper fell to the floor.

I picked it up.

"Yully's little brother, Eustace, drew this for me."

I took it in my hands, careful not to wrinkle the edges. There were two stick people—one, a woman with skin like peaches, yellow hair, and a green dress. The other, a small boy, whose lines were dark brown. The lady in the picture was surely Miss Adams, with her cornflower-blue eyes. The little brown-lined boy was missing an arm, an eye, and a leg. I traced the outline of his drawing with my finger, unable to speak.

What Miss Adams couldn't have known, and what I'd never realized until that moment, was that I had felt the same way my whole life. Broken. Incomplete.

June came over and talked with Miss Adams too, and plenty of white people gawked as we sat talking on the same pews.

The flood had done something that the sun never could. It had brought us together. We all needed shelter to feel protected. A safe place in the storm—despite our differences or even our secrets. We all needed a place on higher ground. It was a good feeling, but the feeling wouldn't last.

Lights appeared on the church wall and a siren came blaring up to the door.

Surely Cordelia had not called the sheriff to have Hutch and the rest of Miss Adams's neighbors removed.

We all looked back, feeling a bit of pain at what could be coming.

The door opened, and Sheriff Teeton burst through with rain pouring like a waterfall over the brim of his hat. His eyes widened as he saw all the folks from Miss Adams's neighborhood there. I waited for him to say something about it, but instead he walked a straight line to our row and spoke directly to Daddy. "I'm sorry, John. Y'all better come with me. It's Isaac."

It was like the moment the snake bit me and the world slowed down. Everything came in waves. As we went down the aisle to the door, Golden reached his hand out and touched my arm. Our eyes locked for a moment, and then I ran out behind the sheriff. Ran out into the rain and the flood and the moment of my life that would change everything else.

38
ANGELS

Dr. Clarke met us in the hallway. He looked exhausted as he cleaned his glasses on his white coat. He put his hand on both Daddy's and my shoulders. We stood there drenched in rain and dread.

"He is losing strength. His blood pressure is low."

Daddy spoke up. "But he was doing better. You yourself said that he might even get to come home soon if he kept improving."

"I was encouraged by his appetite and white blood cell count. I did a new test a few hours ago." He shook his head. "The results are not good. Sometimes, a patient will start to improve and give signs of remission. We were hoping for that. I'm not sure why he improved and then suddenly, a nosedive." He shook his head again. "I'm so sorry."

Daddy knew what he was saying. We all did. But it didn't seem real. I wanted nothing more in the world than for Isaac to sit up in bed and be his old self. To show Dr. Clarke he was wrong, that he could still get better. I wanted to clap my hands over my ears when he said, "I think you should prepare yourself."

Fighting back a catch in his throat, he didn't say any more, but turned and led us to Isaac's room on the second floor. I was shaking so bad my sides hurt.

I prayed each step of the way. I tried to have faith to believe that when we opened the door, there would be something wonderful waiting for us. A wonderful surprise. A miracle. Isaac sitting up in bed.

But when the door opened, he was swallowed up in the mound of white sheets, his skin almost blue. I closed my eyes and imagined being anywhere else but here.

We stood around Isaac's bed, listening to him breathe. Virginia and Daddy sat in the chairs on each side of his bed. There were no masks now to hide our tear-streaked faces. I should have known there was something wrong when Dr. Clarke hadn't asked us to scrub or put on masks and gloves.

It was dark out. The rain had slowed and was tapping softly against the window. It was even peaceful, except for the sounds of the machines beeping, telling us whether Isaac's heart was going too slow or too fast, if he was breathing enough or not. He was sleeping. I wanted to wake him, to open his eyes. He had been doing better. How were we here? Wasn't our faith strong enough for just one miracle? Even if Golden didn't believe—we did!

Virginia put her hand on Isaac's arm. "Isaac, we are here. We're all here."

Isaac opened his eyes and looked at all of us and slowly said, "Hey" in a voice like crepe paper. "Y'all ain't wearing masks anymore." He looked over at me and our eyes met. I knew he understood why.

Daddy answered. "That's right, Son. No masks today." He stroked Isaac's tiny fingers in the palm of his hand. A look passed between Isaac and Daddy. He knew what we knew now.

As I looked at Daddy sitting there in his blue mechanic shirt, with Isaac in his striped pajamas, I saw how much they looked alike. Their eyes had that same sweet sadness. The same braveness.

Sissy came around. "Hey, little brother."

"Hey, Sis." Isaac looked up and smiled at Aunt June. "You gave me the best gift in the whole world when you gave me that ole rooster, June." Aunt June came around to hold his fragile face in her broad, strong hands. "Isaac, you are the best gift Rojo ever had, and me too for that matter." She leaned in a little closer. "I remember him scratching his way out of that little box and how he walked right over to you, like you were old friends."

Isaac's eyes were looking out the window like he was seeing it all for the first time again. "Where is Rojo?"

Daddy ran his hands up and down Isaac's arm, as if trying to warm him. "He is safe and dry at Mr. Jerry's house. Mr. Jerry is looking after him till it stops raining and we can all go home."

"That's nice of Mr. Jerry. You tell him I said thank you. Would you, Daddy?"

Daddy stroked the tiny veins on his wrist. "Yes, Son. I will tell him."

Isaac seemed to get tired, so we waited in the quiet. I wanted to pray but I had no words.

I wanted to run over there and jerk those machines off him. I wanted to scoop him up in my arms and take him to our backyard and push him on that tire swing on our oak tree. Wishing that could fix everything.

It was all happening too fast. What about all our prayers? Where had they gone? Washed down the river with that swing set, I guess. The current was too strong—as much as we all wanted to fight it, we were being swept away.

We heard the door open behind us. It was Reverend Hezekiah. He walked over to us and nodded at Isaac for a moment.

"Hello, Isaac."

"Hey, Reverend." Daddy turned to Virginia and explained that Reverend Hezekiah had been coming to see Isaac from time to time.

"I just want to be here for y'all if you need me. I will be over here by the window."

Isaac seemed so calm. Reverend Hezekiah brought a sense of peace into the room with him. Like everything was gonna be all right.

Suddenly, Isaac, who had seemed to doze off, opened his eyes and looked right at Virginia.

"Mama, do you see them?"

Virginia looked at him, but he was looking off behind her now.

He asked again, a little excited, "Mama, do you see them . . . and . . . do you hear the music?"

When she answered, her voice was strangely serene. "I can't see them, baby, but I can feel them."

"Aren't they beautiful?"

"Yes. So beautiful." Virginia's tears were falling onto the white sheets.

When I looked at Isaac, I saw a glow radiating from his face, as if he had suddenly been filled with the light from another world. He looked past me, past all of us to something else.

Someone else.

Without speaking of it, we all knew what he and Virginia were talking about.

Angels.

I thought of the man in his dream. Was he here?

I felt enveloped in warmth. The way you feel on Christmas when the house is cozy and everything in the world seems right.

I felt more alive than ever and had an overwhelming desire to run in some open field and fill my lungs with air. I was at once aware of the gift of my life and saddened at the moments I had taken it for granted. My body had cold chills all over, and I felt a rush of hope and love and a strange joy mixed in with all the sadness. Sharing the same air, brushing up against the realm of angels.

"Grace, can you come closer?"

I walked over beside him. Daddy stood and had me sit opposite Virginia. Isaac reached over and took my hand in one of his and then brought it together with Virginia's hand that he was holding and placed both of our hands over his heart.

Virginia and I looked at each other, wordless. Our hands were tangled with Isaac's tiny hands, over his small chest. He looked at us both, then lifted his face. His eyes seem to shimmer, fully alive. A smile crossed his lips.

Then he closed his eyes and let out a long breath. And fell asleep.

The sleep of angels.

The rain kept tapping against the windows, but the machines quieted. No beeping. Just the rain speaking his name with each drop.

I looked up at the silver clock on the wall: 10:39. I wanted to turn back the clock, have more time.

Virginia started to hum something while she rocked back and forth, stroking the back of Isaac's hand and touching his face every now and then. It was a song I knew, the song that she sang to all of us when we were little. At once, I knew that it was the song Isaac had been singing that night I held up Rojo in the window when his lips were moving but I couldn't hear. The same song the silver music box played.

Her voice was clear and peaceful, even while her body wept.

"You are my sunshine, my only sunshine. You make me happy when skies are gray. You'll never know, dear, how much I love you. Please don't take my sunshine away."

Reverend Hezekiah stood quietly beside the window but stepped forward to catch Virginia when she stood, then fainted. There was a single river of grief flowing out of us. I wasn't sure if God or a dam in the world could hold it all in.

39

THE YEAR
OF JUBILEE

The sun came out two mornings later, and the water started to drain away from Jubilee. What was left was a mess. Families spent hours clearing away all their goods that had been ruined and hauling them to the dump. Mattresses, couches, and clothes dried in the sun as people tried to salvage anything they could.

When we returned home, you could see that the water had risen to the top of the porch steps, but no further. The grass in the front yard sunk down like a wet carpet as we walked through it, but we were grateful that everything inside the house was dry. The backyard had standing water, as did the shed. Daddy had hung the red wagon up on a nail on the wall of the shed, along with his important tools. Daddy assured us, "It will only take a few days for the water to drain away." We opened all the doors and windows to air out the musty smell of river, mud, and the overwhelming sorrow that not even the brightest sunlight could cure.

Virginia and Daddy had to wade through the mud and muck in town to pick out a casket for Isaac. The caskets were up high on shelves and had been saved from the floodwaters, but the floors were like every other business's near the river—covered with bits of coal and trash from a muddy riverbed. They chose a small, sky-blue coffin with a dark-blue liner. They dressed Isaac in his cowboy boots and his favorite striped pants and a blue cowboy shirt to match his boots.

Daddy plucked off one of Rojo's feathers and put it in the casket with him. He thought Isaac would have liked that.

Isaac's funeral fell on his eighth birthday, less than a week after he died. The weight of the sadness and the irony of it was too heavy to hold. So we just let it lie there, trying not to think of the party we might have had. Like a balloon floating away into the air, we could not recapture what had been lost.

Daddy surprised everyone by asking both Cooter and Reverend Hezekiah to officiate the service. Reverend Hezekiah had offered for us to have the funeral at Bethlehem Church of the Redeemer. Daddy gladly accepted, though some thought it unwise, given all the cross burnings. Isaac's death was like a great wrecking ball that destroyed any of Daddy's fear of the Klan. Rank Gunner was still in the hospital recovering, which had taken some wind out of the Klan's sails. But to Daddy, it didn't matter. Cooter and Reverend Hezekiah had ministered to Isaac in his time of greatest need. Pastor Bluin never came to the hospital once to see him.

When Saturday came, you would have never known the church had been flooded. They must have worked hard to sweep out the water and debris. It was a beautiful little chapel with hardwood floors and windows that opened up to a cross breeze that brought whiffs of jasmine and mint growing somewhere close by.

They placed Isaac's coffin at the front of the church. The tradition in the South was always open casket, but Daddy asked Virginia if we could place a photo of Isaac in a frame up front and close the casket. She agreed, and we were all grateful. The photograph was from the summer before, and it was just like Isaac's dream: smiling and holding the handle of his red Radio Flyer, pulling Rojo in the back.

There were so many beautiful flowers, the smell filled the air with an added sweetness. A lady we'd heard sing with the choir that Sunday a couple summers ago when we sat outside in the car now sang an old song called "Swing Low, Sweet Chariot," strong and sad.

Hutch and Miss Hazel, Eustace, Yully, Theo, and Miss Pearl sat in the pew behind us. In that congregation of beautiful brown, there were also white faces—folks who had decided to take their chances with the Klan. Behind our family's pew, we saw Cooter in a white dress shirt and tie with his mother, who wore a black cotton dress. Miss Adams wore a navy suit with a pillbox hat with netting over her eyes, which seemed bloodshot from crying. Mr. Farris wore a short-sleeved button-down shirt and a tie. He kept wiping his forehead with his small handkerchief. Jerry and Ann looked sadder than anyone except us. Jerry wore his brown overalls with a plaid shirt and a tie. Ann wore a simple brown dress. For as long as I could remember I had never seen Jerry wear anything but overalls. Sheriff Teeton wore his uniform, and Dr. Clarke wore a gray suit, and he and Miss Adams looked like movie stars sitting close together. There was no sign of Cordelia or Pastor Bluin. And no one from the hills had come down.

Cooter spoke first. He told us stories Isaac had told him when he visited in the hospital. How Isaac loved pulling his wagon with Rojo riding in the back. How Isaac dreamed of deep-sea diving and exploring the universe, maybe being an astronaut someday. We sat there lost in the stories. For a few moments, Isaac was alive to us again. We remembered him as he was when life was shining out of him.

After Cooter, Reverend Hezekiah stepped up to the pulpit. He was silent a moment, looking at us. You could see the reflection of our pain staring back from his eyes. When he finally spoke, his voice gave both comfort and strength, putting me in mind of Dr. King.

"Our dear friends, we grieve with you today. Oh, how our hearts are heavy for your loss. Is there any loss so great as the loss of a child? No . . . I don't think so. Why, when we ask and we pray and we believe, yet the answer rings so loud in our ears that we can scarcely bear the word: *No*. That was the answer. We asked and God said no."

His words felt like a hammer to my heart, but the truth of it brought its own kind of comfort.

"We might even feel angry at God. *Why, God? Why would You allow this?* How can a loving God allow a child to suffer? How do we bear it and go on?

"There are some questions that I believe may remain unanswered. At least for a time. And so we wait for the answer. And the waiting is hard.

"I am reminded of the woman with the issue of blood. Twelve years she waited. Went to all those doctors. Did God know that she had been battling this? Of course He did. He knew her story. He knows your story too."

"Yes, He does!" came a raspy voice in the back of the church.

"Why didn't He heal her on day one? Year one? Why wait twelve years? That's a long time."

"Yes, Lord," agreed the church organist.

"Count up those days. That is 4,380 days to suffer like she did. That's a lot of hours of suffering."

"Yes, it is! Too long!" came a voice from the row beside us.

Reverend Hezekiah nodded in agreement. "But she waited, and it wasn't till that moment when she reached out to touch the hem of His garment. What a moment that must have been!

"But why wait that long? The answer, I believe, involves God's understanding of how suffering changes us. Our suffering breaks down walls. Reaches us where deep calls to deep. Sometimes, God's plan for our story, our journey to Him, involves suffering. A part of her suffering was shame. We all carry some sort of shame. It's one of the devil's favorite weapons against us."

"Yes, Lawd," a lady in a large-brimmed hat called out from the row beside us. She looked at me and smiled with tears spilling out of her eyes.

It was as if we were connected in that moment. Like she understood the shame I carried.

"Isaac was special. I had several visits with him while he was in the hospital. We had good talks. It was obvious what an intelligent boy he was. A child genius. In his young life, he had already read more books than most of us grown-ups here today. But he not only had knowledge; he had wisdom. He told me about his family, how much he loved you all."

Reverend Hezekiah looked at us as if it was just our family he was speaking to. "He told me how he loved teasing his two sisters. His special friendship with you, Grace. How he looked up to you, Sissy. He was the kind of boy every father would love to have as a son. He loved his bosom friend, Rojo, a red rooster he received from his beloved aunt June as an Easter present. And, oh, how he loved his mama and daddy, and he knew your deep love for him.

"He told me that he talked to Jesus at night when he would wake up in his hospital bed and everything was dark and quiet. He would ask Jesus when He was coming for him. It was as if he knew.

"But in the midst of his suffering, he had peace. Peace like nothing I have ever witnessed in my years as a pastor.

"Before I said goodbye to him on one of our last visits, we prayed together. We prayed for God's will to be done. Isaac prayed for each of his family members, for Brother Cooter, and he even prayed for Rojo. His thoughts were for others and not for himself. He transcended his suffering and reached for something greater: Instead of seeking the healing, he sought the Healer. That's hard to do when you're suffering.

"Dr. King has often preached on the value of unjust suffering. So many of you here have suffered unjustly. But the times we are living in—there is a wind of change coming, and many don't want to see it. But it's coming!"

This brought an eruption from the crowd. "Yes, it is! Let it come, Lawd!" Miss Adams swished a paper fan that looked like a peacock tail, nodding with a look of intensity on her face as she grasped Dr. Clarke's arm.

"But there is a purpose, and in some cases, justice, that our suffering brings to light. God is working, and His timing is always perfect. My God is an on-time God!"

"Come on! Preach!" called an excited man from the back.

"In Leviticus 25:8-10 it says to count seven times seven years to mark a period of forty-nine years. Then have the trumpet sound. 'And you shall consecrate the fiftieth year, and proclaim liberty throughout all the land to all its inhabitants. It shall be a Jubilee for you.' They called it the 'Year of Jubilee.'

"In the Year of Jubilee, all debts were forgiven. Whatever a man owed, the debt was marked 'paid in full.' The chains of the captives were broken. There was a mercy that trumped everything else. Like a clean slate to begin again. Everything lost was restored. Well, I don't know what year we're in according to the Jewish calendar, but I think 1963 feels like we're due for a new beginning."

"Yes, Lord! Amen" came from the seat behind us.

"God knows that our most debilitating wounds are often not in our bodies but in our hearts and our minds. But there is freedom to be had. Oh yes, there is!"

"Hallelujah!" someone called from the back row.

"I think about Isaac's frail body, how it had become a prison for his enormous spirit that wanted to break free. He has that freedom now. And you know, he was seven years old. He got his Jubilee. This was his Year of Jubilee. But will it be yours?"

He silently gazed at us all. As if he had spiritual X-ray vision to see each of our burdens and struggles.

"As we grieve this loss today, we feel emptied out. But for Isaac, all that was lost has been restored, fully and whole. The angels gently carried Isaac to the loving arms of our Savior. Hallelujah. Let us pray."

I will never forget the men who carried Isaac's small blue casket:

Cooter, Dr. Clarke, Sheriff Teeton, Hutch, Reverend Hezekiah, and Daddy. It was not customary for a parent to be a pallbearer, but Daddy insisted. I wondered if he felt it was his last chance to take care of Isaac. Their faces were wet with tears as they lifted the casket and carried it gingerly across the old wood floor. It must have been light, and it would only have taken two or three men to carry it. But all these men wanted the honor of carrying Isaac. We all followed out the door behind them. As we came to the doors, there on the back pew was a halo of sunlit curls surrounding sad blue eyes. Golden. I didn't want to look away from him, our souls clinging to each other like vines. I wondered what he had risked to be there.

The sheriff led our cars up the steep and winding roads, while other drivers we passed pulled over to the side of the road out of respect. Golden rode with Cooter in the funeral procession. Daddy wanted to bury Isaac close to little baby Josie, right by his mother, Grandma Josie.

There were wildflowers, mushrooms, lilac trees, and morning glories surrounding the place Isaac was to be laid to rest.

Cooter said a prayer. Then Sissy sang "Pass Me Not, O Gentle Savior," and her voice was so sweet and pure it made me ache. Miss Adams put her arm around my shoulders. Golden stood beside me.

When the time came, Theo, Yully, and Golden helped me pick wildflowers to lay on the casket. Others did the same thing. We sang a benediction; then everyone started saying their last goodbyes and walking to their cars.

Mr. Farris shyly approached us as we stood beside the open grave. He was carrying a little brown bag. Out of it he pulled a wooden figurine of a boy pulling a wagon with a little rooster in the back. He handed it to Daddy. As Daddy held it, he knelt by the freshly shoveled dirt of Isaac's grave and wept.

40

GONE

Rojo was gone.

Two mornings after the service, Daddy sat upright in bed around 6 a.m., the hour when Rojo would crow to wake us and the rest of the neighborhood, but that familiar sound never came. I heard Daddy's bare feet walk down the hallway and out the back door. He made whistling sounds to call him.

I jumped out of bed to stare out the back door, as if some alarm was starting to sound in my head. Daddy was turning over buckets and standing a few feet from the area I had prayed he would never see. Whatever trust I had tried to build back was about to be obliterated. I ran out the door, through the yard toward him, trying to think of how to explain. But when I got there, he was already on his knees, staring down at the spot where Rojo and I had dug up the treasure. But instead of the patched-together sod there was a hole, with the top of the old box sticking out of the ground. Daddy opened the lid as I held my breath, knowing nothing I could say would put that hundred dollars back.

I started to explain. "Daddy, I—"

But when he opened the lid, we both froze. Like Rojo, the money, all of it, was gone.

Our eyes met. "Grace, did you . . . ?" I shook my head as if to say, *"I didn't take it,"* which wasn't completely true. Then the answer dawned on us at the same time. The only person more desperate than even me. The only other person who knew about it.

Virginia.

Daddy charged through the yard and burst through the back door, red-faced. "Virginia!"

I was following behind him, awash in fear and nausea.

Sissy and June came out of their rooms, still in their nightgowns.

Virginia lay in bed most days, not getting dressed till one o'clock. Sometimes later. He opened the bedroom door, and as though she already knew, she was sitting up in bed. She turned and looked at him and then at me.

"It's gone. It's all gone."

"Virginia, what did you do?"

She seemed almost robotic, with a vacant stare on her face. "Ask Grace. I wasn't the only one who dug it up."

Daddy looked over at me, confused.

Virginia offered the simultaneous mercy and betrayal of saying, "Gracie dug up about a hundred dollars to give to the parents of the boy healer to come *pray* for Isaac." She spit out the word *pray* like it was poison.

Daddy's eyes found mine, swimming in a cluster of sorrow and what could have been either anger or frustration. I mouthed the words, *"I'm sorry."*

He gave his head a slow nod and closed his eyes, as if remembering something he'd rather forget.

The rise and fall of Virginia's voice as she continued put me in mind of those old horror movies where the villain is always calmest before he murders you.

"I was watching you that night, Grace. I had come home after everyone was in bed. I couldn't sleep and had gotten up to get some air on the porch when I heard Rojo in the backyard, scratching. Then I heard another sound—digging. I hid, then I saw you come around from behind the shed. I watched you sneak back inside. I went to see what you had been doing, and there it was, the money my husband buried and didn't trust me enough to tell me where."

"Where is it, Virginia?"

She took a sip of water from the glass on the bedside table, taking her time. "I used the money to buy medicine. Cordelia's brother, Dr. Oden, told me that there was new medicine, still undergoing trials, but he knew of cases where people were cured after using it. He could buy it, but it would cost me."

Daddy and I looked at each other, then June looked at us. Sissy, who had slunk in without any of us noticing, stared at the floor.

Virginia stopped for a moment, folding her hands in her lap as if she had been waiting for this to be revealed, then continued, "Dr. Oden made some calls . . . He was able to get the drugs, but we had to keep it a secret from the nurses, and especially from Dr. Clarke. They were black-market drugs, not yet approved by the government, but had been performing well in trials. John, can't you see there was no way I could have lived with myself if I hadn't done everything possible to save Isaac?"

Her voice cracked as she spoke his name. "The medicine they were giving him wasn't doing *nothing*. My baby was laying there dying, and we all just sat, watching it happen. I decided I was gonna *do* something. Dr. Oden advised me to switch it out for the pills the nurses gave Isaac. Or sneak it into his food.

"It took every penny from that box to buy that medicine. But how could I not act? I did what any mother would do to save her child."

Daddy's face was so broken, I had to look away. June's face revealed equal parts shock, fury, and sorrow.

Virginia wasn't done.

"In the beginning, he was improving. Grace, you bringing that Miracle Boy was perfect timing. We started giving Isaac his new medicine two days after Golden came. Once I got the money to Dr. Oden . . . It was the perfect excuse to say God was healing him, when I knew all along that it wasn't any miracle but the medicine. I'm not saying that I don't believe in miracles; I just wasn't convinced that Golden could do what everyone claimed he could. But then . . . things changed. Isaac took a turn. I went to Dr. Oden and asked him what was happening. He told me that the medicine did have risks. Risks he had not told me about before. That there was a chance of organ damage because the medicine was so strong."

She took another drink from her glass. "I thought it was the right thing, don't you see? Wouldn't you have done the same?"

The rage I felt—I thought it would overtake me. I wanted to run and grab her by the hair and drag her out of that bed. Why hadn't she told us? Maybe Dr. Clarke could have saved him.

Daddy's voice thundered across the room. "*No!* I wouldn't have done the same. I would have asked questions. I would have told you what I was doing. I wouldn't have kept it a secret and trusted a reprobate like Oden. How could you have done this, Virginia? How could you put Isaac in the hands of a man like that?"

She looked at him, then slid down in bed, closed her eyes, and rolled over with her back to us.

Daddy walked out of the house, the door slamming behind him, and pulled out of the driveway.

41

MISSING
PIECES

Aunt June and I decided to drive down and find a shady spot by the river on the outskirts of town. We were desperate to get away from Virginia and the dark cloud that hung over our house. It had been two days since she had told us the awful story about Dr. Oden. We rode in silence and only started to talk once we had found a spot on the riverbank and settled our feet into the water. The smell of honeysuckle growing nearby filled the air with sweetness, like a little bit of heaven had come down to earth.

June sighed deeply, taking in the smell. "Gracie, I asked your daddy if I could tell you what is happening with this whole awful situation. He can't really talk about it with your mama around. But I told him, I think you're old enough and you have a right to know."

I looked up at June, moved by her loyalty to me. "Thank you, Aunt June." I took her hand and squeezed it against my face.

She gave me a side hug, cheek to cheek. "Okay, so here goes: Your daddy laid out the whole, gruesome story for the sheriff. He took Dr. Clarke down there, who said now in retrospect, he remembered seeing

Dr. Oden sneaking around and looking like he was up to something when Virginia visited Isaac."

I wanted to tell June about seeing Virginia and Dr. Oden arguing outside of the hospital, but I couldn't without revealing the fact that we had taken Emoline there in secret, and without Cordelia's permission, to visit Isaac. Blast all the lies.

"Anyway, the sheriff called your daddy back down to the station yesterday and said that it was a case of Dr. Oden's word against your mama's, and knowing what a weasel he is, he would just deny it all and accuse her of lying. He says we have to get him to admit to it."

"Why would he do that?"

"I have no idea, Gracie. They said something about getting your mama to wear some fancy recording device."

"Like, undercover?"

She nodded. "The big thing right now is, we have to keep it quiet. They are hoping they can dig up some evidence, proof that he bought the drugs."

"Wow!"

"I know, Gracie. Right out of *Perry Mason*."

A hummingbird flew past us and hovered at the stem of one of the honeysuckles, drinking in the nectar. June and I sat and watched in silence before it flew away. Like our Isaac—here for such a short time and then gone. And like Rojo. After Daddy stormed out, June, Sissy, and I had gone looking for Rojo, but he had vanished. Daddy said for me and Sissy to make some posters with a drawing of him, our telephone number and address, and the offer of some reward money for anyone who found him. We had put them up around the neighborhood and in town.

When June and I returned home, there was a package sticking out of the mailbox. I ran to see what it was, never imagining it would be for me.

My dearest Grace, I have mailed this book to Yully as well, in hopes that it would be something the two of you could discuss. It is about a young girl. I think her story will inspire you both.

Love, Miss Adams

I showed June. She held it out in front of her, squinting as she read aloud. "*A Tree Grows in Brooklyn*, by Betty Smith." She opened it to the first page. I leaned against her arm as she read aloud. "'The one tree in Francis's yard was neither a pine nor a hemlock . . .'" The buzzing of her words that reached me through my ear pressed to her shoulder almost lulled me to sleep.

"That Miss Adams sure loves you, and who could blame her. This sounds like a perfect book for you and Yully to read right now." She smiled sweetly. "I'm going to get a glass of tea. You want some?"

"No thanks. I think I'll stay out here and read."

I turned to the page June had already read. I got so lost in the book, I didn't notice the sound of the tires on the gravel driveway till I heard the car door close and about jumped out of my skin.

"You okay?"

"Yes, just didn't hear you."

Daddy sat down beside me on the swing. "What do you have there?" I handed it to him, and he inspected the cover.

"It's from Miss Adams. She left it for me in the mailbox."

"Miss Adams sure does think a lot of you."

I smiled, feeling a little embarrassed by the compliment. "Daddy, I have been wanting to ask something . . . Why is it that you were willing to stand up to the Klan? Weren't you scared?"

He nodded and handed the book to me, then sat back in the swing, letting his body fall into the motion.

"Yes, I was scared, but I was more afraid of being silent. There is a cost for doing nothing, Grace. A part of your humanity dies when you leave evil to flourish. I had a friend in the Navy—a Negro man. I learned a lot from him, seeing how he was treated by the other men on the ship. It was a disgrace. Every person has a right to dignity. Without that, we are no different than barbarians."

I leaned my head against his shoulder, and he took my small hand in his.

"Daddy, I've been wanting to say how sorry I am for . . . taking the money."

He nodded in motion with the swing. "I know, Gracie. I know you are."

And that was all that was ever said about it.

"Gracie, are you still on the porch?" June came around through the gate between the back and front yards.

"I'm here!"

"Oh, hey, John. I didn't hear you drive up."

The phone started ringing in the kitchen. June ran back in to answer it. "John, it's for you. It's the sheriff."

Daddy jumped up quickly, the serious expression returning to his face.

We followed him inside and put our ears to the kitchen door to listen.

We didn't need Perry Mason to figure out what had happened.

Somebody at the station had leaked the story about Dr. Oden. Left town. He was gone.

There was a lot of that going around.

42

ROJO AND REWARDS

Everyone in town was talking about Dr. Oden's disappearance. When his father, John Oden, the bank president, heard what his son was being accused of, he was outraged, as was Cordelia, who sent a letter informing Virginia that her membership in the SWS was terminated, effective immediately.

John Oden did everything possible to assure everyone in town that there wasn't an ounce of truth to Virginia's claims, but after some digging, the sheriff and his deputies found evidence that Dr. Oden's gambling problem had escalated and he was in debt to some very shady characters for thousands of dollars. They also found evidence that the money Virginia had paid him had mostly gone to pay gambling debts. Only a small amount was used to buy the black-market drugs used to treat Isaac.

They put out a warrant for his arrest.

The stress of all this weighed on Virginia. Clumps of her hair started to fall out.

As the town buzzed on about it, Mr. Oden threatened that he would hire a big-city lawyer from Lexington. Said he would prove his son's innocence.

Daddy said he figured Mr. Oden had paid for him to get a new identity and sent him away somewhere.

I remember the way Daddy's jaw tightened as he explained this to June and me—running his hands through his hair. Then without another word, he walked out of the kitchen and out the back screen door and disappeared into the shed.

I was beginning to have just a small taste of what Hutch and his family and neighbors might have felt every time they were wronged but got no justice. It was like having acid in your veins—it burned and churned around your body with nowhere to escape.

Each morning when I woke up, the acid in my veins and the ache in my heart was made worse by the silence in the backyard. Ever since Rojo went missing, our home echoed like a tomb. The constant reminder of loss upon loss.

I went into the kitchen. Daddy and June were sitting at the table drinking coffee. I heard Daddy say, "She'll turn up soon."

"Who will turn up soon?"

Daddy motioned me over to him. "Grace, I think your mama needed to get away. Clear her head from everything."

"Where is she?"

He looked down at the linoleum, taking a deep breath. "I'm not really sure, but I think she went to the hills."

I wondered why she would ever want to go there, given how her family had treated her the last time.

"I don't want you to worry. She'll be back."

I didn't really know how to feel about her. I had the same old guilt I'd carried for years, but now I felt angry at her. There was so much to process. Why didn't she ask more questions about the medicine? Why not at least ask Dr. Clarke? She had lied to all of us.

Daddy called Virginia's people in the hills, but no one had seen her up there either. He sat on the porch every night, looking out, watching for her. Then a few days later, she pulled up in the driveway as if she'd gone out to the store. We were finishing breakfast. Daddy sprang up out of his chair with June behind him. Sissy came out too and stood on the top step, then went to give Virginia a hug.

Daddy put his arms around Virginia as she cried. June came around them and rubbed Virginia's back with her large, gentle hand.

I thought about how Daddy had let go of his anger over the money she took. Virginia looked up into Daddy's face with tears running down her face. I read her lips as she said, "I'm so sorry, John. I'm so sorry."

I sat on the porch, watching at a safe distance. She looked at me the way a wounded animal might as Daddy practically carried her into the house.

I felt nothing.

* * *

The next morning, the first really good thing happened. A redheaded, freckle-faced boy appeared at our door carrying a box. Eli Gunner. And in the box was Rojo.

"I think his l-l-little l-l-leg is broken."

I couldn't believe it. Eli explained that he'd been wandering deep in the forest behind our house and found Rojo tangled up by a net someone must have laid as a trap for a squirrel or groundhog. He carefully unraveled the tangle from around Rojo's leg and carried him home to take care of him in their barn. A few days later, his mother saw the poster in the Green Parrot about a missing red rooster. The good news: there was a reward.

Eli held Rojo so tenderly and was reluctant to accept the reward, but Daddy insisted. He had ridden his bike, pulling a wagon behind him with Rojo in a large cardboard box, sitting softly on a blanket so's not to feel the bumps in the road. When Daddy and I thanked him for saving

Rojo, he shifted from one bare foot to the other, then said, "I-I-I was wondering if you c-c-could t-t-tell Hutch something for me? Could you t-t-tell him I said thank you?"

Daddy put his hand on Eli's shoulder, trying to calm him. "Of course. I'd be glad to tell him."

He struggled with the next words. "I-I-I'm sorry for what my p-p-pa did. It was wr-wrong."

Daddy squeezed his shoulder and said, "You're a fine young man, Eli."

Eli smiled, which seemed to stretch his face strangely, as if his skin was unaccustomed to the upward movement. He rode a little taller as he pedaled his bike and wagon away from us. Like Virginia, I guess he was trying to outrun his father's shadow.

Daddy and I spoke softly to Rojo. Seeing him was like Christmas morning.

Later that day Daddy took him to the vet, who said a chicken with a broken leg was a lost cause and that we should put him down, but Daddy had another idea. He took Rojo over to Mr. Farris, who fashioned a wooden splint to fit Rojo's leg precisely, then sanded it down smooth as silk so it wouldn't give him splinters. Daddy wrapped the leg in white tape and made a comfortable place for Rojo where he could reach his food and water easily while he healed up. It wasn't even a week before we saw Rojo wobbling around on his peg leg. He had survived.

I wondered if maybe we would too. It was too soon to tell.

43

RINGING BELLS

In mid-August the heat continued to rage in the afternoons. I stood in the backyard absorbing the sounds of summer: a barking dog, Rojo clucking as he pecked in the dirt, a slamming screen door in the distance, and the jarflies. They rubbed their wings together, making a sound that rose and fell like an orchestra in perfect synchronization. It reminded me of Virginia scraping a knife in quick, even strokes on the cast-iron skillet when bits of fried chicken got stuck on the bottom of the pan, except in a much higher pitch. It was an oppressive sound that made me want to stick my head in a bucket of ice water.

I noticed that the bees covered up the purple spikes of lavender Aunt June had planted in the beginning of summer. They seemed frantic, darting from one stem to the next, gathering every last bit of nectar they could. I called for June to come and see. She stood on the back steps, squinting against the glaring sun as she watched.

"Aren't they amazing little creatures? They do that because they sense that winter is coming." The phone rang and she ran back inside to answer it. I stood watching them. Why was it that bees, compared to humans, didn't have much of a brain, but they had a sense about danger and when hard times were coming? Had the bees known that Isaac was sick before we had? I wished that I could have asked them.

The magic feeling I felt at the beginning of summer was like a dream you can't quite remember when you wake up. The melancholy comfort of fall still seemed too far away to dream about. I felt lost in this terrible in-between, unable to process everything that had transpired and unable to move forward. Dread of the first day of school loomed, and I wished to go back to the beginning. If I had known those first weeks of summer would be the last days I had with Isaac, would I have spent them any different? I let my toes drag along the warm wood of the porch as my inside thoughts seeped into the air. "I just wish I could've known what was coming."

June put her arm around me. "Oh, my Gracie, I understand what you mean, but it's better not to know."

My breath quivered in my chest and I choked on the tears that gathered at the back of my throat before making their way to my eyes.

I remember hearing an old preacher say that death always comes in threes. In the weeks following Isaac's passing, the second bell rang. It was for Cooter's mama.

Cooter showed up one morning for biscuits and found her lying in her bed with a peaceful smile on her face. It was a good death.

The big news around town was over who had returned for Leola's burial. As we all placed flowers on her pine box, a man with dark hair and a slight limp appeared from the trees and offered a single yellow rose. It was her husband, Jack Conley, back from the dead.

With Cooter's mama's passing, he started visiting our house about every other day. I was dying to know if Cooter had told Daddy anything about Jack Conley's mysterious return, but if he had, Daddy wasn't telling.

Cooter and Sissy would sit out on the porch swing, or he'd help Virginia and Sissy make dinner or Daddy chop wood. Sometimes, on warm afternoons, he'd take Sissy for a ride out in the country. He saw Sissy as the girl he knew she could be instead of the girl that Sissy believed she was. I didn't want to tell Cooter, but one night when Daddy and I had driven to the Tri-Way for a burger, I had seen Sissy flirting with a new boy. He reminded me of Taylor Bluin with his slick car and smooth talk.

I watched Daddy's face as we both saw her.

"Daddy, why do you think Sissy ain't satisfied with Cooter?" I knew I didn't have to explain what I meant.

"She can't tame the horse that's in her."

We ate our burgers in silence, thinking about it all. I knew Cooter loved Sissy and would be steady and safe. I wished she could find it in herself not to destroy the good love Cooter was offering her. Only time would tell.

The gulf between all of us and Virginia was deep. I guess we were all trying to do the best we could. Virginia slept later than everyone except Sissy, then spent a lot of time out in the garden. Now that she was no longer busy with SWS, she had a lot of time on her hands. It seemed cruel that all those women Virginia had spent so much time trying to impress had turned their backs in her greatest moment of need.

She worked for hours each day, turning the backyard into a paradise, with a trellis of white roses and a small bench Daddy built for her so she could read under the shade tree.

June told me that having your hands in the dirt was healing. There was even some science behind it—that digging released something in your brain that made you feel happy. I guess Virginia needed healing more than just about anyone I knew. The one emotion worse than grief was guilt. I knew that well.

June decided to stay awhile to help out on Virginia's dark days. Having her there made me think our life could go on. I told her I hoped she stayed forever.

In the evenings, June and Virginia would make dinner and Daddy would turn on the TV for us to watch while we ate. It helped to fill the awkward silence and the gaping hole that the missing seat at the table left us with. After dinner, Virginia would disappear to the backyard and sit in the garden. I would stare at her out the screen door as she looked up to the sky. Sometimes I saw her lips moving. I knew she was talking to either Isaac or God. Maybe both. I thought of Isaac. He was in paradise. I wondered what he did every day. Maybe he was exploring the galaxies and the ocean depths like he had always dreamed of. If heaven is a perpetual state of peace and happiness, I couldn't help but think that Isaac was getting to do all the things in heaven that he never got to do on earth.

The toll of the third bell came on a Saturday morning.

We were encouraged when Virginia rose early that day, dressed, and went to the garden to gather potatoes and green beans and a few herbs for lunch later. She was rinsing the dirt off the vegetables when Retha and her little daughter, Caroline, knocked on our door. Granny Bee had passed.

We stood there waiting for Virginia to react, but she never did. Maybe she'd cried all her tears for Isaac.

It seemed that heaven was getting full, and the world was feeling empty.

There was a mountain funeral at a country church. Her death, like her life, seemed to leave people cold. As I stared down into the plaster-white face of Granny Bee, it occurred to me that her whole life of nearly eighty years was a disappointment to her. She had married two men who ended up betraying her and had lost the last few years of peace she could've had with her children and grandchildren for the love of a man who would never love her the way she deserved. This was the tragedy of a life lived with what Daddy had called "the poor mind."

I thought of Isaac, so curious and sparkling. He seemed to grasp in his young years what mattered. Even with the drowning sadness for the loss of Isaac, there came with his death a sense of hopefulness and purpose. As I looked down at Granny Bee, I despaired for the waste of a life. Her chance to make a difference in the world was over. I did not want my life to be like that.

After the funeral, June and I went for one of our evening walks.

"June, when do you think Virginia will be normal again?"

"Well, I'm afraid only God knows the answer to that, but I think she's making progress."

"Why do you say that?"

"Remember when your mama left for a few days after Isaac passed?"

"Yes."

"She told me where she went."

"Where?"

"Back to the hills. Said she stayed with an old friend, and each day she'd go to Isaac's grave. She planted roses and lilacs, making it beautiful. And then she would lay across his grave and cry. She doesn't know how to forgive herself for what happened to Isaac. She believes that his death was her fault. That her deception and sin caused it."

And suddenly, for the first time, I understood Virginia. I knew exactly how she felt. I had carried the weight of little baby Josie's death on my shoulders all these years. And as for deception . . . I started counting up the lies that I had told. How could I ever be forgiven?

44

THE
BAKE SALE

Miss Adams had been staying in Middlesboro, but she told me that before she left Kentucky, she would come say goodbye. It was difficult to imagine her not being close by. She had made me believe there was more to the world than our tiny speck on the map. Instead of her coming to say goodbye, though, something else happened that would put Jubilee on the map for the first good thing in a long while. Miss Adams decided that Jubilee should have a part in the March on Washington. She asked Reverend Hezekiah if he could hold a meeting at his church to see which members of the community would be willing to make the trip. Daddy, feeling a great amount of gratitude to Reverend Hezekiah for his kindness to Isaac and our family, decided we should attend the meeting as well. Even Virginia agreed to go.

Reverend Hezekiah started off by thanking Miss Adams for spearheading the bus initiative. "My dear sisters and brothers, it is truly an honor to enter into this historic moment together. We will sponsor a group, possibly even a bus full if funds can be raised, to attend the March on Washington."

"Amen! Hallelujah!" came from different members of the congregation.

"Recent events in Jubilee have affirmed a conviction that we must become active participants in the fight for change by joining the peaceful efforts directed by Dr. King. So, with that said, who would be willing to go?"

At first there were no hands. Then the first hand went up. It was little Eustace. After that, most everyone in the audience raised their hands and stood to their feet. Someone started singing "We Shall Overcome." Then we were all singing.

That night, I heard Daddy and Virginia talking at the kitchen table. I couldn't sleep. Too much excitement from that day. I lay on the creaky wood floor of the hallway with my legs—now very brown from the summer sun—sprawled in front of me.

I heard Virginia clear her throat before saying, "You know, John . . . I have been too hard on Miss Adams."

"There was a lot going on. You were exhausted, Virginia."

"Yes, but still. When I think of all Reverend Hezekiah and his church have done for us . . . I want to do something . . . to help."

"What are you thinking?"

"We could help raise money so that as many people as possible can go."

"And how could we do that?"

"Well, I have been helping with the SWS bake sale for years. You'd be amazed how much money a bake sale can raise. Why not start there?"

It was the first sign of life in weeks.

"Virginia, I think that is a marvelous idea."

I sat there processing what I'd just heard. She had admitted to treating Miss Adams badly and wanted to raise money to help her. It felt strange and new. I didn't like it. It almost felt . . . wrong. The ice cube that had formed around my heart where Virginia was concerned had a hairline fracture. But it could easily freeze back over.

Virginia called Miss Adams the next day and the plan was set in motion. The ladies from Reverend Hezekiah's church turned out the most beautiful pies and cakes you ever laid your eyes on, including some that white folks in town had never even heard of.

Virginia asked Miss Rosalie at the Nickel Thrift if it would be okay for them to do the bake sale in front of her store. She took a risk, telling her where the funds for the bake sale would go. Miss Rosalie didn't hesitate.

"I'm so glad somebody is doing something! What is that quote? 'The only way for evil to triumph is for good men to do nothing'? Well, this woman is tired of doing nothing. I'd love to help!"

The bake sale had amazing baked goods and the best location in town. The sign over the bake sale stand read, *Baked Goods for a Good Cause*. Naturally, people were not only aware of the tragic loss of Isaac, but the word about Dr. Oden had gotten around as well—how he had deceived Virginia to pay off gambling debts and was potentially responsible for Isaac's death. People came in droves and bought cakes and pies and lemonade and sweet tea all day Friday and Saturday. Maybe it was their way of showing support for what had happened to Virginia. We knew if someone asked what the "good cause" was, we would have to tell the truth, but gratefully, no one ever did.

On Saturday as I sat behind the table helping Virginia, I saw Cordelia and Emoline coming out of Handy Hardware. Cordelia looked over for a moment; it could have been my own prejudice against her, but I thought I could see disgust on her face. She walked up Main Street away from us. To my surprise, Emoline walked over.

Cordelia called out, "Emoline!"

Emoline ignored her. Virginia looked up for a moment and winced at the sight of Cordelia. Emoline edged nervously up to the table and I closed the distance between us. Feeling a wave of unexpected sympathy, I said, "Would you like to buy something?"

She had a nickel in her hand. "Yes. Do you have any peanut butter cookies?"

I looked through the basket of cookies and found a peanut butter one, then handed it to her.

She held it in her hands, swaying nervously from side to side. "I'm sorry about Isaac. He was the sweetest, nicest boy I ever knew."

I felt a lump in my throat. I wanted so badly to ask her why she risked getting in trouble with Cordelia to go see him and why even now she was going against Cordelia to support the bake sale. Then she reached out and hugged me. You could have knocked me over. She turned and walked away. Virginia never commented. Whatever secret Emoline and Isaac shared would remain between them.

By Saturday's end, the table was empty and the box that held the money was full. The sale raised enough money to send twenty-five people to Washington.

I thought of Reverend Hezekiah and what he said about suffering and how God uses it to change us. Maybe things were beginning to change, but there was still plenty of healing left for us to do.

Virginia and I kept our distance. When she wasn't in the garden, she spent hours in Isaac's room. Sleeping in his bed. Her face in his pillowcase, trying to breathe in every last bit of him she could.

She did have better days when we would hear her in the kitchen fixing breakfast. There were signs of life, and we were all glad for that, but between me and Virginia, there was still a gaping canyon. There were only two ways I knew of to cross a canyon without dying—you either fly over, or you build a bridge.

45

ORPHANS
AND MOTHERS

Rojo was crowing his lungs out. I opened my eyes to realize it was the morning of my fourteenth birthday. I felt under my mattress for the red journal from Miss Adams and wrote:

August 28, 1963
  Today I am fourteen. It is hard to believe all of the things that have happened in the past year, and especially in the past few months.
  These are the things I wish for:
  I wish for Miss Adams not to move away.
  I wish June could stay forever.
  I wish for Mr. Farris's wife to be nicer to him.
  I wish Sissy would love Cooter.
  I wish for Golden to be free of Mary and Joseph.
  I wish for Virginia and I—

I didn't know how to finish it.
I heard June knock at the door, singing, "Happy Birthday to you,

happy birthday to you, happy birthday, sweet Gracie. Aunt June sure loves you!" She gave me a bear hug. "All right! Time's a wastin'. We've got a party to get ready for!"

The air was like a crisp apple, the first signs of fall in the trees. Leaves turning gold and orange. The lack of humidity agreed with my curls. I spent extra time in the bathroom getting ready. My bangs had grown out nicely. I looked into the mirror, staring at the brown waves around my face. June had bought me a brand-new dress to wear. It was mint-green cotton with a white waistband and white spaghetti straps and a white headband to match. It was perfect. I had never seen anything so pretty.

Even Virginia seemed pleased. "Why, Grace, you look like a young lady."

My stomach did a small flip at her approving words.

Aunt June and Virginia buzzed in the kitchen making sandwiches, potato salad, and homemade ice cream to go with the cake. Daddy and Sissy were in the backyard blowing up balloons. I saw one of the balloons that must have gotten loose float past the kitchen window and move upward toward the trees. I watched and remembered all the birthdays Isaac and I had shared, our birthdays being so close together. He loved to let a balloon go and watch it till it disappeared. *"I miss you, Isaac."* I mouthed the words silently and wiped away a warm tear spilling down my cheek before it hit the frosting on the chocolate cake. Isaac's favorite. I looked around at all the party preparations. The celebration was not only for me, but for the citizens of Jubilee who would stand among the thousands to hear Dr. King speak.

We had decided that we would time the party so that everyone could watch Dr. King speak while we ate cake and ice cream and maybe even catch a glimpse of our own Jubilee representatives—Miss Adams, Reverend Hezekiah, and the other twenty-five that had gone along to the March. Daddy had invited Hutch, Yully, and Eustace to the birthday party. Hutch had decided to send Hazel to Washington, and he stayed home with the kids. Eustace was very disappointed to not be able to go—Hutch said he understood but that he was too young to make such a journey. We had also invited Mr. and Mrs. Farris and Cooter.

We were pretty sure Mrs. Farris wouldn't come. She had taken a fall walking to the mailbox. I had been going over to help with any chores they needed done, and Mr. Farris was teaching me to whittle and carve.

I was in the kitchen helping June put the finishing touches on the chocolate cake, though I was careful not to get any of it on my new dress. I heard footsteps coming up the porch and thought it might be Cooter coming early to help. I ran to the door, excited.

But it wasn't Cooter.

It was him.

He stood there beneath a halo of blond curls with the sun streaming in behind him. I wiped my hands on the kitchen towel I was carrying.

"Happy birthday, Grace." He pulled a handful of wildflowers from behind his back.

"Thank you," I said, breathing in their aroma. We stood with our eyes locked. "How did you know it was my birthday?"

"I have been keeping up with how you're doing through Cooter ever since his mama passed. He moved into her place. I've been seeing him a lot lately."

"We've been seeing a lot of him around here, too. He and Sissy, you know."

"You look nice. I like your dress," he said, smiling. "And, Grace, you have some chocolate icing right here—"

He touched my chin with his index finger.

"Oops. I was helping June with the cake." He smiled as I wiped the icing with my finger then licked it off.

"There's something else." He dug into his pants pocket and pulled out a wad of cash. "Here is your money."

"But how . . . ?"

"I snuck into Mary's purse, before she could spend it, and hid it somewhere safe. Somewhere I knew she'd never look. She tried to get me to admit to taking it, but I decided she could beat me till I was dead before I'd tell her."

I noticed fresh bruises on his arms right below where his sleeve fell. "Did she do that?"

He shrugged and looked away from me for a moment, as if he was remembering. "It doesn't matter. I'm leaving. I'm almost fifteen, old enough to work. I'm not gonna let them use me anymore. I just wanted to come and tell you."

We looked at each other, and I pointed to the swing for us to sit down. We sat in the quiet for a minute, our bodies swaying together.

"Where will you go?"

He shrugged. "I have no idea. I just need to find the moment when I can slip away."

"Are you afraid?"

"Terrified. There's only one thing I'm more terrified of."

"What's that?"

"Staying."

I thought of the wish I had written for him in my red journal. "I will pray for God to make a way."

"Thank you, Grace. I didn't want to leave without saying goodbye."

"Does Cooter know you're going?"

"Yes, he does. It's really helped to be able to talk to him. It gave me courage, I guess."

Then without even meaning to, I said, "I wish I knew that I would see you again."

"It's your birthday. You always get your wish on your birthday."

We stared at one another, and then he leaned in, touching his forehead against mine.

We were both startled at the sound of the screen door opening.

"Grace Mockingbird, move away from that boy."

I stood, then stumbled back. My embarrassment was like a red balloon on my freshly fourteen-year-old face.

"I'm sorry, Mrs. Mockingbird." Golden stood from the swing.

Virginia looked him up and down. His hands were shaking a little.

"I heard what you told Grace." She didn't wait for him to answer. "Did they force you to do the healing? To pretend you have the power to heal?"

He took a deep breath before he answered. "Yes, ma'am. But I have to take some responsibility for that too. I'm old enough to know the truth from a lie. That's why I came to tell Grace. I'm not going to do it anymore. I plan on going out on my own. And not that it makes up for anything, but I brought back the money Grace paid."

Virginia looked over at me and I tried to hand her the money, but she said, "You should give that to your father, Grace." She walked over to the porch swing, sat down, and began to swing as if trying to quiet her nerves. Golden and I stood in front of her, absorbing this strange moment.

Virginia watched a hummingbird drink from the small feeder that hung from the porch as her words rose like a vapor into the air. "There are a lot of things in my life I wish I could do over. I have cared so much about things that didn't matter, trying to forget the past, but the past . . . well, it always comes and finds you."

A redbird flew by the feeder, scaring away the hummingbird, then landed on the edge of the fern pot.

"Would you wait here a minute?"

"Yes, ma'am."

We looked at one another, wondering what was coming next.

Virginia went inside, then returned with something in her hands. "This was Isaac's wallet. Inside is the money he'd saved from his allowances and birthdays and Christmas money. There's nearly twenty dollars in here. I know he would want you to have it, Golden."

"Daniel, ma'am. My real name is Daniel . . . Dunnigan. I was adopted. Grace knows the whole story."

She looked over at me with a knowing look on her face. "Yes, I suppose she does."

"Anyway, ma'am, it's not right. Not after what I did. I don't feel right taking it."

"It's what Isaac would have wanted. For you to have the chance to live. It is a shame to be given a life and never live it. Don't waste it, Daniel Dunnigan."

He nodded, his eyes burning with a fire I had not seen before, as if Virginia's words had kindled something inside him. He turned and looked over his shoulder, probably nervous that Mary or Joseph might be out looking for him. "I guess I'd better go."

He held the wallet tightly in one hand. Virginia stepped back, giving us space. He stepped closer to me, but not too close, since Virginia was standing behind us.

"Goodbye, Grace. I'll write to you when I land somewhere."

"I'd like that."

Then Virginia stepped forward and put her hands on his face and spoke softly. "I heard the voice of the Lord, saying: 'Whom shall I send?'"

He answered, "'Send me.'"

She smiled and raised her eyebrows, obviously impressed that he'd finished the verse she had started.

His blue eyes were flooded with tears, maybe because of Virginia's kindness, or his longing for a mother, his mother. Or maybe both.

He backed down the porch steps, his blurry eyes never leaving mine. I watched as he disappeared, wondering if I would ever see my beautiful golden boy again.

Then Virginia did something she hadn't done in years. As we stood there, side by side on the porch, she put her arm around me, and the very touch of her hand, foreign as it was, opened up a flood within me. As we stood holding each other, the dam inside us gave way. We wept for what was lost. For what would never be. We wept for the forgiveness that seemed to flood our hearts at the very same moment. It was just as June had said. Something beautiful had come from all our brokenness.

And in my heart, a word came to me. Falling softly as if riding on the redbird's wings. It had always been there. But how could I have known our tears would erode the icy stone wall? As the layers crumbled away, the word that had been buried deep within me, nearly lost, had come back to me.

Maybe there was no other way, and only through this suffering could I find it and cherish it as I did in that moment. There had been no way around the pain, only through it and to the other side, which had led us here. I let the word pass through my soul and find its way to my lips, letting it ring into that late summer air like the sound of a rooster crowing, or a church bell ringing. The sound of freedom.

"Mother."

EPILOGUE

Even while laughing a heart can ache.

PROVERBS 14:13

A. Philip Randolph once said, "Freedom is never given; it is won." I can see the truth in this as I turn the pages of my memory back to that summer. I realize there are many kinds of prisons, and the freedom we seek is often elusive. For some, the prison is hate. For others it is the inability to forgive. Even in the face of great injustice, the forgiveness required is the most terrible medicine to swallow, but the aftertaste is like wild honeysuckle. Maybe it all boils down to those two things. Hate is the prison we carry with us. Forgiveness turns the key and unlocks the door. Corrie ten Boom wrote, "To forgive is to set a prisoner free and discover the prisoner was you."

As I close my eyes, I remember faces and try to catch the sound of their voices on the summer wind. I place a fresh bundle of roses on the newest grave I have come to visit, then walk around and see other names: Hutch, Reverend Hezekiah, and of course, Miss Pearl.

343

Some lived a good long life; others, not nearly long enough.

Hutch lived into his eighties, but diabetes took his eyesight for the last couple years of his life. He died at home surrounded by Miss Hazel, Yully, Theo, Eustace, me, Mama and Daddy, and as many of the neighbors as could fit into their living room. He was carried home on the notes of the old spirituals, "Ain't No Grave," "Swing Low, Sweet Chariot," and "Take My Hand, Precious Lord." It was a good death.

They say the most ideal decline is a sharp one—healthy one day, gone the next. That was Miss Pearl's story. She died peeling a peach, the perfect S shape hanging down from her hand when Theo found her in her front porch rocker. Theo and I joke that when we get to the pearly gates, there will be Miss Pearl in a ruby-encrusted rocker with a solid-gold fruit stand to greet each newcomer with a free welcome-to-heaven peach. One can dream.

After everything that happened, Daddy started saving money for a college fund. Sissy wasn't interested, so it all went to me. It wasn't a lot, but along with scholarships, it helped get me through my first semester of college. I decided to follow in Miss Adams's footsteps and apply to the University of Chicago. With the help of a letter of recommendation from her, I was accepted. I worked my way through school and with a generous financial gift from Mr. and Mrs. Farris, I was able to graduate with only a small amount of debt. I studied journalism and have spent much of my adult life traveling and writing. The wanderlust has never left me. Maybe it never will.

Theo and Yully both attended Berea College in Kentucky. It was the very first integrated college in the South. Not only that, but they offered all students the ability to work their way through school. Yully and Theo graduated with honors and then married each other. I was the maid of honor.

Sissy and Cooter eventually married too, but sadly, whatever hole was in Sissy's heart had an appetite for her misery. She divorced Cooter and left one night without a word. We pray, if she is still alive, that one day she will return.

After Sissy left, Cooter married Emoline, who I learned to tolerate and, for Cooter's sake, tried to find anything positive to say about her that I could.

After Isaac's funeral service, we began attending Reverend Hezekiah's church. They became the family we all longed for, and it brought comfort in the difficult years of grief that were to come. Reverend Hezekiah suffered a heart attack in his fifties. It was a devastating loss. Theo took over as the new pastor of his father's church. His eyes are as clear and green as they ever were. Yully teaches tenth grade American history in Middlesboro.

Meanwhile Yully's little brother, Eustace, became one of the brightest young civil rights attorneys in the country. We are all so proud of him.

Mr. and Mrs. Farris lived into their nineties. Though Mrs. Farris was never what you would have considered warm to me, she did improve. Mr. Farris became the only grandfather I ever knew. He showed me how to grow a prize rosebush, and I taught him how to make fried chicken when he was sick of eating liver and onions. After I moved away, as the Farrises aged, Daddy and Virginia watched over them until they finally passed within days of each other. Mr. Farris left all of his treasures, including his little critters and the Victrola, to me. Sarah's music box sits on my dresser and holds what little jewelry I possess.

Miss Adams did join Dr. King in his crusade for equal rights before his tragic assassination. I still dream of his voice and his sermons that forged a fire that would stay with me for the rest of my life.

Miss Adams eventually returned to her home state of Mississippi to work for change in what was considered the most racist state in the nation. She was regularly targeted by the Klan throughout her life but never backed down from speaking out against injustice. I always held out hope that one day Miss Adams and Dr. Clarke would marry, but they never did—not each other or anyone else. Maybe because their passions in life took them in different directions. Dr. Clarke stayed in Jubilee and serves as chief of medicine at Middlesboro General today. Miss Adams got a few glimpses of the promised land that Dr. King had spoken of so eloquently on that historic day in Washington, which she was present to hear.

About a week ago, Miss Adams worked late, as she often did. Just a mile from home, she rounded a blind curve and was hit, head on, by a drunk driver. Her wishes were to be buried in Jubilee, among the people she loved, and who loved her. These beautiful souls that, for a moment, defied the establishment and embraced something so radical that it changed us all—love.

One of my most prized possessions is the photograph Miss Adams took of Yully, Theo, and me that day at her house. Miss Adams wrapped it up as a gift for my birthday that summer. It is a living testimony to the way someone's perspective can change. All these years later, I wonder how different my life would have been if those miraculous, terrible, and awful things had not happened that summer.

Not only in my life, but in the lives of those in Jubilee who grew new eyes.

It began in small ways: simple acts of kindness, a shared lunch counter, holding the door open so another could walk through first. Each step for change was like climbing the face of a great mountain—but like Reverend Hezekiah used to say, sometimes it is the struggle that makes you strong.

Of course, there were those who were so entrenched in their hatred and fear that they wallowed in it for the rest of their days. The men in hoods still spewed their venom on anyone they could. Rank Gunner lost his burned leg and died of an infection a year after the fire. Hutch visited him in the hospital to say he forgave him for everything, but even then, at the end, Rank remained proud and bitter.

But for those who let the sun shine through, their shoulders, void of that awful burden of hatred, felt feather-light. As though they had grown wings. Eli grew up to be the finest veterinarian the town ever had and remains a respected member of the community and a friend to all.

Of all the transformations, Virginia's surprised me most.

We slowly built back the way between us, though it wasn't always easy. After Isaac's death and the death of her mother, Virginia wanted to do something to fill the long, quiet hours and the ache in her heart. She decided the best way to do that was to help others in need. She and Daddy dreamed up the idea of a Help-Mobile. She funded this with bake sales that all the ladies at church were happy to help with. Daddy fixed up an old VW van and put shelves in the back to hold food and clothing for the needy. She would drive it up into the hills and park by the old mountain church she'd attended as a girl. She was reborn. Helping others transformed her into a person of substance who no longer worried about what anyone thought of her.

On some of my visits home, I would come along to lend a hand. It was during these times that I asked questions about her life, the heartache and struggle of growing up the way she did. It was in this way that we built a trust between us. She would ask me questions about my life in Chicago and say she admired my independence. Her willingness to see me as an individual, with my own views, differing from many of hers, and still afford me respect—this is the soil in which something beautiful and unexpected grew: a friendship. One that I cherish.

I call home every Sunday afternoon. Daddy's voice is still my favorite sound in the world.

Rojo lived to the ripe old age of thirteen. Daddy continued to read the King James Bible to him under the old oak tree. He was convinced that Rojo's diet of worms and the Good Book was why he lived so long. One morning when he didn't hear the familiar morning greeting, Daddy came out to find Rojo lying under the tree, gone to be with Isaac.

Aunt June still visits Mom and Dad in Jubilee from time to time. I send her postcards from all the places I travel. She is still as fiery and wonderful as she ever was.

As for Golden and me? I was relieved to go to the mailbox a few months after he came to our house and see a small postcard from Tallahassee, Florida. It read: *God made a way. Will write more when I can.*

I must have checked the mailbox four times a day for the next month, but nothing came until my next birthday. He never sent a return address. It wasn't until I was in college that I saw him again. He was beautiful, kind, and broken.

I want to believe that anything broken can be mended, given enough time and love. But life has taught me that there are some heartaches you have to make peace with. They become like an old pair of jeans that don't fit anymore, but you keep them in the drawer anyway. Some wounds never heal completely without a miraculous touch from the divine. Golden—Daniel—is still waiting on that touch.

Though the loss of Isaac left me angry and confused, the feeling of those angels in the room never left me. For my college graduation, Daddy bought me my own King James Bible, except in red, in honor of Rojo. It seemed only fitting to start with the letters in red. If it hadn't been for Reverend Hezekiah and his church, I might have given up on faith altogether. I'm glad I didn't. I really want to taste that welcome-to-heaven peach one day.

We do the best we can with what we've been given. The mercy that pours out from those red letters that Jesus left behind for a ragged crew of misfits makes me believe that that is enough.

We reach high and bow low to drink the sorrow and the bliss. To taste the bounty of freedom that is as bitter, some days, as it is sweet. It's hard to rewrite your story . . . but not impossible.

A NOTE FROM
THE AUTHOR

Each of us could probably follow a trail back to a moment that set our lives on a path that added different hues to the colors of our core memories and changed the way we would move through the world. Scientists believe that, on average, our earliest memories as children can be traced back to around two and a half years old, though it's earlier for some and later for others.

My first memory, when I was three and a half years old, occurred in October of 1971. My brother Samuel, just shy of his fifth birthday, was dying of lymphoma. He had a beloved pet rooster named Rojo that my Aunt Frieda gave him as a wee chick the Easter before he got sick. As his condition worsened, Samuel requested that he be able to see me and Rojo. Since I was three and Rojo was, you know, a chicken, neither of us was allowed into the ICU. My dad came home, put me and Rojo in his Volkswagen (since he was a Volkswagen mechanic, we always drove Volkswagens), and delivered us to the small hospital where Samuel was being treated. My father lifted me onto his shoulders and had me hold Rojo up to the window so we could both see Samuel. It was the last time I saw him alive. I still dream of running through our small backyard beside Samuel on his Big Wheel with Rojo riding shotgun (as my parents say he loved to do). But the hospital visit is my only clear memory of him.

The town of Jubilee is inspired by the small towns in Kentucky that I passed through as a child, on summer car trips when my parents would take us to visit relatives that lived up in the hills of eastern Kentucky.

You might wonder how much of the story is truth and how much is fiction. That is always a difficult equation to draw, since memories are wont to differ, depending on who is doing the remembering. The details of a memory can shift over time, but the emotion of that memory is the truth of what happened. Much of this novel is a fictional world created to serve the greater truths that a young family wrestles with in the aftermath of the worst possible event: the death of a child. We all deal with loss in different ways. Death casts a heavy shadow that is difficult to outrun. The Mockingbird family's story represents small parts of my own family's story but is mostly a world that came to life in the pages from places unknown. Some of the real stories are present to echo the crisis of faith that my family (and others I've known) maneuvered through in the wake of charlatans who came in sheep's clothing and made promises that only God could keep.

The civil rights narrative of this story is drawn from my passion for this righteous cause and for my near obsession with that part of American history. The enormous courage and sacrifice required by so many citizens to stand up for change is moving and infectious. The actions of each individual during that tumultuous time, including many stories that will never be heralded, started turning the tide that we are still trying to turn today. I hope I have served the cause of equality in some small way.

I have included a photo of Samuel and Rojo, taken before Samuel went into the hospital. Before my father's passing in 1999, it was only on rare occasions that he or my mother spoke of Samuel—it seemed too painful to do so. But in more recent years, my mother has shared some beautiful memories of him with me. I feel the ache in her words and the breathlessness of her brush with the angels the day he died. My father was as pure a soul as any I have ever known, and my mother loves Jesus more than her own breath.

Thank you for taking the hours and days and possibly weeks to read these pages. It means more to me and my family than I can adequately explain.

I am glad Samuel had a chance to live again in these pages.

ACKNOWLEDGMENTS

Entering the mysterious path of novel writing seemed impossible when I began this book more than ten years ago with a clear beginning and only a partial idea of how it might end, but nothing in between. It was my friend and mentor Wayne Kirkpatrick, who has been a success in many different fields of writing and artistry, who suggested, "Just write what you see." I first want to thank Wayne, because if he had not offered those freeing words, I'm pretty sure the story would have never made it out of my head and onto the page.

Deep thanks to my family: Samuel, Mike, Sam, Tammy, Sherry, Haze, Morgan, Myleah, Myka, Betty, Taylor, Martha, Jackson, Jordan, Jes, Sue, Goldie, Frieda, Hazel, Janice, Doris, Linda, Larry, Joel, Heather, and especially my mother, Lola Morgan, and my father, Cova Morgan, (as well as many close friends of our family) for allowing me to borrow from our story to create the world of the Mockingbird family and the people of Jubilee. I want to thank my seventh-grade teacher, Theresa Butler, for birthing a love for poetry and good books. Thank you to the real-life Dr. Clarke, who saved the life of my niece Jes when she was nine years old.

The process of getting to a final manuscript was aided enormously by so many friends, editors, encouragers. Katharine Cluverius, thank you for wading so patiently through this story with me for so long! Without your editorial help, I'd still be on the seat-of-my-pants draft. Thank you!

Also my beloved friend Ginny "Virginia" Owens, who introduced me to Katharine and was an early reader and the most wonderful encourager. On the subject of early believers and editorial help—thank you, Kate Etue, as well as David and Amy Huffman. Thank you also to Dolly Parton for writing, playing, and singing beautiful music and being just amazing. You gave me my first shot back in 1986 that led me to Nashville and all that followed after. Thank you, John Mays, for opening my mind and soul up to the beauty of good books and a new way of seeing the world.

Huge thanks to Chris and Dorena Williamson for your time to read and to share with me about the Black American experience and the wisdom you shared and books you loaned me in my research about the civil rights movement in 1963. I'm forever grateful for your example and for your sermons that have moved and inspired me for decades. Also, thank you for telling me about your precious grandfather Hezekiah. Huge gratitude also to Carole Ford and Vanessa Conner for reading from the perspective of growing up in the Jim Crow South and checking me on accuracy and realism. Thank you also to Lynda Randle for being a reader and for teaching me spirituals and giving me a glimpse of the world through your eyes.

Thank you to dear friends who encouraged me all along the way: Valerie and Eric Arnold, Andrew Greer, Sissy Goff, Melissa Trevathan, Shonda Vaughn, Gretchen and Lucas Thompson, Lesley Burbridge, Michael Closter, Sarah Feldman, Mark Nicholas, Jeremy Bose, Tom Douglas, Sandra McCracken, Amy Alexander, Amy Grant, Phil Madeira, Ian Morgan Cron, Michelle McNeil, and others I am positive I'm forgetting. Each of you helped me keep going in moments when I felt discouraged. Thank you to Jen Cooke, Laureen Smith, Donna Jordan, my Canadian sisterhood, and to Ashley Cleveland, for challenging me at a crucial moment.

Thank you, Carolyn McCready, for believing that I could write this story when all I had was the memory, up until your very important perspective on a close (but not close enough) final draft as a reader.

Thank you, Karen Watson, for being an absolutely incredible human and my East Tennessee sister, and for giving me the great honor of working with you and the amazing people at Tyndale. Thank you also to Jan Stob and Kentucky native Elizabeth Jackson for making a tender home in your hearts for Jubilee. You made me cry in the Wendy's drive-thru!

Thank you, Danielle Egan-Miller, for taking a chance on a songwriter-turned-novelist. Your passion and depth of knowledge for storytelling is a gift. You are a force! I am honored and grateful to work with you. Also, to Ellie Roth-Imbody for our brief but meaningful time working together.

Sarah Rische—your thoughtful, gentle-handed approach to editing *Jubilee* made the final manuscript a joy to write. You have serious editorial fairy dust. Your attention to detail was mind-blowing. Thank you a million times for the compassion, love, and care you took with every word of the story.

Thank you to Jonathan Richardson—my now-fiancé, soon-to-be husband, by the time this is published. You love anyone in need with complete abandon. Thank you for challenging and inspiring me to love more deeply. I am honored to be your partner in life and chaos. I'm so grateful that God showered us both with such a sweet surprise of love.

Finally, thank you to my daughters:

Cova Olivia Brouwer Gentry, your compassion and heart shine through every facet of your life. Matched only by your zest for dinosaurs, turtles, frogs, bad movies, and adventure. Your writing is a light to the world. You slay dragons and save sparrows on a daily basis.

Savannah Brouwer—my lioness, lover of the wind. Your writing makes me weep. Your passion for Jesus, for the marginalized, and for the written word are only a small part of what makes you a beautiful child of God. Maranatha.

Olivia and Savannah, I love you both so much and am so grateful for the gift of being your mother—even though much of the time, you are mothers to me.

Thank You, God, for putting within our hearts the longing to tell stories that bring healing, even to the deepest wounds.

DISCUSSION
QUESTIONS

1. The inspiration for *The Year of Jubilee* came from the author's earliest memory, in which she was held up to her brother's hospital room window, holding his pet rooster. What's the first thing you remember? How has that memory shaped you or the way you see the world?

2. Miss Adams uses a quote from a John Steinbeck novel to encourage her students to expand their perspective and later shares *A Tree Grows in Brooklyn* with Grace. What were your favorite books as a child? What books—in childhood or adulthood—changed how you see the world?

3. Though she lacks affection from Virginia, where does Grace find mothering from others? Have you found friends, mentors, or relatives who fill relational gaps in your own life? Who are they?

4. Remembering the message preached at her husband's funeral, Aunt June tells Grace, "When God says no it's because He wants to give us a greater yes . . . I personally think that God allows suffering because He wants to show us something beautiful." Do you agree with her perspective? How do you answer the question of why suffering exists in this world?

5. Confronted with injustice, Miss Adams and John Mockingbird are both determined to help but take action in different ways. In what ways do they help? What attempts did you feel might be misguided?

6. Aunt June cares for Sissy and Grace through what proves to be a tumultuous summer. What did you think of how she counsels and disciplines (or doesn't discipline) the girls? What might you have done differently?

7. In her desperation to save Isaac, Grace enlists the help of Golden Shepherd, a child evangelist and healer. What does she come to learn about Golden's gifts? Do you believe healings, such as the one Golden attempts for Isaac, are possible? How do you define what a miracle is? Do you believe miracles exist?

8. Though Grace is deeply wounded by her mother's distance and unforgiveness, she gets glimpses into the things that have shaped Virginia, like her family of origin. What did you think of Virginia at the start of the book? Did your perspective change as the story went on? How has your view of your own parents changed as you've gotten older?

9. Grace has spent most of her life without friends outside of her siblings but finds connection with Theo and Yully. Are there people in your life who have become friends despite differences in your backgrounds or beliefs? What are the benefits of these types of friendships? What challenges do they present?

10. In a desperate moment, Hutch acts to save Rank Gunner despite the terror Rank intended to inflict on Hutch and his family. Would you have done the same? Are there other examples in the story of characters loving others who could be considered their enemies? How can we learn to love our enemies better?

11. In the epilogue, Grace reveals the course life takes for many of the book's characters in the years that follow. Which characters have the future you might've expected? Which surprised you?

ABOUT THE AUTHOR

Singer/songwriter **Cindy Morgan** is a two-time Grammy nominee, a thirteen-time Dove winner, and a recipient of the prestigious Songwriter of the Year trophy. An East Tennessee native, her evocative melodies and lyrics have mined the depths of life and love both in her own recording and through songwriting for noteworthy artists around the globe, including Vince Gill, India.Arie, Rascal Flatts, Amy Grant, Sandra McCracken, and Glen Campbell.

Cindy is the author of two works of adult nonfiction—the memoir *How Could I Ask for More: Stories of Blessings, Battles, and Beauty* (Worthy Inspired, 2015) and *Barefoot on Barbed Wire: A Journey Out of Fear into Freedom* (Harvest House Publishers, 2001)—and of the children's picture book *Dance Me, Daddy* (ZonderKidz, 2009). *The Year of Jubilee* is her debut novel.

Cindy is a cocreator of the charitable Hymns for Hunger Tour, which has raised awareness and resources for hunger relief organizations across the globe. She currently resides near Nashville with her two daughters. For more information, visit cindymorganmusic.com.

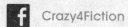
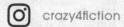
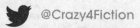

By purchasing this book from Tyndale, you have
helped us meet the spiritual and physical needs of
people all around the world.

Tyndale | Trusted. For Life.

CP1704